I AM

A Novel Approach to the
Gospel of Jesus Christ

JONATHAN E RUOPP SR

Jonathan E Ruopp Sr (signature)

WESTBOW
PRESS®
A DIVISION OF THOMAS NELSON
& ZONDERVAN

WestBow Press books may be ordered through booksellers or by contacting:

WestBow Press
A Division of Thomas Nelson & Zondervan
1663 Liberty Drive
Bloomington, IN 47403
www.westbowpress.com
1 (866) 928-1240

ISBN: 978-1-5127-7420-7 (sc)
ISBN: 978-1-5127-7421-4 (hc)
ISBN: 978-1-5127-7419-1 (e)

Library of Congress Control Number: 2017901764

Print information available on the last page.

WestBow Press rev. date: 8/21/2017

Dedication

I dedicate this work to the memory of my mother, Fay Weber Ruopp, who recently passed at the age of eighty-nine after suffering her last few years with dementia. I often reflect on her and my father, Charles Frederick Ruopp Jr., reading together in our living room when I was growing up. They would read for hours on end, only disturbing the silence to discuss something interesting they had read. They were both veracious readers, but they rarely read from the Bible.

The Bible is a difficult read for most of us, and too often it is read in bits and pieces without an overall understanding of its profound significance. It is for this reason that I endeavored to write this book: to provide a big-picture view of the gospel; one that would read more like a novel, yet include all of the content from each of the four gospels; one that would adequately address the spiritual implications of these historical events; one appropriately set in the context of Jewish culture and Roman politics.

Sadly, my father died many years before the inspiration came to write this book, and my mother's dementia made it impossible for her to read with understanding what had been written.

Agape,
Jonathan E. Ruopp Sr.

About the cover

The background is from a chart of the seventy-two names of God used by Jewish and Christian mystics. The three-letter names or parts of names were derived from a formula using the three consecutive seventy-two-letter verses: Exodus 14:19–21. These names have been used by those Jews who follow the Kabbalah, and by Christian Gnostics in meditation for spiritual insight and to conjure miraculous power from God.

In contrast, the four-letter name of God "I AM" that God gave to Moses at the burning bush supersedes these mystical names and is superimposed onto the forehead of the image of Jesus of Nazareth. Jesus referred to himself by this very name, when interrogated by the High Priest and the Sanhedrin. Already well known for his many miracles before his trial, Jesus backed up his claim of being "I AM" by rising from the dead after he was brutally executed for this very assertion.

Rather than meditating on mystical numerological names of God for spiritual insight and miraculous power, I challenge you to contemplate the profound spiritual message in the words, miracles, and events surrounding the life, death, and resurrection of Jesus the Messiah.

Acknowledgements

I would like to thank my family for their support in this my latest endeavor. My profound gratitude goes out to my wife, Gail, who endured my many frustrations and also shared in the few brief periods of triumph I experienced. She, as always, was and is my greatest sounding board, and she helped me immensely, especially with my initial edits. The candor of my son, Jonathan, was a bit unexpected and greatly appreciated. His level-headedness kept me focused on the needs of my potential audience, and was instrumental in my use of communication indicators to explain the scriptural events in greater depth; my description of Jesus's conversation with Nicodemus was directly affected by our discussions. The considerable artistic talents of my daughter, Emily, and her generous willingness to use those talents for the book cover were a source of great joy to me. She took a concept that I had in my head, and, through her patience and perseverance, brought it to life through her art work and graphic design skills.

Thank you,
from your grateful husband and father.

Contents

Introduction xv

Chapter 1   Salutation and History 1
Chapter 2   Zechariah in the Temple 9
Chapter 3   Immaculate Conception 13
Chapter 4   Signs in the Heavens 17
Chapter 5   Mary's Journey 23
Chapter 6   Mary Visits Elizabeth 25
Chapter 7   Circumcision of John the Baptist............. 28
Chapter 8   Joseph's Decision 32
Chapter 9   Birth of the Messiah................................. 37
Chapter 10   Traditions of the Firstborn 40
Chapter 11   Flight to Egypt.. 42
Chapter 12   Jesus Found in the Temple...................... 45
Chapter 13   John the Baptist 52
Chapter 14   John Baptizes Jesus................................. 54
Chapter 15   Tempted in the Wilderness 57
Chapter 16   Temple Leaders Confront John................ 62
Chapter 17   Introduction to the Messiah 66
Chapter 18   Marriage at Cana..................................... 69
Chapter 19   Passover and Nicodemus......................... 74
Chapter 20   Transition from John to Jesus.................. 80
Chapter 21   To Galilee through Samaria..................... 83
Chapter 22   Galilee Receives Him.............................. 88
Chapter 23   From Nazareth to Capernaum 92

Chapter 24   Gathering Disciples.. 96
Chapter 25   Lessons in Faith.. 103
Chapter 26   Preaching throughout Galilee 111
Chapter 27   Tax Collector at Capernaum..................................115
Chapter 28   Sermon on the Mount.. 126
Chapter 29   Return from the Mount to Capernaum 137
Chapter 30   Raising the Dead at Nain.................................... 144
Chapter 31   Healing at the Bethesda Pool 150
Chapter 32   Back across the Sea... 154
Chapter 33   Return to His Own Country 158
Chapter 34   Return to the Bethsaida Desert........................... 160
Chapter 35   Healing Crowds at Gennesaret 166
Chapter 36   Bread of Life at Capernaum................................172
Chapter 37   A Trip to Tyre and Sidon....................................176
Chapter 38   Feeding Four Thousand at the Sea of Galilee........179
Chapter 39   Seeking a Sign at Magdala and Bethsaida.............. 181
Chapter 40   Visiting the Towns of Caesarea Philippi................ 184
Chapter 41   Mount of Transfiguration................................... 187
Chapter 42   Abiding in Galilee 192
Chapter 43   Through Samaria to Jerusalem............................ 199
Chapter 44   Feast of Tabernacles..205
Chapter 45   The Evil Generation 222
Chapter 46   Feast of Dedication 235
Chapter 47   Encampment at Bethabara................................. 241
Chapter 48   Synagogues Surrounding Jerusalem 249
Chapter 49   Raising Lazarus at Bethany................................. 255
Chapter 50   Through Jericho to Jerusalem 262
Chapter 51   Mary Anoints Jesus 267
Chapter 52   Palm Sunday 271
Chapter 53   Monday after Palm Sunday 278
Chapter 54   Tuesday at the Temple....................................... 281
Chapter 55   Wednesday's End-Time Warning.......................... 291
Chapter 56   Thursday's Passover Preparations........................300
Chapter 57   Friday's Last Supper 305

Chapter 58   The Mount of Olives.. 312
Chapter 59   The Garden Betrayal..317
Chapter 60   Delivered to the High Priest...................................... 321
Chapter 61   Delivered to Pilate.. 325
Chapter 62   The Roman Trial.. 330
Chapter 63   The Crucifixion.. 335
Chapter 64   Burial before the Sabbath...340
Chapter 65   Sunday Morning Resurrection................................... 343
Chapter 66   Jesus Appears to His Disciples.................................. 347
Chapter 67   Pentecost 356

Bibliography.. 361

Introduction

This book is written with the intent of reaching those people who are interested in learning about the gospel of Jesus Christ, but are not yet comfortable reading from the Bible. Hopefully, this book, being written in novel form, will be easier to read than the Bible. It is written in a possible and logical chronology, according to my study, which endeavors to combine the four gospel accounts. Set within the historical context of the time, it follows the events of the gospels, keeping the Jewish calendar in mind. Lastly, I have included my own spiritual insights into Jesus's words and works, inserting them into the gospel accounts, and marrying them with the feasts of the Jewish calendar. In an effort to accomplish this last objective, I have included many possible communication indicators, as well.

In order to accomplish these established goals and yet preserve the integrity of the biblical account, the book has been created as a compilation of self-edited content from the King James Version of the Bible. Nearly all of my edits were done to transform the old English of the KJV into a more reader-friendly version of English. There are a few edits, however, that were made to bring into focus the more spiritual aspects of the text.

It is my hope that this work has something for everyone. For the seeker, it should provide you with a good place to start—the accompanying scripture references are intended to direct you to the true biblical account. For the novice, who knows the basic story about Jesus of Nazareth, but may have gaps in understanding or questions regarding the narrative; this account should go a long way in connecting the dots for you. For the learned, I have no misconception that my spiritual insights will be a challenge to your already substantial knowledge; I encourage you to entertain the possibility of their truth, knowing that iron sharpens iron; hoping that you will also judge the intended nature of the work as a novel.

I would be remiss if I did not include at least a brief explanation of my own profiting through the process of creating this book. There was a tradition that each of the Davidic kings were to write a copy of the Torah, so that they might become eminently familiar with God's Word. This endeavor, though I felt altogether compelled by the Holy Spirit to complete, has been one of the most enjoyable and rewarding projects I have ever undertaken. Every day, through the process, I was in contact with God and his Word, marveling daily over His love and wisdom. From it, I have come away with a new understanding of Christianity: Christianity is a decision-altering worldview founded on an indwelling personal relationship with God—a shared understanding, through the revelation of Jesus Christ, from God's Word, by the Holy Spirit.

I encourage you all to get to know God through his Word, and to share what he has shown to you with someone!

Jonathan E. Ruopp Sr.

Chapter 1

SALUTATION AND HISTORY

In the beginning was the Word, and the Word
was with God, and the Word was God. The same
was in the beginning with God. All things were
made by him; and without him was not anything
made that was made. In him was life; and the life
was the light of men. And the light shines in the
darkness; and the darkness comprehends it not.
—John 1:1–5

And the Word was made flesh, and dwelt
among us, (and we beheld his glory,
the glory as of the only begotten of the
Father,) full of grace and truth.
—John 1:14

In the beginning God created the heaven and the earth ... and he
brought forth life, the host of heaven, and the creatures upon the
earth. And like God, all that he created was good!

And among the host of heaven, God created also Lucifer,
perfect in beauty, and without fear; and God anointed Lucifer, full
of wisdom, to be a covering cherub.

But Lucifer envied God, and said within his heart, "I will exalt my throne above the stars of God: I will be like the Most High."

Corrupting his perfection, he rebelled against God; and he deceived also one third of the host of heaven that they might follow him. So there was a battle in heaven—good versus evil.

Then God formed man from the dust of the earth, and placed him in a garden to care for it. And he gave man authority over the creatures of the earth, that he might have dominion over them. The man, Adam, walked with God, and spoke openly with him there in the garden.

Now Lucifer, also called Satan and the devil, came to the garden in the form of a serpent, and deceived Adam and his wife, Eve, so that they also rebelled against God. Their rebellion set into motion a cycle of sin and death passed down, through the flesh, to all mankind.

And so, as mankind multiplied, so did sin. And, after many centuries of man's rebellion, God saw that the wickedness of man was great in the earth, and that every imagination of the thoughts of his heart was only evil continually. So God brought forth a great flood to destroy all that walked upon the earth, both man and beast, to cleanse the earth of sin. And through the flood, God saved the man, Noah, and his family, for Noah was the most righteous man of his day. Together with them, God saved also a pair of every sort of animal—to preserve them, to restore the earth to its original glory.

In just three generations after the flood, as mankind began to multiply again, they organized so that they might lift themselves up in power before God, for they built themselves a tower, in Babel, that would reach to the heights of heaven. But God saw their evil, and the sinful nature that continued to grow within mankind; and he dispersed them by dividing their language, so that they left off building, and separated to the four corners of the earth.

Then, some two hundred years later, God spoke to the man, Abraham, and blessed him, for Abraham chose to follow God, because he believed his word. And God counted Abraham's belief as righteousness. So God promised to bless Abraham and his seed, that his descendants would become a blessing to all mankind. Through Abraham's seed came Isaac, and Jacob his son, whom God loved and named Israel. Through Abraham came also Jacob's twelve sons, by whom the twelve tribes of Israel are named: Reuben, Simeon, Levi, Judah, Zebulon, Issachar, Dan, Gad, Asher, Naphtali, Joseph, and Benjamin; and Joseph's tribe was divided between his two sons, Ephraim and Manasseh.

It was Jacob's son, Joseph, who brought the children of Israel into Egypt after his brothers sold him into slavery. There, God saved them and all the land from great famine. And Israel prospered there until a king, who knew not Joseph, enslaved them for fear that they had grown too great in number and in strength.

In slavery, the people cried out to God for a deliverer, and God sent them the man, Moses. God appointed Moses to lead Israel in their Exodus from Egypt. By him, God led Israel out of the house of bondage by a strong hand. Triumphing over Pharaoh and all the gods of Egypt by way of ten plagues, God then divided the sea, so his people might pass over upon dry ground.

Then God led Israel through the wilderness of Sin, by a pillar of fire and cloud, and by Moses, and his siblings, Aaron and Miriam. Through Moses, God gave the people the Law; and the tabernacle, a portable dwelling place for God, which allowed him to dwell among his people. Yet the people continued in the idolatry that they had learned in Egypt, so God chose to prove them for forty years, preparing them for the Promised Land, a place where they could dwell and be at rest from all their enemies.

Then God raised up the man, Joshua, to lead them into battle, that they might claim the land promised to them. And God divided the Jordan River, which flooded, so that his people might pass over into the Promised Land on dry ground. Israel conquered the land, dividing it among the twelve tribes, and occupied it in the midst of their enemies. And God raised up judges to lead the people into battle against their enemies, and to lead them back to God when they strayed. This period of the judges lasted some three hundred years.

Then, in the days of the judge, Samuel, the people desired a king, so God raised up for them the man, David. And God established an everlasting kingdom with him, through his seed, that Israel might enter into rest from all their enemies and serve God in peace. Therefore, Solomon, David's son, built God a temple in Jerusalem—as a permanent house unto the Lord, where the people could worship.

Despite all that God had done for Israel, the kings and the people continued in sin and idolatry. So God divided the nation and gave them up to corrupt kings, and after some five hundred years of adulterous rule, he brought them into captivity among the Gentile nations. Nevertheless, in all their journeys, God provided them prophets to proclaim his word—prophets such as Isaiah, Jeremiah, Ezekiel, and Daniel—to show Israel its faithlessness in contrast to God's faithfulness. And to these prophets God showed his will and the events he had planned to carry out his will. Included in what God showed his prophets were the events surrounding the coming Messiah: a prophet, priest, and king to whom was promised an everlasting reign.

Daniel's words foretold the years of Israel's captivity, and the time when the Messiah would come. He spoke of their subjection to Babylon, Media-Persia, Greece, and Rome; and the nation watched as his words unfolded, over the generations, before their eyes.

The Exodus from Egypt occurred around 1446 BCE, and the conquest of Canaan, the Promised Land, began around 1406 BCE. Four hundred and eighty years after the Exodus, Solomon, David's son, began construction on the temple—966 BCE, in the fourth year of his reign. And he was seven years in building it, so that it was completed in 959 BCE, in the midst of Solomon's reign, which lasted for forty years, from 970 BCE to 930 BCE.

Now it happened around 930 BCE, after the death of Solomon, that the nation of Israel was divided into two kingdoms: the northern kingdom of Israel, and the southern kingdom of Judah. Then in 722 BCE, the capital city of the northern kingdom, Samaria, fell to the Assyrians, and Israel was taken into captivity. Later, in 587 BCE, Nebuchadnezzar, king of Babylon, laid siege to Judah; he destroyed Solomon's Temple at Jerusalem, and carried away the people of Judah into captivity.

As prophesied, seventy years later, in 517 BCE, Cyrus, king of Persia, allowed the Jews to return to Jerusalem to rebuild their temple.

In 331 BCE, Alexander the Great, of Greece, defeated Darius III and the Persians, but in 323 BCE, Alexander died suddenly. After some forty years of power struggles, Alexander's vast kingdom was divided into four: the Ptolemaic Kingdom of Egypt, the Seleucid Empire in the east, the Kingdom of Pergamon in Asia Minor, and Macedon.

Then in 165 BCE, the Jewish people from the former nation of Judah, rose up against the Seleucid Empire, freeing the Jewish people for the first time since the Babylonian exile, some four hundred years earlier. The revolt, led by Judah Maccabee, son of Mattathias the Hasmonean, began the Hasmonean Dynasty. Hanukkah celebrates their freedom and the rededication of the temple—and the original event, during which the Menorah, a seven-branched oil lamp containing only enough oil to last for one day, miraculously burned for eight days, allowing them time to obtain more oil before the flame went out.

In 64 BCE, however, a power struggle between two Hasmonean princes, Hyrcanus II and Aristobulus II, invited Roman influence over the region. Aristobulus II sought the help of the Roman general, Pompey, who, a year later, conquered Jerusalem for the prince. But Pompey, seeking treasure, defiled the temple by entering into the Holy of Holies. To his great disappointment, the earthly treasure he sought was not there. It was through such ill-fated circumstances that Roman rule began in Judea. Hasmonean rule reestablished Jewish independence briefly during the Roman civil wars, after the death of Julius Caesar, but was eventually eradicated again in 37 BCE, when the Roman senate installed Herod the Great as king of Judea.

Herod reconquered Judea with the help of the Roman general, Mark Anthony. He then replaced the temple priesthood, and the Sanhedrin, a group of seventy Jewish elders, which had been reestablished by the Hasmonean Dynasty. He also sought to modernize his kingdom, introducing a Hellenistic influence over the region. Despite the many impressive building projects undertaken by Herod that modernized Judea, the Jewish populous, for the most part, resented his rule. He was among a group of relatively new converts to Judaism, forced to convert after the Maccabean conquest lest they lose their land. So, despite the most commendable of his projects, extensive renovations to the temple, Herod's religious ardor was considered inferior by those Jews who could trace their lineage back to Abraham. His allegiance to Rome and his deposing of the Hasmonean Jewish leadership, in their minds, confirmed this belief. All these things together caused resentment, and Herod's reign was marked by discontentment and frequent armed confrontation by his Jewish subjects. To exacerbate the feelings the people had toward his rule, Herod quickly and ruthlessly dispelled any unrest, collaborating with the Romans, employing their use of crucifixion as a deterrent to future rebellion.

It was into this environment that the Messiah, the Anointed One, was to come, armed with grace and truth. The Jewish leaders of the time taught of His coming. Daniel's interpretation of Jeremiah's prophecy set the time of His coming at 490 years after the decree to rebuild Jerusalem. As the time drew near, the nation, well-versed in the scriptures, waited with a heightened sense of anticipation. Every young woman prayed to be the young virgin, prophesied by Isaiah, to give birth to the Messiah. And the young men were enamored with the thought of his coming kingdom. Many envisioned the battles to be won alongside their messianic king. Others sought to promote themselves as prophets and messiahs.

But as the anticipation grew among the common people in Judea, so too, the anxiety grew among the Jewish leadership. Though the scriptures suggested that the former prophets would be sent again to the nation, it was widely viewed among the leaders that there would be no more new prophets. In contrast to the views of the common folk, the religious leaders specifically sought the return of Elijah, whom Malachi prophesied would come to restore all things before the coming Messiah. They considered it their duty, as the priesthood, to keep the people from following all other false prophets and false messiahs. So during this chaotic time, exposing false prophets and false messiahs was a commonplace occurrence among them.

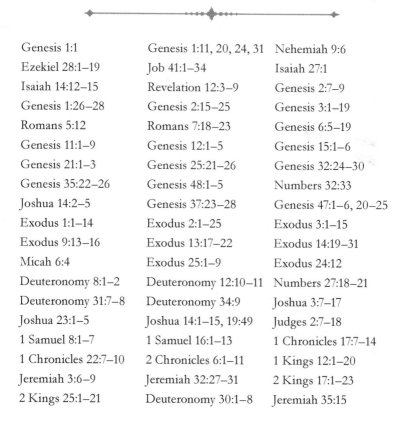

Genesis 1:1	Genesis 1:11, 20, 24, 31	Nehemiah 9:6
Ezekiel 28:1–19	Job 41:1–34	Isaiah 27:1
Isaiah 14:12–15	Revelation 12:3–9	Genesis 2:7–9
Genesis 1:26–28	Genesis 2:15–25	Genesis 3:1–19
Romans 5:12	Romans 7:18–23	Genesis 6:5–19
Genesis 11:1–9	Genesis 12:1–5	Genesis 15:1–6
Genesis 21:1–3	Genesis 25:21–26	Genesis 32:24–30
Genesis 35:22–26	Genesis 48:1–5	Numbers 32:33
Joshua 14:2–5	Genesis 37:23–28	Genesis 47:1–6, 20–25
Exodus 1:1–14	Exodus 2:1–25	Exodus 3:1–15
Exodus 9:13–16	Exodus 13:17–22	Exodus 14:19–31
Micah 6:4	Exodus 25:1–9	Exodus 24:12
Deuteronomy 8:1–2	Deuteronomy 12:10–11	Numbers 27:18–21
Deuteronomy 31:7–8	Deuteronomy 34:9	Joshua 3:7–17
Joshua 23:1–5	Joshua 14:1–15, 19:49	Judges 2:7–18
1 Samuel 8:1–7	1 Samuel 16:1–13	1 Chronicles 17:7–14
1 Chronicles 22:7–10	2 Chronicles 6:1–11	1 Kings 12:1–20
Jeremiah 3:6–9	Jeremiah 32:27–31	2 Kings 17:1–23
2 Kings 25:1–21	Deuteronomy 30:1–8	Jeremiah 35:15

Daniel 9:1–27   Deuteronomy 18:15–19   Genesis 14:14–20
Psalms 110:1–7   Psalms 89:18   Psalms 16:10
Daniel 7:7–18   Daniel 2:1–45   Jeremiah 25:11–14
Jeremiah 51:11   Daniel 8:1–27   Isaiah 7:14
Isaiah 9:2–7   Malachi 4:5–6

Chapter 2

ZECHARIAH IN THE TEMPLE

The old man took the censer in his left hand, carrying the bowl in his right, and moved apprehensively, maneuvering himself behind the veil. Covered in his priestly vestments, he approached reverently, praying very softly into his beard. Fragrance from the incense, which he carried, mingled with the lingering smell of the day's daily sacrifices. The aroma permeated the temple. Gone was the familiar reassuring sound typically emanating from the multitude praying outside. He was alone, on the Day of Atonement, in the Holy of Holies. There he stood, before the Ark of the Covenant, shaking with fear. The old man bowed solemnly, then crept nearer, focusing on the mercy seat atop the ark. He stopped, setting the censer gently down upon the floor. The smoke from the incense mixed with the coals from the altar billowed up from the censer before him.

He remembered from the scriptures that the smoke was to serve as protection for the high priest, while being in the presence of God, and understood that the incense represented the prayers of the people. These thoughts provided him but a thin veil of comfort.

Then dipping his finger into the bowl, he continued, feeling the blood of the bull still warm upon his skin. Raising his eyes and his finger, he sprinkled the front of the mercy seat with the blood, as was the tradition. Then backing away, he created a path of blood as he retreated toward the veil, where he had entered, repeating the act of sprinkling six times more, for a total of exactly seven times. Then, stepping back outside the veil, the old man sighed, grateful to have endured this part of the ritual.

Raised according to the priestly order, he had dreamed from an early age of someday becoming high priest of the temple. This day was the pinnacle of an illustrious career, for the Day of Atonement was the one time of the year that the high priest was to enter the Holy of Holies to atone for the sins of the people.

Having gone through the rituals, painstakingly, to ensure his own purity before God, the sacrifice of the bull, and the sprinkling of its blood, he continued with the sacrifice of the goat for the sins of the people.

He had begun the rituals at the beginning of the day, after the sun had fully set, sending everyone out of the Tent of Meeting. Before slaughtering the bull, he had bathed and put on his priestly garb—the fine linens, the turban, and the sash. Missing from his attire for the Day of Atonement rituals was the breastplate with the precious stones representing the twelve tribes of Israel, and the headpiece, the holy crown of gold bearing the inscription: HOLINESS TO THE LORD. Dressed only in linen, the old man felt lighter without the heavy gold of these items; he also felt old and vulnerable. After dressing, at the door of the Tent of Meeting, he had cast lots over the two goats to determine which goat was the sacrificial goat for God, and which goat was the scapegoat to bear the sins of the people. Only when he had finished this step, did he proceed with the sacrifice of the bull, filling the bowl with its blood.

The high priest continued with his duties, cutting the throat of the sacrificial goat, and holding it as it died, while filling another bowl with its blood. He approached the veil again, entering as before, being very careful not to slip upon the path of the bull's blood dotting the floor. He bowed low as he neared the censer, before the Ark of the Covenant, setting the bowl upon the floor next to it.

Stopping suddenly in his tracks, he sensed the presence of

someone before him. He stretched forth a cautionary hand, which shook violently as the lowered gaze from his steel gray eyes widened into an expression of panic. His head tilted upward, and his shaking intensified, overwhelming his entire body. Before him stood a man clothed in shimmering light. The old man stared, mouth agape, trying to comprehend the details of the vision. But it was like looking at moving light through melted glass. Like looking into a bright white fire, and trying to view a single flame, the features of the man before him eluded his focus. When the man spoke, the sound of his voice, like his visage, was elusive, like the sound of water from a swift-running stream.

"Fear not, Zechariah," said the man, "for your prayer is heard, and your wife, Elizabeth, shall bear you a son, and you shall call his name John. And you shall have joy and gladness, and many shall rejoice at his birth. For he shall be great in the sight of the Lord, and shall drink neither wine nor strong drink, and he shall be filled with the Holy Spirit, even from his mother's womb. Many of the children of Israel shall he turn to the Lord their God. And he shall go before him in the spirit and power of Elijah, to turn the hearts of the fathers to the children, and the disobedient to the wisdom of the just; to make ready a people prepared for the Lord."

Zechariah ceased his shaking. Then understanding the gravity of the words, he lowered his eyes again; his head began wagging slightly from side to side in disbelief. Then he asked in bewilderment, "By what sign shall I know this, for I am an old man, and my wife well stricken in years?"

"I am Gabriel," responded the man, "who stands in the presence of God, and am sent to speak unto you, and to show you these glad tidings. And, behold, you shall be dumb, and not able to speak, until the day that these things shall be performed, because you believe not my words, which shall be fulfilled in their season."

The old man tried to voice his protest, but produced no sound. When he lifted his eyes again, the vision of the man was gone.

Zechariah took some time to regain his composure. Then the

old man, continuing with his duties, repeated the sprinkling ritual with the blood of the goat and stumbled back out through the veil to the safety of the Holy Place.

When he was ready, and all else was completed, he laid his hands upon the head of the scapegoat and prayed, silently rehearsing the sins of the people over it.

Then he opened the door of the Tent of Meeting, and handed the scapegoat to the man entrusted to its care. The scapegoat was given to him to be taken into the desert, there to be released.

From Zechariah's ashen face, the man perceived his discomfort. So did those of the priesthood who were waiting outside with him. The many questions they asked Zechariah were greeted with wild expressions, hand gestures, and an open mouth devoid of sound.

"Have you seen a vision, then?" one of them asked.

Zechariah, wide-eyed, pointed frantically at him. He nodded repeatedly.

"And you have lost your voice?" another inquired.

Zechariah nodded again in his direction, the color returning to his cheeks. Then he raised his hands in a gesture of reassurance, motioning for the somewhat placated assembly to resume their work. They took hold upon the carcasses of the sacrificed bull and goat to take them outside the city to be destroyed by fire. The old man gave the sacrifices no more thought. He smiled thoughtfully, and returned to the business of the temple, wondering all the while about the nature of the vision and the message.

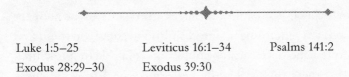

Luke 1:5–25   Leviticus 16:1–34   Psalms 141:2

Exodus 28:29–30   Exodus 39:30

Chapter 3

IMMACULATE CONCEPTION

Slight moonlight from a high window revealed the rich luster of her shiny black hair, still damp from the evening washing. Her shimmering locks hung down around her face as she rocked gently, bowed for some time, reciting her prayers. When she emerged from her position of prayer, she reclined back upon her folded legs, gazing thoughtfully toward the light emanating from the window. As she had done countless evenings before, she ended her prayers by giving thanks for the blessings of the previous day. It was time to climb into bed for her much-needed sleep, but the previous day had not been like other days, and this was reflected in her prayers and in her bittersweet mood.

She had known the day was approaching; her mother had given her plenty of warning. She eventually knew the whole plan, the ritual, the exact day, and the man. She had accepted this all in good turn, as she knew she must. In fact, she heartily approved of the match. This young carpenter was quite handsome, she thought. He was gifted in his trade, and hardworking. He seemed a just man, was considered devout, and was well-liked among the community. When the rabbi joined their hands in betrothal, just a few short hours ago, her joy was full. And the pride and tenderness she had glimpsed in the eyes of her betrothed made her blush. She blushed now, remembering his look.

Yes, her heart was still full of joy at the prospect of their marriage, but she felt sadness, as well. Ever since she could remember, she had wanted to be that young virgin, mother to the coming Messiah. She spent her days imagining what it would be like to raise such a child. These thoughts shaped her whole outlook on life; they shaped her personality. She was only fourteen, but her understanding of the scriptures was extraordinary. She entreated her father about the intricacies of the Law, the message of the Prophets, and the wisdom of the Writings, wanting always to know the spiritual "why." She was kind and joyous, constantly smiling, always the optimist. She was quick-witted, often mixing humor with scripture to make a point. She wondered how her betrothal and impending marriage would change her outlook on life, and her personality. Would her husband appreciate her humor and her love of the scriptures? Would she continue to view the scriptures with the same importance? And what about their children, what would their lives be like? The Messiah would most assuredly be directed by God in every aspect of his life, but her children would be ordinary, struggling with all the temptations that the world had to offer. Raising normal children seemed to her a less glamorous and far more difficult task.

This marriage will change everything, she mused. *It has already changed my prayers.*

Her prayers always contained a request to be the blessed virgin of the Messiah, but tonight that prayer was altered. Instead, she prayed that the virgin whom God would choose would appreciate the gravity of the blessing, and prove worthy of it.

She then added a new prayer, saying, "Bless Joseph and all that he is inclined to do, and bless our future children. May they be righteous and many."

The light from the window gradually intensified, eventually illuminating every corner of the small room. Her deep brown eyes were bright and clear, her olive complexion unblemished. The corners of her mouth were turned up, affording her a pleased, optimistic quality even in this most solemn of her moods. So distracted was she in her thoughts that she did not realize the change in her surroundings. She sat staring, unaware, until disturbed by a strange voice, which seemed to inhabit the room itself.

"Hail," said the voice, and then Gabriel appeared before her, saying, "You who are highly favored, the Lord is with you; blessed are you among women!"

When she saw him, she was startled. But the initial shock of his appearance was almost immediately overshadowed by her bewilderment concerning his perplexing salutation.

Seeing her distress, Gabriel encouraged her. "Fear not, Mary," he said, "for you have found favor with God. And, behold, you shall conceive in your womb, and bring forth a son, and shall call his name JESUS. He shall be great, and shall be called the Son of the Highest, and the Lord God shall give unto him the throne of his father, David, and he shall reign over the house of Jacob forever; and of his kingdom there shall be no end."

His words were like some miraculous medicinal cure for her melancholia, and her heart flooded with joy. She beamed a grateful smile; her cheeks flushed, her eyes welled, and she gasped involuntarily. She tried with great difficulty to temper her emotions, then succumbed to the magnitude of the moment, and blurted out the first thought that came rushing into her mind.

"How shall this be, seeing I know not a man?" she inquired. Her question, though asked with considerable excitement, was one she had pondered often—how would the virgin conceive the Messiah? She was pleased that she had been composed enough to ask this question, but was embarrassed by her delivery.

Gabriel answered her, saying, "The Holy Spirit shall come upon you, and the power of the Highest shall overshadow you: therefore, also, that holy thing which shall be born of you shall be called the Son of God. And, behold, your cousin Elizabeth, she has also conceived a son in her old age, and this is the sixth month with her, who was called barren. For with God nothing shall be impossible."

Mary bowed her head gratefully, digesting the gravity of his answer.

"Behold, the handmaid of the Lord," she whispered.

Then her heart swelled again, and she lifted up her face and her outstretched arms.

"Be it unto me according to your word!" she beamed with joy.

And the angel departed from her, leaving her alone in her room, sparsely lit by the evening sky. She woke early in the morning after a night of light sleep, and gazed out her window at the sunrise, vacantly wondering at the two morning stars set so close to one another. Mercury and Venus, shining brightly, greeted the day.

In the days that followed, Mary feared to share her experience with anyone, choosing rather to spend as much time as possible in prayer. She ended her days early, retiring to her room to pray every evening before the sun went down. Ten days after the visit from the angel, while Mary knelt praying in her room, she was bathed in great light from sunset to moonset for a period of about an hour and a half. She spent that time in a blissful trance, soaking up the majesty of the Creator. She was alone in the house for the evening, by request, while her mother visited neighbors to celebrate the holiday, for it was 1 Tishri, the Jewish New Year, the Day of Trumpets. The year was 3,764 of the Jewish calendar; the year was 3 BCE.

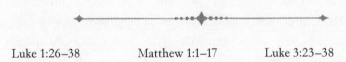

Luke 1:26–38   Matthew 1:1–17   Luke 3:23–38

Chapter 4

SIGNS IN THE HEAVENS

Magi from the East, over whom Daniel once had been elevated chief, roughly six hundred years prior, during the reign of Nebuchadnezzar, beheld Jupiter and Venus in very close proximity in the early morning sky. These Magi originated from a priestly order of the Medes and Persians, similar to that of the Levites of the Hebrew religion. Now they served the court of the Parthian kings. They monitored the night skies, charting the path of the stars to make predictions and interpretations to assist in royal decisions of government. Venus had been tracked in the morning sky for the last six months, moving slowly eastward toward the sun. Jupiter appeared below Venus on the horizon some eleven days prior. The two planets, or moving stars, were considered good omens. Jupiter was considered the star of the kings, and Venus was considered the star of fertility. The convergence of these two moving stars, according to the interpretation of the Magi, signified the birth of a king.

"Balthazar, this could be confirmation of the Hebrew prophecy," said Melchior, poking a finger at the chart.

"The birth of a new king in the constellation of the lion," returned Balthazar, looking at him inquisitively, "the Lion of Judah. Is that what you are thinking?"

"And a strong king, it would seem—Jupiter ascending immediately from the sun," added Caspar.

"Let us not get ahead of ourselves, gentlemen," warned Balthazar, "but we will continue to monitor the movement of these stars. As I have said many times before, the Hebrew prophecies speak of a king of kings. To usher in such a one, the heavens will manifest irrefutable signs."

*****

Within the next month, Mercury, the messenger star, joined Jupiter and Venus in the morning sky. Jupiter passed Venus, rising higher in the sky, as Venus descended toward the horizon. Then Mercury, ascending from the horizon, came into very close proximity to Venus. Eventually, Venus disappeared from the morning sky, beyond the horizon, and into the sun. The Magi were very familiar with the course that the fertility star would take. They knew it would reappear in the evening sky in four months, so they contented themselves charting the progress of Jupiter through the background of the stationary stars.

"Do you think it is significant?" asked Caspar after completing their evening charts.

"I think all things in the heavens are significant," scolded Balthazar, "but what does it mean? That is the question."

"It is 1 Tishri on the Hebrew calendar, the Hebrew New Year. That seems significant," replied Melchior.

"How would *you* interpret the signs as they apply to the Hebrew prophecies?" inquired Caspar, evading any further rebuke from Balthazar by addressing his curiosity directly to Melchior.

"Well," ventured Melchior, "the virgin constellation was enveloped in the waning sun precisely at the time of the new moon, which heralds each Hebrew month—and in this case, their New Year. The sun, representing the supreme king, or the Hebrew God in this case, could have impregnated the virgin as the prophecies foretell, and this may serve to herald a new beginning."

"Your interpretation is interesting and intriguing, but I still believe the signs must prove more spectacular for such an event as the prophecies suggest," reasoned Balthazar. "Would you not agree?"

"I like the interpretation. Let us not dismiss it so easily. Let us agree to consider this a sign, with those we have already witnessed, and be patient to see what will come," Caspar stated emphatically.

The two nodded in assent, but Balthazar looked uneasily at the chart before rolling it up.

*****

Four days later, Jupiter converged with Regulus, the brightest of the stars in the constellation of the lion. This bright star was considered the king of stationary stars, because the arc of its course in the heavens so closely resembles that of the sun.

"Another strong sign, is it not, Balthazar?" prodded Melchior, "the joining of two kingly stars."

"Yes, the evidence mounts, Melchior," Balthazar admitted.

"The time is right, according to the prophecy of Jeremiah, and Daniel's interpretation of it," added Caspar. "Is it too early to alert the court of our findings?"

"I believe so. Let us do our work with diligence," admonished Balthazar. "We must collect all the evidence we can find concerning this Hebrew king of kings. We cannot afford to make a mistake concerning such a great matter."

*****

During the following months, the Magi waited for the annual retrogression of Jupiter, a time when the moving star would stop and reverse its course in the heavens. While waiting, they compiled and scrutinized their charts and writings, searching for any information concerning the Hebrew king of kings. After two and a half months, Jupiter stopped, and then retraced its path toward the east, heading back toward Regulus. Twenty days later, Venus, as expected, appeared in the western evening sky, traveling eastward following Jupiter. Two months passed before Jupiter reached Regulus again. When it did, it joined not only the other star, but the moon, as well. In fact, the two stars straddled the moon. After passing Regulus, in a surprising move, Jupiter completed a second retrogression. It retraced its course again, moving in its original direction westward back toward Regulus and Venus. When it encountered Regulus for the third time, the two king stars again straddled the moon.

"There is no doubt," said Melchior. "I am convinced that the birth of a mighty king is imminent. The two king stars have met three times, and twice they have set astride the moon, mother of the sky. This is very rare. We must approach the court with our findings."

"I agree with you, Melchior. This is strong confirmation that a mighty king will be born," nodded Balthazar. "I am not entirely certain, however, that this is the Hebrew king of the prophecies."

"Balthazar," Caspar protested, "we must inform the court."

Balthazar relented, "Agreed. We will present what evidence we have gathered, and let the king and the court decide what course shall be taken."

*****

The presentation of the Magi before the court of the Parthians was met with skepticism and suspicion. The king, however, trusted Balthazar, and sought his counsel on the matter.

"I suggest sending an envoy to bring tribute to the newborn king of kings," warned Balthazar, "for we have discovered disturbing words within the Hebrew prophecies of Isaiah."

Mechior read from a scroll, "For unto us a child is born, unto us a son is given; and the government shall be upon his shoulder, and his name shall be called Wonderful Counselor, Mighty God, Everlasting Father, Prince of Peace. Of the increase of his government and peace there shall be no end, upon the throne of David, and upon his kingdom, to order it, and to establish it with judgment and with justice from henceforth even forever. The zeal of the LORD of hosts will perform this."

Hearing of the words of the prophecy provoked a murmur within the court. After further scrutiny among those counselors most vocal among them, the king addressed the court, pronouncing his judgment.

"Very well," he said, heeding the counsel of the Magi, which was now echoed by his court, "assemble an envoy and collect a proper tribute. The envoy shall leave within the month."

Balthazar bowed reverently before the king. "If it pleases your majesty," he paused, adding weight to his words, "Melchior, Caspar, and I would like to accompany the envoy to Judea."

The king, in turn, weighed Balthazar's request, and then his own words. "It pleases me well, Balthazar;" said the king, "your presence will add greater homage to the visit. You shall, in fact, head the envoy. Make whatever preparations you deem fit, and upon your return, you will provide a full report."

They planned to leave for Jerusalem within the month, but while they were preparing for their journey, an extraordinary event occurred in the heavens. Venus, having reached its farthest most eastward and brightest point, converged with Jupiter again, forming one brilliant "new" star. Venus then entered its own retrogression, returning westerly with Jupiter. This remarkable occurrence, observed in the western sky on the seventeenth day of June, was accompanied by a full moon in the east. This occurred 280 days after the Jewish New Year—the natural period of human gestation. The Magi hastened their journey with much excitement, heading westward toward Jerusalem, following the star, because they believed the Hebrew king of kings had already been born.

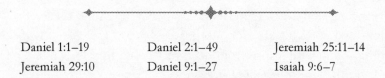

Daniel 1:1–19   Daniel 2:1–49   Jeremiah 25:11–14
Jeremiah 29:10   Daniel 9:1–27   Isaiah 9:6–7

Chapter 5

MARY'S JOURNEY

The oxcart separated from the small caravan at the entrance to Jerusalem, winding its way along the uneven path, up the hill toward the tiny village of Ein Kerem. As it rumbled along, Mary gazed out over the countryside, half admiring the sights and wondering at the adventure the day would bring. The driver, a young man in his mid-to-late twenties, was a potter named Topheth, a friend of the family. He had business in Jerusalem, and promised Mary's mother to drive her the extra distance to the summer house of Zechariah. The young merchant, trying to impress his pretty young companion, had been doubling as a tour guide and minstrel on their three-day journey all the way from Nazareth, and was now whistling some foreign tune he picked up somewhere in his travels. The wooden cart full of earthenware jostled back and forth with every step of the ox. But Mary was oblivious to the jostling, the whistling, and the sounds of the rattling earthenware. Her mind was consumed with other matters; she was still wrestling with her newfound situation.

"Go child, go with my blessings," her mother had told her, forcing an apprehensive smile, "and we shall see if the vision is true."

In the coolness of the early-morning hours, before her journey, her mother had patted Mary's hand nervously. Gazing searchingly into her eyes, she encouraged her, "If Elizabeth is indeed with child, you shall stay with her, attending to her needs as we discussed. But if not, you will return immediately, and we will monitor your own condition."

Mary, who had been absentmindedly rubbing her hand in remembrance of her mother's touch, laid her hand gently upon her stomach.

"I see no need to involve Joseph at this point!" she heard her mother say, her hushed voice rising to a shriek. "We will deal with that when we know more," she continued, lowering her voice again, and straining to relax her deeply furrowed brow. "In God's good time," she had corrected herself, her face returning to her apprehensive smile.

"Don't worry, Mama," Mary had assured her, smiling calmly, "it is all true. I know it is!"

"You're a good girl, Mary," said her mother, and kissed her hand, as the cart began to move forward.

The cart jerked, bringing Mary's thoughts back to the present.

Her mother's final words were, "I believe in you." These words and the genuine smile of her mother's face reassured her. Mary smiled and rubbed her hand again. She knew she would find Elizabeth as the angel had described her—six months pregnant. This meant that Mary would need to stay with Elizabeth for the remaining three months of her pregnancy and at least another month to help while she recovered. This also meant that upon her return to Nazareth, Mary would most certainly be showing.

How will I explain this to Joseph? she wondered. *How will my mother explain to him my sudden disappearance?*

"We're here," interrupted the potter. "Delivered safe and sound," he boasted.

Before fully awakening to the excitement of the moment, Mary finished her thought.

God must have a plan that will fulfill his purpose. I will try not to worry about what is already planned for me, she consoled herself.

Chapter 6

MARY VISITS ELIZABETH

"Oh, thank you for taking such good care of me, my dear friend," said Mary gleefully, kissing Topheth on the cheek as he helped her down from his cart.

She smiled sweetly into his face, which was likewise aglow, reflecting her smile. Then she tugged at him, pulling his big work-hardened hand, and began running toward the gate.

"Come, I will introduce you. You must come meet my cousin. She will want to thank you also," she said, as they bounded past the gate into the small courtyard.

Inside the courtyard, Mary spied a young woman sweeping the walkway. She released the hand of the potter, looking back at him, for he was laboring somewhat to catch his breath. He smiled in consent, and she turned and skipped off to greet the young worker.

"Good afternoon," said Mary. "I seek Elizabeth, the wife of Zechariah. I am her cousin, Mary," she said, smiling.

The woman began to reply, and then turned, looking up.

Mary turned also, and seeing her cousin descending the stone staircase, she greeted her with restrained emotion, "Cousin Elizabeth!"

Elizabeth halted on the staircase, briefly, holding her stomach. She looked upward, at the sky. Mary looked up, as well. The potter and the young woman, who had quit her sweeping, looked skyward with them. At a great distance, a dove circled overhead. Mary's gaze returned to Elizabeth, who was now staring intently into Mary's face with anticipation.

Elizabeth, speaking with great joy and excitement, prophesied aloud, "Blessed are you among women, and blessed is the fruit of your womb. How can it be, therefore, that the mother of my Lord should come to me? For, lo, as soon as the voice of your salutation sounded in my ears, the babe leaped in my womb for joy. And blessed is she that believed, for there shall be a performance of those things which were told her from the Lord."

When she finished her greeting, there was a great pause. The potter and the young woman looked at one another in astonishment.

Then closing her eyes and lifting her hands toward heaven, Mary prophesied, as well, saying, "My soul does magnify the Lord, and my spirit has rejoiced in God my Savior. For he has regarded the low estate of his handmaiden: for, behold, from henceforth all generations shall call me blessed. For he that is mighty has done to me great things, and holy is his name. And his mercy is on them that fear him from generation to generation. He has shown strength with his arm; he has scattered the proud in the imagination of their hearts. He has put down the mighty from their seats, and exalted them of low degree. He has filled the hungry with good things, and the rich he has sent empty away. He has helped his servant Israel, in remembrance of his mercy, as he spoke to our fathers, to Abraham, and to his seed forever."

The cousins hugged at the bottom of the stairs, and the two onlookers drew near to celebrate with them. All four entered the house, and Elizabeth served wheat cakes and new wine while they discussed with joy what they had all witnessed. As the potter was leaving, he was still reveling.

He smiled heartily, raising his voice in excitement as he climbed back onto his cart, "An amazing day! It's not often that God rewards us so quickly and so generously for our kindnesses. For a short trek out of my way, I am rewarded with a pretty young traveling companion, a late lunch with three lovely women, and the joy of witnessing God's work in progress. Yes, I will remember this day always!"

With that, he goaded his ox into service, waved, and yelled, "Good-bye, ladies."

He was a good distance down the road, and he could still be heard saying, "It's not every day that one gets to witness prophesying. I never have before, and perhaps I may never again."

Luke 1:39–56

Chapter 7

CIRCUMCISION OF JOHN THE BAPTIST

Topheth, the potter, who was exuberant in his storytelling, became somewhat of a celebrity having spread his eyewitness account of the prophecies along his trade route. Mary's mother, hearing the confirmation of Elizabeth's condition, was determined to visit her cousin to celebrate the birth of her child. When the time arrived for her to leave, she went to her rabbi, explaining the situation—adding details to the story, which had already reached him through gossip. The rabbi reluctantly consented to confront Joseph with the truth of Mary's condition, before Mary and her mother were to return from their visit. So Mary's mother arranged her own journey with the young pottery merchant to join her daughter in Ein Kerem.

The winter journey was not so pleasant, but they had little time to complain, for they arrived early in the evening on the day of Elizabeth's delivery. She had entered into her labor several hours earlier, and Mary's mother joined the flurry of activity the moment she arrived. Fresh linens were prepared, and water basins repeatedly were filled. In and out of one of the guest chambers, which had been set up as a birthing room, went the parade of women employed in this solemn and joyous work of ushering in life. Their constant good-natured chatter could be heard throughout the entire house.

Zechariah and the potter took turns shifting positions, and moving between rooms, trying to get comfortable. Silently, they observed the scene as it unfolded. Topheth felt he was needed there to support Zechariah. And old Zechariah, as wide-eyed as a child, silently took in everything. Those steel-gray eyes overflowed with tears several hours into the night, when after hearing the first cries of the infant, Mary ushered him into the room to behold his radiant wife and newborn son. All faces were aglow as they beheld the couple who had waited so long for the arrival of this child. Outside the window, low on the western horizon, the first appearance of the evening star, Venus, went unnoticed.

Following the birth of their son, as was the custom, the child was presented to the local rabbi to be circumcised on the eighth day. While performing the rite of circumcision, the rabbi, referring to the child, called him Zechariah, after the name of his father.

"He shall be called John," Elizabeth protested.

The rabbi looked at her with a puzzled expression, and the onlookers began to murmur. Then those closest to Zechariah turned to him. But as he was still unable to speak for himself, he gestured awkwardly for something upon which to write. He scribbled hastily.

"His name is John," read the rabbi, frowning and displaying the note.

A collective gasp filled the synagogue, followed by more murmuring.

"None of his kindred are called by this name," one priestly colleague objected.

In response, as if on cue, the mouth of Zechariah was opened, and he began to prophesy!

"Blessed be the Lord God of Israel, for he has visited and redeemed his people, and has raised up a horn of salvation for us in the house of his servant, David," stammered Zechariah. "As he spoke by the mouth of his holy prophets, which have been since the world began: that we should be saved from our enemies, and from the hand of all that hate us, to perform the mercy promised to our fathers, and to remember his holy covenant; the oath which he swore to our father, Abraham, that he would grant unto us, that we being delivered out of the hand of our enemies might serve him without fear, in holiness and righteousness before him, all the days of our lives," Zechariah continued, growing in strength and conviction. Then he looked long and lovingly at his son, and beamed and said, "And you, child, shall be called the prophet of the Highest, for you shall go before the face of the Lord to prepare his ways; to give knowledge of salvation unto his people by the remission of their sins, through the tender mercy of our God." Then looking briefly at his wife, then at Mary's mother, then at Mary herself, he finished his prophecy with great satisfaction gazing expectantly at the virgin belly, "Whereby the dayspring from on high has visited us, to give light to them that sit in darkness and in the shadow of death, to guide our feet into the way of peace."

All in attendance were equally stunned, though their astonishment manifested itself in various forms of comical awkwardness. The rabbi opened and closed his mouth several times, trying to find the proper words to speak. Zechariah's priestly colleagues waggled scowling looks among themselves, glancing pensively at Zechariah. The women were huddled, hugging and crying joyfully, giving glory to God. And there was Zechariah, who had wrestled his son from the grasp of the immobile rabbi, praising God, laughing aloud, and crying shamelessly while lifting his child high above his head in playful adoration. The remainder of the onlookers stood in bewilderment, marveling at the spectacle. Finally, the rabbi composed himself, and tugging at the arm of Zechariah, regained control of the usually solemn event. The circumcision was concluded quickly, without further incident, and the audience spilled out into the streets of the little village, where eventually the excited conversation diminished, and the attendants dispersed.

But all that had been witnessed that day was told and retold throughout the entire hill country of Judea. Those that heard the testimony wondered in their hearts at what manner of child this would be. From that day, whether through apprehension or genuine joyous expectation, a fear of God came upon the land.

Luke 1:57–80

Chapter 8

JOSEPH'S DECISION

The rabbi at Nazareth struggled within himself, praying and fasting for guidance—not so much about believing Mary's story, but about how to convey such news to Joseph. Over the years, he had dealt with the supernatural beliefs of those who frequented his synagogue, and he found that time had a way of tempering the overzealousness of the impressionable heart. As a young rabbi, he had become flustered and anxious in his dealings with stories of the supernatural, but experience had taught him that these things usually worked themselves out naturally. He found it best not to ignore supernatural beliefs, but to downplay their importance. After a week of prayer and procrastination had passed, he knew he could no longer wait to relate the story to Joseph. Joseph knew that Mary's mother had gone to visit her cousin, and he knew that Mary had been sent there months beforehand to help with Elizabeth's delivery. But the rabbi knew that Mary was pregnant, something that Joseph would need to comprehend sooner, rather than later. He wanted Joseph to have plenty of time to digest the severity of the decision that he would have to make—a decision that would affect many people, deeply, for a long time. His prayers led him to the belief that he should present Mary's story to Joseph as he himself had received it. He called upon him one evening, soon after suppertime.

"Joseph, have you heard any news concerning Mary?" he asked warily.

"No, but *you* have! Haven't you? Is this not the reason for your visit?" he guessed, grinning widely.

"I am here to discuss *old* news," he hesitated, not returning the grin, "but important news." Then taking Joseph's arm, he looked him in the eyes, "And I caution you to hear all that I have to say, considering carefully my counsel, for I have known of the matter for some time now and have been praying diligently for wisdom."

The rabbi's gravity startled Joseph, whose work in the trades had forged him into a man of considerable physical strength. For this reason, the strength of the rabbi's grip was what initially took him by surprise, followed by the almost violent flash in the rabbi's metallic brown eyes. The words of the rabbi, though heard by Joseph's ears, and understood by Joseph's mind, registered only as confirmation as to the importance of the ensuing conversation. Joseph gestured to the cushions on the floor of his modest living quarters, and the two men sat on either side of a low handsomely crafted table.

"A week or so after Mary left for Ein Kerem, her mother came to me to discuss a rather disturbing matter," said the rabbi. "Two days before Mary's departure," he explained, "she came to her mother claiming that she had been visited one night by an angel of the Lord."

The rabbi hesitated, so that Joseph could fully grasp his words. Joseph looked puzzled, and then opened his mouth, wanting to speak. But the rabbi put one hand up before Joseph, with the other at his own lips in a gesture of silence.

Then he continued, "This angel, according to Mary, told her that Elizabeth, who had been barren for many years, was now with child. Her mother, who originally thought the story was nonsense, reconsidered, and the next day decided to send Mary to Elizabeth at Ein Kerem.

"I know, I know, this has all been explained to you," he said to Joseph, trying to continue uninterrupted. "As you also know, the pregnancy was confirmed, and Mary's mother has gone to Ein Kerem, as well," he said, pausing to regroup. "Let me now explain to you the whole matter," continued the rabbi. "I have been told by several people that Zechariah, Elizabeth's husband, was also visited by an angel and that he was struck dumb when told of the imminent birth of their son. I was informed later, that upon Mary's arrival, Elizabeth prophesied about the child. The potter who took her to Ein Kerem witnessed this," he explained. He paused again and then added, "He told me that Mary also prophesied that day!"

Joseph looked thoughtfully at the rabbi. "So you're telling me that Mary believes she has seen an angel, and that she has prophesied." He paused. "Should I be concerned?" he asked, carefully framing his words.

"Let us not judge rashly. Please, there is still more to tell," he said, measuring Joseph's reaction. "The angel that spoke to Mary that night had more *exciting* news. Mary's mother asked me to deliver the news to you before they return," he explained. "As I said before, I have been praying for wisdom to deliver the message, hoping to put off this conversation a little longer. But I received more news today, which has forced my hand. Elizabeth gave birth to a son, and they have named him John. It seems that there was some question about the name, because of Zechariah's inability to speak, but the issue was resolved when his voice miraculously returned, and he began to prophesy."

When he had concluded these words, the rabbi stopped abruptly. He watched Joseph intently, waiting for his reaction.

Joseph started, his physical nerves perceptibly mimicking his thoughts.

"Rabbi, what are all these prophecies about?" Joseph questioned anxiously.

"That their child will be a great prophet, and will prepare the way before the Lord," he said wistfully. "But the foundation of our conversation is even deeper, I'm afraid," said the rabbi, sighing, while mustering courage. He continued, "The day that Mary arrived in Ein Kerem, according to the potter, Elizabeth prophesied about Mary, as well. And the prophecy was a confirmation, according to Mary's story, of what the angel had told her."

The words of the rabbi trailed off here, his voice lowering with his head, while he searched for the proper words. The pause, though strained, was not a long one, however; it ended abruptly, when he blurted out the big news, "That she would become pregnant by the Holy Spirit of God and give birth to the Messiah."

Joseph blinked, put an elbow on the table, and then dropped his head, running his rough hand through a shock of wavy black hair.

"Is there more?" Joseph forced out, as if he had been kicked in the solar plexus.

"No, that is the entire matter," said the rabbi sympathetically, and then added, "as I know it."

"You mentioned counsel, Rabbi," Joseph managed, still looking a bit sick. "Counsel, wisdom, for which you prayed?" he urged.

"My counsel is this, Joseph," said the rabbi, "hold your judgment until the last possible moment, making certain that you have all the facts. We have no confirmation yet that Mary is even pregnant. If she is pregnant, then you will have to decide." "Even then," he added, "there will be things to consider."

"Are you suggesting that she could have possibly conceived a child by the Spirit of God?" Joseph suggested incredulously.

"I am confessing that I do not know the will of God, or his power. We are all looking for a Messiah, Joseph. The girls all pray that God will choose them to be his mother. I suppose, if a Messiah comes, someone will be his mother," the rabbi mused.

"And you think it's Mary?" Joseph said with a tone between hopefulness and incredulity.

"It could be Mary, just as easily as someone else," he offered weakly. Then with conviction, he said, "If she is found to be pregnant, I hope for her sake that her child is the Messiah." Then he lowered his eyes and reluctantly concluded, "The alternative would be tragic."

Joseph knew the Law, and he knew that a woman found to be pregnant outside of marriage would be ostracized by a God-fearing Jewish society. According to the Mosaic Law, she should be put to death by stoning. Stonings were rare, but he had heard the practice of stoning was still being adhered to by some of the most traditional sects of the Jews. In these treacherous times, religious ardor had intensified, and the normally coolheaded restraint of the common folk could no longer be relied upon.

For the next several weeks, before Mary and her mother were to return, Joseph involved himself in a period of extreme soul searching. Taking the advice of the rabbi, he spent much of his nonworking hours in prayer. He fasted often, as well, losing several nonauxiliary pounds. Sleep came sparingly, and was often fitful, with dreams of horribly tragic scenes involving Mary. It was after one of these dreams that Joseph decided within himself that if Mary were found to be pregnant, he would divorce her immediately, hoping that she and her mother would leave the area to conceal their shame. His mind being settled, his strength revived, and his sleep returned to normal. He was, therefore, in good spirits when retiring to his bed one night, just weeks before Mary's return.

But that night, the angel of the Lord appeared to him in a dream, saying, "Joseph, you son of David, fear not to take unto you Mary your wife, for that which is conceived in her is of the Holy Spirit. And she shall bring forth a son, and you shall call his name Jesus, for he shall save his people from their sins."

And when Joseph awoke, he remembered the dream and the words of the prophet Isaiah, which were written, "Behold, a virgin shall be with child, and shall bring forth a son, and they shall call his name Immanuel;" Immanuel being interpreted as, "God with us."

Joseph went early that morning to the rabbi, and told him of the dream, and they read from the scroll together the words of Isaiah. So God softened the heart of Joseph, in that Joseph's resolve was to marry Mary, and to refrain from lying with her until the birth of this wondrous child.

Matthew 1:18–25   Deuteronomy 22:23–24   Isaiah 7:14

Chapter 9

BIRTH OF THE MESSIAH

Rome prepared for the Silver Jubilee, the sixtieth year of the rule of Caesar Augustus. The Senate planned to bestow upon Augustus the highest possible honor, the title *Pater Patriae* (Father of the Country). A decree went out, therefore, into all the empire, that a registration should be performed for the suspension of taxes for one year celebrating this honor. In return for the suspension of these taxes, each Roman subject was to take an oath to be faithful to Caesar Augustus. Quirinius, then procurator of Syria, tolerated the tradition of the Jews to be numbered according to their native tribal families. This produced great upheaval, as travelers clogged the highways, returning to the villages of their tribal nativity to be registered.

Joseph, now understanding the whole of the matter concerning Mary, decided to spare her from long difficult travel and to conceal her condition from the scrutiny of their Nazarene neighbors. To this end, he sent word to her at Ein Kerem that he would join her there. They would marry there and then travel to Bethlehem, only a short trip, where they would register together as husband and wife. So after conspiring with the rabbi, Joseph and the rabbi traveled from Nazareth and joined her early that summer. Joseph and Mary then married before her full term had come.

The Jews were reluctant to take an oath honoring Caesar, and the celebration of the Silver Jubilee had come and gone without their full registration. Roman pressure mounted in the months that followed, and unregistered Jews were being rounded up. Joseph had hoped to somehow avoid taking such an oath, but he now realized the impending danger. He continued to wait, however, hoping that Mary would deliver the baby. Her condition had become increasingly uncomfortable, and Joseph worried over the prospect of her traveling even the short distance to Bethlehem. But Mary, recognizing her husband's torment, convinced him she was capable of making such a small journey.

So they went to Bethlehem in the afternoon, standing in long lines, waiting to be registered. And as the day drew long, Mary became more and more uncomfortable. Joseph had just registered, but before he could read the oath, Mary's water broke, and Joseph was forced to quickly search out accommodations. The only inn of the tiny village was already overfilled with the influx of visitors. The innkeeper seemed to relish the opportunity to turn away the distressed couple, but his wife, taking pity upon them, sent them down the road to a cave containing stables. She promised to come to them later to help, which she did within the hour. The couple was huddled safely inside the cave before the sun went down. But the innkeeper's wife, upon arriving, commented on the strangeness of the sky—for there appeared in the east a full moon, low on the horizon, with an exceedingly bright star above it.

Joseph had fashioned Mary a bed of straw and was trying his best to keep her comfortable. He was visibly relieved when the woman entered the stable with clean linens and a jar of fresh water. She immediately took control, sending Joseph out for firewood while she attended to Mary. When Joseph returned, he was put to work building a fire, putting water on to boil, and arranging a feeding trough with fresh straw. The woman rifled through her stack of linens, separating the larger pieces from the smaller strips, and placed them just so in preparation of the birth. When the critical time arrived, she skillfully instructed Joseph in attending to Mary's comfort, while guiding Mary through the difficult phases of the delivery. The child was born without too much difficulty, and mother and child were cleaned with the larger pieces of the linens. The woman, who was delighted over the health of her two patients, apologized repeatedly for having to wrap the child in the remaining strips of linen. But, she assured the parents that the linen strips would keep their son clean, and that the straw would provide him ample warmth.

That night, in the fields outside the village, shepherds kept watch over their flock. And as they wondered over the uniquely lighted sky, an angel appeared unto them, and the glory of God shone all around them, so that they feared for their lives.

And the angel said to them, "Fear not, for behold, I bring you good tidings of great joy, which shall be to all people. For unto you is born this day in the city of David, a Savior; who is the Messiah, the Lord. And this shall be a sign unto you; you shall find the babe wrapped in swaddling cloths, lying in a manger."

And suddenly, there was with the angel a multitude of the heavenly host praising God, and saying, "Glory to God in the highest, and on earth peace, good will toward men."

Then when the angels had ascended again into heaven, the shepherds said to one another, "Let us now go even unto Bethlehem, and see this thing which is come to pass, which the Lord has made known unto us."

So they came with haste and found Mary, and Joseph, and the babe lying in a manger. And when they had seen it, they made known abroad the saying that was told them concerning this child. And all they that heard it wondered at those things which were told them by the shepherds. But Mary kept all these things, and pondered them in her heart. And the shepherds returned, glorifying and praising God for all the things that they had heard and seen. For all that the angel had told them had come to pass.

Luke 2:1–20

Chapter 10

TRADITIONS OF THE FIRSTBORN

After heartfelt discussion, Joseph and Mary decided to remain in Bethlehem, where their sure-to-be-misunderstood situation could remain undetected. With the help of the innkeeper's wife, who had become quite fond of the family, they secured more permanent lodging.

Now, according to the Law of Moses, there are seven days of separation for a male child. During this time, Mary was considered unclean. On the eighth day, they visited the synagogue at Bethlehem, and presented their son to the local rabbi to be circumcised. As instructed by the angel, they named him Jesus.

Mary continued thirty-three days, fulfilling the days of her purification, before they brought the babe to Jerusalem to present him to the Lord. Then, according to the Law, Mary presented herself, with her sacrifice (a lamb of the first year for a burnt offering and a turtledove for a sin offering), and so she was made clean. And because her first child was a male, sacrifice was made also for him (a pair of turtledoves, one for a burnt offering and one for a sin offering), and so he was separated to the Lord, according to the Law of Moses.

At the temple in Jerusalem was a man named Simeon, who was just and devout. And he waited for the consolation of Israel, and the Holy Spirit was upon him. God had revealed to him by the Holy

Spirit that he should not see death before he had seen the Lord's Messiah. So he came by the Spirit into the temple, when the parents brought Jesus to fulfill the custom of the Law.

And he took the baby up in his arms, and blessed God, and said, "Lord, now let your servant depart in peace, according to your word, for my eyes have seen your salvation, which you have prepared before the face of all people; a light to lighten the Gentiles, and the glory of your people Israel."

And Joseph and Mary marveled at those things that he said.

Then Simeon blessed them also and said to Mary, "Behold, this child is set for the fall and rising again of many in Israel; and for a sign which shall be spoken against; yes, a sword shall pierce through your own soul also, that the thoughts of many hearts may be revealed."

A prophetess was there, as well, one Anna, the daughter of Phanuel, of the tribe of Asher. She was very old, a widow of some eighty-four years, whose husband had died just seven years into their marriage. She remained always at the temple, serving God day and night in fasting and prayer. She, too, came at that time, and gave thanks to the Lord. And she spoke of the child to all them that sought redemption in Jerusalem.

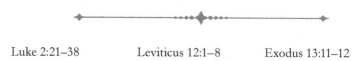

Luke 2:21–38   Leviticus 12:1–8   Exodus 13:11–12

Chapter 11

FLIGHT TO EGYPT

The Magi arrived at Jerusalem near the end of December.

And they sought counsel with Herod, the king, saying, "Where is he that is born king of the Jews? For we have seen his star in the east and have come to worship him."

Then the Magi quoted Daniel's scripture and pointed out the signs still vivid in the night sky overhead. When Herod the king had heard these things, he was troubled, and all Jerusalem with him. And when he had gathered all the chief priests and scribes of the people together, he demanded of them where the Messiah should be born.

And they said to him, "In Bethlehem of Judea, for thus it is written by the prophet, 'And you, Bethlehem, in the land of Judah, are not the least among the princes of Judah, for out of you shall come a Governor, that shall rule my people Israel.'"

Then Herod called Melchior, Balthazar, and Caspar; speaking privately with them, inquiring of them diligently what time the star appeared.

And he sent them to Bethlehem, and said, "Go and search diligently for the young child, and when you have found him, bring me word again, that I may come and worship him also."

When they had heard the king, they departed; and the star, which they saw in the east, went before them, till it came and stood over where the young child was. When the Magi saw the star, they rejoiced with exceeding great joy.

"Do you see how Jupiter and Venus stand still together directly over Bethlehem?" marveled Melchior.

"This very night, Jupiter begins its annual return march back across the sky," said Balthazar. "How marvelous."

"And on the very day that the sun stands still, marking the rebirth of the sun," mused Caspar.

"See, too, where the king star resides, my friends," stressed Balthazar.

"In the very abdomen of Virgo," responded Caspar, "the virgin birth of a king. It must be!"

"This is certainly a sign of the Hebrew prophecy come to pass," added Melchior wistfully.

So they inquired at the inn, and the innkeeper's wife took them to the place where the family dwelled. And when they had come into the house, they saw the young child with Mary his mother and fell down and worshiped him. Then they opened their treasures and presented unto him gifts: gold, frankincense, and myrrh. So Joseph and Mary extended them their hospitality, and the Magi resided with them that night. But being warned of God in a dream that they should not return to Herod, the Magi awoke the next morning, and departed into their own country another way.

That evening, the angel of the Lord appeared also to Joseph in a dream, saying, "Arise, and take the young child and his mother, and flee into Egypt, and remain there until I bring you word, for Herod will seek the young child to destroy him."

When he arose, therefore, Joseph took the young child and his mother that very night and departed into Egypt. And they remained there until the death of Herod: that it might be fulfilled which was spoken of the Lord by the prophet, saying, "Out of Egypt have I called my son."

Two weeks had passed before Herod realized that he was mocked of the wise men. He was exceedingly angry and sent forth soldiers to slay all the children that were in Bethlehem, and in all the coasts thereof. Because the wise men had seen the star on September 11 of the previous year, and because it was not known if this sign heralded the birth or conception of the child, Herod ordered the death of all male children from two years old and under. On the evening his orders were executed, even the moon lamented—hiding as it were, in sackcloth and ashes behind the shadow of the earth, in total eclipse. Then was fulfilled that which was spoken by Jeremiah the prophet, saying, "In Ramah there was a voice heard, lamentation, and weeping, and great mourning, Rachel weeping for her children, and would not be comforted, because they are not."

Within three weeks of the atrocity, Herod died a painful death—his very bowels rotted within him.

And when Herod was dead, the angel of the Lord appeared in a dream to Joseph in Egypt, saying, "Arise, and take the young child and his mother, and go into the land of Israel, for they are dead which sought the young child's life."

So Joseph arose and took the young child and his mother and came into the land of Israel. But when he heard that Archelaus reigned in Judea in the room of his father, Herod, he was afraid to go there; notwithstanding, being warned of God in a dream, he turned aside into the parts of Galilee. And he came and dwelt again in the city of Nazareth: that it might be fulfilled which was spoken by the prophets, "He shall be called a Nazarene." There in Nazareth, Jesus was raised according to the code of a Nazarite, putting no razor to his hair, and partaking of no strong drink or wine. Neither did he partake of anything of the vine or partake in any burial ceremonies of the dead. And the child grew, becoming strong in spirit, filled with wisdom, and the grace of God was upon him.

<hr />

Matthew 2:1–23   Daniel 9:24   Micah 5:2
Hosea 11:1   Jeremiah 31:15   Numbers 6:1–8
Luke 2:39–40

Chapter 12

JESUS FOUND IN THE TEMPLE

Joseph and Mary added to their family, living as peaceably as was possible within the community at Nazareth. Joseph worked as a handyman, able to do all forms of labor, including carpentry, stonework, and brickwork. He built roads for the Romans and worked on the ongoing building projects established by Herod, primarily at Caesarea. In slow times, he took on smaller projects for the villagers around Nazareth, in Galilee. He worked the fields at harvest and planted during planting season. He frequented the fishing towns around the Sea of Galilee, helping the fishermen, when the fishing work was plentiful. He built stone walls and towers for the vineyards and did any odd job he could find. And his sons eventually worked alongside him, sweating in the hot sun, even sleeping among the sheep in the cold of winter, to aid the shepherds when needed. The family endured the hostile Roman rule, and the rule of the corrupt Herodian dynasty. They saw the suffering of the poor, the shrewdness of the corrupt businessmen, the violence rooted in frustration, and the effect of the hard times endured by all. Jesus and his brothers, James, Joseph, Simon, and Judas learned from their father, and eventually helped him in his work. Mary instructed her daughter, Salome, and her sisters in the traditional role of running the household.

Though Jesus obediently learned and worked with his father

and brothers, it was evident to Joseph that his true interests lay in other directions. Joseph and Mary tried their best to provide an environment wrought in righteousness, but even this proved to be a daunting task. Jesus was very watchful of everything around him, very inquisitive, and as a youth, he spoke his mind openly, often to the consternation of his parents. It became apparent, early on, that he was learning much more than they were teaching him. Parenting Jesus became quite the challenge, so much so that it became impossible for the couple to hide their frustration from their other children. Many of Jesus's thoughts seemed odd to the audience of common folk surrounding his everyday life, his concepts being too profound for them to grasp. For this reason, as he matured, he found himself drawn more and more to the clergy, who although they did not always understand or agree with his thoughts, were more willing to discuss them in detail. Still, Joseph persevered; stressing honor, hard work, compassion, and simple direct communication. Jesus became hard-working, relatively quiet among the local folk, and very respectful. For this reason, he was not often noticed, and not well known. His long locks, however, made him stand out as a holy man, separated to God, but one who remained both introspective and to himself.

Jesus developed a special relationship with both parents. Father and son eventually enjoyed a mutual respect for one another, as Jesus became more proficient at simplifying his thoughts into parables using definitions already available in the scriptures. Mary, too, became skillful deciphering his coded speech, which, with her, took on a somewhat playful form of communicating. His siblings, for the most part, however, found his speech irritating, because of the unpopular response it received from the local community.

From the time of Jesus's birth, Joseph felt it his duty to stress piety; adhering strictly to the Law, he observed all of its ordinances and participated in all of its traditions. Accordingly, every year he took his family to Jerusalem to celebrate the feast of Passover. When Jesus was twelve years old, as was their custom, they went up to Jerusalem during the Passover feast. As was typical during these celebrations, they were accompanied by family and friends, who traveled with them from Galilee. Their journey was festive, and many others from local towns and villages joined them along their route. Jerusalem overflowed with visitors at this time, and tent communities sprung up within and just outside the city walls. The children took full advantage of this holiday atmosphere, running in packs, and reveling in camping outdoors. The parents enjoyed their holiday from strict parenting, relying on safety in numbers—the number of the children within their groups, and the number of adults overseeing them. Often, a group of the children slept together in one tent, staying up all hours of the night. In the morning, the tent communities would begin to stir at dawn, as families prepared for their daily ascent to the temple. As was the custom of most visiting parents, Joseph and Mary kept their children with them, entering the Jerusalem throngs as a family unit. After their worship within the temple had concluded, however, the groups of children often reunited to tour the festivities of the city. They would all return to the camp late afternoon, early evening—this went on all week long. Jesus teamed up with his cousin, John, as they always did during these festivals. They were similarly passionate about their beliefs, and enjoyed discussing the scriptures with one another. A few months earlier, John celebrated his thirteenth birthday, entering manhood with the reading of the Torah at his synagogue. John had an extensive knowledge of the scriptures, and a real knack for piecing passages together to garner simple yet profound truths. Jesus, who had surpassed John by his wisdom and knowledge of the scriptures, nevertheless assumed his usual subordinate role to the older, more exuberant cousin in their conversations. Jesus was contented, instead, to ask his cousin pertinent questions designed to expand John's understanding. John, though intrigued by the startlingly challenging questions, was unaware of the subtle change in their communication. He was still feeling the pride and pressure that accompanied the responsibility of his newfound manhood.

"Woman," said Jesus, "there was a great king, who sent his son to a very poor house in a wicked city, saying, 'Go and clean the house, for it is filthy, and the stink of it is an affront to me.'"

"Jesus," scolded Mary, blushing and wearing an embarrassed half-smile, "no one will know you're kidding. A son calling his mother 'woman' sounds so disrespectful."

"Sorry Mama," he snickered, turning toward John. "John and I would like to go to the temple to hear the rabbis speak," he said questioningly.

"Quit teasing your mother," said Joseph, "and we will go together when it is time. I assure you, you will have your fill of hearing from the rabbis."

Jesus and his father returned strategic glances.

"And as for your parable, it came across as arrogant and harsh—not at all worthy of a son of God," he frowned.

"How long must I tolerate you, man?" replied Jesus, feigning his best disgusted look at his father.

"You better run, boy," barked Joseph, laughing heartily and turning on them with a pounce.

"Run," cried John, "the Philistines are upon us!"

And the two boys scrambled out the door into the morning air. They ran a little way from the tent before stopping, realizing that Joseph had not really pursued them. John bent over, laughing and breathing heavily.

"He's funny. It must be fun to have Uncle Joseph as a father," he said, enviously grinning up at Jesus.

Jesus grinned back knowingly, waiting to hear the true heart of the matter from his cousin.

"I mean, I love my father, but he's so old and strict, being a priest and all," he said still looking Jesus in the eyes as he stood upright.

Jesus, feeling compassion, faced John. And grabbing his shoulders, he looked earnestly at him and warmly diverted John's thoughts.

"Yeah, but you can outrun *your* father," he said.

John threw his head back and laughed aloud.

"This is true," he laughed again.

Jesus put his arm around John's neck, and they stumbled back toward the tent, still laughing.

Later that day, John and Jesus sat in a small alcove of the temple surrounded by older men bantering back and forth about the interpretation of scripture.

"The lad has a valid point, Caiaphas," said Annas to the young man. "Isaiah says, 'Your dead men shall live, together with my dead body shall they arise. Awake and sing, you that dwell in dust, for your dew is as the dew of herbs, and the earth shall cast out the dead.'"

Caiaphas gazed, perturbed at the boy, and then quizzically at his mentor, wavering between smile and frown. "Master Annas, this is a hard lesson," he said gravely. "Who will believe it?" he asked, "It is divisive in nature and will divide the faith of an already unstable people."

"Who has believed our report?" offered Jesus, smiling wryly. "Isaiah writes this, also."

"And so he does," returned Annas with a chuckle, briefly glancing at Caiaphas. "Perhaps we should keep this knowledge among ourselves for a while." As his gaze returned to Jesus, Annas, disturbed by the lad's reference to scriptures that had always troubled him, added thoughtfully, "At least until the proper opportunity presents itself."

At this last comment, the group of men returned to their heated debate over the possibility of resurrection from the dead, and its implications.

"Jesus," scolded John in a whisper, "I think you enjoy causing trouble. Your questions always end in heated arguments."

"God's ways are not man's ways," Jesus reassured him, "therefore, man's thoughts will always rage against God's truth.

Even so, we must have the courage to proclaim it. Have faith; eventually they *will* hear it."

"Not today," John scoffed, a little perturbed at the noticeable role reversal evident by the respect the rabbis had been paying to his younger cousin. "Let's tour the city once more. I don't want to spend our last day hanging with adults."

"You go ahead," Jesus returned. "I want, or rather, I *need* to stay here."

"Suit yourself. I'll catch up with you later," said John. He slumped somewhat and sighed, and then turned and headed toward the gate at the far end of the courtyard.

For the next three days, Jesus remained in the temple, praying and provoking with his questions the thoughts of the rabbis who came to discuss the scriptures. Meanwhile, Joseph departed Jerusalem with his wife and family, believing that Jesus also had begun the journey home accompanying his cousins and friends. It wasn't until the end of the first day's journey that they realized he was missing. When asked, John told them he was last seen in the temple, talking with the rabbis. So Joseph and Mary returned with their family to Jerusalem to find him. On the third day, they found him in the temple still among the rabbis.

"I have calculated the times according to Daniel's writings, and the boy is correct," said Nicodemus. "Astonishingly, the Messiah should come in our lifetime." He cautiously surveyed the group of men before him, and then looked warily at Jesus. "He may very well be among us now," he concluded.

"I caution you, Nicodemus, not to speculate aloud about such things," Caiaphas warned. "False messiahs and prophets can be very difficult to control. They tend to lead poor, weak-minded people astray—away from the structure of the Law. Israel needs the Law; it is the Law that binds us together."

"What say you to that, young master?" inquired Nicodemus grinning at Jesus.

Jesus glanced over the shoulder of the young rabbi, seeing

his parents searching the temple. He smiled at the humorous way in which Nicodemus had addressed him, not acknowledging the disapproving responses obvious on the faces of the other rabbis.

"It is the misunderstanding of the Law that binds," he corrected, waiting for his parents to recognize his voice. When they saw him, he added boldly, "and when the true Messiah comes, the son of God, the truth he speaks will free our people from their bonds to serve his Father willingly."

His words pierced the hearts of the rabbis, and their indignation was quite apparent in their flushing cheeks. These men, keepers of the Law, who had been entertaining the inquisitive nature of this boy, were now having their understanding of the Law called into question by him. The effect made them speechless, and afforded an awkward silence allowing his parents to interrupt the discussion.

"Son, why have you dealt with us so? Behold, your father and I have sought you sorrowing," said Mary.

But he said to them, "How is it that you sought me? Know you not that I must be about my Father's business?"

Jesus's parents did not understand the words he spoke to them. The rabbis, however, were troubled by his saying, remembering that Nicodemus warned that the Messiah might be among them. So Jesus went with his parents and came to Nazareth and was subject unto them. Joseph took offence at the words spoken by the boy, believing that Jesus was being disrespectful to him, for they were a stern reminder to Joseph that he was not Jesus's biological father. Mary comforted Joseph but kept the sayings in her heart and pondered their meaning. And Jesus increased in wisdom and stature and in favor with God and man.

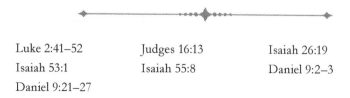

Luke 2:41–52	Judges 16:13	Isaiah 26:19
Isaiah 53:1	Isaiah 55:8	Daniel 9:2–3
Daniel 9:21–27		

Chapter 13

JOHN THE BAPTIST

Thirteen years after the death of Herod the Great, Caesar Augustus also died, and the Roman Senate validated Tiberius Caesar as his successor. Twelve years into his reign, Tiberius retired to Capri, appointing Aelius Sejanus as regent to help him rule from Rome. Sejanus was ruthless with anti-Hebrew views. In his capacity as regent, he made many appointments, including Pontius Pilate to governor of Judea. It was not by accident that Pilate and his other appointees shared his views, for Sejanus was interested in replacing Tiberius as Caesar.

Now in the fifteenth year of the reign of Tiberius Caesar; Pontius Pilate being governor of Judea, and Herod Antipas being tetrarch of Galilee; and his brother Philip tetrarch of Ituraea and of the region of Trachonitis; and Lysanias the tetrarch of Abilene; Annas and Caiaphas being the high priests; the word of God came unto John, the son of Zechariah, in the wilderness. And John had his raiment of camel's hair, and a leather girdle about his loins; and his food was locusts and wild honey. And he came to Bethabara, into the country about the Jordan River, where first the children of Israel entered the Promised Land. It was here, at the "door of the crossing," that the heap of stones stood signifying the miracle, which twelve stones were taken from the dry riverbed when God parted the river Jordan. Here, John dwelt in nearby caves, and preached the baptism of repentance for the remission of sins.

"Repent, all of you, for the kingdom of heaven is at hand," cried John. "Prepare yourselves the way of the Lord; make his paths straight. Every valley shall be exalted, and every mountain and hill laid low, and the crooked ways shall be made straight, and the rough places plane, and all flesh shall see the salvation of God."

Then went out to him Jerusalem and all Judea and the entire region round about the Jordan.

And when they came, he said to them, "Say not among yourselves, 'We have Abraham for our father,' for I say to you that God is able of these stones to raise up children to Abraham."

When the people heard his words, they repented and were baptized of him in the River Jordan, confessing their sins.

For they recognized the boldness of John and the power of his words, and fearing, they asked of him, "What shall we do then?"

He answered them, "He that has two coats, let him impart to him that has none; and he that has food, let him do likewise."

Then came also tax collectors to be baptized, and said to him, "Master, what shall *we* do?"

And he said to them, "Collect no more than that which is commanded you."

The soldiers, likewise, demanded of him, saying, "And what shall *we* do?"

And he said to them, "Do violence to no man, neither accuse any falsely, and be content with your wages."

These and many other things in his exhortation he preached to the people.

Luke 3:1–6	Luke 3:10–14	Luke 3:18
Matthew 3:1–6	Matthew 3:9	Mark 1:1–6
John 1:28	Joshua 4:1–9	Isaiah 40:3–5

Chapter 14

JOHN BAPTIZES JESUS

In late spring, after the Passover, and before his thirty-first birthday, Jesus came to the river Jordan from Nazareth in Galilee to hear John's preaching; and to begin his own ministry, for he knew that John was sent to prepare a way before him. While John was baptizing, he saw Jesus coming to him among the many who came.

Jesus had grown into a strong man, hardened by the many years working as a laborer. Though muscular, he was lean from walking long distances to find work. He looked weather-beaten from the elements; his skin was darkened from the sun, and his long, dark hair was bleached into highlights, as was his beard.

When John saw Jesus entering the water, he had a vision concerning him. The sky became light behind him, and a bright light in the form of a dove descended delicately upon him, where it remained. John realized that this was the Messiah, for God had instructed him, saying, "Upon whom you shall see the Spirit descending, and remaining on him, the same is he who baptizes with the Holy Spirit." When the vision departed, Jesus stood before John in water up to his waist.

"Baptize me, John," he said, beginning to kneel before him, lowering his body farther into the water.

But John, grabbing him by the shoulders, prevented him, saying, "I have need to be baptized of *you*, and you come to *me*?"

And Jesus, answering, said to him, "Allow it to be so, *now*, for thus it becomes us to fulfill all righteousness."

So John released his grip upon him, reluctantly letting go. And Jesus, when he was baptized, went up straightway out of the water; and, lo, the heavens were opened unto him, and he beheld the Spirit of God descending like a dove, and lighting upon him. And, lo, a voice from heaven thundered, "This is my beloved Son, in whom I am well pleased."

The crowd, unaware of the momentous event playing out before them, paid little attention. They noticed only the clouds opening up above them, showering them all in dazzling light. Looking skyward, they did not witness the brilliant white dove, which landed with fluttering wings, settling upon the wet hair of Jesus. But John saw. The prolonged sound of distant rumbling thunder continued to avert all eyes toward the heavens.

And one among the crowd, a Pharisee named Nicodemus, said to himself, "From what origin comes this sound of thunder?"

When the rumbling ceased, the clouds converged and the light faded, and when the crowd looked again upon Jesus and John, the dove was no longer visible.

"Thank you, cousin," said Jesus with a smile, grasping John's shoulders, and shaking them.

John smiled back awkwardly, somewhat stunned by the magnitude of the honor and the surreal nature of the event, not recognizing Jesus as the adult version of his cousin. Jesus waded through the water toward the bank of the river opposite the crowd. When he reached the river's edge, he looked back at John. John waved to him in belated recognition and they traded knowing smiles.

The onlookers marveled only at the direction of Jesus's departure, watching him warily as he left the Jordan heading up river away from them.

Nicodemus, wondering to himself, thought, *Where is this young man going?*

John continued baptizing, looking from time to time in the direction Jesus had gone, his smile lingering long after Jesus had disappeared from view.

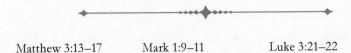

Matthew 3:13–17   Mark 1:9–11   Luke 3:21–22

Chapter 15

TEMPTED IN THE WILDERNESS

Then leaving the Jordan River, Jesus, being compelled by the Holy Spirit, was led into the wilderness to be tempted of Satan.

Jesus had suffered temptation like all men during his lifetime leading up to this moment and had weathered the storms. But the harshness of the years had taken their toll on the once strong faith of his parents. They grew impatient, waiting for Jesus to assume his role as Messiah and redeem the nation Israel from corruption and hardship. The strong ties he had enjoyed with his parents and his siblings became strained as his understanding of God's will became more acute. The more he understood, the freer he became in his relationship with his heavenly Father. Conversely, as Jesus became freer, Joseph became more religious, stressing stricter adherence to the Law. Joseph believed it necessary for Jesus to present himself to the Sanhedrin, the leaders of the temple, to establish his authority as Messiah. He fretted daily over Jesus's unwillingness to do so. But most of all, Joseph feared that he would die before fulfilling what he perceived to be his own mission—that of bringing his son to power. The father-son battle of words and wills became a main topic among the siblings, who often taunted their older brother about his nonexistent ministry. Mary tried to defuse the family turmoil by downplaying the criticisms that Joseph and the other children had toward Jesus, while encouraging Jesus to talk to the temple leaders. She believed, like Joseph did, that Jesus must gain the approval of the Sanhedrin to fulfill his mission. She also believed that when Jesus gained their approval, peace within her family would be restored. Because Jesus was unwilling to go to them, she, from time to time, brought them to him. These meetings usually ended in frustration for all involved, because his views were, more times than not, at odds with those of the rabbis. His strange ideas, and the reluctance of the religious leaders to accept them, became well-known among the inhabitants of the little village and beyond. Still, his appearance, with his long hair, was, in contrast, a constant reminder that he had taken a Nazarite vow and should be afforded some religious latitude. He bore, with grace, the burden of their reproaches, countering them, from time to time, with witty humor to remind his detractors of their own shortcomings. His demeanor also, one of grateful servitude, evoked mixed emotions in all who came in contact with him. He spoke freely of God, always with joy, which, in the midst of such despair, seemed both refreshing and somewhat misguidedly cruel. He and his family were among the lowest of the poor, owning no property and doing the most manual of all labor. Though Joseph possessed skills in several trades, he and his sons were, more often than not, reduced to doing the more menial jobs of common laborers: moving stone and timber to build walls and buildings, working in the fields during planting and harvest seasons, helping the fishermen during their big catches, and tending to the flocks alongside the shepherds. Jesus knew what it was like to travel long distances on foot, and to stand in lines waiting to be chosen for work. He worked hard and long in the hot sun, and slept often among the sheep during cold nights. He endured all these things, as other men, yet without complaining. For he knew his time of ministry was approaching, and he waited patiently for God's direction, being unwilling to proceed of his own accord.

Now, after John's baptism, the Spirit was upon him, and he found his direction, which he followed eagerly into the desert wilderness.

He fasted and prayed for days on end. He watched, as wild beasts approached in the night, without fear of them or aggression toward them. He wept and laughed aloud in his prayers, as he wrestled with God that he might perfectly understand his will. He saw visions during daylight hours and dreamed at night. After forty days of fasting, in constant communication with God, he understood his mission and his Father and knew his Father's will. These were among the many things of which he was now certain: he was truly God's son; his heavenly Father would sustain him, providing him with whatever he needed to accomplish his mission; he must die for the sins of mankind; and he would eventually rule God's kingdom. When he was content in his understanding, he ceased his prayer, desiring to again be among people. His hunger was great. Yet he hungered not only for physical food, but for spiritual food, as well. The Spirit groaned within him for the establishment of his Father's kingdom. He knew that to satisfy his spiritual craving, he must gather the faithful, and present them to his Father.

Only then, when Jesus was most vulnerable, did Satan appear to tempt him.

And when the tempter came to him, he said, "If you are the Son of God, command that these stones be made bread."

Now Satan's challenge addressed several areas of possible doubt. The first was whether Jesus really was the Son of God. The second was his physical hunger. The third addressed his spiritual hunger—Jesus's lack of disciples, for in his teachings, John had said to the people that God could raise children of Abraham from stones. The last was to test Jesus's ability to actually do it. Did he have the power? In essence, Satan wanted a sign.

Jesus had just completed forty days of fasting, so he had no doubt that his Father could physically sustain him indefinitely. And though he had no disciples as yet, this was a temptation of which he was familiar, because his family and neighbors had often painfully reminded him of this fact; now, however, he knew what he must do to gather them. As far as his being God's son, the Father

himself had resolved that issue: in the words spoken, when Jesus
was baptized by John, and in his communication with him these last
forty days. What remained was a test of power, but Jesus recognized
that any power that he had would come from the Father. His power
would come from his faith in God's word. In this, he was like any
other man.

So Jesus answered him, stressing his manhood and belief in
God's word, saying, "It is written, 'Man shall not live by bread alone,
but by every word that proceeds out of the mouth of God.'"

Then the devil took him up into the holy city, set him on a
pinnacle of the temple, and said to him, "If you are the Son of God,
cast yourself down, for it is written, 'He shall give his angels charge
concerning you, and in their hands they shall bear you up, lest at
any time you should dash your foot against a stone.'"

Satan, still not satisfied that Jesus understood he was the Son of
God, tempted him again concerning this point, using God's word
against him. He tempted him also about his understanding of his
own mortality and about his position of authority above the angels.

Looking toward his sacrifice for mankind's sin, Jesus knew that
his faith in God's word would be needed to overcome death. The
Father would certainly resurrect him, so that he could rule over
all creation, including the angels. There was no need to prove the
Father's word by attempting suicide—as a man, he would not tempt
the Father in this manner. But he also wanted Satan to realize that,
though he was man, he was also God, and could not be tempted to
prove himself by the sign that Satan desired.

So Jesus said to him, "It is written again, 'You shall not tempt
the Lord your God.'"

At this response, Satan knew he was beaten. In a rare instance,
Satan revealed his true nature, deciding to offer Jesus all that he
had for the one thing he desired most—to be worshiped as God.
He also tempted Jesus with the one thing for which Jesus, as a man,
had to rely solely upon God—power. So he took Jesus up into a

high mountain, and showed him all the kingdoms of the world in a moment of time.

And Satan bargained with him, saying, "All this power I will give to you, and the glory of these kingdoms, for it is delivered to me, and to whomever I will, I can give it. If you, therefore, will worship me, all shall be yours."

But Jesus answered, and said to him, "Get behind me, Satan, for it is written, 'You shall worship the Lord your God, and him alone shall you serve.'"

When Jesus, by his words, had refused Satan's offer, the devil left him. And when Satan had gone, behold, angels came and ministered unto Jesus.

Matthew 4:1–11	Luke 4:1–13	Mark 1:12–13
Matthew 3:9	Luke 3:8	1 Corinthians 10:16-17
Deuteronomy 8:3	Psalms 91:11–12	Deuteronomy 6:15–16
Exodus 17:7	Exodus 34:14	

Chapter 16

TEMPLE LEADERS CONFRONT JOHN

John did not sleep well in the nights that followed Jesus's baptism; he spent many late hours praying fervently, anticipating the fulfillment of his own mission. He wondered how long it would be before he saw Jesus again and what the appearance and introduction of Jesus as the Messiah would mean to Israel. He also questioned how the ministry of the Messiah would impact his own ministry. These questions were not new to John; he had wrestled with them for some time. But he knew that the time was drawing critically near, and he feared, most of all, not fulfilling his mission properly before God.

Over a month had passed since Jesus's baptism, and the people were growing impatient with John. This was the second year of John's mission, and all men mused in their hearts about John, over whether he was the Messiah. The temple leaders were divided among themselves as to the authenticity of John's mission, so they sent representatives to him to reach a resolution among themselves. Jesus returned to Jordan, where he knew his ministry would begin. While John was baptizing, he saw Jesus walking among the large crowds gathered along the riverbank. John acknowledged him, but Jesus put a finger to his lips signifying his request for anonymity, and then gestured toward the approach of the temple priests. As John glanced their way, Jesus disappeared among the crowd.

Though the temple leaders were still some distance away, the acoustics of the place put them within earshot of John's preaching. John went into one of his familiar sermons, amplifying his voice for the benefit of the approaching visitors, "As it is written in the book, according to the words of Isaiah the prophet, 'Prepare yourselves the way of the Lord; make his paths straight. Every valley shall be exalted, and every mountain and hill laid low; and the crooked ways shall be made straight, and the rough places plane; and all flesh shall see the salvation of God.'" Then speaking toward the direction of the oncoming priests, while he continued baptizing, he shouted, "Oh generation of vipers, who has warned you to flee from the wrath to come? Bring forth, therefore, fruits worthy of repentance, and think not to say within yourselves, 'We have Abraham for our father.'" "For I say unto you," he said, pointing to the twelve memorial stones set up by Joshua, "that God is able of these stones to raise up children unto Abraham. And now also the ax is laid unto the root of the trees; therefore, every tree which bears not good fruit is hewn down, and cast into the fire. I indeed baptize you with water unto repentance, but he that comes after me is preferred before me, for he is mightier than I."

As the priests and Levites approached, the crowd on the riverbank parted, anticipating the gravity of the confrontation between these men of the established religious order and this alleged prophet with his strange mission of repentance, remission of sins, and water baptism. The people wondered whether the leaders would accept his mission or denounce it as heresy. These religious leaders, having been rebuked by John before the people, hardened their hearts and remained unrepentant, not accepting his doctrine. Their intentions were soon evident from the disrespectful way they began to interrogate John.

"Who *are* you?" they demanded. "*You* are not the Messiah," they charged, provoking him.

But John remained calm, searching the crowd; "I am *not* the Messiah," he confessed to them.

So they asked him, "What then? Are you Elijah?"

And he said to them with growing anxiety, "I am not."

"Are you the prophet foretold of by Moses?" they demanded, now following John's gaze over the crowd.

John's demeanor changed; his shoulders slumped somewhat, his head cocked, and he shifted on his feet. Then he answered, "No," his confidence perceptibly wavering from their interrogation.

Finally, perceiving that they had the upper hand, his interrogators asked him point-blank, "Who are you, that we may give an answer to them that sent us? What do you say of yourself? Who do you claim to be?"

Gratefully, John spied Jesus, off to the side, behind the priests; Jesus was staring at him. John straightened, turning directly toward his accusers, defiantly, exuding renewed faith, and said, "I am the voice of one crying in the wilderness; make straight the way of the Lord, as said the prophet Isaiah." And he gestured to them, that they might enter the water to be baptized.

But after conferring among themselves, they refused his baptism—in essence, denying the validity of his mission—and then asked John with renewed distain, "Why do you baptize then, if you are not the Messiah, nor Elijah, neither that prophet?"

John was undeterred by their rebuff, and he answered them boldly, gesturing toward the Jordan. "I baptize with water," he cried. Then opening his arms widely, acknowledging the crowd, he continued loudly, "But there stands one among you, whom you know not; he it is who, coming after me, is preferred before me. It is for a witness to him that I have come, though I am not worthy to unloose the latchet of his shoe."

The temple leaders scanned the crowd critically and looked among themselves with concern.

Their attention turned back to John as he continued, "He shall baptize you with the Holy Spirit, and with fire: whose fan is in his hand, and he will thoroughly purge his threshing floor and gather his wheat into the barn, but he will burn up the chaff with unquenchable fire."

His strong words were alarming to the priests for several reasons. First, the change in John's demeanor was disconcerting—somehow he had regained the upper hand. Second, there was the stunning announcement that the Messiah was already among them. If John was truly a prophet, as the people believed, then his words were a certainty. If John was a false prophet, his words would be problematic in that they would lead the people astray. And third, the prospect of the Messiah purging the threshing floor with fire suggested that he would be at odds with the Jerusalem leadership. The threshing floor represented Jerusalem! David had purchased the threshing floor at Jerusalem, built an altar unto the Lord upon it, and offered sacrifices to stop the plague caused by his numbering the people of Israel. John's words were directed squarely against the temple leadership; at his harsh words, therefore, their representatives turned, and left in humiliation. John saw Jesus standing at some distance. Jesus nodded, then turned and disappeared over a rise in the bank.

Matthew 3:5–12	Mark 1:5–8	Luke 3:3–9
Luke 3:15–17	John 1:19–28	Malachi 4:5
Deuteronomy 18:18	Isaiah 40:3–5	Ruth 4:7
1 Chronicles 21:1–28	2 Chronicles 3:1	

Chapter 17

INTRODUCTION TO THE MESSIAH

The next day, John saw Jesus coming to him again, and said, "Behold the Lamb of God, who takes away the sin of the world. This is he of whom I said, 'After me comes a man who is preferred before me.' For he *was* before me. And I knew him not but that he should be made manifest to Israel; therefore have I come baptizing with water. I saw the Spirit descending from heaven like a dove, and it abode upon him. And I knew him not, but he that sent me to baptize with water, the same said unto me, 'Upon whom you shall see the Spirit descending, and remaining on him, the same is he who baptizes with the Holy Spirit.' And I saw, and I bare record that this is the Son of God."

And his words caused a great commotion among John's followers, as to what was actually said and meant. In the confusion of the moment, Jesus left without fanfare, for no one in the crowd identified him as the source of John's comments. The talk of the day, however, surrounded John's declaration and the significance of it. And everyone wanted to know who this man was that John had come to introduce to Israel.

Again, the next day, before the crowds had gathered, John sat among his closest disciples. Suddenly he stood, and two of his disciples stood also as John stared in the distance.

And looking upon Jesus as he walked, he said to them, "Behold the Lamb of God!"

And when the two disciples heard this, they looked upon John, who nodded toward Jesus; so they gathered their things quickly, and they followed him.

Then Jesus, hearing them approach, turned and saw them following, and said to them, "What do you seek?"

They said to him, "Rabbi, where do you dwell?"

He said to them, "Come and see."

So they went with him, and followed him to a large cave in the garden of Gethsemane, where he had been dwelling, while near the river Jordan. And the two abode with him that whole day, for it was about the tenth hour of the morning.

One of the two who heard John speak, and followed Jesus, was a man named Andrew; the other was a man named John.

Andrew first found his own brother, Simon, and said to him, "We have found the Messiah!"

Then he brought Simon to Jesus.

And when Jesus beheld him, his hardened stature and muscular build, he said, "You are Simon, the son of Jonah. You should be called Peter, the Rock."

Jesus smiled at Peter, and Peter returned the smile. While the others laughed heartily at their expense, an instant bond was formed between the two men.

The day following, Jesus went into Galilee, to Bethsaida, the city of Andrew and Peter.

And there he was introduced to Philip, and said to him, "Follow me."

Then Philip went looking for Nathanael, his friend; who was wrestling with God under his favorite fig tree, as was his habit—this time, over the injustices the Romans were bringing upon Israel. His argument with God ended as it always did, with him repenting of his excessively candid words.

When Philip found Nathanael, he said to him, "We have found

him, of whom Moses in the Law, and the prophets, did write: Jesus of Nazareth, the son of Joseph!"

But Nathanael said to him, "Can there any good thing come out of Nazareth?"

This he said, reciting a famous saying: Nazareth was formerly known for religious zeal and the Nazarite vow of separation, but had since become known for its hypocrisy and religious faithlessness.

Philip chuckled at his skepticism, and said to him, "Come and see!"

When Jesus saw Nathanael coming to him, he said of him, "Behold an Israelite indeed, in whom there is no guile!"

Nathanael said to him, "How do you know me?"

Jesus answered, and said to him, "Before Philip called you, when you were under the fig tree, I saw you."

Nathanael marveled, and said to him, "Rabbi, you *are* the Son of God; you *are* the King of Israel!"

Jesus answered him, "Because I said to you, 'I saw you under the fig tree,' you believe? You shall see greater things than these. Truly, truly, I say unto you, hereafter you shall see heaven open, and the angels of God ascending and descending upon the Son of man."

John 1:29–51   Numbers 6:1–21   Genesis 28:10–22

Chapter 18

MARRIAGE AT CANA

In the morning, Andrew awakened early, as was his custom, and he found that Jesus was not sleeping among the others. Filling a cup of water from the great water jar just inside the door, he stepped out into the predawn light, gulping down a mouthful to quench his morning thirst. He was somewhat bothered by the disappearance of this holy man, whom he had waited so enthusiastically to find. He knew the scriptures, as well as a man might know them without formal training. He had known that the time of the Messiah's coming was drawing near. To hear John's teaching of his imminent arrival excited him, inspired him, and haunted him. Lingering in the doorway, now, he recounted John's words, "Behold, the Lamb of God!"

These may be the greatest words I ever hear, he mused, *that may have been the most significant moment of my life!* Then he thought, *I would so much have liked to become close to Jesus. Perhaps the feeling is not mutual. Perhaps ...*

His thoughts were cut off, for he saw Jesus strolling toward him, with his arms out, as if prepared to hug him.

Still some distance away from the house, Jesus shouted jovially, "It's a beautiful morning; glad to see you awake."

"Good morning. Where were you at such an early hour? I'm usually the first to wake," said Andrew. "I get everyone else up, *usually.*"

"I like to speak to my Father when everything is still," said
Jesus, as he drew close to his new disciple. He studied the puzzled
look on Andrew's face. "I like to pray when it's quiet," he explained.

"Oh," Andrew returned, "Oh!" he reiterated with renewed
understanding. "I get it!" *He calls God his Father*, he thought in
amazement. Before he could wrap his brain around the thought,
Jesus changed the subject.

"There is a wedding in Cana that we must attend. You're all
coming with me!" Jesus beamed.

True to his word, Andrew leisurely woke the others, supervised
the women of the household in the preparation of a hearty
fisherman's breakfast, and coaxed Jesus's newly formed band of
disciples into an organized parade of wedding guests. They arrived
at the house of the bride's parents early in the afternoon. Many
people were milling about, some sitting and talking in groups.
Children were playing. The smell of food was in the air. There was
laughter and music, dancing and wine. As often was the case, this
marriage festival had continued for several days. Guests brought
prepared food, and close relatives and friends brought gifts. As
was also often the case, water and wine was provided entirely by
the bridegroom, and, as you might imagine, after several days the
supply of wine became diminished. To extend the amount of wine,
water was added to it, but eventually even the watered-down wine
ran out. Jesus's parents had attended the wedding and the first
day of the marriage festival. On this day, however, Mary returned
alone with food, and was welcomed by the bride's mother, who had
grown weary from entertaining her guests. Jesus had been greeted
by several of the attendees, who were excited to see him. He had
introduced his disciples, mingling with familiar and unfamiliar
villagers who had come to join the celebration. The group settled
down with several other guests, and was talking casually about
the newly wedded couple. They were listening to some humorous
stories about the earlier days of the festival, when Mary, seeing Jesus,
approached him anxiously.

Excusing herself and acknowledging his disciples, she said with some agitation, "They have no wine."

Jesus, still in a jovial mood from the previous conversation, replied playfully to his mother, "Woman, what have I to do with you? My hour has not yet come."

His playful mood and words were not initially understood by his mother and were not appreciated. She started, looking at him with annoyance, and then realized by his smile that he was joking. She smirked and shook her head. But as she grasped his humor, his countenance changed from cheerfulness to melancholy, and she started, again, grasping the true significance of his words. "My time has not yet come" was a joke about Jesus's death, one that Jesus often used with his mother. But this use of the saying, in conjunction with wine, diminished some of its usual humor. Wine, Mary knew, represented the blood of the grape, and, therefore, blood in general. His joke, in this context, took on an ominous meaning. Mary remembered the words spoken to her by the devout man Simeon, when Jesus was circumcised: "Yes, a sword shall pierce through your own soul also."

Her face was visibly pained by the thought, and she gasped out to those encamped around him, "Whatever he says to you, do it."

Then she hastily turned away from him. Jesus watched her with compassion as she fled his presence.

The others, not comprehending their exchange of words and emotions, watched Mary rushing away, and turned in confusion toward Jesus for clarification. Now there were six large stone water pots arranged along the wall, used for Jewish purification rites, which, when filled, held twenty to thirty gallons apiece.

Jesus motioned to them, saying, "Fill the water pots with water."

Andrew seemed to awaken from the confusion first, and directed the servants nearby to comply with Jesus's demands. The disciples pitched in, as their efforts took some time, and many more guests became interested, watching intently as they painstakingly filled each of the water jars up to the brim.

Then he said to them, "Draw some out now, and take it to the governor of the feast."

The muffled murmur of the inquisitive crowd turned to outright laughter, many believing that he intended to perpetrate a prank on the bride's father. Others, not appreciating the humor in such a prank, were indignant, their comments conveying their disapproval.

The servants looked at him incredulously, but Andrew, sensing something special happening, barked at them laughingly, "Well, take it to him."

So they reluctantly complied, filling an earthenware pitcher, taking it to the father of the bride. The crowd followed behind them, awaiting the reaction. One of the lesser servants, after much coaxing, brought the pitcher to the bride's father, the governor of the feast; and not knowing what to say, without a word, poured the water into his cup. To his amazement, the pitcher poured out deep red wine.

"What is the meaning of this?" demanded the governor. "Where did you get this?"

But the servant remained silent, now speechless from the unexplained change in the liquid. The governor tasted the wine, and slammed his cup down on the table in anger. He began to get up from his seat, but then reconsidered his decision, licking his lips. He looked down at his cup. Then reaching for it, he tasted its contents again, and seemed so well pleased at its flavor that his anger subsided. "Where *did* you get this?" he inquired with delight.

The servant, still confused, smiled at him foolishly, joyously giddy, and motioned toward Jesus.

But the governor of the feast, seeing the bridegroom nearby, called for him, and said, brimming with pride, "Every man at the beginning sets forth good wine; and when men have well drunk, then that which is worse, but you have kept the good wine until now!"

He put his arm around him and began praising his new son-in-law to his guests.

The bridegroom smiled sheepishly, not understanding what was happening, but was clearly enjoying the rare praise his father-in-law was showering upon him. The bride's father had reluctantly allowed the marriage, not fully approving of the young man. The son-in-law had, in turn, resented his father-in-law's feelings toward him. But the unique graciousness of the miraculous gesture had reconciled the two men one to another. The onlookers, who witnessed the event from the beginning, gradually comprehended what had happened to the water in the purification pots. Jesus chose to slip away with his disciples in the excitement. Not wishing to deprive the two men their newfound admiration for one another, their guests did not reveal to them Jesus's part in the matter. They did, however, discuss the incident among themselves with considerable excitement. Many, not able to contain their enthusiasm, left the feast early in order to reflect openly upon the miracle they had just witnessed. Missing from those who had witnessed the miracle was Mary, who had disappeared immediately after her conversation with her son, retreating in anguish. Those who witnessed the event marveled over the power of the miracle, but Mary's soul felt the weight of his words. Jesus, alone, knew what his miracle and words together conveyed—that the purification and reconciliation of his people rested in his blood.

This was the beginning of the miracles Jesus did, there in Cana of Galilee, when he manifested his glory. And his disciples believed in him, because they witnessed this miracle. After this he went down to Capernaum—he, his mother, his brethren, and his disciples—and they continued there not many days.

John 2:1–12   Deuteronomy 32:14   Luke 2:34–35

Chapter 19

PASSOVER AND NICODEMUS

After the marriage feast at Cana, Andrew and Peter invited Jesus and his family to accompany them to Capernaum. From there, they traveled together to Jerusalem for the Passover. The trek was long, but not an unfamiliar one. As at other times, their small group of travelers was joined by others like them, going to the Passover festival at Jerusalem. Trips like these became times of intimate communal living, and afforded an occasion for Jesus's new friends to get to know him and his family. It provided Mary and Jesus's brothers the opportunity to hear the eyewitness accounts of Jesus's miracle. It also allowed Mary to voice her concerns about the direction, or lack thereof, of Jesus's ministry. She confided to John, one late evening when the two of them were the only ones awake by the fire, that she was so looking forward to this time in Jerusalem, because it would provide an opportunity for Jesus to present his mission to the temple priests. Her family witnessed the enthusiasm of his followers, and his followers became acquainted with the dynamics within Mary's family. They saw the pressure put upon Jesus to live up to his divine mission: the parental pressure to seek approval from the religious leaders, and the skepticism heaped upon him by his younger siblings. The disciples found the behavior of Jesus's brothers demoralizing and confrontational when discussing his ministry. James they found especially critical, not wanting to hear the praising words that John the Baptist had declared about Jesus. James's harsh words also soured his brothers over any talk of how Jesus turned water into wine; it no longer became a topic of discussion with them. By the end of the journey, the group had separated to some degree into two camps: the disciples and Jesus, and Jesus's family. The one exception was Mary, who had grown accustomed to trying to keep the peace within her household; she maintained confidential communication with both sides.

When they reached Jerusalem, the two bands within their group remained loosely together, yet only in proximity to one another. Entering the temple, they found merchants selling oxen and sheep and doves, and money changers among them, exchanging common currency for the temple coins. While his divided entourage was occupied with scrutinizing the colorful spectacle of the festive environment, Jesus's anger was growing. He stopped along the way, and finding some discarded cords used to restrain the animals, he fashioned a scourge. Then starting at one end of the row of merchants, he began whipping them violently, driving them from their tables and toward the temple exit. He released the sheep and the oxen as well, stampeding them after the fleeing merchants who owned them. Then he poured out the money changers' coins; they rang out as they hit the stone floor, and they scattered and rolled in every direction. As the money changers leapt to their feet to resist his onslaught, he overturned their tables. They, too, reluctantly fled toward the exit. The disturbance was not at first perceptible in the midst of such a crowd, but grew in magnitude as Jesus, without a word, methodically parted the merchants from their wares. His disciples and family, ahead of him, were slow to take notice.

When he approached the merchants that sold doves, he wrestled with them over their cages, now shouting, "Take these things hence; make not my Father's house a house of merchandise."

When Mary heard his voice, she recoiled in a panic. She grabbed her sons and Peter, the disciple closest to her, and urged them to remove Jesus before the temple guards apprehended him. In the utter confusion of fleeing merchants and animals and people frantically gathering coins from the floor, they were able to usher him away. Outside the temple, he regained his composure, gathered himself, and turned to confront his adversaries.

A few of the temple priests, who had gathered on behalf of the merchants, demanded of him, "What token will you show us to signify your authority to do these things?"

Jesus tossed the scourge at their feet, and answered them, "Destroy this temple, and in three days I will raise it up."

At this, they looked at one another, trying to comprehend his words. Then they replied, "Forty and six years was this temple in building, and will you rebuild it in three days?"

But Jesus responded, not with more words, but with a gesture—he tapped his chest hard with both palms, then lifted his hands out, as if he were trying to embrace the crowd before him. His expression was one of frustration, however. He stood in this pose for several seconds, imploring them to understand. Then he turned on his heels and descended down the temple steps, leaving them wondering what all the commotion was about, for they did not understand that he was signifying to them the temple of his body.

In the days that followed, Jesus taught in the temple about the establishment of God's kingdom. He healed the sick and cast out demons, and the crowds marveled at the miracles he performed.

Now Nicodemus, who was a Pharisee and a ruler of the Jews, had been following the ministry of John the Baptist to understand his mission. He had witnessed Jesus's baptism, and heard the testimony of John concerning him. And he went to the temple to hear Jesus's teaching, and beheld his healing ministry.

Nicodemus then came to Jesus by night, and said to him, "Rabbi, we know that you are a teacher come from God, for no man can do these miracles that you do, except God be with him."

Jesus was intrigued by the words of Nicodemus, for by them he implied that the Jewish leadership was conceding that Jesus came from God, and that he was not merely a man but that God was *with* him.

So Jesus spoke candidly with the man about his own divine birth—being born of God by the Spirit of God, answering him, "Truly, truly, I say unto you, except a man be born from above, he cannot see the kingdom of God."

But Nicodemus, driven by his desire to see the kingdom of God with his own eyes, did not understanding that Jesus spoke of himself. Out of his own desire, therefore, Nicodemus inquired of him, "How can a man be born when he is old? Can he enter the second time into his mother's womb, and be born?"

Jesus, perceiving the misunderstanding, yet willing to answer his question, replied, "Truly, truly, I say unto you, except a man be born of water and of the Spirit, he cannot enter into the kingdom of God. That which is born of the flesh is flesh, and that which is born of the Spirit is spirit. Marvel not that I said unto you, 'You *must* be born from above.' The Spirit breathes upon whom he delights, and you hear his voice, but know not from where it comes and to where it goes: so is *everyone* who is born of the Spirit."

In his explanation, Jesus pointed toward John's baptism of repentance by water; and the baptism of the Holy Spirit, which Jesus would send upon his believers.

These things had been explained, in similar fashion, by Ezekiel, who prophesied, "I sprinkle clean water upon you, and you shall be clean from all your filthiness; and from all your idols, will I cleanse you. A new heart also will I give you, and a new spirit will I put within you, and I will take away the stony heart out of your flesh, and I will give you a heart of flesh. And I will put my Spirit within you, and cause you to walk in my statutes, and you shall keep my judgments, and do them."

But Jesus's words also addressed what had happened at his own baptism, and how, through the event, God had confirmed him as the Messiah.

Isaiah had written of the coming event: "Behold my servant,

whom I uphold; my Chosen One, in whom my soul delights; I have put my Spirit upon him: he shall bring forth judgment to the Gentiles."

Jesus expected this learned man to understand these things. Nicodemus, however, demonstrated his ignorance.

"How can these things be accomplished?" he inquired, bewildered.

The dullness of the question astonished Jesus, and his surprise could be heard in his voice.

"Are you a *master* of Israel and know not these things?" he inquired.

But he didn't wait for Nicodemus to answer him, because Nicodemus's question was a clear reminder that the Pharisees, due to the hardness of their hearts, had rejected John's baptism, and, therefore, John's declaration of Jesus as the Messiah and Son of God.

The surprise in his voice was replaced by agitation as he continued, returning to his initial comments regarding himself being born from above. "Truly, truly, I say unto you, we speak of that which we do know, and testify of what we have seen, and you receive not our witness. If I have told you earthly things, and you believe not, how shall you believe, if I tell you of heavenly things? And no man has ascended up to heaven, but he that came down from heaven, even the Son of man who is in heaven."

Nicodemus was taken aback, not totally understanding the anger in Jesus's voice.

Jesus continued, nonetheless, answering the question put forth by Nicodemus. "As Moses lifted up the serpent in the wilderness, even so must the Son of man be lifted up: that whoever believes in him should not perish, but have eternal life. For God so loved the world, that he gave his only begotten Son, that whoever believes in him should not perish, but have everlasting life. For God sent not his Son into the world to condemn the world, but that the world through him might be saved. He that believes in him is not condemned, but he that believes not is condemned already, because he has not believed in the name of the only begotten Son of God. And this is the condemnation, that light has come into the world, and men loved darkness rather than light, because their deeds were evil. For every one that does evil hates the light, neither comes to the light, lest his deeds should be reproved. But he that does truth comes to the light, that his deeds may be made manifest, that they are wrought in God."

In his explanation of how being born from above would be accomplished, Jesus alluded to his crucifixion—being lifted up upon the cross. He also suggested that his crucifixion would come about because evil men would reject the truth about him being the Son of God. Nicodemus left feeling insulted by his words. Nevertheless, Jesus's words had made a profound impression upon him; they were convicting, cutting him to the soul. They would haunt him, demanding resolution.

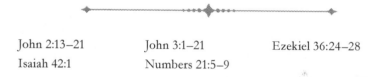

| John 2:13–21 | John 3:1–21 | Ezekiel 36:24–28 |
| Isaiah 42:1 | Numbers 21:5–9 | |

Chapter 20

TRANSITION FROM JOHN TO JESUS

John the Baptist, hearing of Jesus's miracles at the temple, knew that his own mission was nearing completion. And guided by the Holy Spirit, he moved northward to Aenon near to Salim, and continued baptizing there, because there was much water. Now John camped on the eastern side of the Jordan River, south of the Wadi Cherith, because to the west of the Jordan was the land of the Samaritans, and to the north of the Wadi Cherith was the Roman area of Decapolis. Because it was more tolerable to the Jews, he dwelt instead in Perea, the tetrarchy of Herod Antipas, which lay along the eastern border of the river. The place was strategically, geographically, and historically significant. Strategically, it presented John an opportunity to speak to large numbers of Jewish travelers. Geographically, it was located at the intersection between the Great Plain of the Jezreel Valley, which ran from the Mediterranean Sea to the Jordan River; and the Jordan Valley, which ran along the river itself. This was an ancient travel route from the Mediterranean to Jerusalem. Moving here meant that John would encounter those large crowds returning to Galilee from the Passover. Historically, the place was where God sent Elijah to hide from Ahab, when Elijah held back the dew and rain from Israel. While there, Elijah drank from the brook of Cherith, and was fed bread and flesh by ravens.

This brook was really a wadi, a ravine that remained dry except during the rainy season.

Now, after the Passover, Jesus remained in Judea, and returned with his disciples to Bethabara, where John had initially baptized. And those at the Passover, who heard of Jesus's miracles, came to him in great multitudes. They were joined also by those Jews who would return to Galilee by way of the ancient travel route. Jesus used, to his advantage, this captive audience, instructing his disciples to baptize in the water of the Jordan those who would repent of their sins. But he refrained from baptizing by water himself, choosing rather to preach to them of the kingdom of God. He taught them, instead, of the baptism of the Holy Spirit that he would send upon them, and the eternal purification of their souls, and he healed them according to their faith in his words.

Now, because of his teaching, there arose a question between some of John's disciples and the Jewish leaders about purifying. And they came to John, and said to him, "Rabbi, he that was with you beyond Jordan, to whom you bore witness, behold, the same baptizes, and all men come to him and to *his* baptism."

John answered, and said, "A man can receive nothing, except it be given him from heaven. You yourselves bear me witness, that I said, 'I am not the Messiah, but that I am sent before him.' He that has the bride is the bridegroom, but the friend of the bridegroom, who stands and hears him, rejoices greatly because of the bridegroom's voice: for this, my joy, therefore, is fulfilled. He must increase, but I must decrease. He that comes from above is above all: he that is of the earth is earthly, and speaks of the earth; he that comes from heaven is above all. And what he has seen and heard, of that he testifies, and no man receives his testimony. He that has received his testimony has set to his seal that God is true. For he, whom God has sent, speaks the words of God, for God gives not the Spirit by measure unto him. The Father loves the Son, and has given all things into his hand. He that believes in the Son has everlasting life, and he that believes not the Son shall not see life, but the wrath of God abides on him."

Now, when Herod Antipas heard that John had come into the borders of his territory, he went out to hear him, for Herod feared John, knowing that he was a just and holy man. And Herod observed him, and listened to him gladly, and he amended many things, because of his words. Then Herod returned to John in the company of his wife, Herodias, so that she might also hear his words.

But John, seeing them together, prophesied against Herod concerning his invalid kingship over the Jews, saying, "It is not lawful for you to have your brother's wife."

This he said, because he knew that Jesus was the true bridegroom of Israel, but they perceived not that his words were prophecy.

Instead, Herodias, being convicted, and taking offense by his words, sought to have John killed; because she had married Herod, but was formerly the wife of Philip, Herod's brother. Herod, however, prevented her from killing John, because he feared him, believing him to be a prophet. Nevertheless, to appease his wife, Herod sent forth soldiers to lay hold upon John, and had him bound in prison for Herodias's sake.

***

John 3:22–36   John 4:1–3   Mark 6:17–20
Matthew 14:3–5   Luke 3:19–20   1 Kings 17:1–6

Chapter 21

TO GALILEE THROUGH SAMARIA

Now many of the Pharisees rejected John's baptism and, therefore, Jesus's identity as the Messiah. Nevertheless, they feared the growing influence of these two men on the common folk, for they taught a different doctrine concerning purification—one apart from the traditions of Moses and the established order of temple worship. Their new teaching threatened the established control the Jewish leadership had over the people. It also threatened the temple economy. Hearing that the size of the crowds following Jesus exceeded those of John only increased the apprehension of these religious leaders.

Knowing their fear, and not wishing to confront the Jewish leadership openly before the people, Jesus decided to leave Judea. It was his intention to accompany the crowds along the ancient travel route to Galilee. But as Jesus and his disciples prepared their departure, word came to them that John had been imprisoned by Herod Antipas. So, to escape a similar fate, Jesus chose to avoid a risky journey through Herod's territory; they would, instead, return through Samaria to the familiar surroundings of Galilee.

On their way, they came to the Samaritan city of Sychar, near to the parcel of ground that Jacob gave to his son Joseph. And Jacob's well was there. Jesus sent his disciples into the town to buy food. But, being wearied with his journey, Jesus stayed behind, sitting on

the well with his tallit, or prayer shawl, over his head for shade. And
he began to pray, because it was about the sixth hour (noon). For it
was the custom of the Jews to pray three times a day: the third hour
(9:00 a.m.), the sixth hour, and the ninth hour (3:00 p.m.) While he
sat there, a Samaritan woman, wearing the garments of a married
woman, came quietly to draw water, not wishing to disturb him.
And it was her custom to draw water from Jacob's well each day,
at this time, because she believed the ritual was representative of
drawing out knowledge from God.

Without altering his posture, Jesus said to her, "Give to me
drink."

Then the woman of Samaria said to him, "How is it that you,
being a Jew, ask drink of me, a woman of Samaria? For the Jews
have no dealings with the Samaritans."

Jesus answered her, "If you knew the gift of God," referring to
the baptism of the Holy Spirit, "and who it is that said to you, 'Give
to me drink,' you would have asked of him, and he would have given
you living water."

The woman said to him, "Sir, you have nothing to draw with,
and the well is deep: from where then have you that living water?
Are you greater than our father Jacob, who gave us the well, and
drank thereof himself, and his children, and his cattle?"

Then she set a cup of water before him on the well.

Jesus answered her, again, sipping the water, but maintaining
his position. "Whoever drinks of this water shall thirst again, but
whoever drinks of the water that *I* shall give him shall *never* thirst,
but the water that *I* shall give him shall be in him a well of water
springing up unto everlasting life."

The woman said to him, growing impatient with him, for he
looked not upon her when he spoke, "Sir, *give* me this water, that I
thirst not, neither come here to draw."

Then Jesus answered her flippantly, "Go. Call your husband,
and come here." This Jesus said to test her, speaking to her, not

of her personal life, but of the infidelity of the Samaritan people toward worshiping God.

But the woman perceived not his meaning, and answered in a manner bordering on defiant. "I have *held* no husband," she said, for she was a Samaritan prophetess whose life events, like other of the prophets, God had set as an example to mirror the path that Israel had taken. Accordingly, she had been married to several cruel men, and her prophetic message reflected her life experience with them. Unafraid to set herself against such willful men, she positioned herself very near to Jesus, now, provoking him to confrontation.

Finally, Jesus lifted his head toward her, and looking into her eyes, chuckled and replied, "You have eloquently and tactfully expressed yourself, 'A husband I have not *held*,' for five husbands have held *you*—captive! And the one who holds you now is not your husband: in that you've answered truthfully."

The woman, startled at his words, suddenly understood his meaning: how Israel had served in captivity the nations of Egypt, Assyria, Babylon, Media-Persia, and Greece, and now served Rome. The woman looked at him with mouth agape, and then smiled sheepishly, realizing that her garb, which represented her marriage to God, had not fooled him.

She then replied to him, "Sir," feeling she had been beaten at her own game—both discovered and outwitted, "I perceive that you are a prophet!"

They smiled at one another, now both being somewhat exposed.

"Our fathers worshiped in this mountain," she continued, "and you say, that in Jerusalem is the place where men ought to worship."

Jesus said to her, "Woman, believe me, the hour comes, when you shall neither in this mountain, nor yet at Jerusalem, worship the Father. You worship you know not what: we know what we worship, for salvation is of the Jews. But the hour comes, and now is, when the true worshipers shall worship the Father in Spirit and in truth, for the Father seeks such to worship him. God is a Spirit, and they that worship him must worship him in Spirit and in truth."

With growing anticipation, she said to him, "I know that the Messiah comes, who is called the Christ: when he comes, he will tell us all things."

Jesus revealed to her plainly, "I who speak unto you am he."

After these words, came his disciples, clumsily disrupting their intimacy. And they marveled that he talked with the woman, yet no man asked him, "What do you seek?" or "Why do you talk with her?" An awkward silence briefly ensued.

The woman then left her water pot, and looking back several times, hurried away into the city, where she gathered the men and said to them, "Come, see a man, who told me all things that ever I did. Is not this the Messiah?"

So they went out of the city, and came to him.

In the meanwhile, his disciples tried to persuade him with the food they brought, saying, "Master, eat."

But he said to them joyfully, "I have meat to eat of which you know not."

The disciples, confused, inquired one to another, "Has any man brought him anything to eat?"

Jesus said to them, "My meat is to do the will of him that send me, and to finish his work. Do not say, 'There are yet four months, and then comes harvest.' Behold, I say unto you, lift up your eyes, and look on the fields, for they are white already to harvest. And he that reaps receives wages, and gathers fruit unto life eternal, that both he that sows and he that reaps may rejoice together. And herein is that saying true, 'One sows, and another reaps.' I send you to reap on that which you bestowed no labor; other men labored, and you are entered into their labors."

And many Samaritans of that city believed in him for the saying of the woman, who testified, "He told me all that ever I did." So when the Samaritans had come to him, they besought him that he would stay with them, and he abode there two days.

And many more believed because of his own words, and said to the woman, "Now we believe, not because of your saying, for we have heard him ourselves, and know that this is indeed the Messiah, the Savior of the world."

Then, after two days, he departed from there, and continued his journey to Galilee.

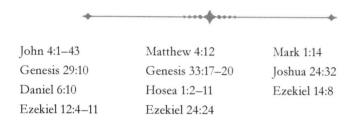

John 4:1–43	Matthew 4:12	Mark 1:14
Genesis 29:10	Genesis 33:17–20	Joshua 24:32
Daniel 6:10	Hosea 1:2–11	Ezekiel 14:8
Ezekiel 12:4–11	Ezekiel 24:24	

Chapter 22

GALILEE RECEIVES HIM

Jesus and his disciples returned to Galilee, where crowds came out to greet him, for the fame of him went out through the entire region, because of the miracles they had seen him perform at the Passover feast in Jerusalem. As he and his disciples went from village to village on his return home to Nazareth, the villagers compelled him to teach in their synagogues, which he did, being glorified of all.

When he reached Nazareth, where he had been brought up, it was the Sabbath day, and as was his custom, he went into the synagogue. Now, although he had attended this synagogue from his youth, it was also in his youth that he had stopped reading from the scriptures, because his interpretations were not well received by the rabbi and the townsfolk. Nevertheless, this day he stood up to read. The rabbi, remembering the misadventures of Jesus's interpretations long past, hesitated momentarily, then delivered to him the scroll containing the book of the prophet Isaiah. His eyes looked into Jesus's eyes as he handed it to him; there was a sense of hopefulness, pleading, and apprehension in the eyes of the rabbi.

When Jesus opened the scroll, he found the appropriate place he sought, and read aloud where it was written, "The Spirit of the Lord is upon me, because he has anointed me to preach the gospel to the poor; he has sent me to heal the brokenhearted, to preach deliverance to the captives, and recovering of sight to the blind, to set at liberty them that are bruised, to preach the acceptable year of the Lord."

Then, he closed the scroll, and kissed it, and gave it again to the rabbi, whose anxiety heightened, anticipating what would come next. Jesus returned to his place among the other attendees and sat down. And the eyes of all that were in the synagogue were fastened upon him, waiting on his interpretation of the matter, for such was the usual custom and order of the reading of scripture.

With great joy, he began by saying, "This day is this scripture fulfilled in your ears!"

And all bare him witness, and wondered at the gracious words, which proceeded out of his mouth. He paused, for some time, so that they might digest the magnitude of his words, expecting to share with them so much more. But in that pause, the people began to focus, not on his words, but on the contrast between the eloquence of his words and the coarse occupation of the man who spoke them. Instead of glorifying God, because of the good news of his message, they judged him and missed the significance of his words.

"Is not this Joseph's son?" they protested. "What shall a common laborer's son teach us about God? His views have not matured in all these years."

And Joseph, who was among them, hoping that the mission of his son had finally begun in earnest, was embarrassed by their hurtful words.

Then Jesus grew angry, and said to them, "You will surely say unto me this proverb, 'Physician, heal yourself: whatever we have heard done in Capernaum, do also here in your country.'" "Truly I say unto you," he continued, quoting a familiar proverb, "'No prophet is accepted in his own country.' But I tell you the truth, many widows were in Israel in the days of Elijah, when the heaven was shut up three years and six months, when great famine was throughout all the land, but unto none of them was Elijah sent, save unto Sarepta, a woman who was a widow of a city of Sidon. And many lepers were in Israel in the time of Elisha the prophet, and none of them was cleansed, saving Naaman the Syrian."

In response, all in the synagogue, when they heard these things, were filled with wrath, because his words justified foreigners above Israel. And they rose up, and thrust him out of the synagogue, and pursued him, forcing him to leave the city. As their rage increased, the mob led him to the brow of the hill on which their city was built, for they sought to kill him by casting him down headlong to his death. But when they reached the summit, Jesus turned upon them in the power of the Spirit, and the spirit of rage, which had taken hold of them, departed from them, so that they were calmed. Then he, passing through the midst of them, went his way. Joseph returned to his house in shame, fearing for the life of his son.

From there, Jesus continued his journey northward, and came with his disciples again into Cana of Galilee, where he made the water wine. And they dwelt at the house of Nathanael, who lived there in Cana.

And there was a certain nobleman, whose son was sick at Capernaum. The man had heard about the miracles Jesus had performed in Jerusalem. So when the man heard that Jesus had come out of Judea into Galilee, he went to him at Cana, and besought him that he would come down to Capernaum to heal his son, for his son was at the very point of death.

But Jesus said to him, "Except you see signs and wonders, you will not believe."

The nobleman pleaded with him, saying, "Sir, come down, or else my child will die."

Then Jesus said to him, "Go your way; your son lives."

The man believed the words that Jesus spoke to him, and he went his way. And as he was returning to his home, his servants met him, and told him, saying, "Your son lives!"

Then the nobleman inquired of them the hour when he began

to get better. And they said to him, "Yesterday, at the seventh hour, the fever left him."

So the father knew that it was at the same hour in which Jesus said to him, "Your son lives." And he believed, and so did his whole household.

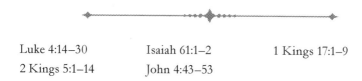

Luke 4:14–30   Isaiah 61:1–2   1 Kings 17:1–9
2 Kings 5:1–14   John 4:43–53

Chapter 23

FROM NAZARETH TO CAPERNAUM

From Nazareth and Cana, they came and dwelt in Capernaum, a fishing village on the Sea of Galilee, in the borders of Zebulon and Naphtali. Peter and Andrew, and John and John's brother James, who were all fishermen by trade, resided there. So entering the village, the group disbanded, each separating to their respective homes. Philip lived in Bethsaida, a sister city to Capernaum, so Jesus and Nathanael continued on to his house, where they remained as his guests.

Now the day before the next Sabbath, in the afternoon as the day wore on, Philip took Jesus and Nathanael to find the others. Peter and Andrew were testing one of their recently mended nets, by casting the net into the sea by the shoreline.

Jesus called to them, "Come, follow after me, and I will make you fishers of men."

They laughed at his greeting, happy to see him, and immediately pulled in their net. Jesus, Philip, and Nathanael sat waiting for them as they returned to shore to join them. When the boat was secured, the five set off farther down the coastline, where they found James and John in their boat among several others docked at a small marina. Zebedee, their father, and his servants worked alongside them mending their nets. Peter, seeing Zebedee, cautioned Jesus about calling James and John away from their work.

Zebedee, he explained, had quite a temper, especially when it came to circumventing work that affected his income. Jesus just smiled at his skepticism.

When they drew near enough for them to hear him, Jesus hailed to them, "Zebedee, send forth your sons to me, for God has work for them to do."

The activity around the boats ceased, and everyone stared at Jesus. Then they scrutinized Zebedee to witness his reaction. At Jesus's address, James and John looked at each other, expecting their father to erupt in anger. Zebedee, startled at the words, looked up from his work to measure the man who dared to shout them for all the world to hear. And seeing Jesus smiling at him, Zebedee considered his words. Then he straightened with pride, looking at his sons, and turned to Jesus, again.

"Take them from me, and let me know if they shirk from their duty," he growled at him.

Then he smiled back at Jesus, who laughed aloud. Zebedee then turned to his sons, swallowed with moistened eyes, and nodded at them his consent. They jumped to their feet. James banged a hardened hand upon his father's shoulder, and looked him in the eye.

"Go on," the old man said in a shallow voice.

So they climbed out of the boat to join the others. John bounded up to Jesus, and greeted the others happily. James followed him slowly, looking back at his father, feeling a mixture of pride, gratefulness, and sadness. The sounds of the fishermen reliving the scene were not lost on James as he moved farther away from the boats, but he did not look back again. Zebedee watched them from time to time as he continued with his work, until they disappeared out of sight.

When the sun went down at the start of the Sabbath, Jesus entered the synagogue and read from the writings of Isaiah to those gathered there: "The land of Zebulon, and the land of Naphtali, by way of the sea, beyond Jordan, Galilee of the Gentiles; the people which sat in darkness saw great light, and to them which sat in the region and shadow of death light is sprung up." And he preached to them: "The time is fulfilled, and the kingdom of God is at hand: repent, all of you, and believe the good news!"

And all who heard him were astonished at his doctrine, for he taught with authority, his words having power behind them—for his words stated emphatically that Isaiah's prophecy was being fulfilled right there and then before them!

Now there was a man among them, in the synagogue, possessed by a demonic spirit.

And he cried aloud, saying, "Let us alone. What have we to do with you, you Jesus of Nazareth? Have you come to destroy us? I know you, who you are, the Holy One of God!"

Jesus rebuked him, saying, "Hold your peace and come out of him."

And the man went into convulsions in the midst of them, and the spirit within him cried with a loud voice, before the man's convulsions ended. His body remained tense for some time, before he relaxed, and peace returned to his face. Then Jesus stooped down beside him and helped him to his feet again. The man looked at Jesus intently, and then turned to those around him to celebrate with them. His arms stretched out high and wide, and tears streamed down his cheeks as he gave glory to God.

And they were all amazed, and said, "What thing is this? What new doctrine is this? For with authority and power of word he commands even the unclean spirits, and they obey him and come out."

Then Jesus and his disciples left the synagogue, while the people were still rejoicing, and went to Peter's house. When they entered the house, they found the mother of Peter's wife lying upon her bed, sick with fever. And those of the household besought Jesus, and told him of her illness. So he came to her bedside; and standing over her, he rebuked the fever. Immediately, the fever left her. Jesus then took her by the hand and lifted her up. She thanked him, sheepishly, regained her composure, and lost no time in ministering to her guests. Jesus and the others were invited to spend the Sabbath at Peter's house—an invitation they all graciously accepted. So they spent the night there, and the next day, eating and drinking, socializing, and reflecting on the events of the past few weeks.

The next evening, when the sun was setting, the Sabbath came to a close. Then, the villagers gathered at the door of Peter's house, bringing to Jesus all who were sick and possessed with demons. Jesus had compassion upon them all, casting out the demons with a word, forbidding them to speak, for they knew him.

Many demons cried out, "You are the Messiah, the Son of God," as they left their victims.

Likewise, having compassion upon the sick, Jesus healed them by laying his hands upon them. All who witnessed these things marveled, for the demonic spirits obeyed him, and those suffering from sickness and disease were healed by his touch.

The people of Capernaum tried to persuade Jesus to stay with them, that they might learn from him and continue to hear his words.

But Jesus declined their urgings, saying, "I must preach the kingdom of God to other cities also, for therefore am I sent."

Jesus and Nathanael followed Philip up the coastline toward Bethsaida, back to his house, where they spent the night.

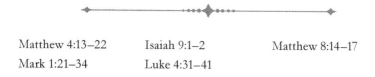

Matthew 4:13–22   Isaiah 9:1–2   Matthew 8:14–17
Mark 1:21–34   Luke 4:31–41

Chapter 24

GATHERING DISCIPLES

In the morning, Andrew rose early, as usual, and woke the others, who were reluctantly coming to life after the long night.

After Jesus had sent the townspeople home, the night before, Peter, Andrew, James, and John, too excited to sleep, decided to go fishing. They needed to unwind, and wished to confer with one another over the magnitude of the day's events. As far as fishing goes, it proved to be a fruitless exercise, but they did manage to unwind by thoroughly discussing all the details of Jesus's healings and exorcisms. And sleep was no longer a problem after the physical rigors of fishing; they were dead tired by the time they got back home.

Andrew, unwilling to miss what might come, now that daylight had arrived, roused them from what amounted to a brief nap, and gathered them together for the short journey to Philip's house. To their surprise, they discovered a small group of people gathered outside their own house speaking in low tones and waiting in one corner of the property for Jesus to emerge.

"If you're waiting for Jesus, he's no longer here," James called to them, and the four disciples set off down the road.

The group conferred briefly among themselves, and then followed James and the others at some distance.

When the disciples got to Philip's house, Philip and Nathanael were still asleep, and Jesus was gone.

"Where is the Master?" they demanded of their groggy friends.

But they had no idea where Jesus was. So after taking some measure of abuse from the others, Philip and Nathanael joined them as they set out looking for him, for they remembered that Jesus liked to rise early to pray.

As they searched, the townspeople gathered in a continually growing number of groups, following at various distances, hoping to get a glimpse of this miracle man. An old merchant driving a wagon laden with pots pointed the disciples in the right direction.

"Jesus? Yeah, I saw him climbing that hill over there," the man said. "The truth of the matter is I know his mother, Mary. When she was but a teenager, I took her all the way from Nazareth to the outskirts of Jerusalem."

"Yes, thank you," said Peter, somewhat annoyed by this unsolicited information.

"One of the best days of my life," the old man muttered, recognizing their noninterest. "Well, glad to be of service, anyway," he finished.

Then Topheth coaxed his ox forward, waving nonchalantly as he drove away. The disciples hurried off in the opposite direction, toward the indicated hill to find Jesus.

When they reached the summit of the hill, they found Jesus kneeling with his head lowered in prayer. They approached him warily, reluctant to disturb him. Looking at one another, they waited for some time for him to acknowledge them. Finally he looked upon them and smiled peacefully. This, too, set them aback.

Peter stammered out, "All men seek for you."

But Jesus said to them, "Let us go into the next towns that I may preach there also, for therefore have I come."

Then he stood, smiled at them all, draped his arms around the shoulders of Peter and Andrew, and led them down the hill.

Moving down the hill, Jesus took them in a different direction, not returning the way the disciples had come, but following a new path toward the sea. Those following the disciples waited at the bottom of the hill for them to return, but did not see Jesus and the others until they had reached the road at the bottom. By then, they were quite some distance away. But the townspeople, in their various groups, had amassed into a very large crowd, and seeing Jesus, they hurried to draw near to him. By the banks of the sea, the crowd overtook Jesus and his disciples. Jesus, seeing Peter's boat nearby, entered into it and requested that Peter maneuver it a little ways offshore, so that he might minister to the crowd by his words. Andrew joined them, jumping in, after shoving the boat from the dock. James, John, Philip, and Nathanael followed their lead, leaving the dock behind and eventually pulling their boat alongside the other, a bit farther out to sea. Then Jesus sat down and spoke to the people from this small ship, teaching them many things by parables.

Stretching his hands high and toward the people, he looked upon them and waited as they became silent.

Then he began his teaching, his voice ringing out clearly over the stillness of the early morning water. "Behold, a sower went out to sow his seed. And it came to pass, as he sowed, that some seed fell by the wayside, and was trodden down, and the fowls of the air came and devoured it up. Some seed fell upon stony places, and immediately it sprang up, because it had no depth of earth. And when the sun came up, because it had no root and lacked moisture, it became scorched, and withered away. And some seed fell among thorns, and the thorns sprang up with it, and choked it, and it yielded no fruit. But other seed fell into good ground, and brought forth fruit that sprang up and increased—some thirtyfold, some sixtyfold, and some a hundredfold." And when he had said these things, he cried aloud with his hands raised toward them, as if embracing them, "He that has ears to hear, let him hear!"

The crowd remained silent, confused by the message, and stunned by his outburst. Then he continued, as before, in the soothing manner of a storyteller. "So is the kingdom of God, as if a man should cast seed into the ground; and should sleep, and rise night and day, and the seed should spring and grow up, he knows not how. For the earth brings forth fruit of herself: first the blade, then the ear, after that the full corn in the ear. But when the fruit is brought forth, immediately he puts in the sickle, because the harvest has come."

After these words, the crowd began to murmur. When the crowd grew silent again, Jesus resumed. "Again, the kingdom of heaven is like unto treasure hid in a field, which when a man has found, he hides, and for joy thereof goes and sells all that he has, and buys that field."

Without stopping for the crowd's reaction, he continued with another parable. "Again, the kingdom of heaven is like unto a merchant man, seeking goodly pearls, who, when he had found one pearl of great price, went and sold all that he had, and bought it."

Then he paused, and his words were followed again by a soft murmur, like the rustling of wind over a field of wheat. Eventually the murmuring ceased, their voices falling silent before he continued.

During the interruption of the crowd, however, Andrew whispered to Jesus, "Why do you speak to them in parables?"

Jesus explained, "Because it is given unto you to know the mysteries of the kingdom of heaven, but to them it is not given. For whoever *has*, to him shall be given, and he shall have more abundance, but whoever has *not*, from him shall be taken away what he *has* or even what he *thinks* he has."

The disciples looked at one another, not understanding that Jesus was contrasting their faith with the faithlessness of those in the crowd; still, they pushed him no further on the subject.

He resumed his teaching. "To what else shall we liken the kingdom of God? Or with what comparison shall we compare it? It is like a grain of mustard seed, which indeed is among the least of all seeds. But when it is sown, it grows up, and becomes greater than all herbs. It becomes a tree, shooting out great branches, so that the fowls of the air may lodge under the shadow of it."

He continued with another parable. "The kingdom of heaven is like unto leaven, which a woman took, and hid in three measures of meal, till the whole was leavened."

Another parable he put forth unto them, saying, "The kingdom of heaven is likened unto a man who sowed good seed in his field, but while men slept, his enemy came and sowed tares among the wheat, and went his way. But when the blade was sprung up, and brought forth fruit, then appeared the tares also. So the servants of the householder came and said unto him, 'Sir, did you not sow good seed in your field? From whence then has it tares?' He said unto them, 'An enemy has done this.' The servants said unto him, 'Will you then have us go and gather them up?' But he said, 'No; lest while you gather up the tares, you root up also the wheat with them. Let them both grow together, until the harvest, and in the time of harvest, I will say to the reapers, 'Gather together first the tares, and bind them into bundles to burn them, but gather the wheat into my barn.'"

At this, the crowd murmured again, yet louder, into a low rumble. Their response continued for a minute or so, before dissipating again.

Jesus, measuring their growing confusion and frustration over his unorthodox mode of conveying his message, concluded his teaching with a parable more relevant to the fishing community he was addressing.

. "I will leave you with one more parable to consider," he said. "The kingdom of heaven is like unto a net, that was cast into the sea, and gathered of every kind, which, when it was full, they drew to shore, and sat down, and gathered the good into vessels, but cast the bad away. So shall it be at the end of the world: the angels shall come forth, and sever the wicked from among the just, and shall cast them into the furnace of fire: there shall be wailing and gnashing of teeth."

Now, when he had left off speaking, he said to Peter, "Launch out into the deep, and let down your nets for a catch."

But Peter answered him out of fatigue. "Master, we have toiled all the night, and have taken nothing." Then he quickly repented, considering who was addressing him. "Nevertheless," he said sheepishly, "at your word, I will let down the net." Then he summoned his tired body into action.

Jesus laughed, and Peter and Andrew laughed along with him.

Now the crowd was expecting Jesus to come ashore after his teaching, to perform more miracles. So, as he sailed out farther to sea, they watched him, unwilling to leave without witnessing some sign. This kept the crowd intact, discussing his miracles of the night before, and also debating the possible meanings of this morning's many parables. The crowd remained anxiously awaiting Jesus's return, therefore, as the disciples went back to fishing.

At Jesus's command, Peter and Andrew brought the boat to a standstill and cast out their net. Having accomplished this, they watched as the net overflowed with a great multitude of fishes: so many that as they strained upon it, their net broke. Struggling to save the catch, they beckoned to their partners, James and John, who were already nearby, following in the other ship.

"Come and help us," they cried.

And they came, and filled both the ships, so that they began to sink.

When Peter saw it, he fell down before Jesus, saying, "Depart from me, for I am a sinful man, Oh Lord." For Peter, and all those who were with him, were astonished at the overwhelming number of fish that they had taken.

"Fear not; from henceforth you shall catch *men*," Jesus said, smiling broadly at him. Peter shook his head incredulously, not knowing whether to laugh or cry. He laughed nervously, somewhat out of control, and his laughter became contagious among the crewmembers of both ships. Jesus laughed with them, relishing in their joy. Peter laughed so hard that tears ran down his face, and he shook violently. He had to look away from Jesus and concentrate on getting the ships to shore, in order to regain his composure. When they finally brought their ships to land, Peter and the others forsook all, and followed him.

And they left the townspeople by the dock, rejoicing over the "miraculous catch," gathering the good fish into vessels and casting the bad away.

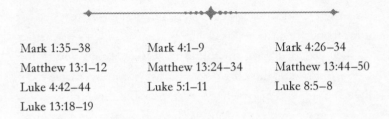

Mark 1:35–38   Mark 4:1–9   Mark 4:26–34
Matthew 13:1–12   Matthew 13:24–34   Matthew 13:44–50
Luke 4:42–44   Luke 5:1–11   Luke 8:5–8
Luke 13:18–19

Chapter 25

LESSONS IN FAITH

With the townspeople occupied at the dock, Jesus and his disciples returned to Peter's house unimpeded. And when he was alone with them, they asked of him the parable of the sower.

So he gathered them around him, and sitting in their midst, he said to them, "As I said to you before, unto you it is given to know the mystery of the kingdom of God: but unto them that are without, all these things are done in parables. As the psalmist has written, 'I will open my mouth in parables; I will utter things which have been kept secret from the foundation of the world.' For this reason I speak to them in parables, because they seeing, see not, and hearing, they hear not; neither do they understand. In them is fulfilled the prophecy of Isaiah, which says, 'By hearing, you shall hear, and shall not understand; and seeing, you shall see, and shall not perceive, for this people's heart has grown fat, and their ears are dull of hearing, and their eyes they have closed; lest at any time they should see with their eyes, and hear with their ears, and should understand with their heart, and should be converted, and I should heal them.'"

When he finished saying this, he paused, weighing their understanding. And seeing their confusion, he added, "and their sins should be forgiven them."

This he phrased as a statement, but the inflection in his voice rendered it a question, a quiz of sorts, for them to note and ponder later. Their blank faces showed their lack of understanding. Jesus dropped his head, his hair falling down around his face. He massaged the back of his neck with one hand, and then smiled, looking up at them. They returned the smile, hesitantly, as if pretending to understand the meaning of some incomprehensible joke.

"Nevertheless," he continued, "blessed are your eyes, for they *shall* see: and your ears, for they *shall* hear. For truly I say unto you, that many prophets and righteous men have desired to see those things which you shall see, and have not seen them; and to hear those things which you shall hear, and have not heard them."

These words had a mesmerizing effect upon the disciples. To be mentioned in the same breath with prophets and righteous men was a dream come true to this small group of faithful believers, but Jesus's comments set their futures beyond even the lives of such heroes of Israel. All in attendance leaned in, and the silence in the room became palpable.

Then he admonished them, "Know you not this parable? And how then will you know *all* parables?"

These words were spoken in stark contrast to the encouraging words that had just preceded them. This quick turnaround was gut-wrenching, for his latter words were heavy with conviction; they cut to the heart. The effect the contrast had upon his disciples was to intensify their concentration and prepare them for the important teaching that followed. Not to be lost in this moment of emotional upheaval felt by the disciples, however, was the idea that understanding all parables somehow hinged upon understanding this particular one. This idea was beyond intriguing; the hearts and minds of his disciples could not have been more prepared to receive his teaching.

"Hear, therefore, the parable of the sower," he said, and began his explanation, "The seed is the word of God, and the sower sows the word. Those by the wayside are they that hear and understand not. But when they have heard, Satan comes immediately and takes away the word that was sown in their hearts lest they should believe and be saved. And these are they, likewise, which are sown on stony ground, who, when they have heard the word, immediately receive it with joy and gladness; yet they have no root in themselves, and so believe for a while, enduring for a time: but in time of temptation and tribulation, when affliction and persecution arise for the word's sake, they are immediately offended and fall away. And these are they which are sown among thorns; such as hear the word, and go forth; but the cares of this world, the deceitfulness of riches, the pleasures of this life, and the lusts of other things entering in, choke the word, so that it becomes unfruitful, bringing no fruit unto perfection. But these are they which are sown on good ground, which out of an honest and good heart, hear the word, understand it, receive it, and keep it; so that the word brings forth fruit with patience, bearing some thirtyfold, some sixtyfold, and some an hundredfold."

Jesus paused, briefly, giving them time to digest his explanation. During this interlude, his disciples silently scrutinized the connections he made between God's word and the roles that the hearers, Satan, and the distractions of the world have upon the ability to understand it. They realized it was important not only to understand it, but to retain that understanding, and apply it to life's decisions. Jesus's words stressed a hidden meaning that would be revealed from God's word, "the mystery of the kingdom of God" that the prophets sought to know. All these ideas came to mind as they pondered his teaching.

Then Jesus took the lamp from its stand, and placed it on the floor, covering it with a ceramic measuring pot with protruding handles. The light was diminished greatly but still glowed beneath the pot where the handles met the floor. The room took on an eerie appearance. He slid the lamp and pot into a corner beneath a bed to make the room even darker.

Then he inquired of them out of the darkened room, "Is a lamp brought to be put under a measuring pot, or under a bed, and not to be set on a lamp stand?"

Not waiting for them to answer, he slid the lamp from beneath the bed, and removed the pot, returning the lamp to its stand. When the lamp was returned, the disciples noticed that the entire household, who were wondering why the room was darkened, had joined them out of curiosity.

Then Jesus answered for them, "No man, when lighting a lamp, covers it with a measuring pot, or puts it under a bed, but sets it on a lamp stand, so that those who come into the brightness may see. For there is nothing kept secret, that shall not be made manifest; neither anything hid, that shall not be known and come abroad. Therefore I say, 'If anyone has ears to hear, let him hear.'"

This final saying he delivered with great conviction, his voice increasing in volume, as when he spoke the same words from the boat to the crowd across the still water.

He followed these words with ones no less impassioned, but softer and entreating, yet in the form of a warning. "Take heed what you hear, for with what standard you measure, it shall be measured to you. Take heed, therefore, *how* you hear, for unto you that hear shall more be given. Whoever has, to *him* shall be given; and whoever has not, from *him* shall be taken that which he has—it shall be taken from him even that which he seems to have."

Again, Jesus's words formed in them a dichotomy of feelings. They were encouraged to know that all the secrets of God's kingdom hidden in his word were available to be understood, yet they felt anxiety over the consequences of perhaps not hearing the word correctly.

Despite dealing with these lingering unsettled feelings, his disciples mustered the courage to prod him further, their spiritual appetites not yet satiated.

"Declare unto us the parable of the tares of the field," they demanded.

Jesus was encouraged by their enthusiasm. He smiled, and continued teaching them. "He that sows the good seed is the Son of man; the field is the world; the good seed are the children of the kingdom, but the tares are the children of the wicked one. The enemy that sowed them is the devil; the harvest is the end of the world, and the reapers are the angels. As, therefore, the tares are gathered and burned in the fire; so shall it be at the end of this world. The Son of man shall send forth his angels, and they shall gather out of his kingdom all things that offend, and them which do iniquity; and shall cast them into a furnace of fire: there shall be wailing and gnashing of teeth. Then shall the righteous shine forth as the sun in the kingdom of their Father. Who has ears to hear, let him hear."

When he had concluded this teaching, he paused again. And finding them satisfied, with no further questions, he asked them, "Have you understood all these things?"

And they replied to him in unison, "Yes, Lord."

In the afternoon, people began to gather again outside of Peter's house. The "miraculous catch," as it was being called, had occupied the townspeople for most of the day. Almost everyone was affected in some way, and most of them were now home relaxing after the unexpected rigors of this unusual morning. Those gathered outside had come despite their fatigue, because they feared Jesus leaving their town, as he suggested the previous evening, before they had a chance to see him again. With them they brought all those who suffered from any number of infirmities hoping to have their loved ones healed by his touch. Inside the house, Jesus communed with the women of the household and other women who had come to follow him. The men had fallen asleep after Jesus finished his teaching, exhaustion having set in due to their late night and early morning fishing.

Jesus, when he was told of those who waited outside, went out to them, having compassion upon them. And he healed them all, one by one as they were brought to him. While his male disciples slept through most of the activity, the women went about organizing those who had come into a manageable and quiet procession. As the men began to wake, they took over this role, allowing the women to return to their household duties. The women enjoyed playing an active role in Jesus's ministry, and reluctantly relinquished their duties to the men.

The afternoon wore on, and eventually the number of people still needing healing dwindled, until Jesus had laid hands upon the last of them. The crowd, still milling about, marveled at his miracles and remained there as spectators in a carnival-like atmosphere. As evening drew near, Jesus sent them home. Jesus, and his intimate group of followers at the house, ate a meal that the women had been preparing all day long.

Then afterward, Jesus made known his intentions of leaving Capernaum immediately, saying, "Let us, now, pass over to the other side of Galilee."

So his disciples gathered their gear, and went down to the dock, where they readied their boats for a night of sailing. Their small group shrank even further, as few were inclined to accompany him on such a journey; they said their good-byes at the dock. Those who were married said good-bye to their spouses, and those who had children bid farewell to them in the cool night air.

Jesus's companions were beginning an exciting new adventure, and they were dealing with many emotions as they climbed into their boats and sailed into the dark void. They were excited by the possibilities, saddened by leaving their former lives and loved ones behind, and apprehensive of the unknown dangers and hardships that they might face. While they were dealing with their overflowing emotions, Jesus was silent. He watched the scene at the dock as a spectator, showing no emotion. All who left with him had someone to whom they said good-bye, but Jesus sat alone—watching. Even after they shoved off, he continued his silence, falling asleep on a pillow in the back part of the ship. Not much was discussed between the others in the ships, either. They took turns alternating between gazing at the shoreline from where they had come, and peering into the darkness ahead. They looked from time to time at the stars above them and into the eyes of one another. There was little comfort to be found no matter where they looked. Little was said, though a sea of feelings was below the surface.

After some time out at sea, clouds began to roll in, covering the stars and making visibility that much more problematic. Each vessel was equipped with a lantern that provided light to the crew. These lights were visible to the other ships, but as the clouds rolled in, so too did the wind, and the distance between the lights became farther apart. The waves, also, rocked the boats more violently, so that the light from the other vessels became sporadic as each ship dipped below the crests of the waves. In the distance, from time to time, they saw flashes of lightning behind the clouds, followed by peals of thunder. It rained in spurts, intermittent showers, and the waves began to crash against the sides of the boats, so that the boats began to take on water. Neither the crashing of the waves, nor the rocking of the boat, the wind, the rain, the thunder, or the lightning awakened Jesus!

Finally, when the boat that he was in became nearly flooded, the disciples awakened him, crying out, "Master, don't you care that we perish?"

And he arose, and rebuked the wind, and said to the sea, "Peace, be still!"

And the wind ceased, and there was a great calm. And shouts of joy could be heard from the other ships off in the distance.

Then Jesus turned on his crew, admonishing them, saying, "Why are you so fearful? How is it that you have no faith?"

And his disciples became very fearful, looking upon him. As they watched, he curled up again upon his pillow, pulled a tarp over his body for a covering, and resumed his sleep. They marveled that he seemed merely annoyed by their near-death interruption, as if someone had awakened him for something so insignificant as to shut an opened window. As he slept, they whispered one to another, "What manner of man is this, that even the wind and the sea obey him?"

A light breeze took them peacefully to shore by morning, where

the boats landed upon the beach. Jesus, apparently refreshed by
the journey, made no other comment concerning their ordeal, as if
nothing had happened. He was jovial and ready to enter the closest
town to find breakfast. His followers were less inspired, wearied
by their night at sea, and shaken by their miraculous near-death
experience. They talked among themselves, but decided not to bring
up the ordeal in the presence of Jesus, for they feared another
admonishment. They also feared knowing the truth behind what
had happened out there.

Mark 4:10–25   Mark 4:34–41   Matthew 13:10–23
Isaiah 6:8–10   Matthew 13:34–43   Psalms 78:2
Matthew 13:51   Matthew 8:23–27   Luke 8:9–18
Luke 8:22–25

Chapter 26

PREACHING THROUGHOUT GALILEE

The storm had taken them to the opposite side of Galilee, to the shores of the country of the Gadarenes. There, they met a man from the city, who had been possessed by demons for a long time. He wore no clothes; nor did he live in a house, but dwelled in the tombs. And when anyone approached him, he would come out of the tombs and become exceedingly fierce, so that no one could pass by that way. Neither could he be restrained, not even with chains, because he had often been bound with shackles and chains, but the chains had been pulled apart by him, and the shackles broken in pieces. Neither could anyone tame him. He could be heard always, night and day, in the mountains and in the tombs, crying out and cutting himself with stones.

When he saw Jesus from afar, he ran and fell down before him and worshiped him.

Jesus, recognizing that the man was tormented by demons, said, "Come out of the man, unclean spirit!"

But the man cried out with a loud voice, "What have we to do with you, Jesus, Son of the Most High God? Have you come here to torment us before the time? We implore you by God that you do not torment us."

Then Jesus demanded, "What is your name?"

And the man cried out, "My name is Legion, for we are many."

Many demons had entered him, and they begged Jesus that he would not command them to go out into the abyss. Now, a good way off, a herd of many swine was feeding there on the mountain.

So the demons begged Jesus that he would permit them to enter them, saying, "If you cast us out, permit us to go away into the herd of swine." They cried as one, "Send us to the swine, that we may enter them."

And he permitted them, commanding them, "Go."

Then the demons went out of the man and entered the herd of swine, which numbered about two thousand. And suddenly, the whole herd of swine ran violently down the steep embankment into the sea, and drowned, perishing in the water. When those who kept the swine saw what had happened, they fled and told the people of the area everything they had witnessed, in the city and in the country, including what had happened to the demon-possessed man. And behold, the whole city came out to meet Jesus to confirm what had happened. When they arrived, they found the man from whom the demons had departed, sitting at the feet of Jesus, clothed and in his right mind. And they were afraid. They who had seen it, told them also by what means the demon-possessed man had been healed. So the whole multitude of the surrounding region of the Gadarenes begged Jesus to depart from them, for they were seized with immense fear. Jesus complied with their wishes, and returned to the boat. Then, the man from whom the demons had departed begged Jesus that he might go with him.

But Jesus sent him away, saying, "Go home, return to your own house and to your friends, and tell them what great things the Lord has done for you, how God has had compassion upon you."

And the man went his way and proclaimed throughout the whole city and in all the region of Decapolis what great things Jesus had done for him; and all marveled.

So Jesus and his disciples departed from there, and they sailed from coast to coast, and town to town, around the Sea of Galilee. And he taught in their synagogues, and preached the gospel of the kingdom, and healed all manner of sickness and all manner of disease among the people. And he cast out devils. So his fame went throughout all Syria, as well, and they brought unto him all sick people that were taken with various diseases and torments, and those that were possessed with devils, and those that were lunatic, and those that had the palsy, and he healed them.

And their voyages on the sea, unlike their first, became a respite from the chaos of the crowds.

Now, when they came to a certain city, there came a leper, who seeing Jesus, kneeled down before him, and then fell on his face, and worshiped him; and he besought him, saying, "Lord, if you will, you can make me clean."

And Jesus, moved with compassion, put forth his hand, and touched him, saying, "I will: you are clean."

And as soon as he had spoken, immediately the leprosy departed from him, and he was cleansed.

And Jesus charged him, saying, "See that you tell no man, but go and show yourself to the priests, and offer for your cleansing the gift that Moses commanded, for a testimony unto them."

But the man went out, and began to publish it much, and to blaze abroad the matter, insomuch that Jesus could no more openly enter into the city. The people received the man's testimony, for he was a Pharisee named Simon, who had been well-respected among the Jewish leadership. From this point forward, Pharisees began to follow Jesus's ministry with great interest. In fact, because of his testimony, the overall fame of Jesus increased abroad, and great multitudes came together to hear, and to be healed by Jesus of their infirmities. They came from Galilee and Decapolis, from Jerusalem and Judea, and from beyond Jordan. His fame was such that he found no more respite in the sea, for they followed him even in boats, and great multitudes met him whenever he reached shore. So he withdrew himself into the wilderness, into desert places to pray, and they came to him, even there, from every quarter.

Mark 5:1–20   Luke 8:26–39   Matthew 8:28–34
Matthew 4:23–25   Mark 1:39–45   Matthew 8:2–4
Luke 5:12–16

Chapter 27

TAX COLLECTOR AT CAPERNAUM

And, again, Jesus entered Capernaum after some days, and it was
heard that he was in the house. Immediately many gathered together,
so that there was no longer room to receive them, not even near the
door. And Jesus preached the Word to them. Now it happened as
he was teaching that there were Pharisees and teachers of the Law
sitting among them, who had come out of every town of Galilee,
Judea, and Jerusalem. And the power of the Lord was present to
heal them. While Jesus spoke, a man named Thomas and three of
his friends came carrying a paralytic upon a bed, whom they sought
to bring in to lay before him. And when they could not find how
they might bring him in, because of the crowd, they went up onto
the housetop, and uncovered the roof above where he was. And
when they had broken through, they let down the bed on which the
paralytic was lying, into the midst of them, before Jesus.

When Jesus saw their faith, he said to the paralytic, "Son, be of
good cheer; your sins are forgiven you."

And some of the scribes and Pharisees who were sitting there
began to reason within themselves, *This man blasphemes! Why does this
man speak blasphemies like this? Who can forgive sins but God alone?*

But immediately, Jesus perceived in his spirit their thoughts,
and he said to them, "Why do you think evil in your hearts? For
which is easier, to say, 'Your sins are forgiven you,' or to say, 'Arise,

take up your bed and walk?' But that you may know that the Son of man has power on earth to forgive sins," he turned, and said to the man who was paralyzed, "I say unto you, arise, take up your bed, and go to your house."

Immediately the man arose before them, took up the bed he had been lying upon, and went out in the presence of them all, departing to his own house, and glorifying God. Now when the multitudes saw it, they were all amazed and glorified God, who had given such power to men.

Thomas, amazed at the miracle performed on his friend, said, "Had I not seen it with my own eyes, I would not have believed it. He is truly the Messiah of God!" And Thomas purposed in his heart to follow him thereafter.

But the Pharisees and teachers of the Law were filled with fear, saying, "We have never seen anything like this!"

After these things, Jesus went out from the house, walking by the sea, and Peter followed him. Now there was a man named Matthew, the son of Alphaeus, sitting at a tax booth collecting taxes. For the Romans, when they had heard about the "miraculous catch," had set up a tax booth by the dock.

And Matthew pointed out Peter to the Roman guards, who were guarding the booth. "There is Simon Barjonas," said Matthew. "He is a disciple of Jesus, who worked the miracle."

And seeing Peter, they came to him and brought him back to the booth, asking of him, "Doesn't your master pay tribute?"

Peter answered them, "Yes," and promised to return to them after getting the tax money from his house.

As soon as he had stepped away from the booth, still in the hearing of Matthew and the Romans, Jesus met him, asking him, "What are you intending to do, Peter? Of whom do the kings of the earth take custom or tribute? Of their own children or of strangers?"

Peter answered, "Of strangers."

Jesus replied, "Then are the children free!"

Peter glanced warily at the Romans.

"Notwithstanding," Jesus continued, "lest we should offend them, go to the sea and cast a hook, and take up the fish that first comes up, and bring it here."

So Peter ran off to do some fishing, while Matthew and the guards discussed the conversation mockingly, and returned to their duties. Jesus remained at the booth, lounging on the dock. As he sat there, those who came to pay their taxes recognized him, and a small crowd began to form at some distance around him. Now among the crowd was a group of Pharisees discussing their disappointment that Jesus could be found in the company of Romans and tax collectors.

And Jesus, knowing their thoughts, sat upon one of the posts of the dock, motioning the crowd to draw near. Then he spoke to them a parable in the hearing of them all.

"Two men went up into the temple to pray," he began, "the one a Pharisee, and the other a tax collector."

This he said not looking at Matthew or the group of Pharisees.

"Now the Pharisee," Jesus explained, "stood and prayed thus with himself, 'God, I thank you, that I am not as other men are, extortionists, unjust, adulterers, or even as this tax collector. I fast twice in the week, and I give tithes of all that I possess.'"

He paused for effect, glancing briefly at the Pharisees, who seemed satisfied by the prayer offered by their representative character.

Jesus continued with his story, "And the tax collector, standing afar off, would not lift up so much as his eyes unto heaven, but smote upon his breast, saying, 'God be merciful to me, a sinner.'"

He paused, again, letting his hearers contemplate the contrast. Matthew, he noticed, was sitting with his head down and his cheeks flushed.

Still watching Matthew, he continued, "I tell you, this man went down to his house justified rather than the other."

Matthew's head jerked up, and his eyes looked right into the eyes of Jesus, who managed a hint of a smile.

Then averting his eyes from Matthew, Jesus focused on the Pharisees, who were frowning disapprovingly.

His gaze seemed to go right through them, as he added, "For everyone that exalts himself shall be abased!"

Then moving his gaze back to Matthew, he concluded, "And he that humbles himself shall be exalted!"

Now the Roman guards, who were scrutinizing the scene, recognized the irony of his parable, and began to laugh at the Pharisees. It took a few moments before the crowd caught on, as well. But when it did, the Pharisees felt compelled to walk away from the stares of the people to avoid further embarrassment. The crowd, not knowing exactly how to react, dispersed, following the lead of the Pharisees.

The leader of the Roman guard assigned to the tax booth was a centurion. He found little humor in the situation, viewing Jesus's words as the words of a troublemaker. He wondered what further trouble Jesus might cause, and hoped that there would not be a problem with his payment of tribute, when his friend returned. He didn't have to wonder long, because, just then, Peter came running back to the dock. In one hand he held a good-sized fish by the gill. In the other, he held a small pole—still attached to the fish by line and hook. The guards broke out into laughter, again, as they awaited what might transpire.

Jesus laughed with them over the silliness of the sight, as he rose to his feet.

"Peter," said Jesus, "now, when you have opened his mouth, you will find a piece of money."

They all looked at him as if he had lost his mind. Peter's look changed to hope, as he looked at the fish, then back to incredulity as he returned his gaze to Jesus. Jesus smiled at him, nodded, and then laughed aloud. They all laughed with him, and then waited anxiously as Peter began to take the hook out. Peter took the hook out slowly, hesitating from time to time. He was hedging, afraid of how the guards might react when no money was found in the fish. The hook eventually came out, without any money. Everyone looked at everyone else. They all laughed, again, this time due to nervous energy. Then Jesus gestured for Peter to slap the back of the fish. Peter, repeated the gesture, and everyone laughed, again. Peter picked up the fish in one hand, cradling and balancing it. He gave Jesus another look, and they all laughed, again. Then he gave the fish a good whack on the back, and out popped a *stater*, a shiny silver Greek coin, worth the exact amount to pay the tax for the two of them! Everyone went silent!

Then Jesus chuckled and said nonchalantly, "Now take that coin, and give it to them for me and you."

Peter picked up the coin, looking at it, but not fully comprehending. He looked back at Jesus, who gestured for him to give it to Matthew. Peter looked at Matthew, who was still staring at the coin with his mouth open, and shaking his head. The Romans were doing the same, trying to speak, but not finding the words. Finally, Jesus put his arm around Peter.

"You can do it; give him the coin," he said encouraging him.

Peter looked at him, and then lifted the coin before Matthew, who held up his palm to receive it. Matthew looked at the coin intently, felt it, and then put the coin in the box. He looked up at Jesus with an expression of wonder. A guard picked up the coin and passed it among the other soldiers, then gave it to the centurion, who frowned and tossed it back into the box.

Then Jesus looked Matthew in the eyes and said, "Follow me."

Matthew shut the box. He handed it to the centurion. Then he rose up, left all, and followed Jesus.

Now Andrew and the other disciples met Jesus, Matthew, and Peter as they came up from the dock, and they continued on their way, away from the direction of the sea.

Unbeknownst to them, when Matthew left his post with Jesus and Peter; the centurion guarding the tax office, taking offense, followed them. And catching up to them farther down the road, he accosted them, with his men looking on.

"Hey *you*, big guy," he said gruffly, confronting Peter. "I'm traveling down the road; carry my gear. It's only about a mile."

And his men began to laugh. Peter sheepishly consented, humiliated by the gesture.

Then Jesus spoke up, speaking to Peter, but in the hearing of them all. "Whoever shall compel you to go a mile, go with him two."

And he took the bundle from Peter's hands, shifting his gaze into the eyes of the centurion. The centurion, perceiving his words as insolence, approached Jesus, while the other guards readied for a violent confrontation. He stopped in front of him, turned to look at his soldiers, and then backhanded Jesus hard across the cheek. The centurion hit him so hard that he lost his own balance momentarily. When he recovered, he saw Jesus still before him, hardly moved by the blow.

Jesus's eyes searched the eyes of the centurion, then turned to Peter as he continued, "I say unto you, that you resist not evil, but whoever shall smite you on your right cheek, turn to him the other also."

Then he returned his gaze to the centurion, and cocked his head, offering his other cheek to the full force of his forehand. At this, the centurion was clearly angered, yet humbled. He started to grab for the bundle, then stopped. He glared at Jesus, frowning. Then turning his palms up, he accepted the bundle back from Jesus, his face changing to a look both apologetic and bewildered.

Then, he turned and looked at his men. "What?" he growled.

And his men retreated, averting their eyes from his. Peter stared at Jesus, and then glanced at the other disciples in amazement; then he looked back at Jesus with newfound respect.

Now, across the road, coming from the other direction, stood two gruff-looking men, and they witnessed this entire encounter with the Roman soldiers. Though they did not recognize Jesus and his disciples, their interest was piqued by the coarse way these Roman soldiers were treating their countrymen. Simon, the older man, a hardened patriot for decades, was a member of the Zealots.

His reputation for his hatred of the Roman occupation was well-known in the region; he was known as Simon the Zealot. The younger man, his son Judas, notorious in his own right, was known for his affiliation with a more sinister patriotic group of assassins called the Sicarii. The group got its name from the small knives that they wore attached to their wrists or forearms.

When the Romans had gone, the two approached Jesus.

"I heard your words to the centurion," Simon said. "Your wise words were spoken in foolishness," he growled sternly. "They could have caused you great trouble." Then he smiled. "But they were very effective," he said, chuckling and shaking his head from side to side. "They made me proud to be a son of Abraham."

Jesus just grinned back at him. He glanced at Judas, but he was not smiling.

"Where are you headed?" Simon asked. "Perhaps we should accompany you; we wouldn't want such courage and wisdom to be snuffed out by the Romans.

"I'm Simon," he continued, and gestured toward his son, "and this is Judas."

"I'm Jesus, and we are going to the house of our new friend, Matthew. By all means, join us," Jesus replied.

Simon recognized the name, now famous throughout the region. He was visibly impressed; his eyes widened, as his eyebrows rose. Then he swallowed hard, and he glanced at his son. The disciples looked at one another, a bit uneasy over the prospect of traveling with these two new companions. Judas's facial features remained stoic, not betraying his underlying feelings, but his father recognized the disapproval in his eyes. The two, however, followed Jesus to Matthew's house. And they continued to follow him thereafter.

When they arrived at the house, Matthew arranged a great feast to honor Jesus. He invited all those he knew, including family, friends, and colleagues; his new friends, Jesus's disciples, were among them. And a great number of tax collectors and others that followed Jesus sat down together with Jesus and his disciples.

But when the scribes and Pharisees saw Jesus eating with the tax collectors and sinners, they complained to his disciples, "How is it that you and your teacher eat and drink with tax collectors and sinners?"

When Jesus heard it, he said to them, "Those who are well have no need of a physician, but those who are sick do. But go and learn what this means: 'I desire mercy and not sacrifice.' For I have not come to call the righteous, but sinners, to repentance."

Then came James, the brother of Matthew, with some of the disciples of John the Baptist, for James also followed John. They had come to hear the words of Jesus but would not partake of the feast, for they were fasting. The Pharisees, likewise, refrained from eating, not because they were fasting, but because they disapproved of those who were participating.

And the Pharisees, seeking to align themselves with John against Jesus, came to Jesus, protesting, "Why do the disciples of John fast often and make prayers, and likewise those of the Pharisees, but yours do not fast, but eat and drink?"

And Jesus said to them, "Can you make the friends of the bridegroom mourn while the bridegroom is with them? As long as they have the bridegroom with them, they cannot fast. But the days will come when the bridegroom will be taken away from them; then they will fast in those days."

Noting their continued disapproval, he spoke a parable to them. "No one sews a piece of new unshrunk cloth on an old garment, otherwise the new piece pulls away from the old, and the tear is made worse, and also the patch that was taken out of the new does not match the old." Another parable he spoke to them. "And no one puts new wine into old wineskins; or else the new wine will burst the wineskins; the wine will be spilled, and the wineskins will be ruined. But new wine must be put into new wineskins, and both are preserved. And no one, having drunk old wine, immediately desires new, for he says, 'The old is better.'"

Now on the Sabbath that followed Matthew's feast, Jesus and

his disciples were walking through the grain fields. And when his disciples were hungry, they plucked off the heads of the grain, and rubbing them in their hands, they began to eat.

And when the Pharisees saw it, they said to Jesus, "Look, your disciples are doing what is not lawful to do on the Sabbath!"

But Jesus said to them, "Have you not read what David did when he was in need and hungry, he and those who were with him: how he entered the house of God, in the days of Abiathar the high priest, and ate the showbread, which was not lawful for him to eat nor for those who were with him, but only for the priests? Or have you not read in the Law that on the Sabbath the priests in the temple profane the Sabbath, and are blameless? Yet I say to you that in this place there is One greater than the temple. But if you had known what this means, 'I desire mercy and not sacrifice,' you would not have condemned the guiltless. For the Son of Man is Lord even of the Sabbath."

Now when Jesus left the grain fields, he entered immediately into their synagogue to teach them. And behold, there was a man who had a withered right hand. So the Pharisees watched him closely, to see whether he would heal him on the Sabbath, so that they might find an accusation against him.

But Jesus knew their thoughts, and said to the man with the withered hand, "Arise and stand here."

And he arose, and stood before him.

Then Jesus turned to the Pharisees and inquired of them, "Is it lawful on the Sabbath to do good or to do evil, to save life or to kill?"

But they kept silent.

And when he had looked around at them with anger, being grieved by the hardness of their hearts, he demanded of them, "What man is there among you who has one sheep, and if it falls into a pit on the Sabbath, will not lay hold of it and lift it out? Of how much more value then is a man than a sheep? Therefore it *is* lawful to do good on the Sabbath!" Then he turned again to the man, and said, "Stretch out your hand."

And he stretched it out, and it was restored as whole as the other. And the man and all in attendance glorified God.

But the Pharisees were filled with rage, and discussed with one another what they might do to Jesus. Then they went out and immediately plotted with the Herodians against him, how they might destroy him.

There was a division, therefore, among the Jews over him.

Jesus withdrew with his disciples to the sea, and went up into a nearby mountain to pray, and continued all night in prayer to God. When the people heard how many things he was doing, a great multitude came to him, and waited for him at the base of the mountain near the sea. They came from Judea and Jerusalem, from Idumea and beyond the Jordan; and from as far as Tyre and Sidon. So he told his disciples that a small boat should be kept ready for him, because of the multitude, lest they should crush him, for he had healed so many that those who had afflictions pressed about him just to touch him.

Mark 2:1–12	Luke 5:17–26	Matthew 9:2–8
Mark 2:13	Matthew 17:24–27	Luke 18:9–14
Mark 2:14	Matthew 9:9	Luke 5:27–28
Matthew 5:41	Matthew 5:39	Luke 6:29
Luke 6:15	Acts 1:13	John 6:71
John 12:4	John 13:2	John 13:26
Luke 5:29–32	Matthew 9:10–13	Mark 2:15–17
Matthew 9:14–17	Matthew 10:3	Mark 3:18
Luke 6:15	Acts 1:13	Mark 2:14
Mark 2:18–22	Luke 5:33–39	Luke 6:1–5

1 Samuel 21:1–6   Mark 2:23–28   Matthew 12:1–8

Hosea 6:6   Mark 3:1–6   Luke 6:6–11

Matthew 12:9–14   Matthew 12:15   Luke 6:12

Mark 3:7–10

Chapter 28

SERMON ON THE MOUNT

Now, when it was day, Jesus called upon his disciples to meet him on the mountain. There were over a hundred of them who had left everything to follow him. These came to him, separating themselves from the multitude, which was waiting at the base of the mountain. From this loyal assembly, Jesus chose twelve. First among the twelve was Simon, whom Jesus also named Peter, and Andrew his brother; James the son of Zebedee and John his brother, to whom Jesus gave the name Boanerges, that is, "Sons of Thunder"; Philip, and Nathanael who was also known as Bartholomew; Thomas, called Didymus by his fellow disciples; Levi the tax collector, known as Matthew, and James his brother, sons of Alphaeus; and Judas the son of James, also known as Thaddaeus, whom Jesus named Lebbaeus, which means "a man of heart"; Simon the Canaanite, also known as Zelotes, because he was a Zealot, and Judas his son, known as Iscariot, because he was a member of the Sicarii, a radical group of Jewish assassins. Jesus presented these twelve to the other disciples as appointed apostles, whom he intended to send out, with power, to preach the good news, to heal sicknesses, and to cast out demons.

After presenting the twelve to them, he sat down among them and taught them, saying, "Blessed are *you*, poor in spirit, for the kingdom of God is yours! Blessed are *you*, who hunger and thirst after righteousness, for you shall be filled with the Spirit of Righteousness! Blessed are *you*, who mourn, when the bridegroom is taken from you, for the Comforter will come unto you! Truly, I say to you, blessed are *you*! When men hate you, and when they exclude you, and revile you, and cast out your name as evil, for the Son of man's sake, rejoice in that day and leap for joy! For indeed your reward is great in heaven, for in like manner did their fathers unto the prophets before you!"

Standing, again, Jesus assembled his disciples and led them partway down the mountain, where they gathered around him on a level place before the great multitude of people. This diverse crowd from the four corners of Israel and beyond its borders had come together to hear him, to be healed of their diseases, and to be cleansed from the unclean spirits that tormented them.

Standing before them, then, Jesus opened his mouth and taught them, saying, "Blessed are the poor in spirit, for theirs is the kingdom of heaven. Blessed are those who mourn, for they shall be comforted. Blessed are the meek, for they shall inherit the earth. Blessed are those who hunger and thirst for righteousness, for they shall be filled. Blessed are the merciful, for they shall obtain mercy. Blessed are the pure in heart, for they shall see God. Blessed are the peacemakers, for they shall be called the sons of God. Blessed are those who are persecuted for righteousness's sake, for theirs is the kingdom of heaven."

He paused, lifting his hands to the crowd, then continued, saying, "Blessed are you, therefore, when they revile and persecute you, and say all kinds of evil against you falsely for my sake. Rejoice and be exceedingly glad, for great is your reward in heaven, for so they persecuted the prophets, who were before you."

The pace of his speech was slow and deliberate, and the contour of this area of the mountain carried his voice to all who came to hear.

After another brief pause, he continued with an encouraging tone. "You are the salt of the earth!" Then he challenged their faithfulness. "But if the salt loses its flavor, how shall it be seasoned? It is then good for nothing but to be thrown out and trampled underfoot by men." Again, he encouraged them. "You are the light of the world!" Then he challenged them. "A city that is set on a hill cannot be hidden. Nor do they light a lamp and put it under a measuring pot, but on a lamp stand, and it gives light to all who are in the house." He followed this by encouragement, again. "Let your light so shine before men, that they may see your good works and glorify your Father in heaven."

As he spoke, the crowd shifted, and he watched as a small group of religious leaders maneuvered their way toward the front.

Jesus paused, until the crowd settled, again. Then, the tone of his speech shifted, reflecting his anger, suited to his altered audience. "But I say, woe unto you who are rich, for you have received your consolation. Woe unto you who are full, for you shall hunger. Woe unto you who laugh, for you shall mourn and weep. Woe unto you when all men speak well of you, for so did their fathers to the false prophets."

When his rage subsided, he paused again, and then confronted the religious leaders openly before the crowd. "Do not think that I have come to destroy the Law or the Prophets. I have not come to destroy but to fulfill. For assuredly, I say unto you, till heaven and earth pass away, not one of the smallest letters nor one of the least grammatical accent marks shall by any means pass from the Law till all is fulfilled. Whoever, therefore, breaks one of the least of these commandments, and teaches men to do so, shall be called least in the kingdom of heaven; but whoever does and teaches them, he shall be called great in the kingdom of heaven. For I say unto you that unless your righteousness exceeds the righteousness of the scribes and Pharisees, you shall by no means enter into the kingdom of heaven."

These comments drew a great murmur from the crowd, and the religious leaders were fidgeting uncomfortably.

Jesus, again, shifted his speech, in the form of an explanation.

"You have heard that it was said to those of old, 'You shall not murder, and whoever murders will be in danger of the judgment.' But *I* say to you that whoever is angry with his brother without a cause shall be in danger of the judgment. And whoever says of his brother, 'Raca!' (meaning empty) shall be in danger of the council. But whoever says, 'You fool!' shall be in danger of hell fire. Therefore, if you bring your gift to the altar, and there remember that your brother has something against you, leave your gift there before the altar, and go your way. First, be reconciled to your brother, and then come and offer your gift. Agree with your opponent at law, quickly, while you are with him on the way to judgment, lest your opponent deliver you to the judge, the judge hand you over to the officer, and you be thrown into prison. Truly, I say to you, you will by no means come out from there till you have paid the last bit of your debt."

He paused again, letting the audience digest his radical interpretation of this portion of the Law. He took his cue from the scribes and Pharisees, who had discussed his words animatedly. Eventually, they settled down again to listen, agreeing that his interpretation of the word *murder* must be a spiritual one.

He continued, "You have heard that it was said to those of old, 'You shall not commit adultery.' But *I* say to you that whoever looks upon a woman to lust after her has committed adultery with her already in his heart. If, therefore, your right eye causes you to sin, pluck it out and cast it from you, for it is more profitable for you that one of your members perish, than for your whole body to be cast into hell. Likewise, if your right hand causes you to sin, cut it off and cast it from you, for it is more profitable for you that one of your members perish, than for your whole body to be cast into hell. Furthermore, it has been said, 'Whoever shall put away his wife, let him give her a certificate of divorcement.' But *I* say to you that whoever puts away his wife for any reason except unfaithfulness causes her to commit adultery, and whoever marries a woman who is divorced commits adultery."

At his interpretation to this portion of the Law, the religious leaders, again, became animated, for they discussed at some length and ferocity whether he spoke of literal male-female marital union or the spiritual relationship between the Jewish religious leadership and members of the Jewish faith. It took some time before they calmed down, the rest of the crowd becoming agitated by the disruption.

Jesus waited until peace was restored, then he continued, "Again, you have heard that it was said to those of old, 'You shall not swear falsely, but shall perform your oaths to the Lord.' But *I* say to you, swear not at all: neither by heaven, for it is God's throne; nor by the earth, for it is his footstool; nor by Jerusalem, for it is the city of the great king. Nor shall you swear by your head, because you cannot make one hair white or black. But let your 'Yes' be yes, and your 'No' be no. For whatever is more than this comes from evil."

He paused briefly, without interruption, then continued, "You have heard that it was said, 'An eye for an eye and a tooth for a tooth.' But *I* say unto you, resist not evil. But whoever shall strike you on your right cheek, turn to him the other also." This he said glancing at Peter, who smiled at him in recognition of their encounter with the Romans.

Directing his next words back at the religious leaders, he said, "If anyone shall judge you according to the Law to take away your clothes, let him have your coat also." Then, seeing the centurion standing off to the side, beneath a tree, he nodded to him, saying, "And whoever compels you to go one mile, go with him two." The centurion frowned uncomfortably yet somehow was not overly offended by his comments. Jesus continued with great passion, speaking to the crowd, "Give to everyone who asks of you. From him who would borrow of you, turn him not away. And from him who takes away your goods, do not ask for them back. As you would like others to do to you, do, likewise, to them."

He paused again, momentarily, looking intently at the crowd, as if instructing his own beloved children, and then he resumed in a tone of compassion, "You have heard that it was said, 'You shall love your neighbor and hate your enemy.' But *I* say to you, love your enemies, bless those who curse you, do good to those who hate you, and pray for those who despitefully use you and persecute you, that you may be sons of your Father in heaven; for he makes his sun to rise on the evil and on the good, and sends rain on the just and on the unjust. For if you love those who love you, what benefit have you? Do not even tax collectors and sinners do the same? If you lend to those from whom you hope to receive back, what enduring gratitude is there for you, for the tax collectors and sinners do as much? And if you greet your brethren only, what do you achieve more than others? Do not even tax collectors and sinners do so? But love your enemies, do good, and lend, hoping for nothing in return, and your reward will be great, and you will be the sons of the Most High, for he is kind to the unthankful and the evil. Therefore, I say unto you, be perfect in mercy; even as your Father in heaven manifests his perfection through mercy."

Now, after Jesus spoke these words concerning tax collectors and sinners, the religious leaders, feeling justified by their works, puffed out their chests in pride.

Jesus, recognizing their arrogance, adjusted his approach to accommodate them. "Take heed that you do not do your charitable deeds before men, to be seen by them. Otherwise you have no reward from your Father in heaven. Therefore, when you do a charitable deed, do not sound a trumpet before you as the hypocrites do in the synagogues and in the streets, that they may have glory from men. Assuredly, I say unto you, they have their reward. But when you do a charitable deed, do not let your left hand know what your right hand is doing, that your charitable deed may be in secret; and your Father who sees in secret will himself reward you openly."

The religious leaders got the message, their prideful feelings morphing into shame, but Jesus continued his message to them. "And when you pray, you shall not be like the hypocrites, for they love to pray standing in the synagogues and on the corners of the streets, that they may be seen by men. Assuredly, I say unto you, they have their reward. But you, when you pray, go into your room, and when you have shut your door, pray to your Father in secret, and your Father who sees you in secret will reward you openly. And when you pray, do not use vain repetitions as the heathen do, for they think that they will be heard for their many words. Therefore, do not be like them, for your Father knows the things you have need of before you ask him."

Though the religious leaders experienced the humiliation meant for them, Jesus's words were more than merely an attack on their pride; they were words of power and conviction, piercing down to the very soul.

Jesus, knowing the conviction of their hearts, demonstrated compassion toward them, speaking words designed to turn them toward the Father. "In this manner, therefore, pray: Our Father in heaven, hallowed be your name. Your kingdom come. Your will be done, in earth, as it is in heaven. Give us this day our daily bread. And forgive us our debts, as we forgive our debtors. And lead us not into temptation, but deliver us from the evil one, for yours is the kingdom and the power and the glory forever. Amen."

When he finished his prayer, he looked directly at the religious leaders, adding, "It is mandatory that you forgive! For if you forgive men their trespasses, your heavenly Father will also forgive you. But if you do not forgive men their trespasses, neither will your Father forgive your trespasses."

Jesus paused briefly, watching the reaction of the religious leaders, who were somewhat subdued by Jesus's spiritual lesson. Recognizing their genuine humility, he returned to words of power and conviction, to drive home his teaching. "Moreover, when you fast, do not be like the hypocrites, with a sad countenance, for they disfigure their faces that they may appear to men to be fasting. Assuredly, I say unto you, they have their reward. But you, when you fast, anoint your head and wash your face, so that you do not appear to men to be fasting, but fast to your Father who is in secret, and your Father who sees you in secret will reward you openly."

He continued in this vein, speaking to the whole crowd, and expanding the theme to include the difference between all godly values and the values of mankind. "Do not, therefore, lay up for yourselves earthly treasures, where moth and rust destroy and where thieves break in and steal, but lay up for yourselves treasures in heaven, where neither moth nor rust destroys and where thieves do not break in and steal. For where your treasure is, there your heart will be also."

Then he returned his gaze, looking directly at the religious leaders. "The lamp of the body is the eye. If, therefore, your eye is good, your whole body will be full of light. But if your eye is bad, your whole body will be full of darkness. If, therefore, the light that is in you is darkness, how great is that darkness! No one can serve two masters, for either he will hate the one and love the other, or else he will be loyal to the one and despise the other. You cannot serve God and worldly treasure."

These words were not lost on many of the religious leaders, whose nods of approval seemed to now express the leadership standards required to lead God's people.

So Jesus shifted his words back to the crowd, explaining how they should expect to be led. "Therefore, I say unto *you*, be not preoccupied with your own life, what you will eat or what you will drink; nor with your own body, what you will put on. Is not life more than food and the body more than clothing? Look at the birds of the air, for they neither sow nor reap nor gather into barns; yet your heavenly Father feeds them. Are you not of more value than they? Which of you by obsessing can add to your stature by increasing your height? Which of you can add to your stature by changing one hair from black to white? If you cannot add to the very least of these, why be concerned about the rest? And why be obsessed with clothing? Consider the lilies of the field, how they grow: they neither toil nor spin; and yet I say to you that even

Solomon, in all his glory, was not arrayed like one of these. Now if God so beautifully adorns the grass of the field, which today is, and tomorrow is thrown into the oven, will he not much more clothe you, Oh you of little faith? Therefore do not worry, saying, 'What shall we eat?' or 'What shall we drink?' or 'What shall we wear?' For after all these things do the faithless Gentiles seek. Be not like them, for your heavenly Father knows that you have need of these things. But seek first the kingdom of God and his righteousness, and all these things shall be added unto you. Likewise, be not concerned with tomorrow, for tomorrow will be concerned with the things of itself. Sufficient unto the day is the evil thereof."

Jesus paused briefly before he continued. "Judge not, that you be not judged. Condemn not, and you shall not be condemned. Rather, forgive, that you may be forgiven. Give, and it shall be given to you; good measure, pressed down, shaken together, and running over will it be put into your bosom. For with what judgment you judge, you will be judged, and with the same standard that you use to measure, it will be measured back to you.

"Will you be my disciples? A disciple is not above his teacher, but everyone who is perfectly instructed will be like unto his teacher. Can the blind lead the blind? Will they not both fall into the ditch? Again, I say unto you, judge not! Why do you scrutinize the speck in your brother's eye, but do not consider the plank in your own eye? Or how can you say to your brother, 'Let me remove the speck from your eye;' and not perceive the plank that is in your own eye? Hypocrite! First remove the plank from your own eye, and then you will see clearly to remove the speck from your brother's eye. Do unto others as you would have them do unto you, for this is the Law and the Prophets."

Jesus paused again briefly, for he felt troubled in his soul; then he turned and glanced at Judas Iscariot, before returning his attention to the religious leaders.

He frowned, glancing briefly at the centurion, and then proceeded. "Do not give what is holy to the dogs; nor cast your pearls before the swine, lest they trample them under their feet, and turn and tear you to pieces. Be not offended in me! But ask, and it shall be given to you; seek, and you shall find; knock, and it shall be opened unto you. For everyone who asks, receives, and he who seeks, finds, and to him who knocks, it shall be opened. For what man is there among you, who, if his son asks for bread, will give him a stone? Or if he asks for a fish, will give him a serpent? If you then, being evil, know how to give good gifts to your children, how much more will your Father who is in heaven give the Holy Spirit to those who ask him?"

After these words, his troubled countenance returned again to one exuding peace, and he spoke thoughtfully to the crowd. "But you must enter by the narrow gate, for wide is the gate and broad is the way that leads to destruction, and there are many who go in by it. Because narrow is the gate and demanding is the way that leads to life, and there are few who find it. Beware, therefore, of false prophets, who come to you in sheep's clothing, but inwardly they are ravenous wolves. You will know them by their fruits. Do men gather grapes from thorn bushes or figs from thistles? Even so, every good tree bears good fruit, but a bad tree bears bad fruit. A good tree cannot bear bad fruit, nor can a bad tree bear good fruit. Every tree that does not bear good fruit is cut down and thrown into the fire. Therefore, by their fruits you will know them. A good man out of the good treasure of his heart brings forth good, and an evil man out of the evil treasure of his heart brings forth evil. For out of the abundance of the heart his mouth speaks. Know, therefore, that not everyone who says to me, 'Lord, Lord,' shall enter the kingdom of heaven, but he who does the will of my Father in heaven. Many will say to me in that day, 'Lord, Lord, have we not prophesied in your name, cast out demons in your name, and done many wonders in your name?' And then I will declare to them, 'I never knew you; depart from me, you who work apart from righteousness!'"

He concluded his teaching, projecting his audience into his last parable. "Whoever, therefore, hears these sayings of mine, and

does them, I will liken him unto a wise man building a house, who
dug deep and laid the foundation, and built his house upon a rock:
and the rain descended, the floods came, and the winds blew and
beat vehemently against that house, and could not shake it, for it
was founded upon a rock. But everyone who hears these sayings
of mine, and does not do them, shall be likened to a foolish man
who built his house upon the earth, without a foundation: and
the rain descended, the floods came, and the winds blew and beat
vehemently against that house, and immediately it fell. And great
was its fall!"

When Jesus had finished these words, he turned his back upon
the crowd, gathered his disciples, and again ascended the mountain.
Many of the religious leaders did not receive his teaching, for they
were offended by his words. Many others among them heard his
message, and acknowledged the wisdom and righteousness in it.
Likewise, the crowd, who looked to the leaders for guidance, was
divided in its understanding and acceptance of this radical, new
teaching.

Everyone in attendance, however, was astonished at the manner
in which Jesus taught, for he taught with such authority. All who
heard and believed, that day, were also miraculously healed of their
infirmities, for his words were imbued with power.

Mark 3:13–19   Luke 6:13–49   Matthew 5:1–48
Matthew 6:1–34   Matthew 7:1–29   1 John 3:15

Chapter 29

RETURN FROM THE MOUNT TO CAPERNAUM

Now, after Jesus's sermon on the mount, Capernaum was overrun with visitors ignited by his words and desperate to see the miracles about which everyone was talking. Great multitudes surrounded Peter's house, in particular, so that it was difficult to move for the push of the crowd. Jesus's mother and brothers had come to see him at Capernaum with bad news concerning his father, Joseph. Joseph and his sons were working on a tower at Siloam, in Jerusalem, building it with great stones. But before the mortar was set, and while they were still working, an earthquake shook the tower, collapsing part of it; which fell upon the laborers, killing many, and Joseph among them. So they came to Jesus to tell him of the tragedy, expecting him to join them for his burial. Mary and the family were still wrestling with Jesus's behavior at the temple, and were very much disturbed to find Capernaum in such a chaotic state, caused by Jesus's unorthodox ministry. Mary was particularly upset with the path his ministry was taking. She had visited the religious leaders often to discuss his mission, hoping to persuade them to acknowledge it, and to help him seamlessly incorporate it into the established Jewish order. Arriving late, because of the tragedy, they were confined to the back of the crowd, at the base of the mountain.

Though they heard his sermon, and their hearts were filled with hope at his words, Mary and the others were concerned with how the religious leaders would interpret them. Would they accept them or reject them? They were not alone in wondering these things; much of the crowd wondered also, but his family's wonder was also filled with worry and apprehension. Added to these thoughts was the pall that hung over them concerning Joseph's death, and how Jesus would receive the news. When the sermon ended, they were forced to wait longer, because of the crowd. Mary maneuvered her way toward the religious leaders as they went by them, and she approached them anxiously.

"What did you think of his sermon?" she asked.

Nicodemus spoke first. "Fascinating, Mary; his interpretation is immersed in wisdom and righteousness—on a very spiritual level!"

"It's nonsense," growled another among them.

"Not everyone is in agreement, as you can see," said Joseph of Arimathaea, "but there are those among us who were quite taken with your son's teachings."

"This is madness!" another said, trying to push through the sea of spectators. "What are we to make of this total lack of order? Are we to conclude that this is God's will—all this chaos?"

Mary cringed at his remarks, but Nicodemus put a comforting arm around her waist.

"Come, now," he said to her, loud enough for the others to hear, "God's ways are above man's ways. He made great sense; a tree is known by its fruit, and so far, all he has done is good."

"Is chaos good, Nicodemus? Am I imagining all these people?" the man retorted.

"Be careful, Annas, that you do not fall into a ditch!" Nicodemus teased him. "These people are genuinely interested in hearing God's word."

"We shall see, in good time, whether his words are of God or not," said Annas. "On that subject, I intend to reserve judgment."

The family and the religious leaders pushed through the crowd, arriving at Peter's house. Of course, Jesus and his disciples had not yet arrived, for they had remained on the mountain, waiting for the great multitude of people to return to their homes.

As the crowd diminished at the base of the mountain, Jesus and his disciples made their way back to Peter's house. News of their return spread quickly, and soon the crowds began to gather around them as they walked.

Entering Capernaum, they were met by a delegation of Jewish elders, who came to Jesus on behalf of a centurion.

And they said to him, "A certain centurion has come to us beseeching us to approach you, because a servant who is dear to him is sick and ready to die. He asked us to speak these words to you, 'Lord, my servant is lying at home paralyzed, and dreadfully tormented.'"

Then the men besought Jesus to come with them, saying, "He is worthy, for he loves our nation, and has built us a synagogue."

So Jesus went with them. And when they drew near to his house, the centurion sent word to Jesus, by his friends, saying, "Lord, trouble not yourself, for I am not worthy that you should enter under my roof, for neither felt I worthy to come unto you myself, but say the word, and my servant shall be healed. For I am a man set under authority, having soldiers under me, and I say to one, 'Go,' and he goes, and to another, 'Come,' and he comes, and to my servant, 'Do this,' and he does it."

When Jesus heard these things, he marveled at his words, and turned around to address those who followed him.

"I say unto you," he exclaimed, "I have not found so great a faith, no, not in Israel. And I say unto you that many will come from the east and the west and sit down with Abraham, Isaac, and Jacob in the kingdom of heaven. But the sons of the kingdom will be cast out into outer darkness. There will be weeping and gnashing of teeth."

Then Jesus said to the friends of the centurion, "Go your way, and tell the centurion, 'As you have believed, so let it be done unto you.'"

So they that were sent returned to the house, and found the servant, who had been sick unto death, made well and whole, in that same hour. And this centurion, the same who had accosted Jesus upon the road, believed with all his household, for his servant's sake.

Jesus returned with his disciples to Peter's house, winding his way through the crowds. The people pressed upon him, just wanting to be near him, to touch him, for they sought of him to be both healed and blessed.

At the house, his kinsmen, his mother and brothers among them, came hoping to dine with him, so that they might break the news gently of his father's demise. But they found him not there, for he had gone off to heal the centurion's servant. And when the crowd pressed also into the house, so that they could not even eat, they decided to go out again to find him.

Believing that he must have gone mad, they were determined to seize him by force, for they reasoned among themselves, saying, "Who in their right mind would promote such chaos?"

Once outside, however, they could not find him. And when Jesus and his disciples returned to the house, his kinsmen were pushed aside by the crowd, so that they could not approach him.

When Jesus entered the house, he directed the twelve to form a loose ring around him. Inside the ring, he called others of his disciples to sit tightly packed together so that no one uninvited could approach him. This arrangement created a sense of order in the midst of the chaos, and made it possible for those outside the ring to see what Jesus was doing. In the center of all this turmoil, Jesus calmly stood, calling to him those in need—healing the sick and casting out demons. Outside the house, the crowd raged on in loud tones, but inside, Jesus and those to whom he ministered could be heard clearly. Occasionally, eruptions of joy and amazement, due to his miracles, disturbed the serenity within.

Eventually, fear and awe struck all those who witnessed him

exorcizing demons, for the victims were often thrown about, and the demons cried out. Included among those witnesses were several scribes who had come from Jerusalem.

Unable to grasp God's plan in all of this, they accused Jesus, saying of him, "He has Beelzebub, and by the prince of the devils he casts out devils."

So Jesus called them to him, and said to them in parables, "How can Satan cast out Satan? If a kingdom is divided against itself, that kingdom cannot stand. If a house is divided against itself, that house cannot stand. And if Satan rises up against himself, and is divided, he cannot stand, and will, therefore, come to an end. No man can enter into a strong man's house and spoil his goods unless he first binds the strong man; then he will spoil his house.

"And take heed unto your own selves," he continued, "for truly, I say unto you, all sins shall be forgiven the sons of men, and blasphemies with whatever they blaspheme, but he that shall blaspheme the Holy Spirit shall never be forgiven but is in danger of eternal damnation."

Eventually, his kinsmen were able to relay a message to John, who interrupted Jesus, saying, "Your mother and brothers are outside, seeking to speak with you."

But Jesus, still burdened by the responsibility of his immediate ministry, would not interrupt the flow of the Spirit of God.

"Who," he asked his listeners emphatically, "*is* my mother and my brothers?"

And the room became silent, as they looked at him with puzzled expressions.

He looked around the room, and then at his closest believers, who sat before him.

Then opening wide his arms, he gestured toward them and exclaimed, "Behold, my mother and my brothers. For whoever shall do the will of God, the same is my brother, and my sister, and my mother."

Many of the listeners were aghast at his strange words, for they felt great sympathy for his kinsmen, and especially his mother; who, in the silence, had heard every word clearly.

Then the message was relayed, again to Jesus through John, who said, "Master, your father, Joseph, is dead—killed in the collapse of a tower being built at Siloam. Your kinsmen have come to inform you of his death, and to bring you home for his burial."

Then a scribe, who was standing just outside the circle of believers, said, "Teacher, go and bury your dead. *I* will follow you wherever you go."

To him, Jesus replied, "Foxes have holes and birds of the air have nests, but the Son of Man has nowhere to lay his head."

Jesus said this, because he knew that this man's veiled loyalty was intended to spoil his ministry of delivering his Father's message; Jesus knew that Satan was behind the man's intent.

Then from the crowd, just outside the door, the voice of Jude, Jesus's younger brother could be heard, saying, "Lord, let us go and bury our father."

This, too, Jesus knew was intended to interrupt him, so he responded, so that all who heard would know the importance of his ministry, "Follow me, and let the dead bury their own dead."

These words divided the onlookers, for his words seemed harsh, lacking compassion, mercy, and love. His kinsmen left together to bury Joseph. Mary's heart was pierced by his words; they troubled her, so that she continued to scrutinize her beliefs about the direction of her son's ministry. She wondered what she truly believed about him, asking herself if she was truly spiritually dead, as his words suggested. Those who were offended by the way Jesus treated his family left off from following him. Those who understood the importance of following him remained. And, though he was truly grieving in his heart over Joseph and his family, Jesus remained faithful to his Nazarite vow, and returned to attending to the needs of the people present.

Matthew 8:1	Luke 13:1–5	Luke 7:1–10
Matthew 8:5–13	Mark 3:20–35	Matthew 12:24–32
Matthew 8:18–22		

Chapter 30

RAISING THE DEAD AT NAIN

Early the next day, Jesus traveled to a city called Nain, and many of his disciples went with him, and a large crowd followed them. Now when they came near to the gate of the city, they beheld a dead man being carried out, the only son of his mother, and she was a widow. A long procession followed her, for many people of the city came out to mourn with her.

When Jesus saw her, he had compassion upon her, and stopped her, saying, "Weep not."

Then he came and touched the funeral bed upon which her son was carried, and those who carried him stood still, allowing Jesus to pay his respects to the young man. But Jesus spoke to the man, in the hearing of them all.

"Young man," he called to him, "I say unto you, arise!"

Before anyone had time to react to his strange words, the dead man sat up and began to speak.

"I will, Lord!" he said, looking gratefully at Jesus. Then he looked around him, and at his mother. "Put me down, put me down," he demanded, "that I may comfort my mother."

So the pallbearers lowered the bier to the ground, and Jesus lifted the man up. When he rose to his feet, Jesus delivered him to his mother. In the arms of her son, his mother sobbed uncontrollably, groaning within herself, and uttering mostly words that were unintelligible.

Then fear gripped them all, and they glorified God, saying, "A great prophet is risen up among us, for God has visited his people."

This report of him went forth throughout all Judea and throughout the entire region round about. And the disciples of John the Baptist reported to John all these things.

Now when John heard in the prison the works of the Messiah, he called two of his disciples that he might send them to Jesus, saying, "Are you he that should come or should we look for another?"

And he sent them in haste to find him. Now Jesus and his disciples had journeyed to Bethany, on their way to Jerusalem to celebrate the Festival of Weeks. When the disciples of John arrived there, they found him ministering to the crowds—healing, casting out demons, and preaching the good news of the kingdom.

After Jesus had finished ministering to the people, John's two messengers approached him, saying, "John the Baptist has sent us unto you, saying, 'Are you he that should come or should we look for another?'"

Then Jesus, answering, said to them, "Go your way, and tell John what things you have seen and heard—how the blind see, the lame walk, the lepers are cleansed, the deaf hear, the dead are raised, and to the poor the gospel is preached." "Tell John," he said to them earnestly, "blessed is he who shall not be offended in me."

As the messengers of John were departing, Jesus began to speak to the people concerning John, and the messengers, hearing his words, stopped to consider them.

"What went you out into the wilderness to see?" he asked. "A reed shaken by the wind? But what went you out to see? A man clothed in soft raiment? Behold, they who are gorgeously appareled, and live delicately, are in king's courts. But what went you out to see? A prophet? Yes, I say unto you, and much more than a prophet. This is he, of whom it is written, 'Behold, I send my messenger before your face, which shall prepare your way before you.' For truly I say unto you, among them that are born of women there has not risen a greater than John the Baptist; notwithstanding, he that is least in the kingdom of God is greater than he. And from the days of John the Baptist until now, the kingdom of heaven has suffered violence, and the violent take it by force. For all the prophets and the Law prophesied until John. And if you will receive it, this is Elijah, who was to come. He who has ears to hear, let him hear."

And the common people who heard Jesus, including the tax collectors, justified God, being baptized with the baptism of John. But the Pharisees and lawyers had rejected the counsel of God against themselves, being not baptized of him. Jesus paused, measuring the crowd, and especially the religious leaders.

Then Jesus smiled at John's messengers, and continued, "To what then shall I liken the leaders of this generation, for what are they like? They are like children sitting in the marketplace, and calling one to another, and saying, 'We have piped unto you, and you have not danced; we have mourned unto you, and you have not wept.' For John the Baptist came neither eating bread nor drinking wine, and you say, 'He has a devil.' The Son of Man has come eating and drinking, and you say, 'Behold a gluttonous man, and a winebibber, a friend of tax collectors and sinners!' But wisdom is justified of her children."

When Jesus concluded these words, he nodded to the messengers, who smiled and waved, then continued on their way to make their report to John.

Now, as the crowd began to disperse, Jesus was approached by several of the Pharisees, one of which desired that he would eat with him. And he went into the Pharisee's house, and sat down to dine. At the table sat his host, Simon, the leper, whom Jesus had healed of leprosy. His son Lazarus sat beside him, and they were joined by several other Pharisees together with Jesus and the twelve. Simon's daughter, Martha, served them.

With Simon's leprosy gone, his stature among the Pharisees was restored, and he reestablished his habit of inviting several of them to dine with him on a regular basis. On the spur of the moment, after hearing Jesus's preaching, and witnessing his ministry, Simon decided to invite him, as well. When he approached him with his invitation, he was apprehensive, and surprised to find that Jesus remembered him—and relieved that Jesus had accepted.

Simon remembered well Jesus's words to him, after he had healed him. "See that you tell no man, but go and show yourself to the priests, and offer for your cleansing the gift that Moses commanded, for a testimony unto them."

He had not heeded his words to keep the miracle silent, and Simon felt somewhat responsible for the chaos that resulted. He had, eventually, presented himself to the priests and offered his gift according to the Law. The temple priests did not, however, like his explanation of the healing, and they interrogated him over the matter. This, too, he thought, had resulted in a negative response to Jesus's ministry. He was truly grateful that Jesus did not bear a grudge.

As they sat, a woman from the city, a prostitute, entered the room. When she knew that Jesus was dining at her father's house, she came bearing an alabaster box of ointment. There she stood at the feet of Jesus, behind him, weeping. All were silent, observing her torment. Eventually, she kneeled down, and began to wash his feet with her tears, wiping them off with her hair. Then she began kissing his feet, and afterward she anointed them with the ointment.

Now when Simon, the Pharisee who had bidden Jesus, saw it, he spoke within himself, saying, *This man, if he were a prophet, would have known who and what manner of woman this is that touches him, for she is a sinner.*

But Jesus knew their history, for Simon's daughter, Mary, had been seduced by a Roman soldier. Simon, being strict in his adherence to the Law, judged her harshly, denying her existence as his daughter. When the soldier discarded her, she turned to prostitution to care for herself, for the people judged her worthy of no other work. Shortly thereafter, Simon contracted leprosy, and was judged by the people as cursed of God.

Knowing their history, and discerning Simon's thoughts, Jesus answering, said to him, "Simon, I have something to say to you."

And he said, "Master, say on."

"There was a certain creditor," Jesus said, "which had two debtors: the one owed five hundred denarii, and the other fifty. And when they had nothing to pay, he frankly forgave them both. Tell me, therefore, which of them will love him more?"

Simon answered, and said, "I suppose that he to whom he forgave more."

And Jesus said to him, "You have rightly judged."

Then he turned to the woman, while he continued speaking to Simon. "Do you see this woman? I entered into your house, and you gave me no water for my feet, but she has washed my feet with her tears, and wiped them with the hairs of her head. You gave me no kiss, but this woman, since the time I came in has not ceased to kiss my feet. My head you did not anoint with oil, but this woman has anointed my feet with ointment. So, I say unto you, her sins, which *are* many, are forgiven, for she loved much, but to whom little is forgiven, the same loves little." And still looking upon her, he said to her, "Your sins are forgiven."

And they that sat at the table with him began to say within themselves, *Who is this that forgives sins, also?*

And he said, again to the woman, "Your faith has saved you; go in peace."

And she looked at Jesus, and smiled, then at her father and brother with swollen eyes, searching for any hint of forgiveness. Then Martha, her sister, ran to her and hugged her tightly. And Simon and Lazarus rose from the table and embraced her, and gave praise to God for their family that was restored. There was a great overflowing of peace and joy within their home that evening, as family and friends, Pharisees, and the disciples of Jesus rejoiced in the goodness of God's Spirit.

Luke 7:11–50   Matthew 11:2–19

Chapter 31

HEALING AT THE BETHESDA POOL

Now Jesus had come to Jerusalem to attend Shavu'ot, or Pentecost, the fiftieth day following the Feast of Weeks. It marked the end of the barley harvest, which completed the yearly agricultural cycle. It also marked the beginning of the wheat harvest and a new agricultural cycle. This festival was, therefore, a celebration of the first fruits, and because of its timing, the giving of the Torah or Law of Moses at Mount Sinai. The festival counted a period of seven weeks from Passover, numbering fifty days to Shavu'ot, at which time the men were to present themselves to God at the temple to hear the reading of the Ten Commandments. The night before was to be spent studying the Torah, followed by early morning prayer.

Jesus led his disciples to the pool at Bethesda to perform the ritualistic purification, before entering the temple that evening. Now the pool had five porches, and all around these porches lay a great multitude of helpless people: the blind, the lame, and the paralyzed, who were all waiting for the moving of the water. For an angel went down at certain times into the pool, and disturbed the water, so that whoever entered the water immediately afterward was made whole of whatever disease he had. Now there was a certain man lying there, who had been afflicted with an illness for thirty-eight years.

When Jesus saw him lying there, he knew that he had been

suffering in that condition for a long time, and he asked him, "Would you like to be made whole?"

The man looked at him warily, and answered, "Sir, I have no one, when the water is troubled, to put me into the pool, but while I am attempting to enter, someone else enters before me."

Jesus replied to him, "Rise, take up your bed, and walk."

And immediately the man was made whole, and took up his bed, and walked. Now the sun had not yet set, and the day was the Sabbath before Shavu'ot.

When the religious leaders, therefore, saw the man carrying his bed, they said to him that was healed, "It is the Sabbath day: it is not lawful for you to carry your bed."

And the man feared their judgment; so rather than testify to them of the glorious miracle that God had bestowed upon him, and suffer their criticism, he chose to place blame on the one who healed him.

So the man answered them, "He that made me whole, the same said to me, 'Take up your bed, and walk.'"

Then they asked him, "What man is *that*, who said to you, 'Take up your bed, and walk'?"

But the man didn't know, for Jesus had disappeared into the crowd surrounding the place.

Later, Jesus found the man in the temple, and warned him, "Behold, you have been made whole; sin no more, lest a worse thing come upon you."

But the man did not heed his warning; he left, and told the religious leaders that it was Jesus who had made him whole. For this reason, the Jewish leadership persecuted Jesus, and sought to slay him, because he had done these things on the Sabbath day.

When they confronted him about his work on the Sabbath, Jesus answered them, "My Father works even now, and so I work, also."

Therefore, the Jewish leaders sought the more to kill him,

because he not only had broken the Sabbath, but said also that God was his Father, making himself equal with God.

When they attacked him on this point, also, Jesus answered, and said to them, "Truly, truly, I say unto you, the Son can do nothing of himself, but what he sees the Father do, for whatever things he does, these also does the Son, likewise. For the Father loves the Son, and shows him all things that he does, and he will show him greater works than these, that you may marvel. For as the Father raises up the dead, and quickens them, even so the Son quickens whom he will. For the Father judges no man, but has committed all judgment unto the Son, that all men should honor the Son, even as they honor the Father. He that honors not the Son, honors not the Father who has sent him.

"Truly, truly, I say unto you, he that hears my word, and believes in him who sent me, has everlasting life, and shall not come into condemnation, but is passed from death unto life. Truly, truly, I say unto you, the hour is coming, and now is, when the dead shall hear the voice of the Son of God, and they that hear shall live. For as the Father has life in himself, so has he given to the Son to have life in himself, and has given him authority to execute judgment also, because he is the Son of man. Marvel not at this, for the hour is coming, in which all that are in the graves shall hear his voice, and shall come forth—they that have done good, unto the resurrection of life; and they that have done evil, unto the resurrection of damnation.

"I can do nothing on my own: as I hear, I judge, and my judgment is just, because I seek not my own will, but the will of the Father who has sent me. If I bear witness of myself, my witness is not true. There is another that bears witness of me, and I know that the witness, which he witnesses of me, is true. You sent unto John, and he bore witness unto the truth. But I receive not testimony from man, but these things I say, that you might be saved. He was a burning and a shining light, and you were willing for a season to rejoice in his light. But I have a greater witness than that of John: the works which the Father has given me to finish; those same works that I do bear witness of me that the Father has sent me. And the Father, himself, who has sent me, has borne witness of me. You have neither heard his voice at any time, nor seen his shape. And you have not his word abiding in you, for whom he has sent, him you believe not.

"Search the scriptures, for in them you think you have eternal life, and they are they which testify of me. And you will not come to me, that you might have life. I receive not honor from men. But I know you, that you have not the love of God in you.

"I am come in my Father's name, and you receive me not; if another shall come in his own name, him you will receive. How can you believe, you who receive honor one of another, and seek not the honor that comes from God only? Do not think that I will accuse you to the Father; there is one that accuses you, even Moses, in whom you trust. For had you believed Moses, you would have believed me, for he wrote of me. But if you believe not his writings, how shall you believe my words?"

John 5:1–47	Deuteronomy 16:9–12	Deuteronomy 16:16–17
Exodus 23:14–16	Leviticus 23:9–17	Exodus 34:22

Chapter 32

BACK ACROSS THE SEA

Following the trip to Jerusalem, Jesus and his disciples returned to Galilee, and crossed over the sea to the desert to escape the crowds and the rage of the temple leaders. Now, when Jesus crossed back over the sea, again returning from the desert, a great multitude had gathered, waiting to welcome him.

And there came to him one of the rulers of the local synagogue, a man named Jairus, whose only daughter was dying, and she was about twelve years old.

When he saw Jesus, he fell down at his feet, and worshiped him, and begging him, said, "My little daughter lies at the point of death. Come and lay your hand on her, and she will live."

So Jesus and his disciples went with him, and the multitude followed along with them, surrounding him.

Now a certain woman, who had a blood flow disorder for twelve years, and spent all her livelihood on physicians, had heard about Jesus's healing powers. She had suffered many things at the hands of the physicians, who could not cure her; neither had her condition improved, but rather worsened. When she heard that Jesus was approaching her village, she followed the crowd to greet him.

Pushing her way through the crowd, she came up suddenly from behind him, touching the hem of his garment, for she said to herself, "If only I may touch the hem of his garment, I shall be made well."

She considered that Jesus was that "Sun of righteousness" that Malachi had written about, who would "arise with healing in his wings." Now, as she reached out, she tugged at the *tzitzit*, or tassel woven into the hem of his *tallit*, or prayer shawl. It was these wing-like projections that God instructed Israel, through Moses, to have woven into the borders of all their garments. These tassels were to be reminders to keep all the commandments of the Lord. This she grabbed, and when she did, she was instantly healed. Immediately, her flow of blood was dried up, and she felt in her body that she was healed of the affliction. Feeling the power of healing go through her body, the woman gasped, and fell to the ground. Then, as the crowd pushed by her, she rose to her feet and examined her abdomen with her hands. She looked up, watching Jesus disappearing behind the crowd, before raising her hands and looking to heaven in gratitude.

Jesus stopped.

Then he turned around facing the crowd, and shouted to them, "Who touched me?"

The people following him stopped and became silent. Jairus, who had continued farther down the road, in haste, turned to survey the scene, agitated at the interruption.

Then Jesus repeated his interrogation, asking, "Who touched my clothes?"

But the people in the crowd began denying touching him. When all had denied, Peter and others with him answered Jesus in amazement, "Master, the multitudes surround you and press up against you, and you say, 'Who touched me?'"

But Jesus insisted, "Somebody touched me, for I perceived power going out from me!"

Then he scanned the crowd intensely to find the one who had done this thing. As he did, the crowd pulled back to avoid his scrutiny, hoping to see who had actually touched him. When the woman realized that what had happened to her was no longer hidden, she came forward, fearing and trembling, and fell down before him. In the presence of all the people, she declared to him the truth of the matter, the reason she had touched him, and how she was healed immediately.

And when he saw her, and heard her testimony, he had compassion upon her, saying, "Be of good comfort, daughter of Israel; your faith has made you whole. Go in peace, and be healed of your affliction."

While Jesus was speaking to her, members of Jairus's household came to him and said, "Your daughter is dead. Why trouble the Master any further?"

When Jesus heard their words, he turned to Jairus, and reassured him, saying, "Be not afraid, only believe, and she shall be made whole."

They arrived at Jairus's house, where they were greeted by flute players and a tumult of those who wept and wailed loudly.

Entering into the house, Jesus said to them, "Why make this clamorous noise, and weep? Weep not! Make room, for the girl is not dead, but sleeping."

And they ridiculed him, laughing him to scorn, for they knew that she was dead. So Jesus permitted no one to enter into her room with him, other than Peter and James and John, and her father and mother. And when he had put them all out, he took her by the hand, and said to her, "*Talitha, cumi*," which means, "Little girl, arise." And her spirit came again, and she immediately arose and walked, and he commanded them to feed her. And her parents were overcome by a combination of great fear and wonder. But Jesus charged them, strictly, that they should tell no one what was done, for the crowds had become unmanageable. Nevertheless, the report went out into all that land.

When Jesus departed from there, two blind men followed him, crying out and saying, "Son of David, have mercy on us!"

But the crowds were such that he could not reach them. When

he had come again to Peter's house, therefore, the blind men came to him.

And Jesus said to them, "Do you believe that I am able to do this?"

They said to him, "Yes, Lord."

Then he touched their eyes, saying, "According to your faith, let it be unto you."

And their eyes were opened. And Jesus sternly warned them, saying, "See that no one knows it."

But these men, also, when they had departed, spread the news about him in all that country. As Jesus left the house, again, the townspeople brought to him a man, mute and demon-possessed. And when the demon was cast out, the mute man spoke.

And the multitudes marveled, saying, "It was never seen like this in Israel!"

But the Pharisees, fearing Jesus's power and his influence over the multitude, sought to turn the crowd against him, saying to them, "He casts out demons by the ruler of the demons."

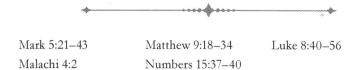

Mark 5:21–43   Matthew 9:18–34   Luke 8:40–56
Malachi 4:2   Numbers 15:37–40

Chapter 33

RETURN TO HIS OWN COUNTRY

Jesus left the Sea of Galilee and came into his own country; and his disciples followed him. And when the Sabbath had come, he began to teach in the synagogue.

And many hearing him were astonished, saying, "Where did this man get these things? And what wisdom is this, which is given to him, that such mighty works are performed by his hands! Is this not the laborer, the son of Mary, and brother of James, Joses, Judas, and Simon? And are not his sisters here with us?"

And they were offended by him.

But Jesus said to them, "A prophet is not without honor, except in his own country, among his own relatives, and in his own house."

Now he could do no mighty work there, in his own hometown. And he marveled, because of their unbelief. Only a few sick people, upon whom he laid his hands, were healed by him.

So Jesus went about all the nearby cities and villages, in a circuit, teaching in their synagogues, preaching the gospel of the kingdom, and healing every sickness and every disease among the people; for he saw the multitudes, and was moved with compassion for them, because they were weary and scattered, like sheep having no shepherd.

Then he said to his disciples, "The harvest truly is plentiful, but the laborers are few. Therefore, pray the Lord of the harvest to send out laborers into his harvest."

And he called the twelve to himself, and began to send them out two by two, and he gave them power over unclean spirits, to cast them out, and to heal all manner of sickness and disease.

These twelve, Jesus sent out and commanded them, saying, "Go not into the way of the Gentiles, and enter not into any city of the Samaritans. But go, rather, to the lost sheep of the house of Israel. And as you go, preach, saying, 'The kingdom of heaven is at hand.' Heal the sick, cleanse the lepers, raise the dead, cast out demons. Freely you have received; freely give. Take nothing for your journey: no staff, no bag, no bread; neither gold nor silver nor bronze coins in your belt. Take only one pair of sandals, and do not pack a second tunic, for a worker is worthy of his hire.

"Now, whatever city or town you enter, inquire who in it is worthy, and stay there till you go out. And when you go into a household, greet it. If the household is worthy, let your peace come upon it. But if it is not worthy, let your peace return to you. And whoever will not receive you or hear your words, when you depart from that house or city, shake off the dust from your feet as a testimony against them. Truly, I say to you, it will be more tolerable for the land of Sodom and Gomorrah in the Day of Judgment than for that city!"

So they departed, and went throughout the towns of Israel, preaching the gospel. And they cast out many demons, and anointed with oil many who were sick, healing people everywhere they went.

Mark 6:1–13   Matthew 9:35–38   Matthew 10:1–15
Luke 9:1–6

Chapter 34

RETURN TO THE
BETHSAIDA DESERT

Now the festival of Purim followed the feast of the dedication of the temple, and Herod threw a feast to commemorate Esther and Israel's victory over Haaman. And as was the custom at the feast, the story was recited from the scriptures. Shortly thereafter, Herod celebrated his birthday, inviting essentially the same guests for a similar feast. They included nobles, high officers, and chief men from Galilee. And, for his birthday, Salome, Herodias's daughter danced before them, and her dance pleased Herod very much.

Therefore, he promised with an oath to give her whatever she asked for, saying, "Ask me whatever you want, and I will give it to you." Then, remembering the story of Esther, and the king of Persia's oath, Herod quoted the oath of King Ahasuerus, "What is your petition? For it shall be granted to you. And what is your request? Even to the half of the kingdom, it shall be performed."

Herod's guests were, indeed, impressed by the flamboyance of his oath.

Now, when the girl did not know what to ask for, she went to her mother and asked, "What shall I ask?"

And Herodias, still harboring hatred in her heart for John's

RETURN TO THE BETHSAIDA DESERT

misunderstood words against Herod, replied, "The head of John the Baptist!"

So the girl returned to Herod, and demanded of him, "I want you to give me, at once, John the Baptist's head!"

At this, his guests all laughed.

Then she lifted up a silver platter from the table, and thrust it toward the king. "Here, on a platter," she said.

His guests became silent, dumbfounded by the apparent seriousness of the demand, both in the tone of the girl's voice, and in her gesture. Herod was immediately sorry; yet, because of his oath, and to save face before those with whom he sat, he was reluctant to refuse her. Then those at the table began to laugh incredulously to see what Herod would do. All eyes were glued to him.

So Herod sent word to the executioner that John was to be beheaded. And, as instructed, to the horror of his guests, John's head was brought to the girl on a platter, and she presented it to her mother.

When John's disciples heard of the horrific news, they came to Herod and took John's body, and buried it; then they went and told Jesus. When Jesus heard it, he departed by boat to the wilderness to be by himself.

And he sent word to the twelve that John had been beheaded, saying, "Come by yourselves into the wilderness, and rest for a while."

So they returned to him there, by boat, to a deserted place near Bethsaida. Seeing them depart, the multitudes followed them on foot, hoping the twelve would lead them to Jesus. When the twelve came to him, they found him on a mountain, in the shelter of a cave. There he sat with them, and they told him all that they had done and taught.

Now when he emerged from the cave, he beheld a great multitude, and was moved with compassion for them, saying, "They are like sheep having no shepherd."

So he began to teach them many things, and healed their sick; and he spoke to them about the kingdom of God.

Now the Passover was at hand, and the hour grew late; and as evening approached, the twelve came to Jesus, and said to him, "We are in the wilderness, and the hour is already late. Send the multitudes away, that they may go into the surrounding villages, to lodge, and to buy for themselves bread, for they have nothing to eat."

But Jesus answered them, "They do not need to go away. You give them something to eat."

Judas, after checking his bag, announced that it held only two hundred small silver coins, called *denarii*.

Philip, therefore, asked Jesus, "Shall we go and buy two hundred denarii worth of bread and give them something to eat?"

Jesus, testing him, asked, "Philip, where shall we buy bread that these may eat?"

Philip, who chuckled, realizing the magnitude of the problem, responded, "Two hundred denarii worth of bread is not sufficient for them, that every one of them may have even a little."

But Jesus said to them, "How many loaves do you have? Go and see."

So they left him there, and when they returned from searching the crowd for food, Andrew offered, "There is a lad here, who has five barley loaves and two small fish, but what are they among so many?"

Philip inquired incredulously, "We have no more than five loaves and two fish?" Then thinking aloud, he mumbled, "Impossible, unless we go and *buy* food for all these people."

This he added before remembering how little money they had. He acknowledged his error in thinking, by holding up his hand and shaking his head, while rolling his eyes. The others ignored the foolishness in his comment, acknowledging, however, the impossibility of Jesus's demand that they should feed the people. They looked among themselves, frowning at one another. Realizing that the group had exhausted all of their apparent resources, they looked to Jesus for direction.

Then Jesus smiled at them, and said, "Bring them here to me, and make them sit down in groups of fifty."

Now there was much grass in the place, and shepherds sometimes grazed their flocks there, when grass was scarce, using the cave for their shelter. So the disciples made the people sit down on the green grass, in ranks of fifties and hundreds, and they were numbered about five thousand men, besides women and children. Jesus then took the five loaves and the two fish, and, looking up to heaven, he blessed them. And when he had given thanks, he broke the loaves and gave them to his disciples to set before the people, and the two fish he divided for them all. When he had distributed them to the disciples, his disciples gave them to the multitude, the bread and the fish, as much as they wanted.

The feast went on for some time; the people were laughing among themselves, discussing the words of Jesus, and rehearsing his many miracles. The meal was an unusual one, and the participants lost track of time, introducing themselves to new acquaintances and enjoying the fellowship as they ate.

Now when they had all eaten and were filled, Jesus said to his disciples, "Gather up the fragments that remain, so that nothing is lost."

So they gathered them up, and filled twelve baskets with the fragments of the barley loaves and fish.

When the multitude realized the sign that Jesus had performed, they said, "This is truly the Prophet who is to come into the world."

When Jesus, therefore, perceived that they were going to take him by force to make him their king, he immediately gathered the twelve, instructing them, "Go ahead of me, across the sea, after the multitude has gone."

Then he spoke to the people, sending them away; and departed from them to the top of the mountain, by himself, to pray alone. When the disciples had convinced the last of the multitude to go, and evening had fallen, they got into their boat and departed down the coastline in the direction of Capernaum, leaving Jesus alone on the mountain.

Out at sea, after the sun had fully set and darkness had taken hold, the wind picked up, tossing the waves into a never-ending series of deep troughs and whitecaps. The wind was blowing in gusts, spraying foamy seawater into the faces of the disciples. So hard was the wind that they began to row, straining against the oars and the elements, and Jesus, still on land, saw their travail. It was about the fourth watch, around 3:00 a.m., when they had rowed about three to four miles, that Jesus came to them walking on the water.

When the disciples saw him walking on the sea, and drawing near to their boat, they cried out in fear, "It is a ghost!"

But Jesus immediately spoke to them, comforting them, saying, "Be of good cheer! It is I; do not be afraid."

Then Peter answered him, "Lord, if it is you, command me to come to you on the water."

So he said to Peter, "Come."

And Peter climbed down out of the boat with great joy, and began walking toward Jesus on the water.

The others in the boat, watching the event, began cheering Peter, who looked back at them with a great big smile on his face, as if to say, "Look at me!"

But the others, in amazement, began looking down at Peter's feet to understand the workings of the miracle. He, too, looked down, then out at the sea with all of its blustering wind and rolling waves. Having his attention diverted from Jesus, Peter's heart began to sink; then, so did he.

"Lord, save me," he cried.

Jesus instantly stretched out his hand and caught him, and he raised him up again, saying, "Oh you of little faith, why did you doubt?"

Then Jesus helped him back into the boat with the assistance of the others. When Jesus entered the boat, after him, the storm ceased—the wind and waves were stilled, and the sea became silent. The disciples looked up at the clear night sky, and out at the calm sea, then back at Jesus.

Then, one by one, they fell to their knees before him, and, with their heads bowed, they worshiped him, saying, "Truly, you *are* the Son of God."

When they lifted their heads to behold him again, the boat glided gently to rest upon the sandy shoreline of Gennesaret.

Esther 5:2–3   Mark 6:18–53   Matthew 14:6–34
John 6:1–21   Luke 9:10–17

Chapter 35

HEALING CROWDS AT GENNESARET

When the boat carrying Jesus and his disciples came to rest on the shore, they dropped anchor and set off up the coastline in the direction of Gennesaret. But as soon as they came out of the boat, the people of the land recognized Jesus. So the people ran ahead of them, throughout the surrounding region, and they gathered the sick on beds, bringing them to wherever they heard he was going. Consequently, whenever Jesus and his disciples entered into villages, cities, or the surrounding countryside, the people laid the sick before him in their marketplaces. And due to the recent fame of the woman healed of her blood issue, they begged him that they might just touch the hem of his garment. And all those who touched him were made well.

Then some of the scribes and Pharisees, who had gathered together after traveling all the way from Jerusalem, came to see Jesus. But when they saw some of his disciples eating bread in the marketplace with defiled, unwashed hands, they found fault with him, for the Pharisees, and all the Jews, would not eat unless they washed their hands in a special way, holding the tradition of the elders. Traditionally, when they came from the marketplace, they would not eat unless they washed. Likewise, there were many other traditions that they received and held regarding cleanliness when eating, such as the washing of cups, pitchers, and copper vessels, and mealtime reclining couches.

When the scribes and Pharisees found Jesus, therefore, they asked him, "Why do your disciples transgress the tradition of the elders? For they do not wash their hands when they eat bread."

Now they asked this question not to be taught by Jesus but to judge him, and their judgment was typically according to the flesh, because they had a natural tendency to understand the Law literally, as it applied to the physical world. But Jesus sought to teach them, and those around them, spiritually, for he concerned himself rather with the spiritual wellbeing of all. At the heart of this, their tradition, he knew, is the desire to relieve ones conscience, through purification, in order to receive God's blessing; in essence, to justify oneself to be worthy of the blessing. Now the application of this premise, according to these religious leaders, was a literal one, focusing on the literal eating of physical food; they judged Jesus's disciples for not purifying their hands, taking no thought regarding the purification of the conscience.

Jesus formed his reply, however, to address the more important spiritual application. Spiritually speaking, eating was a time of communion, a time of sharing in the blessing of receiving God's word—the bread from heaven. This occurred during the feasts and Sabbaths, at the temple and especially in the synagogues. These were times to bring offerings to God from the blessings he had given—spiritual tithes. In the synagogues, they would read from the scriptures, and then offer their interpretation. These interpretations were to be blessings to all those hearers in attendance—washing them by the water of the Word.

But, the religious leadership, which included the scribes and Pharisees, despised any spiritual contribution from the common people, and it was, therefore, being taken away. Instead of receiving the interpretations of the common people, the leaders ruled over them, replacing the spiritual offerings from the common people with merely monetary ones. The monetary offerings were meant to release the giver from spiritual responsibility. The religious leaders had their pockets padded by the money, while their religious stature was puffed up by their own unchallenged interpretations. The practice did serve to relieve the conscience of the giver, but it afforded no further blessing to the assembly.

Malachi prophesied about this very issue, the misappropriation of the Lord's spiritual communion, saying, "Even from the days of your fathers you are gone away from my ordinances, and have not kept them. Return unto me, and I will return unto you, says the LORD of hosts. But you said, 'In what manner shall we return?' Will a man rob God? Yet you have robbed me. But you say, 'In what manner have we robbed you?' In tithes and offerings. You are cursed with a curse: for you have robbed me, even this whole nation. Bring all the tithes into the storehouse, that there may be food in my house, and prove me now with this, says the LORD of hosts, if I will not open you the windows of heaven, and pour you out a blessing, that there shall not be room enough to receive it."

To address this spiritual issue, Jesus brought the scribes and Pharisees to the core of the Law, the Ten Commandments. Here, God gave the command to "honor your father and mother."

"Why do you also transgress the commandment of God, because of your tradition?" Jesus asked them.

They looked at him puzzled.

"For God commanded, through Moses," he continued, "'honor your father and mother,' and 'he who curses father or mother, let him be put to death.' But *you* say, 'Whoever says to his father or mother, "Whatever monetary profit you might have received from me, *that* is my gift to God," that he need not honor his father or mother, otherwise.' By this practice, in fact, you no longer *allow* him to do anything for his father or his mother. Thus, you have made the commandment of God of no effect by your tradition. Hypocrites! Well did Isaiah prophesy about you, saying, 'These people draw near to me with their mouth, and honor me with their lips, but their heart is far from me. And in vain they worship me; teaching, as doctrines,

168

the commandments of men.' For laying aside the commandment of God, you hold the tradition of men—the washing of pitchers and cups, and many other such things you do. All too well you reject the commandment of God, that you may keep your tradition."

To the unlearned, Jesus's response to their accusation seemed almost unrelated. The multitude who heard his words made only an ambiguous connection, believing that he spoke of two entirely different traditions. But the most learned of these religious leaders understood his meaning, though they had never considered the connection Jesus proposed, in quite the same way. In essence, Jesus was accusing them of replacing spiritual washing by the Word of God with physical washing and monetary gifts. These men had been raised on the scriptures, and knew them very well. Jesus's answer to them, with his quote from Isaiah, brought to mind two other passages in Isaiah, which defined father and mother as the Messiah and a spiritually restored Jerusalem.

"I will commit your government into his hand, and he shall be a father to the inhabitants of Jerusalem, and to the house of Judah," wrote Isaiah in one passage; and in the other, "Rejoice with Jerusalem and be glad with her ... you shall be born upon her sides, and be dandled upon her knees. As one whom his mother comforts, so will I comfort you, and you shall be comforted in Jerusalem."

And a third passage, from Malachi, connected them, "A son honors his father, and a servant his master: if then I be a father, where is my honor?

"You offer polluted bread upon my altar," the passage continues, "if you offer the blind for sacrifice, is it not evil? And if you offer the lame and the sick, is it not evil?"

Those who knew the scriptures most fully saw these spiritual connections in his response, and becoming conscious of their current surroundings among the blemished who were brought to Jesus for healing, they were silenced. They stood dumbfounded. Looking at Jesus, and at one another, they struggled with the possibility that the Messiah might actually be standing before them, meanwhile feeling the full weight of his rebuke. When one of the younger scribes sought to speak, the eldest of the group restrained him.

When Jesus saw that the scribes and Pharisees were silenced, he gathered the entire multitude to himself, speaking to them on a less scriptural, though no less spiritual, basis.

"Come to me, and hear! Every one of you, and understand," he said to them. "There is nothing that enters a man from the outside, which can defile him. It's not what goes into the mouth that defiles a man! The things which come out of him; what comes out of his mouth, *those* are the things that defile a man. If anyone has ears to hear, let him hear!"

Then after looking long and hard at Jesus, trying to measure him, whether he was merely a man, or perhaps more; the eldest of the scribes gathered the scribes and Pharisees, and escorted them away from him. As they returned to Jerusalem, they discussed these things in detail, debating whether Jesus could truly be the Messiah. As always, their differing levels of understanding his words caused division among them.

So the level of understanding had great bearing on how his words were received. Those who understood them fully were burdened with the decision to believe or reject them, while those who understood them vaguely often grew angry and hostile; still others, who did not understand them at all, went away confused and frustrated. But his words, as definitive as they always were, silenced all who heard them.

When Jesus had left off speaking to the people, he departed from them and entered into a house. There, his disciples came and said to him, "Do you know that the Pharisees were offended when they heard your words?"

But he answered, and said, "Every plant which my heavenly Father has not planted will be uprooted. Let them alone. They are blind leaders of the blind. And if the blind leads the blind, both will fall into a ditch."

Then Peter, realizing that *he* still did not fully understand, pleaded with him in frustration, "Explain this parable to us."

Jesus looked at Peter, then around the room at their confused faces, and replied to them all in amazement, "Are you also still without understanding? Do you not yet understand that whatever enters the mouth cannot defile a man, because it does not enter his heart but his stomach, and is eliminated, thus purifying all foods? But those things which proceed out of the mouth come from the heart, and they defile a man. For from within, out of the heart proceed evil thoughts, murders, adulteries, fornications." As he listed these, one by one, he looked around the room, slowing his speech to drive the message home, "covetousness, thefts, false witness, wickedness, deceit, lewdness, an evil eye, pride, foolishness, blasphemies, and the like. All these evil things come from within and defile a man, but to eat with unwashed hands, this does not defile a man."

Mark 6:53–56   Matthew 14:34–36   Mark 7:1–23
Matthew 15:1–20   Ephesians 5:25-27   Genesis 20:12
Genesis 21:17   Isaiah 29:13   Isaiah 22:20–25
Isaiah 66:5–13   Malachi 1:6–8   Malachi 3:7-10

Chapter 36

BREAD OF LIFE AT CAPERNAUM

When the people from Bethsaida, where he fed the five thousand, saw that Jesus and his disciples were not still among them, they too entered into ships, and sailed toward Capernaum, seeking them.

Finding them on the other side of the sea, they said to Jesus, "Rabbi, how is it that you have come here?"

Jesus answered them, and said, "Truly, truly, I say unto you, you seek me, not because you saw the miracles, but because you did eat of the loaves, and were filled."

Now the Feast of Unleavened Bread followed immediately after Passover, and the Law, according to Moses, called for bread without leaven to be eaten for seven days. And knowing the significance of the feast, and the recent miracle of feeding the multitude with loaves of bread, Jesus began to preach on the subject.

"Labor not for the food that perishes," he said, "but for that food that endures unto everlasting life, which the Son of man shall give to you, for him has God the Father sealed."

Then they said to him, "What shall we do, that we might work the works of God?"

Jesus answered, and said to them, "This is the work of God, that you believe in him whom he has sent."

They said to him, therefore, "What sign do you show, then, that we may see and believe you? What work do *you* do? Our fathers did eat manna in the desert; as it is written, 'He gave them bread from heaven to eat.'"

Then Jesus said unto them, "Truly, truly, I say unto you, Moses gave you not that bread from heaven, but my Father gives you the true bread from heaven. For the bread of God is he who comes down from heaven, and gives life unto the world."

Then they said to him, "Lord, evermore, give us this bread."

So Jesus said to them, "I AM the bread of life: he who comes to me shall never hunger, and he who believes on me shall never thirst. But I said unto you that you also have seen me, and believe not. All that the Father gives me shall come to me, and he who comes to me I will in no way cast out. For I came down from heaven, not to do my own will, but the will of him that sent me. And this is the will of the Father who has sent me, that of all which he has given me I should lose nothing, but should raise it up again at the last day. And this is the will of him that sent me, that everyone who sees the Son, and believes in him, may have everlasting life, and I will raise him up at the last day."

The Jewish leaders then murmured at him, because he said, "I AM the bread, which came down from heaven." And they said, "Is not this Jesus, the son of Joseph, whose father and mother we know? How is it then that he says, 'I came down from heaven?'"

Jesus, therefore, answered, and said to them, "Murmur not among yourselves. No man can come to me, except the Father who has sent me draws him, and I will raise him up at the last day. It is written in the Prophets, 'And they shall all be taught of God.' Every man, therefore, that has heard, and has learned of the Father, comes to me. Not that any man has seen the Father, save he who is of God; he has seen the Father. Truly, truly, I say unto you, he that believes in me has everlasting life. I AM that bread of life. Your fathers did eat manna in the wilderness, and are dead. This is the bread which comes down from heaven, that a man may eat thereof, and not die. I AM the living bread, which came down from heaven; if any man eat of this bread, he shall live forever, and the bread that I will give is my flesh, which I will give for the life of the world."

The Jewish leaders, therefore, strove among themselves, saying, "How can this man give us his flesh to eat?"

Then Jesus said to them, "Truly, truly, I say unto you, except you eat the flesh of the Son of man, and drink his blood, you have no life in you. Whoever eats my flesh, and drinks my blood, has eternal life, and I will raise him up at the last day. For my flesh is food indeed, and my blood is drink indeed. He that eats my flesh, and drinks my blood, dwells in me, and I in him. As the living Father has sent me, and I live by the Father: so he that eats me, even he shall live by me. This is that bread which came down from heaven: not as your fathers did eat manna, and are dead; he that eats of this bread shall live forever."

Now he spoke of his flesh as the Word of God, which, like bread, would be broken, rightly divided for the healing of mankind. And of his blood, which would be shed as atonement, to cover the sins of the world. And of eating, as believing, as a means of sustaining one's life. But, again, the religious leaders received his words literally; rather than spiritually, as Jesus intended them.

All these things he said in the synagogue, as he taught in Capernaum.

Many, therefore, of his disciples, when they had heard this, said, "This is a hard saying. Who can hear it?"

When Jesus knew in himself that his disciples murmured at it, he said to them, "Does this offend you? What and if you shall see the Son of man ascend up where he was before? It is the Spirit that quickens; the flesh profits nothing: the words that I speak unto you, they are spirit, and they are life. But there are some of you that believe not."

For by this Jesus knew from the beginning who they were that believed not, and who should betray him.

And he told them, "For this reason, I said unto you, that no man can come unto me, except it were given unto him of my Father."

From that time, many of his disciples went back, and walked no more with him.

Then Jesus said to the twelve, "Will you also go away?"

But Peter answered him, "Lord, to whom shall we go? You have the words of eternal life. We believe, and are sure that you are the Messiah, the Son of the living God."

Jesus answered them, "Have I not chosen you twelve? And even one of *you* is a devil!"

He spoke of Judas Iscariot, the son of Simon, for it was he that should betray him, being one of the twelve.

John 6:24–71	Leviticus 23:5–6	Exodus 16:1–15
Nehemiah 9:14–15	Isaiah 54:13	Isaiah 48:17
Jeremiah 31:31–34		

Chapter 37

A TRIP TO TYRE AND SIDON

When Jesus realized that the crowds in Galilee had left off from following him, he arose, and went into the borders of Tyre and Sidon, and entered into a house, secretly. But his whereabouts could not be hidden from a certain woman, whose young daughter had an unclean spirit, for the mother had heard of him, and came diligently seeking him that he might heal her daughter.

The woman was a Phoenician named Adonia, which means "My Lord is God," who lived alone with her daughter on the border of Phoenicia and the northwestern corner of Galilee. Her husband, a well-to-do merchant, had died suddenly, leaving her with plenty of money and a troubled child to raise by herself. Shortly after his death, the child grew moody, increasingly quiet and unruly, and had recently stopped speaking altogether. The mother had taken her to several physicians, who could do nothing to cure her. As time passed, the mother became more and more desperate to help her daughter, until one day she heard about a holy man from Galilee, who was traveling close to the town where she lived. It was said of him that he could truly be the Messiah of Israel, the One of whom the prophets foretold, of the lineage of David. Great stories were being circulated about this man, that he was healing the lame, the blind, and the lepers. It was also told that he could cast out demons, which was of particular interest to her, because she now believed her daughter, Melita, was possessed by one. So she rushed to meet him, and found a small group of people following this man named Jesus. His followers tried to send her away, because she was a foreigner, but she was persistent, to the point of becoming a nuisance. So the disciples consulted Jesus, hoping that *he* would send her away.

After pushing her way into the house to Jesus, she stood before him and cried out, "Have mercy on me, Oh Lord, you Son of David; my daughter is grievously vexed with a devil."

But Jesus sat silently before her, not even looking up.

Then his disciples came directly to him, putting themselves between Jesus and the woman, beseeching him, "Send her away, for she cries continually after us."

But he answered, and said to them all, "I am not sent, but unto the lost sheep of the house of Israel."

Then she pushed her way farther, fell at his feet, worshiped him, and wept, saying, "Lord, help me."

But he answered, and said, "Let the children first be filled. It is not appropriate to take the children's bread, and to cast it to the dogs."

Then she lifted her head, and looking into his eyes with great conviction, said, "Truth, Lord; yet even the dogs eat of the crumbs, which fall from their masters' table."

Then Jesus had compassion upon her, and answered her, "Oh woman, great is your faith: let it be unto you even as you will it. Go your way. For this saying, the devil is gone out of your daughter."

And when she came to her house, she found the devil gone out, and her daughter lying upon her bed.

After Jesus healed her daughter, the two sought to follow him. They followed him to the hills of Galilee, where he miraculously fed four thousand people. But immediately afterward, he boarded a ship and crossed the sea. Though they could not keep up with him initially, they were able to follow his movements to a town called Magdala, a fishing village on the Sea of Galilee. There, they took up residence, hoping to see him again when he returned to the town. Shortly after they arrived, however, the mother became ill. Melita, her daughter, cared for her as best she could, but her mother, anticipating her impending death, instructed Melita to join Jesus's followers after she died. So Melita buried her mother in Magdala, and set out to find Jesus and to join his followers. When Jesus returned to Capernaum, she joined his disciples there, and the women, including the mother of Jesus, accepted her into their company. And so she joined them, providing for the needs of Jesus and his disciples. Her Phoenician name was Melita, which means "bitter," but the women gave her the Hebrew name Mary, which also means "bitter." And they surnamed her Magdalene, because she buried her mother in Magdala.

Mark 7:24–31   Matthew 15:21–28

Chapter 38

FEEDING FOUR THOUSAND AT THE SEA OF GALILEE

Jesus and his disciples departed from Tyre and Sidon, and came again to the region near the Sea of Galilee, and he went up into a mountain and sat down there. And great multitudes followed him there, having with them those that were lame, blind, dumb, and maimed. And there were many others, also, which they cast down at Jesus's feet, and he healed them all. The multitude was filled with wonder, when they heard the dumb speak, and saw the maimed made whole, the lame walk, and the blind see; even those foreigners, who came to see, glorified the God of Israel.

Among those brought to him was one who was deaf, and had an impediment in his speech, and those who brought him before Jesus begged him to put his hand upon him.

So Jesus took him aside from the multitude, and put his fingers into his ears, and he spit, and touched his tongue, and, looking up to heaven, he sighed, and said to the man, "Be opened." Immediately the man's ears were opened, and the string of his tongue was loosed, and when the man understood the magnitude of what was done to him, the man spoke plainly, bearing witness to God's glorious loving kindness and mercy.

And Jesus charged those few who witnessed the affair that they should tell no one what was done, but his humility in the matter made them publish it all the more, for they were astonished beyond measure, saying, "He has done all things well: he makes both the deaf to hear, and the dumb to speak."

The news of this wonderful healing spread quickly among the multitude, so that all became partakers in the glory and the joy of it.

Then Jesus called his disciples to him, and said, "I feel compassion for all these people, because they have continued with me now for three days, and have nothing to eat. I will not send them away to their own houses still fasting, lest they faint along the way, for many have traveled a great distance."

But his disciples said to him, "From what source can a man satisfy so great a multitude with bread, here, in the wilderness?"

So Jesus inquired of them, "How many loaves do you have?"

And they replied, "Seven."

Then Jesus stood before the people, and commanded the multitude to sit down on the ground. And he took the seven loaves, and gave thanks, and broke them. Then he gave them to his disciples, and the disciples distributed them to the multitude. And as his disciples passed the bread, they were given a few small fishes, which Jesus also blessed, and commanded that they likewise be shared among the people. And they all ate, and were filled. Afterward, they gathered up the broken pieces that remained, and there was left seven full baskets. Of those that had eaten, there were some four thousand men, besides women and children. And when the people were thoroughly filled, he sent them all away.

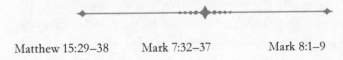

Matthew 15:29–38   Mark 7:32–37   Mark 8:1–9

Chapter 39

SEEKING A SIGN AT MAGDALA
AND BETHSAIDA

After Jesus sent away the multitude, he entered into a ship with his disciples, and came into the coasts of Magdala. The Pharisees and the Sadducees came seeking him, tempting him with questions, and desiring of him that he would show them a sign from heaven.

Displaying outward signs of his aggravation at their lack of faith, Jesus turned slowly upon them, and sighed deeply within his spirit, then answered them, "Why does this generation seek after a sign? When it is evening, you say, 'It will be fair weather, for the heaven above is glowing red.' And in the morning, you say, 'It will be foul weather today, for the heaven above is red and menacing.' Oh you hypocrites, you can discern the face of the heaven. Can you not, also, discern the signs of the times? A wicked and adulterous generation seeks after a sign; truly I say unto you, there shall no sign be given unto it, but the sign of the prophet Jonah."

Now Jonah was a prophet sent by God to preach to the Assyrian city of Nineveh. He had fled from God, not being willing to preach to a city in a hostile Gentile nation. By an act of God, he was swallowed by a great fish, and was spit out upon the shores of Nineveh, where he reluctantly preached to the city; whereupon hearing his words, its residents repented from their wickedness.

Jesus left off speaking to these religious leaders, leaving them wondering at the connection he was making between Jonah and himself.

"Would he leave and preach to the Gentiles?" they questioned. "Would he too be swallowed by a great fish?"

They pressed him to understand his comparison, but Jesus left them pondering his words; and entering into the ship again, he departed to the other side.

And when they had come to the other side, Jesus charged his disciples, saying, "Take heed, and beware of the leaven of the Pharisees, and of the leaven of Herod and the Sadducees!"

Hearing his words, his disciples reasoned among themselves, and being convicted by their own feelings of inadequacy, they answered him, saying, "It must be, because we have taken no bread," for they had forgotten to take bread with them, and had no more than one loaf in the ship.

But, when Jesus perceived the true nature behind their thoughts, he said to them, "Oh you of little faith, why reason you among yourselves, because you have brought no bread? Do you not yet understand? Are your hearts yet hardened? Having eyes, do you not see? And having ears, do you not hear? Don't you remember the five loaves of the five thousand, and the seven loaves of the four thousand? When I broke the five loaves among five thousand, how many baskets full of fragments did you take up?"

His disciples answered him, "Twelve."

"And when I broke the seven loaves among four thousand, how many baskets full of fragments did you take up?" Jesus demanded.

And they said, "Seven."

Then he said to them, "How is it that you do not understand that I am not speaking to you about bread, but that you should beware the leaven of the Pharisees and the Sadducees?"

Finally, they understood that he was not warning them to beware the leaven of bread but to beware the doctrine of the Pharisees and the Sadducees.

Then leaving the ship, they journeyed again to Bethsaida, and the people there brought a blind man to Jesus. And they pressed around Jesus to touch him, that they might see the man healed. But Jesus took the blind man by the hand, and led him out of the town, privately. Then he spit upon the man's eyes, and laid his hands upon him, and asked the man if he could see anything.

The man lifted his head up toward Jesus, straining his eyes to see. Then he moved his head slowly from side to side, squinting to discern the nature of Jesus's disciples through the light.

His spiritual vision restored, the man said to Jesus, "I see men as trees, walking."

Jesus then laid his hands again upon the man's eyes, and instructed him to look up once more, and the man was physically restored, and saw everything in its fullness.

When the man was fully healed, Jesus sent him home, privately; for Jesus discerned that the people of Bethsaida, still unhearing, unrepentant, and seeking a sign, would come again to make him their king.

Therefore, Jesus admonished the man before sending him away, saying, "Neither go into the town, nor tell it to anyone in the town!"

Matthew 15:39	Matthew 16:1–12	Mark 8:10–26
Jonah 1:1–3	Jonah 1:17	Jonah 2:10
Jonah 3:4–5	Jonah 3:10	Deuteronomy 8:3
Amos 8:11		

Chapter 40

VISITING THE TOWNS OF CAESAREA PHILIPPI

Jesus and his disciples separated, and went out into the towns of Caesarea Philippi preaching the gospel. When they came together again, along the way, the disciples found Jesus praying. And it was in the midst of the high holy days, between the Feast of Trumpets and the Day of Atonement, the second day of the month, Tishri. When he had finished his time of prayer, he asked them, saying, "Who do men say that I, the Son of man, am?"

And they said, "Some say that you are John the Baptist; some, Elijah; and others, Jeremiah, or one of the old prophets risen again."

He said to them, "But who do *you* say that I am?"

And Peter answered, and said, "You are the Messiah, the Son of the living God."

And Jesus answered, and said to him, "Blessed are you, Simon Barjona, for flesh and blood has not revealed this unto you, but my Father who is in heaven. And I say also unto you, that you *are* Peter, and upon this rock I will build my church, and the gates of hell shall not prevail against it. And I will give unto you the keys of the kingdom of heaven, and whatever you shall bind upon the earth shall be bound in heaven, and whatever you shall release upon the earth shall be released in heaven."

Then he charged his disciples that they should tell no man that he was Jesus the Messiah. From that time forward, Jesus began to teach his disciples that he, the Son of man, must go to Jerusalem.

"The Son of man must suffer many things," he told them. "He will be rejected by the elders and the chief priests and the scribes, and be crucified and killed, and be raised again on the third day."

These things he spoke to them plainly. When the twelve heard these things, they conferred among themselves. Then Peter rose taking Jesus aside, and standing over him, he grabbed him by the shoulders and forcibly turned Jesus around so that Jesus's back was to his disciples—putting Peter in a place of power.

Then speaking to him in a low, harsh voice, Peter began to rebuke him, saying, "Be it far from you, Lord; this shall not happen to you."

But Jesus looked at Peter's hands, which were gripping his shoulders, then piercingly into Peter's eyes.

"Get behind me, Satan," he said.

Peter squirmed, his gaze lowered, and he released his grip, his hands falling to his sides. Jesus turned around again facing his disciples, his back to Peter—in essence dividing Peter from the others and reaffirming his own position of power over his disciples.

Addressing the eleven, he said, "You are an offense unto me, for you savor not the things that are of God, but those that are of men."

After these words, Jesus called all of his disciples to him, with the twelve including Peter. Jesus then returned Peter's gesture, grasping his shoulders firmly—not harshly, but to strengthen him.

"If any man will come after me," he said to Peter in the hearing of everyone, "let him deny himself, and take up his cross daily, and follow me." Then looking past Peter to address them all, he continued, "For whoever will save his life shall lose it, but whoever shall lose his life for my sake and the gospel's, the same shall save it. For what shall it profit a man, if he shall gain the whole world, and lose his own soul or be cast away?" He looked again at Peter, then back at the rest of his disciples before continuing, "Or what shall a man give in exchange for his soul? Whoever, therefore, shall be ashamed of me and of my words, aligning himself with this adulterous and sinful generation, of him also shall the Son of man be ashamed, when he comes in the glory of his Father with the holy angels. Then, he shall reward every man according to his works. Truly I say unto you that there be some standing here who shall not taste of death till they see the kingdom of God come with power, and the Son of man coming in his kingdom."

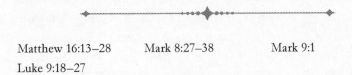

Matthew 16:13–28   Mark 8:27–38   Mark 9:1
Luke 9:18–27

Chapter 41

MOUNT OF TRANSFIGURATION

Now, on the morning prior to the Day of Atonement, Jesus took Peter, James, and John up into a high mountain apart by themselves. There, they fasted and prayed, all of the next day. On that day, the Day of Atonement, Jesus separated himself further, going a short distance from them. As he continued to pray, Peter, James, and John grew heavy with sleep. And while they slept, Jesus's appearance was transfigured so that his face shone as the sun, and his clothing became white as light, shining, white as snow, whiter than any fuller on earth could make them. Now, while Jesus remained in this transfigured state, the three awoke, and beheld him in his glory. And seeing, they beheld Moses and Elijah, who also appeared before them talking with Jesus concerning his death and what he would accomplish at Jerusalem. Looking on, the disciples became speechless with fear. When Jesus, Moses, and Elijah had finished their conversation, Moses and Elijah began to depart. But seeing them leaving, Peter found the courage to speak, though he did not know exactly what to say.

Knowing that the Feast of Tabernacles was shortly upon them, and not wanting them to leave, he blurted out, therefore, "Lord, it is good for us to be here. If you will allow us, let us make three tabernacles, one for you, one for Moses, and one for Elijah."

While Peter was speaking these words, a bright cloud appeared, overshadowing them all, and from the cloud a voice spoke, saying, "This is my beloved Son, in whom I am well pleased; hear him."

Hearing the voice as they entered the cloud, the disciples immediately fell to the ground upon their faces for fear.

Then Jesus came to them and touched them, saying, "Arise, and be not afraid."

When they lifted up their eyes and looked around, they saw no one besides themselves and Jesus.

As they came down from the mountain, Jesus charged them, saying, "Tell the vision to no one, until the Son of man is risen again from the dead."

So the three men kept the incident to themselves, discussing only with one another what the rising from the dead should mean.

As they struggled to understand, they asked him, saying, "Why, then, do the scribes say that Elijah must first come?"

And Jesus answered, and said to them, "Elijah truly shall first come, and restore all things, and it is written of the Son of man, that he must suffer many things, and be set at naught. But I say unto you, that Elijah has come already, and they knew him not, but have done to him whatever they willed, as it is written of him. Likewise, also, shall the Son of man suffer by them."

Then the disciples understood that he spoke to them of John the Baptist.

The next day, when they came to the base of the mountain, they found Andrew and the other disciples, in the midst of a great multitude, being questioned by the scribes. When the people saw Jesus, they were greatly amazed, for his face still shone from the presence of God, and they ran to him, saluting him.

So Jesus asked the scribes, "What is your dispute against them?"

Then, from the multitude, there came to him a certain man, kneeling down to him, and saying, "Lord, I have brought unto you my son, who has a deaf and dumb spirit. I beseech you, look upon my son and have mercy upon him, for he is my only child. He is lunatic, and sorely vexed, for oftentimes he falls into the fire, and often into the water. Wherever the spirit takes him, he tears him, so that he suddenly cries out; then he foams at the mouth and gnashes his teeth, and is left bruised and very depressed. I spoke to your disciples that they should cast him out, but they could not cure him."

Jesus glanced at Andrew and the others sympathetically, and then at the scribes, frowning; then he gazed disapprovingly over the crowd, and answered and said to them all, "Oh faithless and perverse generation, how long shall I be with you? How long must I tolerate you?" Then looking again at the man with compassion, he said, "Bring your son here, to *me.*"

So they brought his son to Jesus, and as he was coming, when he saw Jesus, the spirit began to tear him. The boy fell hard upon the ground and wallowed, foaming.

Then Jesus asked his father, "How long ago is it since this came upon him?"

And the father replied, "From a child. And oftentimes the spirit has cast him into the fire, and into the waters to destroy him, but if you can do anything, have compassion upon us and help us."

Jesus said to him, "If you can believe, all things are possible to him that believes."

Then the father cried out to him, entreating him with tears, "Lord, I believe." Then lowering his eyes in fear and his head in shame, the man surrendered, saying, "Help, Lord, my unbelief."

Jesus looked up, and saw many more people running to join the growing multitude.

Then he looked upon the child, again, and rebuked the foul spirit, saying to him, "You deaf and dumb spirit, I charge you, come out of him, and enter no more into him."

Then the devil cried out, and convulsed the child greatly before departing from him. The young man lay upon the ground, in a contorted position, still and silent, as if dead. The crowd was watching intently, looking from Jesus to the young man's body lying unmoving upon the ground.

They began to murmur among themselves, many insisting aloud, "He is dead!"

Jesus looked at the body of the child, lying motionless, bruised and battered by the ordeal. In the child, he envisioned himself—silent, and at the mercy of forces he could not fight and overcome, alone. Then Jesus looked upon the multitude, realizing that, spiritually, they too were like the child and himself, like lambs before the slaughter.

He renewed his resolve, raising his hand to still their fears. Then he took the child by the hand and lifted him up, and he arose. Jesus delivered him, again, to his father, and he was cured from that very hour. And the people were all amazed at the mighty power of God.

But while everyone wondered at the thing that Jesus had done, he said to the twelve, "Let this account sink down into your ears, for, in like manner, the Son of man shall be delivered unto the power of men."

The twelve looked among themselves in confusion, for they did not understand how this episode might possibly equate to the future of Jesus. Though the connection was hidden from them, they feared to ask him concerning it; rather, their pride was hurt because they were unable to cast out the demonic spirit.

So Andrew and the others came to Jesus privately, as he and the twelve were about to enter into a house, questioning him, "Why could *we* not cast him out?"

And Jesus said to them, "Because of your lack of faith."

And they implored him, "Lord, increase *our* faith!"

Now Jesus and the twelve stood before the house, apart from the multitude, with a sycamore fig tree between them and the crowd. Behind the crowd stood the mountain, where Jesus had been transfigured.

So Jesus, gesturing in the direction of the sycamore tree, and the multitude behind it, said to them, "If you had faith as a grain of mustard seed, you might say to this sycamore tree, 'Be plucked up by the roots, and planted in the sea,' and it would obey you."

And they looked at him incredulously.

Then gesturing, again, in the direction of the multitude and the mountain beyond, he continued, "Truly, I say unto you, if you have faith as a grain of mustard seed, and you shall say to this mountain, 'Depart from this place to another,' it will depart! And nothing shall be impossible unto you."

By these words, their incredulity became even more seasoned with wonder and hope.

He concluded with words of encouragement to them. "Even so, this kind does not depart except by prayer and fasting."

This he said regarding the unbelievers of Israel, who like the deaf and dumb child, are unable to hear God's word and testify to its truth. Only God's power and grace, through prayer and fasting, can move the hearts of unbelievers.

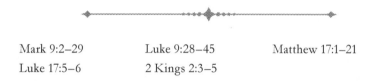

Mark 9:2–29   Luke 9:28–45   Matthew 17:1–21
Luke 17:5–6   2 Kings 2:3–5

Chapter 42

ABIDING IN GALILEE

Jesus and his twelve disciples departed from the area of Caesarea Philippi, and passed through northern Galilee on their way to Capernaum. Along the way, his disciples wondered at his teaching, for he had told them that "the Son of man is delivered into the hands of men, and they shall kill him, and after that he is killed, he shall rise the third day." Though they wondered and discussed it among themselves, they were afraid to ask him concerning his words. But their discussions led them in other directions, also; they wondered what was to become of the kingdom after Jesus was dead, for they couldn't fathom what he meant by rising from the dead. As they speculated who might be left in charge of the kingdom upon his death, there arose a dispute among them, which of them would be greatest in the kingdom.

Now, when they reached Capernaum, after entering into the house where they were staying, Jesus perceived the thoughts of their hearts, and asked them, "What was it that you disputed among yourselves by the way?"

But his disciples feared, and out of embarrassment they held their peace. So Jesus sat down and gestured the twelve to gather around him.

Then he said to them, "If any desire to be first, the same shall be last of all and servant of all."

Then they asked him bluntly, "Who, then, is the greatest in the kingdom of heaven?"

At this, Jesus gestured for one of the children of the household to come to him, and the smallest among them ran to him, stretching out her little arms to be picked up.

Jesus brought the child before them, taking her in his arms, and he answered them, "Truly, I say unto you, except you be converted, and become as little children, you shall not enter into the kingdom of heaven!"

When his disciples heard his answer, they became confused and insulted.

"Whoever shall humble himself," Jesus continued, "as this little child, the same shall be greatest in the kingdom of heaven."

And they all looked upon the child with envy, who was perched comfortably upon the lap of Jesus, smiling, with her fingers in her mouth. Jesus kissed the child, and the child giggled. Then Jesus smiled at the twelve, knowing their envy.

He said to them, "Whoever receives one such child in my name, receives me, and whoever receives me, receives not me only, but him who sent me, for he that is least among you, the same shall be great."

Then John spoke up, confessing to him, "Lord, we saw one casting out devils in your name, and he did not follow us, so we forbade him, because he did not follow us."

But Jesus said to him, looking to all of them, "Forbid him not, for there is no one who shall do a miracle in my name that can easily speak evil of me. For he that is not against us is for us and on our side. For whoever shall give you a cup of water to drink in my name, because you belong to the Messiah, truly I say unto you, he shall not lose his reward."

Then he said to them, sternly, "Know *this* also, that whoever shall offend one of these little ones who believes in me, it would be better for him that a millstone were hanged about his neck, and that he were drowned in the depths of the sea."

"Woe unto the world because of offenses!" he said animatedly with hands and voice raised, looking out the window into the unseen distance above and beyond them, "For it is impossible that no offenses should come!"

Then his gaze returned to them, as his voice also dropped.

"It is also *necessary* that offenses should come," he said soberly, his eyes narrowing, and settling upon Judas Iscariot, "but woe unto *him* by whom they come!"

Jesus paused there briefly, and Judas became uneasy, looking away to avoid Jesus's gaze.

Then Jesus's gaze and tone shifted again, looking at the remaining eleven. "If, therefore, your hand offends you, cut it off and cast it from you; it is better for you to enter into life maimed, than having two hands to go into hell, into the fire that never shall be quenched: where their worm dies not, and the fire is not quenched. If your foot offends you, cut it off and cast it from you; it is better for you to enter lame into life, than having two feet to be cast into hell, into the fire that never shall be quenched: where their worm dies not, and the fire is not quenched. Likewise, if your eye offends you, pluck it out and cast it from you; it is better for you to enter into the kingdom of God with one eye, than having two eyes to be cast into everlasting hell fire: where their worm dies not, and the fire is not quenched. For everyone shall be salted with fire, and every sacrifice shall be salted with salt. Salt is good, but if the salt has lost its saltiness, how will you season it? Have salt in yourselves, and have peace one with another."

The salt of which he spoke represented the wisdom and grace granted to those who follow God. Though his disciples did not fully understand, he taught them that those who follow God are prepared by wisdom and grace through the fire and sacrifice of persecution. Furthermore, if the wise, having lost their wisdom and grace, begin offending others by persecuting them, they have no other way to prepare themselves before God! He instructed them, therefore, to hold onto God's wisdom and grace within themselves, and maintain peace with one another.

"Take heed to yourselves, therefore," he explained, "for if your brother trespasses against you, rebuke him, and if he repents, forgive him. And if he trespasses against you seven times in a day, and seven times in a day turns again to you, saying, 'I repent,' you shall forgive him. Take heed, I say, that you despise not one of these little ones, for in heaven their angels do always behold the face of my Father which is in heaven. For the Son of man has come to save that which is lost. What do you think? If a man has a hundred sheep, and one of them goes astray, does he not leave the ninety-nine, and go into the mountains to seek that which has gone astray? And if he finds it, truly I say unto you, he rejoices more of that sheep, than of the ninety-nine which went not astray. Even so, it is not the will of your Father in heaven that one of these little ones should perish.

"However, if your brother *does* trespass against you, go and tell him his fault between you and him alone. If he hears you, you have gained your brother. But if he will not hear you, then take with you one or two more, that in the mouth of two or three witnesses every word may be established. And if he neglects to hear them, tell it to the entire assembly. But if he neglects to hear the assembly, let him be unto you as a heathen and a tax collector.

"Truly, I say unto you, whatever you shall bind upon the earth shall be bound in heaven, and whatever you shall release upon the earth shall be released in heaven. Again, I say unto you, that if two of you shall agree upon earth as touching anything that they shall ask, it shall be done for them of my Father who is in heaven. For where two or three are gathered together in my name, there I am in the midst of them."

When he had finished speaking, he sent the child away with a kiss, and stood up, signifying the end of his teaching.

Peter stood also, and came to him, asking, "Lord, how often, then, shall my brother sin against me, and I forgive him? Till seven times?"

Jesus said to him, and for the others to hear as well, "I say not unto you, until seven times but until seventy times seven."

This he said to signify that forgiveness should be readily available to the end of time, as prophesied by Daniel—the seventy *weeks* of years. This they understood.

Jesus kept them attentively assembled by following his statement with a parable. "Therefore, is the kingdom of heaven likened unto a certain king, who would take account of his servants. And when he had begun to examine his accounts, one was brought to him that owed him ten thousand *talents* (one talent being worth roughly sixteen years' wages.) But forasmuch as this servant had nothing to pay, his lord commanded him to be bound and sold, and his wife, and children, and all that he had, and payment to be made. The servant, therefore, fell down and worshiped him, saying, 'Lord, have patience with me, and I will pay you everything.' Then the lord of that servant was moved with compassion, and released him, forgiving him the debt. But the same servant went out, and found one of his fellow servants, who owed him a hundred denarii (one denarii being worth a day's wages), and he laid hands on him, and took him by the throat, saying, 'Pay me what you owe.' And his fellow servant fell down at his feet, and besought him, saying, 'Have patience with me, and I will pay you everything.' But he would not listen, and had him bound and cast into prison, till he should pay the debt. So when his fellow servants saw what was done, they were sorely distressed, and came and told their lord all that was done. Then his lord, when he had called again his servant, said to him, 'Oh you wicked servant, I released you, forgiving you all that debt, because you desired it of me. Should not you also have had compassion on your fellow servant, even as I had mercy upon you?' And his lord was enraged, and delivered him bound to the tormentors, till he should pay all that was due him. So, likewise, shall my heavenly Father do also unto you, if you from your hearts forgive not everyone his brother their trespasses."

After Jesus ended his parable, he looked at the doorway, where his mother and the other women of the household were standing. Mary ushered Jesus's brothers before her, so that they might speak to him. They had come to find him, because the Feast of Tabernacles was about to begin, and they wished to bring Jesus to Jerusalem with them.

"Depart from here," they said to him, challenging him, "and go into Judea, so that your disciples, there, may also see the works that you do. For there is no man that does anything in secret, while he seeks himself to be known openly. If you, indeed, do these things, show yourself to the world."

Now his brothers still did not believe in all the talk of his great miracles, for they had continued in their lives around Nazareth, and had yet to see his works. Mary had hoped for reconciliation between Jesus and his brothers, and had strategically maneuvered them before him at a most appropriate time, she felt, when Jesus had just spoken about brotherly forgiveness. Her other sons' words, she realized, were meant to challenge and mock Jesus's ministry. She braced herself, therefore, for Jesus's response, hoping beyond hope that it would be tendered with mercy.

Jesus responded to them, at first, as he had many times before, saying to them, "My time is not yet come."

He paused briefly, and Mary exhaled, grateful for his compassion. Then he exclaimed, "But your time is always ready!"

Mary cringed, and his brothers smirked, for they had baited him, and he was taking the bait. They knew that their challenge presented a no-win situation for their arrogant older brother, and they were gloating, because they had embarrassed him before his devoted followers—and their mother. But this time Jesus did not hold back, despite the natural kinship to his brothers. They were mocking God's power, and Jesus's allegiances were not earthly ones. He spoke to them as the Messiah to unfaithful nonbelievers, which they were, putting their souls and the faith of all those present before his earthly upbringing.

"The world cannot hate you," he continued, "but me it hates, because I testify of it, that its works are evil. *You* go up to the feast! I go not up to this feast, yet, for my time is not yet fully come!"

The harshness of his words cut deep; they had turned his brothers' smugness into their own profound embarrassment and humiliation. They glared at their mother as they pushed their way from the room and the house into the fresh air outside. Mary sunk into despair, and the other women surrounded her in comfort. All those who witnessed the scene could not help but weigh their own beliefs against Jesus's stern sermon and the harsh judgment he weighed against his own family.

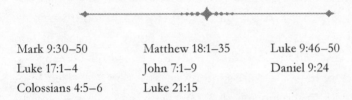

Mark 9:30–50	Matthew 18:1–35	Luke 9:46–50
Luke 17:1–4	John 7:1–9	Daniel 9:24
Colossians 4:5–6	Luke 21:15	

Chapter 43

THROUGH SAMARIA TO JERUSALEM

When Jesus knew that the time had come for him to be received back up to his Father, he resolved himself, unwaveringly, to go to Jerusalem. So he sent messengers ahead, and they went, and entered into a village of the Samaritans, to make ready for him. But the people, there, would not receive him, because he intended only to pass through their town on the way to Jerusalem.

When his disciples, James and John, realized this, they said, "Lord, will you have us command fire to come down from heaven, and consume them, even as Elijah did?"

But Jesus turned and rebuked them, and said, "You know not of what manner of spirit you are. For the Son of man has not come to destroy men's lives, but to save them."

So they continued on to another village, instead.

And as he entered into a certain village, there met him ten lepers, which stood afar off, and they lifted up their voices, and said, "Jesus, Master, have mercy on us."

And when he saw them, he said to them, "Go; show yourselves to the priests."

Now the lepers, knowing the Law of Moses, set off to present themselves to the priests, for they expected to be healed before they arrived. And it came to pass, that as they went, they were cleansed. And one of them, when he saw that his leprosy had ceased, turned back, and with a loud voice glorified God. And he fell down on his face at Jesus's feet, giving him thanks—and he was a Samaritan.

And Jesus, answering him, said, "Were there not ten cleansed, but where are the other nine?" Then turning to the crowd, he said, "There are none found that returned to give glory to God, save this stranger!" And as the crowd marveled at this strange turn of events, Jesus turned again to the man and said, "Arise, go your way; your faith has made you whole."

And the man's flesh was altogether restored, and his spirit also was renewed.

It came to pass, afterward, as they continued along the way, that a certain man, having witnessed these events, said to Jesus, "Lord, I will follow you wherever you go."

And Jesus said to him, "Foxes have holes, and birds of the air have nests, but the Son of man has nowhere to lay his head." And he said to another man, "Follow me."

But the man said, "Lord, allow me first to go and bury my father."

Jesus said to him, glancing at his mother, Mary, "Let the dead bury their dead, but *you* go and preach the kingdom of God."

Mary looked back at Jesus, understanding his glance and sharing his pain. She went to the man and explained that Jesus could not even bury his own father, because his mission to God was too important to interrupt. She convinced him, after much consoling and coaxing, to continue to follow her son.

Another man also said, "Lord, I will follow you, but let me first go home to bid farewell to those at my house."

And Jesus said to him, "No man, having put his hand to the plough, and looking back, is fit for the kingdom of God."

The other women, following the example of Mary, came to the man to encourage him. They were then joined by several of the men, who welcomed him into the fold.

Before entering into the land of Judea, Jesus appointed seventy others, sending them two by two ahead of him into every city and place where he was determined to go.

So he separated them, and in the hearing of all his disciples, he said to them, "The harvest truly is great, but the laborers are few; pray, therefore, that the Lord of the harvest will send forth laborers into his harvest. Go your separate ways; behold, I send you forth as lambs among wolves. Carry neither purse, nor scrip, nor shoes, and salute no one along the way. Into whatever house you enter, first say, 'Peace be upon this house.' And if the son of peace is there, your peace shall rest upon it; if not, it shall return to you again. In the same house remain, eating and drinking such things as they provide, for the laborer is worthy of his hire. Go not from house to house. Into whatever city you enter, and they receive you, eat such things as are set before you. Heal the sick that are there, and say to them, 'The kingdom of God is come nigh unto you.' But into whatever city you enter, and they receive you not, go out into the streets of that city, and say, 'Even the very dust of your city, which cleaves to us, we do wipe off against you: notwithstanding be sure of this, that the kingdom of God is come nigh unto you.' But I say unto you, that it shall be more tolerable in that day for Sodom, than for that city."

Then, as if to explain the type of cities he meant, Jesus went on a rant complaining about the cities he had already visited, and would not visit again. "Woe unto you, Chorazin! Woe unto you, Bethsaida! For if the mighty works had been done in Tyre and Sidon, which have been done in you, they would have a great while ago repented, sitting in sackcloth and ashes. But it shall be more tolerable for Tyre and Sidon at the judgment, than for you. And you, Capernaum, which are exalted to heaven, you shall be thrust down to hell."

When he finished his rant, his gaze, which had overshadowed his crowd of followers, descended again, returning to them. Now many who heard his rebuke were cut to the heart by his words, for they had grown up in these very cities.

Jesus recognized their heartache, so he said, reassuring them,

"He that hears you, hears me; and he that despises you, despises me; and he that despises me despises him that sent me."

The seventy, somewhat consoled by these words, were then dispersed throughout the towns of Judea, being sent to prepare his way toward Jerusalem.

When they returned again, they reported to him with joy, saying, "Lord, even the devils are subject unto us through your name."

And Jesus replied to them, "I beheld Satan as lightning fall from heaven. Behold, I give unto you power to tread on serpents and scorpions, and over all the power of the enemy, and nothing shall by any means hurt you. Notwithstanding in this rejoice not, that the spirits are subject unto you; but rather rejoice, because your names are written in heaven."

In that hour Jesus rejoiced in spirit, and said aloud with his hands and face raised toward heaven, "I thank you, Oh Father, Lord of heaven and earth, that you have hid these things from the wise and prudent, and have revealed them unto babes: even so, Father, for so it seemed good in your sight."

Then he turned to the seventy, speaking to them directly, but in the hearing of all, "All things are delivered unto me of my Father, and no man knows who the Son is but the Father, and who the Father is but the Son, and he to whom the Son will reveal him. Blessed are the eyes which see the things that you see. For I tell you that many prophets and kings have desired to see those things which you see, and have not seen them; and to hear those things which you hear, and have not heard them."

Those who heard envied the seventy for the apparent blessing that God had bestowed upon them.

Then a certain lawyer stood up, and speaking from envy, tempted Jesus, saying, "Master, what shall *I* do to inherit eternal life?"

Jesus, reading in his question his faulty attitude, quizzed him. "What is written in the Law? How do you read it?"

The man smiled shrewdly, and answered, "You shall love the

Lord your God with all your heart, and with all your soul, and with all your strength, and with all your mind." He paused, then thoughtfully added, "And your neighbor as yourself."

Then Jesus said to him, "You have answered right; this do, and you shall live."

Jesus stopped and looked at the man, waiting for his response, knowing that this answer would not satisfy the man's envy.

Then, as if on cue, the man smirked, and asked sarcastically, "And who *is* my neighbor?"

Now, taking advantage of the man's exposed attempt to justify himself, Jesus instructed him with a parable, "A certain man went down from Jerusalem to Jericho, and fell among thieves, who stripped him of his clothes, wounded him, and departed, leaving him half dead. By chance, a certain priest came down that way, and when he saw him, he passed by on the other side. Likewise, a Levite, when he was at the place, came and looked at him, then passed by on the other side. But a certain Samaritan, as he journeyed, came where he was, and when he saw him, he had compassion on him. He went to him, and bound up his wounds, pouring in oil and wine. Then he set him on his own beast, brought him to an inn, and took care of him. The next day, when he departed, he took out two denarii, and gave them to the host, and said to him, 'Take care of him, and whatever more you spend, I will repay, when I come again.' Which now of these three, do you think was a neighbor to him that fell among the thieves?"

And the man, now humbled, replied honestly, "He that showed mercy on him."

Then said Jesus to him, "Go, and *you* do likewise."

Now it came to pass, as they came near to Jerusalem, that Jesus entered into the village of Bethany. And they came to the house of Simon the leper, the Pharisee whom Jesus had healed. Simon's son, Lazarus, and his daughter Martha, lived there with him. Simon's other daughter, Mary, who had anointed the feet of Jesus, had joined his disciples, and was also there among them. While there, Mary continued with his disciples, sitting at the feet of Jesus, to hear his words.

But Martha was cumbered about with much serving, and came to Jesus, and said, "Lord, do you not care that my sister has left me to serve alone? Bid her, therefore, that she help me."

Jesus looked at her with tender sympathy, and answered her, "Martha, Martha, you are careful and troubled about many things. But one thing is necessary, and Mary has chosen that good part, which shall not be taken away from her."

Luke 9:51–56   Luke 17:11–19   Luke 9:57–63
Luke 10:1–42   Deuteronomy 6:5   Leviticus 19:18
2 Kings 1:9–15   Revelation 13:11–18

Chapter 44

FEAST OF TABERNACLES

The Feast of Tabernacles had already begun, when Jesus reached Bethany; and his brothers, who had gone on ahead of him, were celebrating with the multitudes at Jerusalem.

The Jewish religious leaders, seeking Jesus, came to his brothers, asking them, "Where is he?"

His brothers, still upset with Jesus over his harsh words in Galilee, answered them roughly, out of envy and spite, "We do not know; nor do we care."

The people in Jerusalem were still divided concerning Jesus and his ministry.

Some said, "He is a good man."

Others said, "No, he deceives the people."

But these things they spoke quietly among themselves, murmuring privately, fearing hostility from the religious leaders.

It was the middle of the feast week, on the fourth day, that Jesus went to the temple and began to teach.

When the Jewish leaders found him teaching, they marveled, questioning, "How does this man know the scriptures, having never learned from them?"

Jesus answered their incredulity by saying, "My doctrine is not mine, but of the One who sent me. If anyone desires to do his will, he shall know of the doctrine, whether it is of God or whether I speak of myself. Anyone speaking of himself seeks his own glory, but he that seeks glory for the One that sent him, the same is true, and no unrighteousness is in him."

At these words, the religious leaders grumbled. Jesus continued, therefore.

"Did not Moses give you the Law?" he asked them, "And yet none of you keep the Law. If you did, would you go about trying to kill me?"

The people from the crowd answered him, while the leaders, being convicted of their maliciousness, backed down.

"You have a devil!" the crowd shouted. "Who goes about trying to kill you?"

But Jesus stayed focused on the leaders, disregarding the hostility of the crowd, which was apparently ignorant of the intentions of its leaders.

Directing his gaze at the most authoritative among them, he answered them vigorously. "I have done one work, and you marvel. Moses, *for this very cause*, gave you circumcision! Yet this originated not from Moses, but from the patriarchs. And you on the Sabbath day circumcise a man. If a man on the Sabbath day receives circumcision that the Law of Moses should not be broken, why are you enraged at me, because *I* have made a man completely whole on the Sabbath day?"

This he said referring to the lame man he healed at the Bethesda pool, for this was when the leaders began to seek his life.

"Judge not according to appearance, but judge righteous judgment," he exhorted them in conclusion.

Then he disappeared through the crowd.

Hearing his words concerning healing on the Sabbath, some in the crowd remembered that the leaders had sought to kill him for healing the man at the pool.

And they began to discuss it among themselves, saying, "Isn't this the man whom *the leaders* seek to kill? But now he speaks boldly, and they say nothing to him. Do the rulers know, indeed, that this is the true Messiah?"

Others said, "How is it, though, that we know where he's from? When the Messiah comes, no one will know where he's from."

Then Jesus, who had resumed teaching elsewhere in the temple, cried out loudly, so that his voice could be heard throughout the entire temple, "You both know me, and you know from where I am; I am not come of myself, but he that is true has sent me, whom you know not. But I know him, for I am from him, and he has sent me."

At these words, the rage of the leaders was rekindled, and they sought to take him, but could not lay hands upon him, because he disappeared again into the crowd, sliding quickly among those who believed his words.

Many of the people who believed, reasoned, saying, "When the Messiah comes, will he do more miracles than these, which this man has done?"

When the Pharisees and chief priests of the temple heard the murmurings of the people, they became the more enraged. Immediately instructing the officers of the temple guard to take Jesus into custody, they accompanied them to see that his arrest was carried out. But when they found him, he was on his way out of the temple, surrounded by his followers.

Jesus, seeing them approaching, called to them before leaving, "Yet a little while I am with you, and then I go unto him who sent me. You shall seek me, and you shall not find me, for where I am, there you cannot come."

But the Jewish leaders did not understand what he meant. So they bickered among themselves, saying, "Where will he go that we shall not find him? Will he go to the dispersed among the Gentiles, and teach the Gentiles? What manner of saying is this that he said, 'You shall seek me, and shall not find me, and where I am, there you cannot come?'"

On the last day, the great day of the feast, Jesus returned to the temple. And he stood before a great multitude of people, and cried out, saying, "If anyone thirsts, let him come to me and drink. He that believes in me, as the scripture has said, 'out of his belly shall flow rivers of living water.'"

No one fully understood that Jesus spoke concerning the Holy Spirit, whom he intended to send to his believers once he was raised from the dead. They did, however, recognize his reference to the Song of Songs, "A garden enclosed, is my sister, my spouse; a spring shut up, a fountain sealed. Your plants are an orchard of pomegranates, with pleasant fruits; henna, with spikenard, spikenard and saffron; calamus and cinnamon, with all trees of frankincense; myrrh and aloes, with all the chief spices: a fountain of gardens, a well of living waters, and streams from Lebanon. Awake, Oh north wind; and come, you south; blow upon my garden, that the spices thereof may flow out. Let my beloved come into his garden, and eat his pleasant fruits."

From their understanding of the scriptures, his listeners knew the "belly" to be closely associated with the womb and the soul. They also equated "living water" with the Lord and salvation; from the words of Jeremiah, "Oh LORD, the hope of Israel, all who forsake you shall be ashamed, and they that depart from me shall be written in the earth, because they have forsaken the LORD, the fountain of living waters. Heal me, Oh LORD, and I shall be healed; save me, and I shall be saved, for you are my praise."

So, though they could not fully understand his meaning, they recognized the magnitude of his words, nonetheless.

Many of the people, therefore, when they heard this saying, said, "Of a truth this is the Prophet."

Others said, "This is the Messiah."

But some said, "Shall the Messiah come out of Galilee? Has not the scripture said that the Messiah comes of the seed of David, and out of the town of Bethlehem, where David was?"

So there was a division among the people, because of him. And though some of them wanted to take him, still, no man laid hands upon him.

The temple officers, who were also listening to Jesus's teaching, came to the chief priests and Pharisees; and the religious leaders asked them, "Why have you not brought him?"

The officers answered, "Never did a man speak like this man."

Then the Pharisees answered them, "Are you also deceived? Have any of the rulers or the Pharisees believed in him? But this people who know not the Law are cursed."

Nicodemus, he that came to Jesus by night, being among them, said to them, "Does our Law judge any man before it hears him, and knows what he does?"

And the others answered him, "Are you also of Galilee? Search, and look, for out of Galilee arises no prophet."

So they were divided, and every man went to his own house.

That night, Jesus went to the Mount of Olives with the twelve, and stayed in a cave used by the olive growers.

Jesus rose early, before the sun, venturing down the mountain toward Bethphage to pray. In the darkness, he met a young man feeding his donkeys, for it was his vocation to raise and train them.

"You are up early," said the young man.

"I must be about my Father's business," Jesus returned. "I go to speak with him, now."

"I am about my father's business, as well," said the young man. "I raise and train donkeys."

"Mother and son?" asked Jesus of the two donkeys being immediately attended to by the young man.

"Yes," said the young man, "the colt is her foal; he just turned five years old, nearly ready to be trained for riding."

"Noble creatures," pondered Jesus, laying his hand upon the cross formed on the colt's back.

"And a noble profession," said the young man, amazed that the colt had not objected to this stranger's unfamiliar touch. "The Messiah King, David's descendant, will ride into Jerusalem someday on one of these noble creatures. I know it's silly, but I imagine myself training the very colt."

"Have faith, my friend. Work, training your donkeys as unto the Lord. Someday the Lord may well have need of them," Jesus answered him.

"I will remember your kind words," said the young man.

"And I will remember *you*," answered Jesus.

Jesus departed without either of them introducing themselves, the young man wishing they had after it was too late. When he had finished his early-morning chores, however, the young man rehearsed their encounter to his father and mother.

After praying, Jesus returned to the cave, and gathered his disciples, while it was still morning. Then he came again into the temple, and when all the people came to him, he sat down and taught them.

In the midst of his teaching, the scribes and Pharisees brought him a woman taken in adultery, and when they had forcibly set her before him, in the midst of his listeners, they said to him, "Master, this woman was taken in adultery, in the very act."

The woman stood there, defiant, scowling at her accusers. She hardly noticed the man sitting before her with his head bowed and his hand over the back of his neck.

"Now Moses, in the Law, commanded us that such should be stoned," they continued, "but what do *you* say?"

This they said, tempting him, that they might have something by which to accuse him. At these words, several among them bent down and picked up stones. Jesus stood reluctantly, scrutinizing the faces of the woman's accusers. The woman looked at Jesus, trying to place his familiar face. Then he stooped down, and many watching him expected him to pick up a stone, also. Instead, with his finger, he began writing on the ground the names of her accusers, apparently intending not to answer them.

But when they persisted in asking him, he lifted up his head, and looked at the woman with compassion; and looking upon him, also, she recognized Jesus, and immediately felt ashamed. Her countenance changed; she blushed agonizingly, and lowered her head.

Jesus stood, turned to her accusers, and said, "He that is without sin among you, let him cast the first stone."

Then he stooped down, again, and wrote on the ground, continuing his list of their names.

When they heard his words, and saw their names written in the earth, they remembered what he had spoken earlier, "out of his belly shall flow rivers of living water." And they perceived, more fully, how it related to Jeremiah's words, "They that depart from me shall be written in the earth, because they have forsaken the LORD, the fountain of living waters." Each of them, knowing that they were not without sin, and not wanting to be among those who depart from the Lord, dropped their stones. And being convicted by their own consciences, one by one they departed, beginning at the eldest, even unto the last. So Jesus and his listeners were left alone, with the woman standing in their midst.

As the scribes and Pharisees shuffled away, Jesus lifted his head again, and saw no one standing there but the woman.

Then he said to her, "Woman, where are your accusers? Has no man condemned you?"

She looked at him remorsefully, and then whispered to him, warily, "No *man*, Lord."

Then Jesus stood erect, looking into her eyes, and said to her with compassion, "Neither do *I* condemn you. Go, and sin no more."

After hearing his encouraging words, the woman also stood erect, with a renewed sense of dignity. She smiled at him through moistened eyes, and then turned to go. As she departed, Jesus saw the scribes and Pharisees looking back at him, as they made their way slowly through his crowd of followers.

Then he turned to his listeners, speaking in a loud voice, so that these religious leaders could also hear him, "I AM the light of the world; he that follows me shall not walk in darkness, but shall have the light of life."

The woman turned back to look at Jesus, when she heard these words—and several times afterward, before leaving the temple. When outside, she determined in her heart that she would return again to follow him.

The scribes and Pharisees, when they heard his words, reacted quite differently to them, for Jesus had used the words, "I AM," which was reserved among the Jews for the name of God. Moses was given this name by God, himself. When Moses was at the burning bush, God told him, "I AM THAT I AM." The Jews, therefore, purposely avoided using "I AM," to keep from inadvertently defiling God's name by using his name in vain. When they heard Jesus say, "I AM," therefore, they stopped, looked back at him, and decided to return to hear more, still hoping to find something to use against him. Jesus paused, acknowledging their return.

In the interim, the twelve, who sat before Jesus, began talking among themselves.

"Oh, watch this," Peter said chuckling. "This should be good."

The others turned with anticipation to see the scribes and Pharisees returning.

"What do you mean?" asked Nathanael.

"He's baiting them," replied the big fisherman.

Nathanael didn't look convinced, but James and John nodded to Peter, and then smiled at one another.

"Jesus is calling back the scribes and Pharisees! Usually, he is content in seeing them leave," Peter explained. "This time he has intentionally incited them to return."

Peter signaled for the others to stand in preparation for a confrontation from which they would most likely have to flee.

When the religious leaders drew near enough to him, they shouted to Jesus, accusing him, "You bear record of yourself; your record is not true."

"Here we go," James snickered.

Jesus answered them, "Though I bear record of myself, yet my record is true, for I know from where I came, and to where I go, but you cannot tell from where I come, and to where I go. You judge after the flesh; I judge no man. And yet *if* I judge, my judgment is true, for I am not alone in judgment, but I and the Father that sent me. It is also written in your Law that the testimony of two men is true. I AM one being witness of myself, and the Father that sent me bears witness of me."

Then they said to him, "Where is your father?"

Jesus answered, "You neither know me, nor my Father; if you had known me, you should have known my Father also."

At this, his adversaries became quiet. Now Jesus was speaking in the treasury as he taught in the temple, and the twelve were strategizing how they might conduct Jesus away without anyone laying hands on him.

"Why does he provoke them, so?" Judas Iscariot asked, growing agitated.

"You're not feeling sorry for them, are you, Judas?" asked Philip.

"Do you care so much for the poor Pharisees, Judas?" teased Peter.

Judas scowled at them, then turned to Mary, Jesus's mother, and said, "Is it wise to provoke them? Shouldn't he seek to gain their trust?"

John, overhearing his words, asked him incredulously, "Judas, who do you imagine has provoked whom?"

But Mary nodded to Judas. "Only they can legitimize his ministry. I don't know why he treats them so."

John looked at Peter, who also heard the conversation. Peter just shook his head in disbelief.

Then Jesus addressed the leaders again. "I go my way, and you shall seek me, and shall die in your sins; where I go, you cannot come."

Then the leaders of the Jews questioned among themselves,

"Will he kill himself? because he said, 'Where I go, you cannot come.'"

But Jesus answered them, still further, "You are from beneath; I am from above; you are of this world; I am not of this world. I said, therefore, unto you, that you shall die in your sins, for if you believe not that I AM, you shall die in your sins."

Peter nearly burst out laughing, "He becomes bolder and bolder, and still they hold their tongues. How much more plainly can he explain it? They will not hear, yet they will not confront him."

Jesus realized that to reach these proud Jewish leaders, it was necessary to humble them, first. Humbling them openly before the people would make them an example to the people, as well. To make this tact work, he would have to walk a fine line between humbling them and enraging them. He knew he must measure well their tolerance, as he bluntly ministered to them the truth.

After some discussion among themselves, the leaders arrived at a simple yet pertinent question, "Who *are* you?"

Jesus would not take the bait, for they hoped he would blaspheme, calling himself God; instead he said to them, "Even the same that I said to you from the beginning. I have many things to say and to judge of you, but he who is true has sent me, and I speak to the world those things which I have heard of him."

They still did not understand that he spoke to them of the Father.

Knowing their confusion, Jesus added, "When you have lifted up the Son of man, *then* you shall know that I AM, and that I do nothing of myself; but as my Father has taught me, I speak these things. And he that sent me is with me; the Father has not left me alone, for I do always those things that please him."

As he spoke these words, many believed in him. The twelve, except Judas, began to see the humor in the situation. Jesus had all but declared himself the Messiah, the Son of God, yet the exalted religious leaders either could not see it or refused to see it.

"He is so masterful with his words. This is like watching a cat play with a mouse," said Thomas.

"More like a lion playing with a little bird," snickered John, using more scriptural equivalents.

They all covered their faces to muffle their laughter.

Then Jesus said to those Jews that believed in him, "If you continue in my word, then are you my disciples, indeed; and you shall know the truth, and the truth shall make you free."

Though he spoke to the believers among the crowd, it was the Pharisees, who took offense at his comments, that answered him, "We are Abraham's seed, and were never in bondage to any man. How can you say, 'You shall be made free?'"

Jesus answered them, "Truly, truly, I say unto you, whoever commits sin is the servant of sin. The servant abides not in the house for ever, but the Son abides forever. If the Son, therefore, shall make you free, you shall be free indeed. I know that you are Abraham's seed, but you seek to kill me, because my word has no place in you. I speak that which I have seen with my Father, and you do that which you have seen with *your* father."

They answered and said to him, "Abraham is our father."

Jesus said to them, "If you were Abraham's children, you would do the works of Abraham. But now you seek to kill me, a man that has told you the truth, which I have heard of God; this did not Abraham. You do the deeds of *your* father."

Then they said to him, indignantly, "We were not born of fornication; we have one Father, even God."

Jesus said to them, "If God were your Father, you would love me, for I proceeded forth and came from God; neither came I of myself, but *he* sent me. Why do you not understand my speech? Even because you cannot hear my word. You are of *your* father, the devil, and the lusts of your father you will do. He was a murderer from the beginning, and abode not in the truth, because there is no truth in him. When he speaks a lie, he speaks of his own, for he is a liar, and the father of it. And because I tell you the truth, you believe me not. Which of you convinces *me* of sin? And if I say the truth, why do you not believe me? He that is of God hears God's words; you, therefore, hear them not, because you are not of God."

"Get ready boys," said Simon Zelotes. "We will need to be going soon."

While the Jewish leaders decided how to respond to Jesus, the twelve maneuvered themselves into position for a quick getaway.

When the Jewish leaders had finished their discussion, they answered Jesus again, "Say we not well that you are a Samaritan, and have a devil?"

Jesus laughed at this, and answered, "I have not a devil; but I honor my Father, and you do dishonor me. And I seek not my own glory; there is one that seeks and judges. Truly, truly, I say unto you, if a man keeps my sayings, he shall never see death."

Then the Jewish leaders said to him, "Now we know that you have a devil. Abraham is dead, and the prophets, and you say, 'If a man keeps my sayings, he shall never taste of death.' Are you greater than our father Abraham, who is dead, and the prophets, who are dead? Whom do you make yourself?"

Jesus answered, "If I honor myself, my honor is nothing: it is my Father who honors me; of whom you say, that he is your God. Yet you have not known him, but I know him, and if I should say, 'I know him not,' I shall be a liar like you, but I know him, and keep his sayings. Your father Abraham rejoiced to see my day, and he saw it, and was glad."

Then the Jewish leaders laughed back at him, and said, "You are not yet fifty years old, and you have seen Abraham?"

Jesus said to them, "Truly, truly, I say unto you, before Abraham was, I AM."

Finally, the light broke through upon them, and they understood his words, and became enraged. Then the scribes and Pharisees took up stones to cast at him, but Jesus hid himself behind the twelve, and went out of the temple, going through the midst of his believers, and so passed by them.

When they were safely away, while leaving the temple, they passed by a man who had been listening in the wings to Jesus's teaching. He was blind from his birth, and was trying, with some difficulty, to stay within listening distance to them.

As Jesus's disciples passed by the man, they asked Jesus, "Lord, who did sin, this man, or his parents, that he was born blind?"

Jesus answered, "Neither has this man sinned, nor his parents, but that the works of God should be made manifest in him. I must work the works of him that sent me, while it is day; the night comes, when no man can work. As long as I am in the world, I am the light of the world."

When he had thus spoken, he stopped before the man, spat on the ground, and made clay of the spittle.

Then he anointed the eyes of the blind man with the clay, and said to him, "Go; wash in the pool of Siloam."

He went his way, therefore, and washed, and came seeing.

The man's neighbors, therefore, and they which had seen that he was blind before, said, "Is not this he that sat and begged?"

Some said, "This is he."

Others said, "He is like him."

But the man answered their question bluntly and truthfully, telling them, "I am."

Therefore, they said to him, "How were your eyes opened?"

He answered and said, "A man that is called Jesus made clay, and anointed my eyes, and said to me, 'Go to the pool of Siloam, and wash,' and I went and washed, and I received sight."

Then they said to him, "Where is he?"

He said, "I know not."

So they brought the man who was formerly blind to the Pharisees. And it was the Sabbath day when Jesus made the clay, and opened his eyes. Then, again, the Pharisees also asked the man how he had received his sight.

And he said to them, "He put clay upon my eyes, and I washed, and do see."

Therefore, said some of the Pharisees, "This man is not of God, because he keeps not the Sabbath day."

Others said, "How can a man that is a sinner do such miracles?"

So there was a division among them.

They said to the blind man again, "What do you say of him that has opened your eyes?"

"He is a prophet," said the man.

But the Jewish leaders did not believe concerning him, that he had been blind, and received his sight, until they called the man's parents.

And they asked them, saying, "Is this your son, who you say was born blind? How then does he now see?"

His parents answered them, and said, "We know that this is our son, and that he was born blind, but by what means he now sees, we do not know. Who has opened his eyes, we do not know. He is of age; ask him. He shall speak for himself."

These words spoke his parents, because they feared the Jewish leaders, for the leaders had agreed, already, that if anyone confessed that Jesus was the Messiah, he would be put out of the synagogues.

Therefore, his parents said, "He is of age; ask him."

Then, again, they called the man that was blind, and said to him, "Give God the praise; we know that this man is a sinner."

He answered and said, "Whether he is a sinner or not, I do not know. One thing I do know; that, whereas I was blind, now I see."

Then they asked him again, "What did he do to you? How did he open your eyes?"

He answered them, "I have told you already, and you did not hear. Why must you hear it again? Will you also be his disciples?"

Then they reviled him, and said, "You are *his* disciple, but we are Moses's disciples. We know that God spoke to Moses; as for this fellow, we know not from where he is!"

The man answered, and said to them, "Why, herein is a marvelous thing, that you know not from where he is, and yet he has opened my eyes. Now we know that God hears not sinners, but if any man be a worshiper of God, and does his will, him he hears. Since the world began, it was not heard that any man opened the eyes of one that was born blind. If this man were not of God, he could do nothing."

They answered, and said to him, "You were altogether born in sins, and do *you* teach us?"

And they cast him out of the synagogue.

Jesus heard that they had cast the man out of the synagogue, and when he had found him, he said to him, "Do you believe in the Son of God?"

He answered, and said, "Who is he, Lord, that I might believe in him?"

And Jesus said to him, "You have both seen him, and it is he that talks with you."

Then the man said, "Lord, I believe."

And he worshiped him.

Jesus then spoke to the crowd surrounding them. "For judgment I have come into this world, that they which see not, might see; and that they which see, might be made blind."

And some of the Pharisees who were there with him heard these words, and said to him, "Are we blind also?"

Jesus said to them, "If you were blind, you should have no sin, but now you say, 'We see;' therefore, your sin remains."

He began to walk away from them, then turned, and said, "Truly, truly, I say unto you, he that enters not by the door into the sheepfold, but climbs up some other way, the same is a thief and a robber. But he that enters in by the door is the shepherd of the sheep. To him the porter opens; and the sheep hear his voice, and he calls his own sheep by name, and leads them out. And when he puts forth his own sheep, he goes before them, and the sheep follow him, for they know his voice. And a stranger they will not follow, but will flee from him, for they know not the voice of strangers."

This parable spoke Jesus to them, but they understood not what things they were which he spoke to them.

Then Jesus said to them, again, "Truly, truly, I say unto you, I AM the door of the sheep. All that ever came before me are thieves and robbers, but the sheep did not hear them. I AM the door: by me if any man enters in, he shall be saved, and shall go in and out, and find pasture. The thief comes not, but for to steal, and to kill, and to destroy: I have come that they might have life, and that they might have it more abundantly. I AM the good shepherd; the good shepherd gives his life for the sheep. But he that is a hireling, and not the shepherd, whose own the sheep are not, sees the wolf coming, and leaves the sheep, and flees, and the wolf catches them, and scatters the sheep. The hireling flees, because he is a hireling, and cares not for the sheep. I AM the good shepherd, and know my sheep, and am known of mine. As the Father knows me, even so I know the Father, and I lay down my life for the sheep. And other sheep I have, which are not of this fold; them also I must bring, and they shall hear my voice, and there shall be one fold and one shepherd. Therefore does my Father love me, because I lay down my life, that I might take it again. No man takes it from me, but I lay it down of myself. I have power to lay it down, and I have power to take it again. This commandment have I received of my Father."

And many of them said, "He has a devil, and is mad. Why do you listen to him?"

Others said, "These are not the words of him that has a devil. Can a devil open the eyes of the blind?"

There was a division, therefore, again, among the Jews for these sayings.

John 7:10–53	Exodus 20:13	Genesis 17:10–13
Isaiah 49:1–7	Song of Songs 4:12–16	Job 3:11
Psalms 22:10	Isaiah 46:3	Psalms 31:9
Psalms 44:25	Proverbs 13:25	Jeremiah 17:13–14
Deuteronomy 18:22	Micah 5:2	John 8:1–59

Zechariah 9:9
Exodus 20:7
Job 41:1–5
John 10:1–21

Leviticus 20:10
Deuteronomy 19:15
Genesis 22:1–18

Exodus 3:14
Isaiah 31:4
John 9:1–41

Chapter 45

THE EVIL GENERATION

Jesus left the temple, after the Feast of Tabernacles, and went to Bethabara, the place where John first baptized—the "door of the crossing," where Israel first entered the Promised Land.

It came to pass that Jesus was praying there, and when he ceased, one of his disciples said to him, "Lord, teach *us* to pray, as John also taught *his* disciples."

And he said to them, "When you pray, say, 'Our Father who is in heaven, hallowed be your name. Your kingdom come. Your will be done, as in heaven, so in earth. Give us day by day our daily bread. And forgive us our sins, for we also forgive everyone who is indebted to us. And lead us not into temptation, but deliver us from evil.'"

Then he spoke a parable to them, to this end, that men ought always to pray, and not to faint; saying, "There was in a city a judge, who feared not God, neither regarded man, and there was a widow in that city, and she came to him, saying, 'Avenge me of my adversary.' And he would not for a while, but afterward, he said within himself, 'Though I fear not God, nor regard man; yet, because this widow troubles me, I will avenge her, lest by her continual coming she wearies me.'" Then Jesus said, "Hear what the unjust judge says! And shall not God avenge his own elect, who cry day and night unto him, though he bear long with them? I tell you that he will avenge them speedily. Nevertheless, when the Son of man comes, shall he find faith on the earth?"

And he asked them, "Which of you shall have a friend, and shall go to him at midnight, and say to him, 'Friend, lend me three loaves, for a friend of mine, in his journey, has come to me, and I have nothing to set before him?' And he from within shall answer and say, 'Trouble me not; the door is now shut, and my children are with me in bed; I cannot rise and provide for you.' I say to you, though he will not rise and provide for him, because he is his friend, yet because of his troublesome urgency he will rise and give him as much as he needs.

"So I say unto you, ask, and it shall be given to you; seek, and you shall find; knock, and it shall be opened to you. For everyone that asks, receives; and he that seeks, finds; and to him who knocks, it shall be opened. If a son shall ask bread of any of you that is his father, will you give him a stone? Or if he asks for a fish, will you instead of a fish give him a serpent? Or if he shall ask for an egg, will you offer him a scorpion? If you, then, being evil, know how to give good gifts to your children, how much more shall your heavenly Father give the Holy Spirit to them that ask him?"

As he finished his teaching; the devil, seeking to discredit his profoundly significant words, attacked the most vulnerable among Jesus's inner circle of followers. Mary Magdalene, who had grown into a beautiful young woman, and was favored greatly by Jesus and his disciples, began flailing her arms wildly, directing her shaking hands about her neck and mouth, in apparent agony, while making the most disturbing of guttural sounds. Mary, Jesus's mother, pulled her toward Jesus; who when he saw her, recognized that she had returned to the original state of speechlessness from which she had suffered as a child. He immediately cast out the demons from her, and her demeanor became calm again. She stood there, bent over for several seconds, breathing heavily, for the ordeal left her sore and shaken.

"I'm fine," she said finally, in a shallow, hoarse voice.

The women rallied around her, with Mary, the mother of Jesus, leading the way. They sat her down, and provided her water to drink. As she sat upon the ground resting, and trying to catch her breath, the crowd began to murmur.

Some of the scribes and Pharisees said, "He casts out devils through Beelzebub, the chief of the devils."

But Jesus, when he knew their thoughts, turned to face them, saying, "Every kingdom divided against itself is brought to destruction, and household upon household falls. Therefore, if Satan also is divided against himself, how shall his kingdom stand?" Shifting his body sideways, so that his accusers could see his disciples, he presented the twelve and the seventy to them, continuing, "For you say that I cast out devils through Beelzebub. But if I by Beelzebub cast out devils, by whom do your sons cast them out?"

He paused for effect, for the stories of the miraculous healings and exorcisms by his disciples had been a constant topic of conversation among the people for some time.

"For this cause," he scolded them, "*they* shall be your judges."

He turned, then, again to face his accusers, adding, "But if I with the finger of God cast out devils, there is no doubt that the kingdom of God has come upon you."

When he had concluded these words, he explained to all the people, by a parable, what happens to someone who is possessed by demons.

"When a strong man arms himself to protect his dwelling, his possessions are safe;" he said, "but when one stronger than he comes upon him, and overpowers him, he takes from him all the protection in which he trusted, and divides his spoils."

Then he looked at his accusers, again, and told them, "He that is not with me is against me, and he that gathers not with me scatters chaff to the wind."

After his warning, he returned to his teaching, explaining to the crowd, in plain words, what happens to a person who has been delivered from a demon.

"When the unclean spirit is gone out of a man," he said, "he walks through dry places, seeking rest; and finding none, he says, 'I will return to my house, from where I came.' And when he comes, he finds it swept and furnished. Then he goes, and takes with him seven other spirits more wicked than himself; and they enter in, and dwell there, so that the last state of that man is worse than the first. Even so shall it be also unto this evil generation."

From his explanation, Jesus's disciples understood what had just happened to Mary Magdalene. Mary, who was still being attended to by Jesus's mother, understood, as well. Then seeking to help the situation, and to quiet the doubt concerning Jesus's relationship to God, Magdalene cried out, "Blessed is the womb that bore you, and the breasts from which you nursed."

Her words were familiar ones, for they were part of a prayer circulated among the young women who had hoped to bear the Messiah. At her words, Mary, the mother of Jesus, blushed and smiled shyly, then bowed her head. Jesus, recognizing the efforts of Mary Magdalene, turned to her, smiled, and nodded.

He traded thoughtful glances with his mother, then turned back to Magdalene, and concluded his teaching, as it pertained to her own spiritual condition, "Even more blessed are they that hear the word of God, and keep it."

Magdalene, smiled sweetly back at him, and returned a nod of understanding, before being helped to her feet.

But the scribes and Pharisees, unwilling to believe his words only, sought of him a sign from heaven, tempting him to prove his power was truly from God.

As the crowds gathered closer together around him, Jesus pointed to the scribes and Pharisees, and said of them scathingly, "*This* is an evil generation! It seeks a sign, and there shall no sign be given to it, but the sign of Jonah the prophet. For even as Jonah became a sign to the Ninevites, so shall also the Son of man be to *this* generation. For as Jonah was three days and three nights in the great fish's belly, so shall the Son of man be three days and three nights in the heart of the earth.

"The queen of Sheba, who journeyed from the south, shall rise up in the Judgment with the *men* of this generation, and condemn them, for *she* came from the utmost parts of the earth to hear the wisdom of Solomon, and, behold, here, more than Solomon!"

As he said these last words, he turned among them, raising his hands out, palms up, indicating that he was referring to himself. His words and gesture exuded ease and confidence, rather than arrogance. The women in the crowd took particular notice of the intriguing emphasis Jesus used in his comparison between the *men* of 'this evil generation' of scribes and Pharisees, and this *woman* queen.

Looking at the men in the crowd, who were evidently astonished at his teaching, as well, he continued, "Men, *Nineveh* shall rise up in the Judgment with *this* generation, and shall condemn it, for they repented at the preaching of Jonah." "And, behold, here," he said turning, while raising his hands again, "more than Jonah!"

Then Jesus turned to the twelve, and the seventy, those whom he had sent out to minister.

And holding out his hands to them, he said so all could hear, "No man, when lighting a lamp, puts it in a secret place, neither under a measuring pot, but on a lamp stand, so that those who come into the brightness may see. The lamp of the body is the eye; therefore, when your eye is unobstructed by guile, your whole body also is enlightened."

He then turned to face the scribes and Pharisees, and held up one arm toward them, indicating them in disgust, and then said, "But when your eye is evil, your body also is full of darkness. Take heed, therefore, that the light, which is in you, is not darkness."

He frowned at these religious leaders disappointedly, and then turned back to the crowd. "If your whole body, therefore, is enlightened, having no part dark, all will be enlightened, as when the lamp with its bright shining enlightens you!"

When he had said these things to them, the scribes and the Pharisees began to urge him vehemently, to provoke him into saying something by which they might accuse him. To this end, a certain Pharisee, who had been among those who accosted Jesus at the marketplace, brought up, again, the issue of Jesus and his disciples not washing before they ate.

So Jesus responded to the accusation by revealing to them their true nature, saying, "Now you Pharisees cleanse the outside of the cup and the platter, but the inside part of you is full of extortion and wickedness. You fools! Did not he that made the outside, make that which is inside, also?"

His look questioned them with all sincerity, but no one responded.

"But give alms to be within the Law," he raged at them, "and, behold, all things are clean unto you!"

These last words were delivered with sarcasm, and as he said them, he raised his hands in derision.

"Woe unto you, Pharisees!" he shouted, his anger growing, "For you tithe mint and rue and all the herbs, and pass over judgment and the love of God; these things were necessary for you to have done, and not to have left the others undone. Woe unto you, Pharisees! For you love the best seats in the synagogues, and greetings in the marketplace. Woe unto you, scribes and Pharisees, hypocrites! For you are as concealed graves, upon which men walk without knowing."

Jesus ended his speech, turning from them. But his accusers, still lying in wait for some slipup, were not ready to give up yet.

To keep him talking, one of the lawyers, answered him, "Master, by saying this you reproach us also."

Jesus took the bait. Turning on the lawyer, he raged, "Woe unto you also, you lawyers! For you weigh down men with burdens grievous to be borne, and you yourselves touch not the burdens with one of your fingers. Woe unto you! For you build the tombs of the prophets, whom your fathers killed. Truly, you bear witness that you condone the deeds of your fathers, for they, indeed, killed them, and you build their tombs. Therefore, also said the wisdom of God, 'I will send them prophets and apostles, and some of them they shall slay and persecute: that the blood of all the prophets, which was shed from the foundation of the world, may be required of *this* generation; from the blood of Abel to the blood of Zachariah, who perished between the altar and the temple.' Truly, I say unto you, it shall be required of *this* generation. Woe unto you, lawyers! For you have taken away the key of knowledge; you entered not in yourselves, and them that *were* entering in, you hindered."

During his outburst, there were gathered together an innumerable multitude of people, insomuch that they trampled upon one another.

When he finished, he turned to the twelve and the seventy, and speaking to them directly, he said, "Beware the leaven of the Pharisees, which is hypocrisy. For there is nothing covered, that shall not be revealed; neither hid, that shall not be known. Know, therefore, whatever you have spoken in darkness shall be heard in the light, and that which you have spoken in the ear in closets shall be proclaimed upon the housetops. And I say unto you my friends, be not afraid of them that kill the body, and after that have nothing more that they can do. But I will forewarn you whom you shall fear: fear him, which after he has killed, has power to cast into hell; yes, I say unto you, fear him. Are not five sparrows sold for two of the least of coins? And not one of them is forgotten before God. But even the very hairs of your head are all numbered. Fear not, therefore; you are of more value than many sparrows.

"Also, I say unto you, whoever shall confess me before men," he said to the twelve and seventy, moving to the side slightly, allowing them to see their adversaries, the religious leaders, in full retreat toward the back of the crowd, "him shall the Son of man also confess before the angels of God."

He turned still further; and indicating the scribes, Pharisees, and lawyers with his outstretched arms, he denounced them, adding, "But he that denies me before men shall be denied before the angels of God. And whoever shall speak a word against the Son of man, it shall be forgiven him, but to him who blasphemes against the Holy Spirit it shall not be forgiven."

"And when *they*," he continued, pointing accusingly at the religious leaders, "shall bring you unto the synagogues, and unto magistrates, and powers, take no thought how or what you shall answer, or what you shall say, for the Holy Spirit shall teach you in that same hour what you ought to say."

Now, while Jesus was busy berating the scribes, Pharisees, and lawyers, his mother and Judas Iscariot were cringing over his all-out verbal attack. When his rant had subsided, therefore, Judas spoke up, hoping to somehow repair the damage done.

"Master," he said to him, in a conciliatory tone, imploring him to look favorably upon the religious leaders, "speak to my brother, that he divide the inheritance *with* me."

His request suggested that there was an opportunity for Jesus and his disciples to share the religious authority with the established Jewish leadership. His suggestion provided a diplomatic solution that seemed reasonable.

But Jesus, knowing the true covetous nature and intent of Judas, said to him, "*Man*, who made me a judge or a divider over you?"

Then he turned from Judas toward the crowd, saying, "Take heed, and beware of covetousness, for a man's life consists not in the abundance of his possessions."

And he spoke a parable to them, saying, "The ground of a certain rich man brought forth plentifully. And he thought within himself, saying, 'What shall I do, because I have no room where to bestow my fruits?' And he said, 'This will I do: I will pull down my barns, and build greater, and there will I bestow all my fruits and my goods. And I will say to my soul, "Soul, you have much goods laid up for many years; take your ease, eat, drink, and be merry.'" But God said to him, 'You fool, this night your soul shall be required of you. Then whose shall those things be, which you have provided?' So is he that lays up treasure for himself, and is not rich toward God."

Then turning back to his disciples, he taught them. "Therefore, I say unto you, take no thought for your life, what you shall eat; neither for the body, what you shall put on. The life is more than food, and the body is more than clothing. Consider the ravens, for they neither sow nor reap, which neither have storehouse nor barn, and God feeds them. How much more are you better than the fowls? And which of you, by taking thought, can add to his height or length of life one measure? If you then are not able to do that which is least, why take thought for the rest? Consider the lilies how they grow; they toil not, they spin not, and yet I say unto you, that Solomon in all his glory was not arrayed like one of these. If, then, God has so clothed the grass, which is today in the field, and tomorrow is cast into the oven, how much more will he clothe you, Oh you of little faith? Seek not what you shall eat, or what you shall drink, neither be of doubtful mind. For all these things do the nations of the world seek after, and your Father knows that you have need of these things. But, rather, seek the kingdom of God, and all these things shall be added unto you. Fear not, little flock, for it is your Father's good pleasure to *give* you the kingdom. Sell what you have, and give alms; provide yourselves bags which become not old, a treasure in the heavens that fails not, where no thief approaches, neither moth corrupts. For where your treasure is, there will your heart be also."

He paused briefly, considering how to proceed, then encouraged them, saying, "Let your loins be girded about, and your lights burning; and be like men waiting for their lord to return from the wedding; that when he comes and knocks, they may open to him immediately. Blessed are those servants, whom the lord, when he comes, shall find watching. Truly I say unto you, that he shall gird himself, and make them to sit down to food, and will come forth and serve them. And if he shall come in the second watch, or come in the third watch, and find them so, blessed are those servants. And this know, that if the good man of the house had known what hour the thief would come, he would have watched, and not have allowed his house to be broken into. Be, therefore, ready also, for the Son of man comes at an hour when you think not."

Then Peter said to him, "Lord, do you speak this parable to us, or even to all?"

And Jesus said to him and to all, "Who then is that faithful and wise steward, whom his lord shall make ruler over his household to give them their portion of food in due season? Blessed is that servant, whom his lord when he comes shall find so doing. Of a truth, I say unto you that he will make him ruler over all that he has. But if that servant says in his heart, 'My lord delays his coming,' and shall begin to beat the menservants and maidens, and to eat and drink, and to be drunken; the lord of that servant will come in a day when he looks not for him, and at an hour when he is not aware, and will cut him asunder, and will appoint him his portion with the unbelievers. And that servant, which knew his lord's will, and prepared not himself, neither did according to his will, shall be beaten with many stripes. But he that knew not, and did commit things worthy of stripes, shall be beaten with few stripes. For unto whom much is given, of him shall be much required, and to whom men have committed much, of him they will ask the more."

When Jesus had said these words, he paused, and glanced again at the religious leaders; then he continued with passion, saying, "I have come to send fire on the earth, and what do I care if it be already kindled? But I have a baptism to be baptized with, and am hard-pressed till it be accomplished! Do you suppose that I have come to give peace on earth? I tell you, no; but, rather, division, for from henceforth there shall be five in one house divided, three against two, and two against three. The father shall be divided against the son, and the son against the father; the mother against the daughter, and the daughter against the mother; the mother-in-law against her daughter-in-law, and the daughter-in-law against her mother-in-law."

His last words echoed those of Micah, which told of 'the day of the watchmen and the visitation,' when the Messiah would come; so Jesus turned again in the direction of the religious leaders, though his focus was still on the crowd. "When you see a cloud rise out of the west, straightway you say, 'There comes a shower,' and so it is. And when you see the south wind blow, you say, 'There will be heat,' and it comes to pass. You hypocrites, you can discern the face of the sky and of the earth, but how is it that you do not discern this time?"

After asking this question, he looked directly at the religious leaders, who lingered at the back of the crowd; they recognized the reference to Micah, and felt the full weight of his criticism.

Then looking back at the crowd, he continued, "Yes, and why do you not judge *for yourselves* what is right?"

"When you go with your adversary," he said, putting his hand up to signify the religious leaders, "and are taken to the magistrate; when you are still in the way, give diligence that you may be delivered from him, lest he hails you to the judge, and the judge delivers you to the officer, and the officer casts you into prison. I tell you, you shall not depart from there, till you have paid the very last amount."

At his comments, some of the religious leaders, wishing to make Jesus and his disciples out to be the adversaries, reminded him of the Galileans, whose blood Pilate had mingled with their sacrifices. They told him this also to see his reaction to the execution of his countrymen, for they believed their executions were justified, and hoped to incite him into some incriminating words toward Pilate.

But Jesus, answering, said to them, "Do you suppose that *these* Galileans were sinners above all the Galileans, because they suffered such things? I tell you, no; but, except you repent, *you* shall all likewise perish! Or those eighteen, upon whom the tower in Siloam fell and slew them: do you think that *they* were sinners above all men that dwelled in Jerusalem? I tell you, no; but, except you repent, *you* shall all likewise perish."

This comment was not lost on Mary, Jesus's mother, for Joseph had died in this tragedy. She was somewhat comforted by his remarks, which somehow briefly realigned her and her son against the judgmental and unsympathetic religious leaders. She looked at her son with pride, but he did not avert his eyes from the religious leaders, though he felt her gaze.

Instead, he spoke to them this parable. "A certain man had a fig tree planted in his vineyard; and he came and sought fruit from it, and found none. Then he said to the dresser of his vineyard, 'Behold, these three years I have come seeking fruit from this fig tree, and found none. Cut it down. Why should it render the ground unproductive?' And his vinedresser, answering, said to him, 'Lord, let it alone this year also, till I shall dig about it, and dung it, and if it bears fruit, well, but if not, then after that you shall cut it down.'"

At the conclusion of this parable, the religious leaders, recognizing that it presented a thoroughly damning evaluation of their ministry, departed from the encampment at Bethabara in anger.

As they departed, they could hear the words of Jesus beckoning the crowd, "Come unto *me*, all you who labor and are heavy laden, and *I* will give you rest. Take my yoke upon you, and learn of me; for I am meek and lowly in heart: and you shall find rest unto your souls. For my yoke is easy, and my burden is light."

These words, in stark contrast to the heavy burdens imposed on the people by the religious leaders, answered also those harsh words spoken by Rehoboam after the death of his father, Solomon, "My father made your yoke heavy, and I will add to your yoke: my father also chastised you with whips, but I will chastise you with scorpions." Jesus's words promised a more gracious form of leadership, that of a servant leader, and one characterized by mercy rather than sacrifice. They were words of reconciliation in the face of those that had ultimately divided the nation.

This time, the people remained; the religious leaders were not accompanied in their departure.

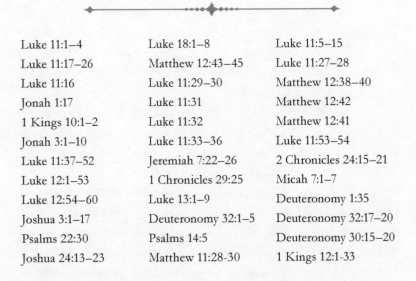

Luke 11:1–4	Luke 18:1–8	Luke 11:5–15
Luke 11:17–26	Matthew 12:43–45	Luke 11:27–28
Luke 11:16	Luke 11:29–30	Matthew 12:38–40
Jonah 1:17	Luke 11:31	Matthew 12:42
1 Kings 10:1–2	Luke 11:32	Matthew 12:41
Jonah 3:1–10	Luke 11:33–36	Luke 11:53–54
Luke 11:37–52	Jeremiah 7:22–26	2 Chronicles 24:15–21
Luke 12:1–53	1 Chronicles 29:25	Micah 7:1–7
Luke 12:54–60	Luke 13:1–9	Deuteronomy 1:35
Joshua 3:1–17	Deuteronomy 32:1–5	Deuteronomy 32:17–20
Psalms 22:30	Psalms 14:5	Deuteronomy 30:15–20
Joshua 24:13–23	Matthew 11:28-30	1 Kings 12:1-33

Chapter 46

FEAST OF DEDICATION

Jesus returned to the house of Simon the leper, one of the chief Pharisees, whom Jesus had healed. There, Jesus and the twelve ate with Simon's family and friends. Among those in attendance sat several religious leaders, who observed Jesus carefully, for it was the Sabbath day. Now there was a certain man among Simon's guests that suffered from dropsy, an acute swelling in his lower legs. When Jesus saw the man's condition, he felt compassion toward him, and desired to heal him. Knowing, however, the mind-set of Simon's guests, he decided to use the opportunity to minister to them, as well.

So Jesus questioned the lawyers and Pharisees, saying, "Is it lawful to heal on the Sabbath day?"

But they held their peace, for Simon's sake, not wanting to start an argument.

Then Jesus took the man, and healed him, releasing him from his infirmity, saying, "Which of you shall have an ass or an ox fallen into a pit, and will not immediately pull him out on the Sabbath day?"

But they had no answer for him to these things, either.

When Jesus noticed how those invited had chosen the chief seats at the table, he instructed them, saying, "When you are invited to a wedding, sit not down in the highest place nor choose the uppermost room, lest someone more honorable than yourself is also invited; and the host brings them, saying to you, 'Give this man your place,' and you begin with shame to take a lower seat or lower room. But when you are invited, choose the lowest room and sit down in the lowest seat, that when the host comes, he may say to you, 'Friend, go up higher.' Then shall you have worship in the presence of them that attend the wedding and sit at the meal with you. For whoever exalts himself shall be abased, and he that humbles himself shall be exalted."

Simon's guests, when hearing his instruction, began to debate his teaching. For many said that the moving of guests at feasts and weddings was not a common practice. But the debate ended, when one guest, a man named Samuel, who owned several inns, which were rented for such occasions, corroborated the practice.

"The Lord is correct in his assessment of my business," Samuel said, receiving a nod from Jesus, "for oftentimes this happens, especially when an important guest decides at the last minute to attend unannounced. If I am to continue to receive business from the most prestigious of clients, I must make accommodation to their needs."

Jesus smiled at the man, who sat quietly after having quelled the debate.

Then Jesus said also to Simon, his host, "When you make a dinner or a supper, call not your friends, nor your brethren, neither your kinsmen, nor your rich neighbors; lest they also invite you again, and a repayment be made to you. But when you make a feast, call the poor, the maimed, the lame, and the blind; and you shall be blessed, for they cannot repay you, and you shall be repaid at the resurrection of the just."

Now Lazarus, Simon's son, sat at dinner with him, and when he heard these things, he said, "Blessed is he that shall eat bread in the kingdom of God."

Lazarus was following in his father's footsteps, preparing himself to join the Jewish leadership among the Pharisees. Though he saw that his father had been healed of leprosy, he did not actually witness the healing. In fact, he had never seen any of the healings or miracles that Jesus was reported to have performed—until now, on the Sabbath. He had, however, listened to Jesus teaching—often. He had spoken to Jesus one-on-one, asking him questions, and had received from him provocative answers. But Lazarus struggled with the teachings of Jesus, being influenced heavily by his Pharisaic teachings. He was, in essence, being tutored by two often opposing teachers, while also being counseled by his father. Up until recently, his future seemed clear; he would become a leader in the community following the Pharisaic teachings, and inherit his father's wealth, which was, in fact, considerable. Now, with the addition of the teachings of Jesus, Lazarus stood at a crossroads of sorts. And, as such, he often found himself, as did his father, wanting to keep the peace between the Pharisees and Jesus. Lazarus's comment, about eating in the kingdom of God, was meant to do just that.

But Jesus was unconcerned with their efforts of keeping the peace; answering Lazarus's comment, he taught them, instead, saying, "But which of you, having a servant plowing or feeding cattle, will say to him by and by, when he has come from the field, 'Go and sit down to food?' And will not rather say to him, 'Make ready so that I may eat; gird yourself, and serve me, till I have eaten and drunken, and afterward you shall eat and drink?' Does he thank that servant, because he did the things that were commanded him? I think not. So likewise you, when you shall have done all those things which are commanded you, say, 'We are unprofitable servants, for we have done that which was our duty to do.'"

At these words, the religious leaders took offense, and began to mock him.

And when the Pharisees demanded of him when, in his estimation, the kingdom of God should come, he answered them and said, "The kingdom of God comes not with observation: neither shall they say, 'Lo here! or, lo there!' for, behold, the kingdom of God is within you."

His words dumbfounded them, for his interpretation was so foreign to their own understanding. His adversaries were reduced to a brief period of muffled laughter, followed by confused silence. They waited upon him for further explanation.

Jesus passed over his own frustration with them, teaching them further with a parable. "A certain man made a great supper, and invited many, and sent his servant at suppertime to say to those invited, 'Come, for all things are now ready.' But they all, with one consent, began to make excuses. The first said to him, 'I have bought a piece of ground, and I must go and see it. I pray you, have me excused.' And another said, 'I have bought five yoke of oxen, and I must go to prove them. I pray you, have me excused.' And another said, 'I have married a wife, and, therefore, I cannot come.' So the servant came, and explained to his lord these things. Then the master of the house, being angry, said to his servant, 'Go out quickly into the streets and lanes of the city, and bring in the poor, and the maimed, and the lame, and the blind.' And the servant returned and said, 'Lord, it is done as you have commanded, and yet there is room.' And the lord said to the servant, 'Go out into the highways and byways, and compel everyone to come in, that my house may be filled. For I say unto you, that none of those men which were invited shall taste of my supper.'"

At this apparent rebuff, the room grew embarrassingly silent, and the faces of Simon and Lazarus reddened. Jesus rose and graciously thanked his host for the meal. Then he excused himself, and departed.

Lazarus's struggle intensified each time Jesus saw fit to berate his colleagues. He was trying, somehow, to incorporate Jesus's teachings into the established order of things, but finding it increasingly difficult to do so. This latest rebuff left him quite bewildered, and on the verge of rejecting Jesus's teachings.

Now it was some three months after the Feast of Tabernacles, in winter, when Jesus went back to Jerusalem for the Feast of the Dedication. And as he walked in the temple, in Solomon's porch, there came to him the Jewish religious leaders, many of whom had dined with him at Simon's house, though neither Simon nor Lazarus was with them. These men encircled Jesus round about, and said to him, "How long do you make us to doubt? If you are the Messiah, tell us plainly."

Jesus answered them, "I told you, and you believed not; the works that I do in my Father's name, they bear witness of me. But you believe not, because you are not of my sheep, as I said to you. My sheep hear my voice, and I know them, and they follow me, and I give unto them eternal life, and they shall never perish, neither shall any man pluck them out of my hand. My Father, who gave them to me, is greater than all, and no man is able to pluck them out of my Father's hand. I and my Father are one."

Then the Jewish leaders took up stones, again, to stone him. Peter and the twelve maneuvered themselves defensively between Jesus and his adversaries, bearing their own stones.

Jesus stood his ground, and answered them, "Many good works have I shown you from my Father; for which of those works do you stone me?"

The leaders answered him, saying, "For a good work we stone you not, but for blasphemy, because that *you*, being a *man*, make yourself *God*."

Jesus answered them, "Is it not written in your Law, 'I said, you are gods?' If *he* called them gods, unto whom the word of God came, and the scripture cannot be broken, say you of *him*, whom the Father has sanctified, and sent into the world, 'You blaspheme,' because I said, 'I am the Son of God?' If I do not the works of my Father, believe me not. But if I *do*, though you believe not me, believe the works, that you may know, and believe, that the Father is in me, and I in him."

For these words, also, the leaders sought again to take him, but he escaped out of their hand, being ushered away by his disciples. And he went again, beyond Jordan, to Bethabara, the place where John first baptized; and there he dwelled with his disciples. Many people went to him, there, remembering the words that John had spoken concerning him.

And they discussed John's words among themselves, saying, "John did no miracle, but all things that John spoke of this man were true."

And many believed in him, there.

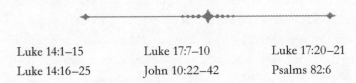

Luke 14:1–15	Luke 17:7–10	Luke 17:20–21
Luke 14:16–25	John 10:22–42	Psalms 82:6

Chapter 47

ENCAMPMENT AT BETHABARA

As they journeyed to Bethabara, there went great multitudes with
him, and he turned, and said to them, "If anyone comes to me,
and hates not his father, and mother, and wife, and children, and
brothers, and sisters; yes, and his own life also, he cannot be my
disciple. And whoever does not bear his cross, and come after me,
cannot be my disciple. For which of you, intending to build a tower,
sits not down first, and counts the cost, whether he has sufficient
funds to finish it? Lest haply, after he has laid the foundation, and
is not able to finish it, all that behold it will begin to mock him,
saying, 'This man began to build, and was not able to finish.' Or
what king, going to make war against another king, sits not down
first, and consults whether he is able with ten thousand to meet
him that comes against him with twenty thousand? Or else, while
the other is yet a great way off, he sends an ambassador, and desires
conditions of peace. So likewise, whoever of you that forsakes not
all that he has, cannot be my disciple. Salt is good, but if the salt has
lost its savor, with what shall it be seasoned? It is neither fit for the
land, nor yet for the dunghill; but men cast it out. He that has ears
to hear, let him hear!"

When they arrived at Bethabara, they encamped there, and
many of the tax collectors and sinners drew also near to him to hear

his words. A group of Pharisees and scribes followed him, as well, at a distance, and Lazarus was numbered among them.

As the Pharisees and scribes drew near to Jesus, they murmured among themselves, saying, "This man receives sinners, and eats with them."

And Jesus spoke this parable to them, saying, "What man of you, having a hundred sheep, if he loses one of them, does not leave the ninety-nine in the wilderness, and go after that which is lost, until he finds it? And when he has found it, he lays it on his shoulders, rejoicing. And when he comes home, he calls together his friends and neighbors, saying to them, 'Rejoice with me, for I have found my sheep which was lost.' I say unto you, that, likewise, joy shall be in heaven over one sinner that repents, more than over ninety-nine just persons, which need no repentance. Or what woman having ten pieces of her wedding silver, if she loses one piece, does not light a candle, and sweep the house, and seek diligently till she finds it? And when she has found it, she calls her friends and her neighbors together, saying, 'Rejoice with me, for I have found the piece which I had lost.' Likewise, I say unto you, there is joy in the presence of the angels of God over one sinner that repents."

Then, instructing them still further, he told them another parable. "A certain man had two sons, and the younger of them said to his father, 'Father, give me the portion of goods that falls to me.' So the father divided unto them his living. Not many days afterward, the younger son gathered all his inheritance together, and took his journey into a far country, and there wasted his substance with riotous living. Now, when he had spent all that he had, there arose a mighty famine in that land, and he began to be in want. He went, therefore, and joined himself to a citizen of that country, who sent him into his fields to feed swine. His hunger became so great that he longed to fill his belly with the husks that the swine were eating; still, no one gave him any. When he came to his senses, he said to himself, 'How many hired servants of my father have bread enough and to spare, yet I perish with hunger! I will arise and go to my father, and will say to him, "Father, I have sinned against heaven, and before you, and am no more worthy to be called your son; make me as one of your hired servants.'" So he arose, and came to his father. But when he was yet a great way off, his father saw him, and had compassion upon him. He ran to him, and fell upon his neck, kissing him. Then the son said to him, 'Father, I have sinned against heaven, and in your sight, and am no more worthy to be called your son.' But the father said to his servants, 'Bring forth the best robe, and put it on him, and put a ring on his hand, and shoes on his feet. Bring here the fatted calf, and kill it. Let us eat, and be merry, for this my son was dead, and is alive again. He was lost, and is found.' And they began to be merry. Now his elder son was in the field, and as he came and drew near to the house, he heard music and dancing. So he called one of the servants, and asked what these things meant. And the servant answered him, 'Your brother has come home; and your father has killed the fatted calf, because he has received him safe and sound.' But the older son became angry, and would not enter in. So his father came out to him, and pleaded with him. But the son answered his father, 'Lo, these many years I have served you, neither transgressed I at any time your commandment, and yet you never gave me even a kid that I might make merry with my friends. But as soon as this, your son, has come; who has devoured your living with harlots, you have killed for him the fatted calf.' Then the father said to him, 'Son, you are at all times with me, and all that I have is yours. But to be merry and rejoice is appropriate, for this, your brother, was dead, and is alive again; he was lost, and is found.'"

At his words, the Pharisees became silent, and withdrew themselves again, some distance from him.

When he had finished teaching the Pharisees directly, he turned also to his disciples, saying, "There was a certain rich man, who had a steward, and this man was accused of wasting his goods. So he called him, and said to him, 'How is it that I hear this of you? Give an account of your stewardship, for you may no longer be steward.' Then the steward said within himself, 'What shall I do, for my lord takes away from me the stewardship? To dig is not my strength. To beg, I am ashamed. I am resolved what to do, that, when I am put out of the stewardship, they may receive me into their houses.' So he called every one of his lord's debtors to him, and said unto the first, 'How much do you owe to my lord?' And he answered him, 'A hundred measures of oil.' So the steward said to him, 'Take your bill, and sit down quickly, and write fifty.' Then the steward said to another, 'And how much do you owe?' And he answered, 'A hundred measures of wheat.' So the steward said to him, 'Take your bill, and write eighty.' And the lord commended the unjust steward, because he had done wisely, for the children of this world are in their *generation* wiser than the children of light. And I say unto you, make to yourselves friends by the false riches of unrighteousness; that, when *you* fail, they may receive you into everlasting habitations. He that is faithful in that which is least is faithful also in much. And he that is unjust in the least is unjust also in much. If, therefore, you have not been faithful in the false riches of the unrighteous, who will commit to your trust the true riches? And if you have not been faithful in that which is another man's, who shall give to you that which is your own? No slave can serve two masters, for either he will hate the one, and love the other, or else he will hold to the one, and despise the other. You cannot be enslaved to God and false riches."

And the Pharisees also, who were covetous, heard all these things, and they ridiculed him, for they did not understand his teaching.

So Jesus answered their ridicule, teaching them further, "You justify yourselves before men, but God knows your hearts, for that which is highly esteemed among men is abomination in the sight of God."

But the Pharisees were offended at both his words and his followers; and seeking to justify their desire to separate themselves from them, they asked him, "Is it lawful for a man to put away his wife for every cause?"

Jesus answered, and said to them, "The Law and the Prophets were until John: since that time the kingdom of God is preached, and every man presses into it. And it is easier for heaven and earth to pass away, than for one dot written in the Law to fail." He asked them, therefore, "What did Moses command you?"

And they said, "Moses permitted to write a bill of divorcement, and to put her away."

Then he answered them, "Have you not read, that he which made them at the beginning of the creation made them male and female, and said, 'For this cause shall a man leave father and mother, and shall cleave to his wife, and they two shall become one flesh?' So then, they are no more two, but one flesh. What, therefore, God has joined together, let not man put asunder."

They said to him, "Why, then, did Moses command to give a writing of divorcement, and to put her away?"

He said to them, "Moses, because of the hardness of your hearts, wrote you this precept, allowing you to put away your wives: but from the beginning it was not so. And I say unto you, whoever puts away his wife, except it be for fornication, and marries another, commits adultery; and whoever marries her that is put away from her husband commits adultery."

This Jesus spoke concerning the recent practice of the Jewish leaders whereby they cast out his followers from their synagogues. His answer silenced his adversaries, and his disciples took this opportunity to ask him privately about the matter.

Answering them, he repeated his words to emphasize their significance, "Whoever shall put away his wife, and marry another, commits adultery against her."

Then his disciples said to him, "If the case of the man be so with his wife, it is not good to marry."

Knowing they still did not understand, he added, "And if a

woman shall put away her husband, and be married to another, she commits adultery."

When he had added this last statement, they understood that he spoke to them of more than the Law of Moses, for Moses provided no legal means for a woman to divorce her husband. Though no one asked him anything more, Jesus could see that they were beginning to understand his meaning was not literal.

So he explained to them, "All cannot receive this saying, save they to whom it is given. For there are some eunuchs, which were so born from their mother's womb, and there are some eunuchs, which were made eunuchs of men, and there are eunuchs, which have made themselves eunuchs for the kingdom of heaven's sake. He that is able to receive it, let him receive it."

When they heard his explanation, they understood that his message to the Pharisees was not one of literal marriage between a man and woman, but of the relationship between God's leaders and those whom God had entrusted them to lead. Because all are not called to lead, not all can receive his saying. His statement concerning a woman divorcing her husband now made sense to them, in light of the disparity between the old leadership of the Pharisees, scribes, and temple priests, and the new leadership Jesus was establishing in his disciples.

After sharing these things privately with the twelve, Jesus took notice of the young man Lazarus, who stood there contrasted among the older religious leaders. Having compassion upon him, he spoke to him a parable.

"There was a certain rich man," said Jesus, scrutinizing Lazarus and his attire, "who was clothed in purple and fine linen, and fared sumptuously every day."

At his words, Lazarus blushed, reluctantly looking down at his purple robe. Jesus instantly had his full attention.

"And there was a certain beggar, named *Lazarus*," Jesus continued, "who was laid at his gate, full of sores, and desiring to be fed with the crumbs which fell from the rich man's table."

At this startling juxtaposition of characters, Lazarus grew even redder in the face, as his colleagues looked back and forth between him and Jesus, wondering where this story was going.

"Moreover," Jesus added, as embellishment to the story, "the dogs came and licked his sores!

"And it came to pass," he continued, "that the beggar died, and was carried by the angels into Abraham's bosom. The rich man also died, and was buried; and in hell he lifted up his eyes, being in torment, and saw Abraham afar off, and Lazarus in his bosom. And he cried and said, 'Father Abraham, have mercy on me, and send Lazarus, that he may dip the tip of his finger in water, and cool my tongue, for I am tormented in this flame.' But Abraham said, 'Son, remember that you in your lifetime received your good things, and likewise Lazarus evil things. But now he is comforted, and you are tormented. And beside all this, between us and you there is a great gulf fixed: so that they who would pass from here to you cannot; neither can they pass to us, who would come from there.' Then the man answered Abraham, 'I pray you therefore, father, that you would send him to my father's house, for I have five brothers, that he may testify unto them, lest they also come into this place of torment.' Abraham said to him, 'They have Moses and the prophets; let them hear them.' And he said, 'No, father Abraham: but if one went to them from the dead, they will repent.' But Abraham said to him, 'If they hear not Moses and the prophets, neither would they be persuaded, though one rose from the dead.'"

When Jesus concluded his parable, the Pharisees, rallying around Lazarus, left the encampment. They discussed the parables that Jesus spoke to them that day, not understanding them, fully. The last parable, however, tormented Lazarus continually, for he struggled greatly afterward concerning what path he should take— one of humility or one of affluence.

John 10:39–42

Luke 16:1–15

Luke 16:16–17

Luke 16:18

Mark 10:12

Deuteronomy 24:1

Luke 14:25–35

Mark 10:1–2

Mark 10:3–9

Mark 10:10–11

Matthew 19:11–12

Luke 15:1–32

Matthew 19:1–3

Matthew 19:4–9

Matthew 19:10

Luke 16:19–34

Chapter 48

SYNAGOGUES SURROUNDING JERUSALEM

The encampment at Bethabara had become a vibrant community of sorts. Villagers from across the Jordan River, from Galilee, Samaria, and Judea, came there daily to hear Jesus speak. And they brought infants to Jesus, so that he would put his hands upon them and pray for them. Now when his disciples saw it, they rebuked those who brought them.

But when Jesus saw what his disciples did, he was very displeased, and called them to him, saying, "Allow the little children to come unto me, and forbid them not, for of such is the kingdom of God. Truly, I say unto you, whoever shall not receive the kingdom of God as a little child, he shall in no way enter therein."

And he took the children up in his arms, and laid his hands upon them, and blessed them.

Then, using Bethabara as a base camp from which to minister, he departed from there, teaching in a nearby synagogue on the Sabbath. And, behold, a woman there, who had a spirit of infirmity eighteen years, was bowed down, and could no longer lift herself up.

When Jesus saw her, he called her to him, and said to her, "Woman, you are released from your infirmity."

Then he laid his hands on her, and immediately she was made straight, and glorified God.

But the ruler of the synagogue answered with indignation, because Jesus had healed on the Sabbath day, and said to the people, "There are six days in which men ought to work: in *them*, therefore, come and be healed, and not on the Sabbath day."

Jesus, then, answered him, and said, "You hypocrite, does not each one of you on the Sabbath release his ox or his ass from the stall, and lead him away to watering? And ought not this woman, being a daughter of Abraham, whom Satan has bound, lo, these eighteen years, be released from her bonds on the Sabbath day?"

When he had said these things, his adversaries were ashamed, and all the people rejoiced for the glorious things that were done by him.

Then he said to his disciples, "Unto what is the kingdom of God like? And to what shall I compare it? It is like a grain of mustard seed, which a man took, and cast into his garden, and it grew, and became a great tree; and the fowls of the air lodged in the branches of it." And again he said, "To what shall I liken the kingdom of God? It is like leaven, which a woman took and hid in three measures of meal, till the whole was leavened."

His disciples remembered the saying from Jesus's earlier teaching, and understood: though the kingdom is founded upon faith, it will grow so large that hypocrisy and demons will infiltrate its borders.

And he went through the cities and villages of Judea, teaching, and journeying closer and closer to Jerusalem.

As he went along the way, Lazarus, seeking to relieve the torment regarding his decision, came running to him. And he kneeled down before him, asking, "Good Master, what good thing shall I do, that I may inherit eternal life?"

And Jesus said to him, "Why do you call me good? There is none good but one, that is, God. But *you* know the commandments; if you will enter into life, keep the commandments."

Lazarus, seeking to justify himself, said to him, "Which?"

Jesus answered him unsympathetically, "You shall do no murder, you shall not commit adultery, you shall not steal, you shall not bear false witness, honor your father and mother." Then Jesus paused, and with obvious irritation in his voice, summarized, "You shall love your neighbor as yourself."

The young man ignored Jesus's irritability toward his line of questioning; pushing forward, he said to him, "Master, all these have I observed from my youth. What, yet, do I lack?"

Then Jesus, considering the young man's earnest struggle more closely, loved him, and said to him enthusiastically, "One thing you lack, if you will be *perfect*: go your way; sell whatever you have, and give to the poor, and you shall have treasure in heaven: and come, take up the cross, and follow me."

But, Lazarus, when he heard his answer, went away grieving, for being very rich, he had hoped he could follow Jesus without having to give up his great wealth.

When Jesus saw that he was very sorrowful, he looked round about, viewing the multitude of the poor that had gathered to him, and he said to his disciples, "How hardly shall they that have riches enter into the kingdom of God!"

And the disciples were astonished at his words.

But Jesus answered again, and said to them, "Children, how hard is it for them that trust in riches to enter into the kingdom of God! It is easier for a camel to go through the eye of a needle, than for a rich man to enter into the kingdom of God."

They were astonished beyond measure, saying among themselves, "Who then can be saved?"

But Jesus, looking upon them, said, "The things which are impossible with men are possible with God, for with God all things are possible!"

Then one of them asked, "Lord, are there few that will be saved?"

And he said to them, "Strive to enter in at the strait gate, for many, I say unto you, will seek to enter in, and shall not be able. When once the master of the house is risen up, and has shut the door, and you begin to stand without, and to knock at the door, saying, 'Lord, Lord, open unto us;' and he shall answer and say unto you, 'I know you not, from where you are:' then shall you begin to say, 'We have eaten and drunk in your presence, and you have taught in our streets.' But he shall say, 'I tell you, I know you not, from where you are; depart from me, all you workers of iniquity.' There shall be weeping and gnashing of teeth, when you shall see Abraham, and Isaac, and Jacob, and all the prophets, in the kingdom of God, and you yourselves thrust out. And they shall come from the east, and from the west, and from the north, and from the south, and shall sit down in the kingdom of God."

Then Peter said to him, signifying the twelve, "Behold, *we* have forsaken all, and have followed you. What shall we have, therefore?"

And Jesus answered, and said to them, "Truly, I say unto you, that you who have followed me; in the *regeneration*, when the Son of man shall sit in the throne of his glory; you also shall sit upon twelve thrones, judging the twelve tribes of Israel. And everyone who has forsaken houses, or brothers, or sisters, or father, or mother, or wife, or children, or lands, for my name's sake and the gospel's; shall receive a hundredfold now in this present time: houses, and brothers, and sisters, and mothers, and children, and lands, with persecutions, and in the world to come inherit eternal life. But many that are first shall be last, and the last shall be first."

Then he explained this last teaching further, in the form of a parable, saying, "For the kingdom of heaven is like unto a man that is a householder, who went out early in the morning to hire laborers into his vineyard. When he had agreed with the laborers for one denarius for the day, a small silver coin, he sent them into his vineyard. And he went out about the third hour, and saw others standing idle in the marketplace, and said to them, 'Go also into the vineyard, and whatever is right I will give to you.' And they went their way. Again, he went out about the sixth and ninth hour, and did likewise. And about the eleventh hour he went out, and found others standing idle, and said to them, 'Why do you stand here all the day idle?' They said to him, 'Because no man has hired us.' He said to them, 'Go also into the vineyard, and whatever is right, that shall you receive.' So when evening was come, the lord of the vineyard said to his steward, 'Call the laborers, and give them their hire, beginning from the last unto the first.' And when they came that were hired about the eleventh hour, they received every man one denarius. But when the first came, they supposed that they should have received more, and they likewise received every man one denarius. And when they had received it, they murmured against the good man of the house, saying, 'These last have worked but one hour, and you have made them equal unto us, who have borne the burden and heat of the day.' But he answered one of them, and said, 'Friend, I do you no wrong: didn't you agree with me for one denarius for the day? Take what is yours, and go your way: I will give to this last, even as to you. Isn't it lawful for me to do what I will with my own? Is your eye evil, because I am good?' So the last shall be first, and the first last, for many are called, but few chosen."

The same day, there came certain of the Pharisees to the encampment, threatening him, so that he would leave the area, for they feared the growing influence he had over the people. Now Bethabara was in Perea, the tetrarchy of Herod Antipas, which lay along the eastern border of the Jordan River; these Pharisees, therefore, came to Jesus, saying, "Get out, and depart from here, for Herod will kill you."

But Jesus answered them, in defiance, "*You* go, and tell that fox, 'Behold, I cast out devils, and I do cures today and tomorrow, and the third day I shall be perfected.' Nevertheless, I must walk today, and tomorrow, and the day following, for it cannot be that a prophet perishes outside of Jerusalem. Oh Jerusalem, Jerusalem, which kills the prophets, and stones them that are sent unto you, how often would I have gathered your children together, as a hen does gather her brood under her wings, and you would not! Behold, your house is left unto you desolate, and truly I say unto you, you shall not see me, until the time comes when you shall say, 'Blessed is he that comes in the name of the Lord.'"

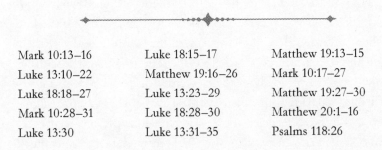

Mark 10:13–16	Luke 18:15–17	Matthew 19:13–15
Luke 13:10–22	Matthew 19:16–26	Mark 10:17–27
Luke 18:18–27	Luke 13:23–29	Matthew 19:27–30
Mark 10:28–31	Luke 18:28–30	Matthew 20:1–16
Luke 13:30	Luke 13:31–35	Psalms 118:26

Chapter 49

RAISING LAZARUS AT BETHANY

Now Lazarus found the thought of giving away his wealth unbearable. Still being tormented by Jesus's parable, however, he began to fast and pray over the path he should take for his future. His fasting made him weak physically, which eventually made him sick. So determined was he that he should receive an answer directly from God that he vowed not to eat again until he received one. Simon understood his son's torment, and prayed continually that God would grant him his request. Martha, who could not comprehend her brother's stubbornness or her father's lack of concern for his son's health, sent for Mary, who returned home to help Martha plead with their brother. They believed that Jesus was the Messiah, and they knew that their father did, as well. They also saw how close Lazarus had become to Jesus; in fact, they envied the relationship their brother had with him. Despite their insistent counsel, however, Lazarus refused to go to him again.

Therefore, his sisters sent word to Jesus, saying, "Lord, behold, the friend whom you love is sick."

When Jesus heard their message, he said to the messengers, in the hearing of his disciples, "This sickness is not unto death, but for the glory of God, that the Son of God might be glorified thereby!"

For this reason, though Jesus loved Martha and her sister, and

Lazarus; when he heard that he was sick, he remained in Bethabara two days longer.

Then on the morning of the third day, he said to his disciples, "Let us go into Judea again."

His disciples murmured among themselves; then Judas Iscariot said to him, "Master, the Jews of late sought to stone you, and you will go there, again?"

Jesus answered him, "Are there not twelve hours in the day? If any man walks in the day, he stumbles not, because he sees the light of this world. But if a man walks in the night, he stumbles, because there is no light in him." Then he said to them all, "Our friend Lazarus sleeps, but I go that I may wake him from that sleep."

Then his disciples said, "Lord, if he sleeps, he shall do well."

Jesus spoke to them concerning his death, but they thought that he meant he was recuperating through sleep.

Then Jesus said to them plainly, "Lazarus is dead! And I am glad for your sakes that I was not there, to the intent that you may believe; nevertheless, let us go to him."

Then Thomas said to his fellow disciples, "Let us also go, that we may die with him."

He said this jokingly, but they all understood the truth behind his words; Jesus's latest clashes with the religious leaders were enraging them to the point of desperation, and the twelve all knew it.

When Jesus drew near to their house in Bethany, he was told that Lazarus had lain in the grave four days already. Now Bethany was near to Jerusalem, less than two miles away, and many of the religious Jews came from there to Martha and Mary to comfort them concerning their brother. Martha, as soon as she heard that Jesus was coming, went and met him, but Mary sat still in the house with their guests.

Then Martha said to Jesus, "Lord, if you had been here, my brother would not have died. But I know that even now, whatever you will ask of God, God will give it to you."

This she said to him, hoping beyond hope that Jesus would bring him back to life.

Jesus confirmed to her, "Your brother shall rise again."

Martha, not wanting to misunderstand his meaning, and trying to buffer herself from disappointment, said to him, "I know that he shall rise again, in the resurrection, at the last day."

Jesus grasped her by the shoulders, looking her directly in the eyes, and said to her, "I am the resurrection, and the life; he that believes in me, though he were dead, yet shall he live, and whoever lives and believes in me shall never die." He studied her expression, and then asked, "Do you believe this?"

Martha's heart leapt, for his answer confirmed her hope that he would bring her brother back to life. She said to him, "Yes, Lord: I believe that you are the Messiah, the Son of God, who was to come into the world!"

And when she had said so, she went away quickly, and called Mary, her sister, secretly, saying, "The Master has come, and calls for you."

When Mary heard these words, she arose quickly and came to him. Now Jesus was not yet come into the town, but remained in the place where Martha met him.

The Jewish mourners, then, who were with Mary in the house to comfort her, when they saw her rise up hastily and go out, followed her, saying, "She goes to the grave to weep, there."

Then, when Mary came to where Jesus was, and saw him, she fell down at his feet, saying, "Lord, if you had been here, my brother would not have died."

When Jesus, therefore, saw her weeping, and the Jews also weeping that came with her, he groaned in the Spirit, and was troubled.

And he said to them, "Where have you laid him?"

They said to him, "Lord, come and see."

When Jesus saw the tomb, he was overcome with the monumental task at hand. In that moment, he saw his own physical end laid out before him: rejection from the religious leaders and harsh treatment from the Romans, leading to crucifixion and burial. As much as he tried to prepare himself for the ordeal that lay ahead, he despised the inevitability of his surrender to these evil men and their intentions. And then there was the spiritual implications he feared most, separation from the Father, for he knew this was coming. When he took upon himself the sins of the world, he knew his Father would turn away from him briefly, but this, he knew, would be the worst thing he must endure. Seeing Lazarus's tomb brought this rushing into his mind, vividly. He saw his own image, broken, naked, and humiliated, hanging upon a cross, and he knew for certain that all would forsake him. He dropped to the ground over the weight of this realization, and he wept.

Those around him understood none of this. They misunderstood his anguish as mere grieving over the loss of a friend. Some wondered if he wept out of frustration that he hadn't prevented his death.

The mourners said, "Behold how he loved him!" Others added, "Could not this man, who opened the eyes of the blind, have caused that even this man should not have died?"

Their words revived him, and he looked up at the mourners with a mixture of pity, frustration, and anger.

"Let the *dead* bury the dead," he muttered to himself.

Then he groaned, again, within his spirit. In this humbled state, even now, the Father called upon him to serve him. Jesus recognized then that at the moment of his greatest service, when called upon to sacrifice himself to sin, he would be alone—as he was now among so many people. Only, then, even the Father would abandon him. But the Father was with him now, and drawing upon his strength, Jesus rose to his feet and strode purposefully nearer to the grave. It was a hewn-out cave with a large stone rolled before its mouth to seal it.

Jesus commanded them, "Take away the stone!"

At his command, several men from among the mourners, along with a few of his disciples, moved toward the tomb to comply.

But Martha said to him, "Lord, by this time he stinks, for he has been dead four days."

At her comments, the men halted, turning to await further instructions.

Jesus answered her, "Did I not say to you that if you would believe, you should see the glory of God?"

So the men removed the stone from its place before the cave, where the dead body of Lazarus was laid. And the stench was unbearable, so that they covered their noses, and quickly moved away to some distance from the opening. Jesus did not move. Neither did he cover his nose. He peered into the utter darkness of the cave, envisioning it as the very depths of hell itself.

Then he lifted his eyes toward heaven, saying in a loud voice, so all could hear him, "Father, I thank you that you have heard me. And I know that you hear me always, but, because of the people which stand by, I say it that they may believe that you have sent me."

Then he cried out with all the force of his voice, "Lazarus, come forth!"

His voice startled the somber mourners, many who had just arrived, and because of the lack of foliage in the surrounding area, the acoustics were such that his words echoed repeatedly. The mourners looked at one another in confused indignation over the apparent irreverence and insensitivity of his gesture at such a solemn occasion.

But when they looked, again, at the mouth of the open tomb, they beheld someone bound hand and foot in grave clothes with his face bound by a napkin. Gasps of air echoed, emanating from multiple sources around the cave, coming not from the apparent dead man, who stood before them, but from their own mouths. Their chests heaved as they tried to comprehend what their eyes were communicating to their too sluggish brains.

Jesus was still looking toward the heavens when he summoned Lazarus from his slumber. When he looked at the tomb, again, he saw an Israelite slave bound in Egyptian fetters. Then the vision passed, and he beheld Lazarus wrapped in swaddling cloths, the clothes of the dead.

Jesus broke the spell for all of them, commanding them, "Release him, and let him go!"

So the men who had removed the stone, and backed away because of the stench, returned to release Lazarus from his bonds, and welcome him back from the dead.

There was a great celebration that night at Simon's house. And many of the mourners, who had come from Jerusalem and different parts of Judea, who had witnessed the resurrection of Lazarus, believed in Jesus. But some of them went to the Pharisees, and told them what he had done.

While the believers at Simon's house celebrated, the chief priests and the Pharisees gathered to form a council, and said, "What shall we do? This man does many miracles. If we let him alone, all men will believe in him, and the Romans shall come and take away both our place and the nation."

And one of them, named Caiaphas, being the high priest that same year, said to them, "You know nothing at all, nor consider that it is expedient for us that one man should die for the people, that the whole nation perish not."

This he spoke not of himself: but being high priest that year, he prophesied that Jesus should die for the nation, and not for the nation only, but that he should gather together, in one, the children of God that were scattered abroad. From that day forward, they took counsel together to put him to death. Jesus left Simon's house, therefore, and walked no more openly among the Jews, but went from there to a region next to the wilderness, toward a city called Ephraim, and there he continued with his disciples. Now the Passover was approaching, so many went from that region up to Jerusalem, before the Passover, to purify themselves. While there, they sought Jesus, for they had accepted him into their community, many believing him to be the Messiah.

And as they stood in the temple, they spoke among themselves, speculating, "What do you think, that he will not come to the feast?"

This they said aloud, to aggravate the chief priests of the temple, who together with the Pharisees had issued a commandment: whoever knew the whereabouts of Jesus must tell them, so that they might take him.

John 11:1–57

Chapter 50

THROUGH JERICHO TO JERUSALEM

When Jesus had determined that it was time to go up to Jerusalem, he gathered the twelve together, and set out walking, as he had so many times before. As at other times, a multitude followed him, as well.

Now, along the way, he took the twelve aside, and said to them, "Behold, we go up to Jerusalem, and all things that are written by the prophets concerning the Son of man shall be accomplished."

When they heard this, they were overwhelmed by the magnitude of the moment, and they were shaken, fearing what was to come. So Jesus went before them, and as they followed; he explained again to them, "The Son of man shall be betrayed unto the chief priests and scribes, and they shall condemn him to death, and deliver him to the Gentiles to be mocked and spitefully entreated. They shall spit upon him, and scourge him, and put him to death by crucifixion, and the third day he shall rise again."

But their perspective was so clouded by their fear that they understood none of these things, for the importance of the resurrection in this saying was hid from them; neither could they comprehend the spiritual implications of the things that were spoken to them.

Then, fearing that all his disciples would be killed alongside

Jesus at Jerusalem, the mother of Zebedee's children came with her sons, worshiping Jesus, and desiring a certain thing of him.

And he said to her, "What is it that you want?"

She said to him, "Grant that these my two sons may sit, the one on your right hand, and the other on the left, in your kingdom."

But Jesus answered her, "You know not what you ask!"

Then James and John spoke up for themselves, saying to him directly, "Master, *we* would that you should do for us whatever *we* desire."

And he said to them, "What would *you* have me to do for you?"

Then they asked him again, for themselves, "Grant unto us that we may sit, one on your right hand, and the other on your left hand, in your glory."

But Jesus repeated to them, also, "You know not what you ask. Are you able to drink of the cup of which I drink, and be baptized with the baptism of which I am baptized?"

They looked at him earnestly, and said to him, "We are able."

Jesus smiled at their belief, and conceded, "You shall, indeed, drink of my cup, and be baptized with the baptism of which I am baptized, but to sit on my right hand and on my left is not mine to give, for it shall be given to them for whom it is prepared by my Father."

And when the ten heard their request, they were moved with indignation against James and John.

But Jesus called them to him, and said, "You know that they which are accounted to rule over the Gentiles exercise lordship over them; and their great ones exercise authority upon them. But it shall not be so among you: but whoever will be great among you, let him be your minister; and whoever will be chief among you, let him be the servant of all: even as the Son of man came not to be ministered unto, but to minister, and to give his life a ransom for many."

Now as he departed down the road, Jesus approached Jericho with his disciples and a great number of followers. There, a blind man named Bartimaeus, the son of Timaeus, sat with another blind man by the side of the road begging. And hearing the multitude pass by, Bartimaeus asked what it meant. And they told him that Jesus of Nazareth was passing by.

When he heard that Jesus was passing by, he began to cry out, and say, "Jesus, Son of David, have mercy on me."

And many charged him that he should hold his peace, but he cried a great deal more, shouting, "Son of David, have mercy on me."

Then he was joined by the other, and the two blind men cried out together, saying, "Have mercy on us, Oh Lord, Son of David."

And the multitude rebuked them both, because they thought they should hold their peace.

But their protests made the two men cry out even louder, yelling with all their might, "Have mercy on us, Oh Lord, Son of David."

Then Jesus, hearing them, stood still, and commanded them to be called.

And his disciples called the blind men, saying to them, "Be of good comfort; rise, he calls for you."

As the two men rose, Bartimaeus cast away his beggar's garment, and they came to Jesus.

Then Jesus said to them, "What do you want that I should do unto you?"

They said to him, "Lord, that our eyes may be opened, so that we might receive our sight."

So Jesus had compassion on them, and touched their eyes, saying, "Receive your sight, and go your way; your faith has saved you and made you whole."

Immediately their eyes were opened, and they received their sight, and they followed Jesus down the road glorifying God. All the people, when they saw it, gave praise to God.

As Jesus entered and passed through Jericho, behold, there was a man named Zacchaeus, who was the chief among the tax collectors, and he was rich. And he sought to see who Jesus was, and could not for the press of the crowd, because he was little of stature.

So he ran before the multitude, and climbed up into a sycamore tree to see Jesus, anticipating that he was to pass by that way.

When Jesus came to the place, he looked up, and saw him, and he said to him, "Zacchaeus, make haste, and come down, for today I must abide at your house."

So Zacchaeus made haste, and came down, and received him joyfully.

When his followers saw it, they all murmured, saying that he was going to be a guest with a man that is a sinner.

But Zacchaeus stood, and said to Jesus, "Behold, Lord, the half of my goods I will give to the poor, and if I have taken anything from any man by false accusation, I will restore it to him fourfold."

Then Jesus, looking upon Zacchaeus with great joy, said to his followers, "This day has salvation come to this house, for as much as he also is a son of Abraham. For the Son of man has come to seek and to save that which was lost."

As they contemplated these things, Jesus taught them with a parable of his imminent departure and his prolonged return, because they had drawn near to Jerusalem, and because they thought that the kingdom of God should immediately appear.

He said, therefore, "A certain nobleman went into a far country to receive for himself a kingdom, and to return. And he called his ten servants, and delivered to them ten sums of money, each servant receiving three months wages, and he said to them, 'Occupy till I come.' But his citizens hated him, and sent a message after him, saying, 'We will not have this man to reign over us.' And it came to pass that when the nobleman returned, having received the kingdom, he commanded these servants to be called unto him, to whom he had given the money, that he might know how much every man had gained by his occupation. Then came the first, saying, 'Lord, your sum has gained ten times more.' And he said to him, 'Well done, good servant: because you have been faithful in a very little, have authority over ten cities.' And the second came, saying, 'Lord, your sum has gained five times more.' And he said likewise to him, 'Be also over five cities.' And another came, saying, 'Lord, behold, here is your sum, which I have kept laid up in a napkin, for I feared you, because you are an austere man: you take up what you laid not down, and reap what you have not sown.' And he said to him, 'Out of your own mouth will I judge you, you wicked servant. You knew that I was an austere man, taking up what I laid not down, and reaping what I have not sown. Why then did you not give my money to the money exchangers, that at my coming I might have received my own money with interest?' And he said to them that stood by, 'Take from him the sum, and give it to him that has ten times more. For I say unto you, that to everyone who *has*, more shall be given; and from him that has not, even that which he has shall be taken from him. But those who are my enemies, who would not have me to reign over them, bring them here, and slay them before me.'"

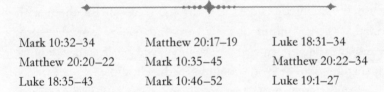

Mark 10:32–34	Matthew 20:17–19	Luke 18:31–34
Matthew 20:20–22	Mark 10:35–45	Matthew 20:22–34
Luke 18:35–43	Mark 10:46–52	Luke 19:1–27

Chapter 51

MARY ANOINTS JESUS

Jesus and his disciples continued their journey from Jericho to Bethany, to the house of Simon the leper. They arrived in the afternoon, before sunset and the beginning of the Sabbath, six days before the Passover. Martha and Mary, Simon's daughters, prepared them a dinner, and Lazarus, his son, whom Jesus had raised from the dead, dined with them. Many people who knew that Jesus was there came to dine with them, though not for Jesus's sake only, but that they might see Lazarus also, whom he had raised from the dead. While they dined, they discussed the intentions of the chief priests, who had consulted among themselves how they might put Lazarus also to death, because by reason of him, many of the Jewish people departed from the teachings of the priests, and believed in Jesus.

Now Jesus's mother, Mary, when it was confirmed that the Jewish leadership sought to kill Jesus and Lazarus, her heart was changed within her, for she saw that Jesus's predictions of his betrayal and death would surely come to pass. So she brought out the precious ointment that the wise men had given her so many years before, and she gave it to Mary, Simon's daughter, explaining to her privately that it was meant for anointing Jesus for his burial.

Then she instructed her, "Go to him, and prepare his body, now, for his time has surely come."

And Judas Iscariot observed them whispering, and saw Jesus's

mother hand over the box to Mary. And he looked at Jesus's mother
questioningly. When she noticed his gaze, she shook her head,
signaling that she no longer wanted to follow through with their
plan. Judas became angry, but he tried to control his demeanor.

He watched as Mary, Simon's daughter, crossed the room with
the alabaster box containing the very precious ointment of spikenard,
made from myrrh and other costly spices. She came to Jesus, sitting
behind him, while he reclined at the table. Positioning his head
upon her lap, she broke open the box. And pouring the precious
ointment over his head, she anointed him with it. The house was
immediately filled with the heavy fragrance of the ointment. All
eyes were upon them, while the dinner party tried to comprehend
the meaning and appropriateness of her seemingly erotic display of
affection. The combination of this expression of intimacy and the
odor of the ointment was intoxicating. The ointment oozed slowly
over his forehead, down his temples, and she massaged it into his
hair and beard with her fingertips, until his scalp and jaw line were
covered by it. Removing his head from her lap, and laying it back
upon a pillow, Mary shifted her body toward his feet. Then, with the
remainder of the ointment, she anointed his feet also, and wiped his
feet with her hair. The entire household was silent and still, except
for Judas, who was visibly annoyed. Pacing the floor, he stopped
several times anxiously to watch, then began pacing again.

As Mary concluded her ritual, Judas could contain himself no
longer; sitting again at the table, he broke the silent spell with great
indignation. "Why was this waste of the ointment made? For it
might have been sold for more than three hundred denarii, and have
been given to the poor."

As he said these words, his glance went from Mary to Jesus, to
the guests around the table, and finally to Mary, Jesus's mother, who
stood by the door. Jesus's mother shot a look back at him—one of
defiance. The look between them was not unnoticed by Jesus. His
mother then looked at Jesus, and her expression turned from one of
defiance to one of anguish; then she disappeared outside the door.

Judas's anger was felt on many levels. Though he cared not for the poor, he had the bag and managed the money for Jesus and his disciples, so his show of concern for the poor was not an unreasonable complaint. This he used to cover up his true feelings. Deep down, he was a thief, a character flaw he could not seem to shake, even in the presence of Jesus and his teachings. Seeing anything of intrinsic value that he could not obtain was always an issue with him. Mary's erotic display was unsettling, as well. Then there was the envy he felt toward Jesus. He couldn't help it. He wondered what it must feel like to command such power, wisdom, and adoration. But, perhaps, what angered him the most was the realization that Jesus's mother had betrayed him. He knew that she had abandoned their plan of arranging a meeting between Jesus and the chief priests of the temple. He didn't know if he could continue the plan without her; yes, this was what angered him the most. He was good at manipulating others into doing his bidding for him, but rarely, if ever, had he mustered the fortitude to follow through with anything on his own. All these things were gnawing at him as he spewed his venomous words.

Now the others at the dinner began to murmur against Mary, also, not that they cared for the poor, either, but because they did not understand her erotic display.

When Jesus understood the matter fully, he said to them, "Why do you trouble this woman, for she has carried out a good work upon me? Let her alone; against the day of my burying has this ointment been kept. For the poor you always have with you, and whenever you will, you may do them good, but me you have not always. She has done what was in her power to do: she has come beforehand to anoint my body for burying, for in that she has poured this ointment on my body, she did it for my burial. Truly I say unto you, wherever this gospel shall be preached throughout the whole world, this thing also that she has done shall be spoken of as a memorial to her."

Judas got up from the table, saying, "I can no longer breathe in here; the odor is overpowering," and then he stormed out of the house.

That Sabbath night, Satan entered into Judas, and he traveled to the temple to conspire with the chief priests, scribes, and captains to betray Jesus. When he arrived, they were already meeting, discussing how they might kill him, for they feared the people. And when they heard his intent, they were glad.

He said to them, "What will you give me, for I will deliver him to you?"

And they covenanted with him for thirty pieces of silver, and promised to give him the money. In return, he promised to find an opportunity to betray Jesus and deliver him up to them in the absence of the multitude.

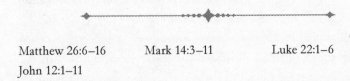

Matthew 26:6–16   Mark 14:3–11   Luke 22:1–6
John 12:1–11

Chapter 52

PALM SUNDAY

Jesus and his disciples spent the entire Sabbath, evening to evening, with Simon and his family. They remained with them, after the Sabbath sun set, staying a second night, as well.

The next day, Jesus and the twelve set out for Jerusalem, and were joined by a growing multitude of disciples along the way.

When they had traversed the short distance from Bethany to the outskirts of Bethphage, at the Mount of Olives, Jesus sent two of his disciples ahead, saying, "Go your way into the village before you, and as soon as you enter into it, you shall come upon an ass tied, and a colt with her, on which man has never sat: release them, and bring them to me. And if any man asks you, 'Why do you release them?' This shall you say unto him, 'The Lord has need of them,' and immediately he will send them here."

So they that were sent went their way, and did as Jesus commanded them, and found it even as he had said to them. When they came to a place in the road where two paths met, they found the ass and her colt, outside a house, tied by the door.

And as they were releasing the colt, the owners thereof came out, and restrained them, saying, "What are you doing? Why do you release them?"

So his disciples answered them even as Jesus had commanded, saying, "The Lord has need of them."

When the owners of the donkeys heard their words, they let the disciples go. Then the two, father and son, prepared the animals, and brought them to Jesus. When they arrived, the young man recognized Jesus as the man who spoke so kindly to him, that early morning, while feeding his donkeys. The son immediately introduced himself, and his father, and was not surprised to find that the man he met that morning was Jesus of Nazareth, for he had pondered often their encounter, speculating about his identity.

The two men went quickly to work, leading the donkeys to a large square rock on the side of the road that could easily be used for mounting purposes.

The colt, which had still not been ridden, was, however, being trained for this purpose. Daily, the son had worked with him, separating the colt from the colt's mother. The young man worked him with a harness, and draped his own clothes over the colt, to get the colt used to the smell of him on his back. The plan was to mount the colt within a week or so, after repeating, daily, this part of the training. Then, after a week or so more of mounting training, the young man would begin teaching the colt riding commands; he would need his father to lead the colt by the harness for this phase of the training. Training donkeys was a slow process, but a well-trained donkey could offer over twenty years of good service.

The father and son looked at one another apprehensively, wondering how things would go. Donkeys were known to buck, sometimes violently, when entering the mounting stage of training, and they were attempting to skip entirely the riding commands phase. Repeating his familiar training, the son draped his coat over the back of the colt; the father added his, also, hoping this might help to calm the animal further. The son took the colt's reins, and the father took the reins of the mother, positioning her in front of and slightly to the side of the colt. The colt was used to following the mother's lead, so they hoped that this, too, would calm the colt. They cautioned Jesus, and his disciples, regarding the possibility of the colt bucking violently. Jesus stepped onto the rock, stroking the side of the colt's face with the back of his hand. His disciples moved back several paces. Before the father and son instructed him, while they were still looking apprehensively at one another, Jesus sat upon the colt. And the colt received him, graciously. No one close to the animals actually saw him mount the colt. Only those viewing from some distance away were watching the scene in its entirety. They let out a collective sigh, which made the twelve disciples and the two donkey trainers glance up to see Jesus. He was comfortably seated upon the apparently contented colt. The father and son smiled at one another. Then they turned to Jesus, and together they let out a muffled laugh. Jesus raised his eyebrows and returned to the men a broad smile. The twelve and his disciple onlookers joined in a brief moment of levity, while trying, through hushed laughter, not to disturb the calm demeanor of the colt.

The road ahead was difficult; it led up one side of a winding ridge and down the other to the temple. The father looked at Jesus for approval to try the first few steps, to see if the colt would cooperate by following their lead. Jesus nodded, and the father moved ahead, tugging gently on the reins of the mother donkey. She followed the father's lead. Then the son took a few steps forward, leading the colt by the reins, hoping he would follow. The colt took a step, and then hesitated. Jesus, who was sitting with both legs to one side, touched the other side of the colt reassuringly. The colt responded, moving forward, steadily, following his mother. The journey to the temple was uneventful—for the donkeys; they strode along at a modest pace. The father and son donkey trainers viewed this as a miracle, especially considering the way the people were behaving around them.

The disciples that followed them, repeatedly ran ahead casting their garments in the way before them as they made their way to the top of the ridge.

As they went along, they joined in singing a familiar song, "Hosanna to the Son of David: blessed is the King of Israel that comes in the name of the Lord; Hosanna in the highest."

Reaching the top of the ridge, they paused, as Jesus beheld the city. The singing stopped, and the crowd became silent, for they beheld him weeping.

"If you had known, even you, at least in this your day, the things which belong unto your peace!" he said, regaining his composure, "But now they are hid from your eyes. For the days shall come upon you, that your enemies shall cast a trench about you, and compass you round, and keep you in on every side, and shall lay you even with the ground, and your children within you; and they shall not leave in you one stone upon another; because you knew not the time of your visitation."

At these words, the people were sorrowful, remaining quiet for a prolonged moment.

Now there were those in Jerusalem who had witnessed the resurrection of Lazarus, who bore record of these things. And for this reason, a very great multitude of people who had come to the Passover feast, when they heard that Jesus was coming to Jerusalem, took branches cut down from palm trees, and went forth from the city to meet him.

And when they saw him, there, at the crest of the Mount of Olives, this whole multitude let out a great cheer, and began to rejoice and praise God with a loud voice for all the mighty works that they had seen him perform.

Then as he began his descent down the Mount of Olives, they joined in spreading their garments before him; others cast their palm branches upon the path. In so doing, they creating a welcome mat all the way to the temple; and the multitudes that went before, and that followed, cried aloud together, saying, "Blessed is the King of Israel that comes in the name of the Lord; peace in heaven, and glory in the highest."

When some of the Pharisees from among the multitude heard the shouts of the people, they said to Jesus, "Master, rebuke your disciples."

But he answered, and said to them, "I tell you, that if these should hold their peace, the stones would immediately cry out."

The Pharisees, therefore, said among themselves, "Perceive how we prevail at nothing? Behold, the world has gone after him."

All this was done, that it might be fulfilled which was spoken by the prophet, Zechariah, saying, "Rejoice greatly, Oh daughter of Zion; shout, Oh daughter of Jerusalem: behold, your King comes unto you: he is just, and having salvation; lowly, riding upon an ass; upon a colt, the foal of an ass."

Even so, while his disciples were doing all these things to Jesus, they did not recognize the fulfillment of the scriptures in them.

Now there were certain Greeks among them that came up to worship at the feast: the same came, therefore, to Philip, whom they knew from Bethsaida of Galilee, and they desired of him to say, "Lord, Jesus, *we* desire to know you."

Philip came and told Andrew, and, again, Andrew and Philip told Jesus.

But Jesus answered them, saying, "The hour has come that the Son of man should be glorified. Truly, truly, I say unto you, unless a kernel of wheat falls into the ground and dies, it abides alone: but if it dies, it brings forth much fruit. He that loves his life shall lose it; and he that hates his life in this world shall keep it unto life eternal. If *any* would serve me, let him follow me; and where I am, there shall my servant be also: if *any* would serve me, him will my Father honor. Now is my soul troubled; and what shall I say? 'Father, save me from this hour:' but for this reason I came unto this hour. Father, glorify your name."

Then came there a voice from heaven, saying, "I have both glorified it, and will glorify it again."

The people, therefore, that stood by and heard it, said that it thundered; others said, "An angel spoke to him."

Jesus answered and said, "This voice came not because of me, but for your sakes. Now is the judgment of this world: now shall the prince of this world be cast out. And I, if I be lifted up from the earth, will draw *all* unto myself."

This he said, signifying what death he should die, being lifted up upon a cross.

The Greeks, therefore, who were distressed, because he spoke of his impending death; were, nonetheless encouraged that even they, being Greeks, might follow him.

But the other people listening to him, answered him, "We have heard, out of the Law, that the Messiah lives forever, and why do you say, 'The Son of man must be lifted up?' Who is this Son of man?"

Then Jesus said to them, "Yet a little while is the light with you. Walk while you have the light, lest darkness come upon you, for he that walks in darkness knows not where he goes. While you have light, believe in the light, that you may be the children of light."

These things spoke Jesus after he dismounted from the colt; then he departed into the crowd, and hid himself from them.

And when he came into Jerusalem, all the city was moved, saying, "Who is this?" And the multitude with him said, "This is Jesus, the prophet of Nazareth, of Galilee."

Then Jesus went into the temple of God, and when he had looked round about upon all things, he cast out all them that bought and sold in the temple. For he overthrew the tables of the money changers, and the seats of them that sold doves, and said to them, "It is written, 'My house shall be called the house of prayer,' but you have made it a den of thieves."

And the blind and the lame came to him in the temple, and he healed them.

When the chief priests and scribes saw the wonderful things that he did, and the children crying in the temple, and saying, "Hosanna to the Son of David;" they were extremely displeased, and said to him, "Do you hear what these say?"

Jesus answered them, saying, "Yes. Have you never read, 'Out of the mouth of babes and sucklings you have perfected praise?'"

When he had silenced his critics with these words, he gathered the people together, teaching all that day and into the evening, even after the sun had set. It was then that the tenth day of Nisan began, when the people were to choose their Passover lamb. Many of those that heard the teaching of Jesus had decided that he was the One, the Messiah. Others were convinced of their decision that he should be killed.

When he had finished his teaching, that evening, he left them, and went out of the city with the twelve to Bethany, and there he lodged.

Matthew 21:1–17   Mark 11:1–11   Luke 19:29–46
John 12:12–36   Isaiah 56:7   Jeremiah 7:11
Zechariah 9:9   Psalms 118:26   Isaiah 9:6
Psalms 16:8–11   Psalms 8:2

Chapter 53

MONDAY AFTER PALM SUNDAY

The next day, in the morning, as he was returning into the city from Bethany, Jesus was hungry. And he saw a fig tree on the way, far in the distance, having leaves. So he came to it, hoping to find some fruit on it. But when he got to it, he found nothing but leaves, for the time of its figs was not yet.

Then Jesus answered, and said to it, "Let no fruit grow on you, that no man eat of your fruit—henceforth and forever."

Some of his disciples heard his words, and beheld that immediately its leaves began to wither, as at the change of the season.

Then others of his disciples, who heard not his words, took notice of it, and they marveled, saying, "How soon is the fig tree withered away!"

And they came to Jerusalem, and Jesus went into the temple, and began to cast out, again, them that bought and sold inside the temple. As before, he overthrew the tables of the money changers, and the seats of them that sold doves, and would not allow anyone to carry any vessel through the temple. These disgruntled merchants gathered up their wares and joined many others who had endured a similar fate the previous day, and had moved their business outside.

As they collected their things, Jesus taught them, scolding them,

"Is it not written, 'My house shall be called of all nations the house of prayer?' but you have made it a den of thieves."

The chief priests and the scribes, and many of the chief of the people, when they heard what he had said and done, sought how they might destroy him; but they could not decide what they should do. Though Jesus had done so many miracles before them, yet they believed not in him. And they feared him, because all the people were very attentive to hear him, being astonished at his doctrine. Even among the chief rulers, many believed in him, but because of the Pharisees, they did not confess him openly, lest they should be put out of the synagogue, for they loved the praise of men more than the praise of God.

Jesus, knowing the intentions of the religious leaders, spoke out of frustration, under his breath, "'Lord, who has believed our report? And to whom has the arm of the Lord been revealed?'" Then quickly, he answered his own thoughts, "They cannot believe, because, 'He has blinded their eyes, and hardened their heart, that they should not see with their eyes, nor understand with their heart, and be converted, and I should heal them.'" Then he reminded himself, saying with a wry smile, "Isaiah saw my glory."

Refocusing on the needs of the multitude, Jesus cried and said, "He who believes in me, believes not in me, but in him that sent me. And he that sees me, sees him who sent me. I have come as a light into the world, that whoever believes in me should not abide in darkness. And if anyone hears my words, and believes not, I judge him not, for I came not to judge the world, but to save the world. He that rejects me, and receives not my words, has one that judges him: the word that I have spoken, the same shall judge him in the last day. For I have not spoken of myself; but the Father which sent me, he gave me a commandment, what I should say, and what I should speak. And I know that his commandment is life everlasting: whatever I speak, therefore, even as the Father said unto me, so I speak."

And he began to teach them of the kingdom of God, and he

taught and healed them, until the evening came; then he went out of the city.

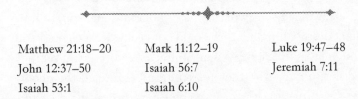

Matthew 21:18–20	Mark 11:12–19	Luke 19:47–48
John 12:37–50	Isaiah 56:7	Jeremiah 7:11
Isaiah 53:1	Isaiah 6:10	

Chapter 54

TUESDAY AT THE TEMPLE

In the morning, as they passed by, on their way back to Jerusalem, they saw the fig tree dried up from the roots.

And Peter, calling to remembrance, said to Jesus, "Master, behold, the fig tree that you cursed is withered away."

And Jesus, answering, said to them, "Have faith in God. For truly I say to you, if you have faith, and doubt not, you shall not only do this which is done to the fig tree. But whoever of you, also, shall say to this mountain, 'Be removed, and be cast into the sea;' and shall not doubt in his heart, but shall believe that those things which he said shall come to pass; he shall have whatever he said. Therefore, I say to you, whatever things you desire, when you pray, believe that you receive them, and you shall have them. For all things, whatever you shall ask in prayer, believing, you shall receive. And when you stand praying, forgive, if you have anything against anyone: that your Father also who is in heaven may forgive you your trespasses. But if you do not forgive, neither will your Father who is in heaven forgive your trespasses."

So they came again to Jerusalem, and as he taught the people in the temple and preached the gospel, there came to him the chief priests, and the scribes, and the elders, and said to him, "Tell us, by what authority do you do these things? And who gave you this authority?"

And Jesus answered, and said to them, "I will also ask of you one question, which if you tell me; I, likewise, will tell you by what authority I do these things. Answer me. The baptism of John, from what origin was it? Was it from heaven, or of men?"

And they reasoned with themselves, saying, "If we shall say, 'From heaven,' he will say to us, 'Why, then, did you not believe him?' But if we shall say, 'Of men,' all the people will stone us, for they are persuaded that John was a prophet, indeed."

So they answered Jesus, and said, "We cannot tell."

And Jesus said to them, "Neither do I tell *you* by what authority I do these things." Scrutinizing their disappointment at their failed attempt to entangle him in his words, Jesus seized the opportunity to teach them, saying, "But what do you think? A certain man had two sons; and he came to the first, and said, 'Son, go work today in my vineyard.' And the first son answered his father, 'I will not:' but afterwards he repented, and went. The father came to the second son, and said likewise. And the second son answered his father, '*I* will go, sir:' and went not. Which of the two did the will of his father?"

The chief priests, scribes, and elders replied, "The first."

Jesus then scolded them, "Truly, I say unto you, that the tax collectors and the harlots go into the kingdom of God before you. For John came to you in the way of righteousness, and you believed him not: but the tax collectors and the harlots believed him; and *you*, when you had witnessed this, repented not afterward, that you might also believe him."

Then he began to speak to the people this parable: "There was a certain householder, who planted a vineyard, and hedged it round about, and dug a place for the winepress, and built a tower, and let it out to vinedressers, and went into a far country for a long time. And when the time of the fruit drew near, he sent to the vinedressers a servant, that he might receive from them of the fruit of the vineyard. And they caught him, and beat him, and sent him away empty. And, again, he sent to them another servant, and at him they cast stones, and wounded him in the head, and sent him away shamefully handled. And, again, he sent another, and him they killed, and many others, beating some, and killing some. Then the lord of the vineyard said, 'What shall I do?' Having yet, therefore, one son, his well beloved, he sent him also unto them, last of all, saying, 'I will send my beloved son: it may be that they will reverence him, when they see him.' But when the vinedressers saw the son, they reasoned among themselves, saying, 'This is the heir; come, let us kill him, and let us seize on his inheritance, that it may be ours.' So they took him, and cast him out of the vineyard, and killed him. When the lord of the vineyard comes, what, therefore, shall he do to those vinedressers?"

The people said to him, "He will miserably destroy those wicked men, and will lease out his vineyard to other vinedressers, which shall render him the fruits in their seasons."

And Jesus confirmed their answer, saying, "Yes. He shall come and destroy these vinedressers, and shall give the vineyard to others."

When the chief priests and scribes heard this parable, they perceived that he spoke of them, and responded, "God forbid!"

And Jesus beheld them, and said, "Did you never read this in the scriptures? What is this, then, that is written, 'The stone which the builders rejected, the same has become the head of the corner. This is the Lord's doing, and it is marvelous in our eyes'? Therefore, I say to you, the kingdom of God *shall* be taken from you, and given to a nation bringing forth the fruits thereof." "And whoever shall fall on *this* stone," he said, tapping his chest with his palms, and lifting his hands to indicate himself, "*shall* be broken, but on whomever it shall fall, it will grind him to powder."

Then the chief priests and the scribes sought to lay hands on him, but did not, for they feared the multitude, because the people believed that Jesus was a prophet. So the religious leaders turned to leave him, working their way through the crowd.

But Jesus, knowing their treachery, turned to the people again, and speaking to them in the hearing of his enemies, by parable, he said, "The kingdom of heaven is like unto a certain king, who made a marriage for his son, and sent forth his servants to call them that were bidden to the wedding, and they would not come. Again, he sent forth other servants, saying to them, 'Tell them which are bidden, "Behold, I have prepared my dinner: my oxen and my fatlings are killed, and all things are ready; come unto the marriage."' But they made light of it, and went their ways, one to his farm, another to his merchandise, and the remnant took his servants and entreated them spitefully, and slew them. But when the king heard thereof, he was enraged, and he sent forth his armies, and destroyed those murderers, and burned up their city. Then said he to his servants, 'The wedding is ready, but they which were bidden were not worthy. Go, therefore, into the highways, and as many as you shall find, bid to the marriage.' So those servants went out into the highways, and gathered together all, as many as they found, both bad and good, and the wedding was furnished with guests. And when the king came in to see the guests, he saw there a man which had not on a wedding garment, and he said to him, 'Friend, how did you come in here not having a wedding garment?' And the man was speechless. Then said the king to the servants, 'Bind him hand and foot, and take him away, and cast him into outer darkness;' there shall be weeping and gnashing of teeth. For many are called, but few are chosen."

Angered, even more so, over this parable directed toward them, the chief priests and Pharisees went out, and took counsel how they might entangle him in his talk. So they sent to him certain of the Pharisees and of the Herodians, their disciples, as spies, who pretended to be just men. These watched him, to catch him in his words, so they might deliver him unto the power and authority of the governor.

For this reason, they came to Jesus, and said to him, "Master, we know that you are true, and teach the way of God in truth; neither care you for any man, for you regard not the person of men. Tell us, therefore, what do you think? Is it lawful for us to give tribute unto Caesar, or not? Shall we give, or shall we not give?"

But Jesus, knowing their hypocrisy, perceived their wickedness, and said to them, "Why do you tempt me, you hypocrites? Show me the tribute money. Bring me a coin, that I may see it."

So they brought him a denarius.

And he said to them, "Whose is this image and superscription?" They answered him, "Caesar's."

Then he said to them, "Render, therefore, unto Caesar the things which are Caesar's, and unto God the things that are God's."

When they had heard these words, they marveled, and held their peace, for they could not take hold of his words before the people; so they left him, and went their way back to the chief priests and Pharisees who sent them.

The same day, the Sadducees, who say that there is no resurrection; came to him, inquiring, "Master, Moses wrote to us, 'If a man dies, having no children, his brother shall marry his wife, and raise up seed unto his brother.' Now there were with us seven brothers, and the first took a wife, and died without children. And the second took her to wife, and he died childless. Likewise, the third unto the seventh had her, and left no seed. Last of all, the woman died, also. In the resurrection, therefore, when they shall rise, whose wife shall she be of them? For the seven all had her to wife."

This hypothetical story was commonly used by the Sadducees to refute the teachings of the resurrection from the dead, the idea originating from the story of a woman named Sarah in the book of Tobit.

Jesus answered their questions regarding this hypothetical scenario, saying, "You do err, not knowing the scriptures, nor the power of God. The children of this world marry, and are given in marriage. But they which shall be accounted worthy to obtain that world, even the resurrection from the dead; neither marry, nor are given in marriage. Neither can they die anymore, for they are equal unto the angels of God in heaven, and are the children of God, being the children of the resurrection. Now as touching the resurrection: and the dead, that they rise: have you not read in the book of Moses, how, in the bush, God spoke to him, saying, 'I am the God of Abraham, and the God of Isaac, and the God of Jacob?' God is not the God of the dead, but the God of the living, for all live unto him. You, therefore, do greatly err."

And when the multitude heard this, they were astonished at his doctrine. But when the Pharisees, who had come to hear for themselves, after their spies had failed, saw that Jesus had put the Sadducees to silence, they gathered together again.

Then one of them, who was a lawyer, came, having heard them reasoning together, and perceiving that Jesus had answered them well, asked Jesus, testing him further, "Master, which is the great commandment in the Law?"

Jesus said to him, "The first of all the commandments is: 'Hear, Oh Israel; the Lord our God is one Lord. And you shall love the Lord your God with all your heart, and with all your soul, and with all your mind, and with all your strength.' This is the first and great commandment. And the second is like unto it, namely this: 'You shall love your neighbor as yourself.' There is no other commandment greater than these. On these two commandments hang all the Law and the Prophets."

And the lawyer said to him, "Well, Master, you have said the truth, for there is one God, and there is no other god but he. And to love him with all your heart, and with all your understanding, and with all your soul, and with all your strength, and to love your neighbor as yourself, is more than all whole burnt offerings and sacrifices."

When Jesus saw that he answered discreetly, he said to him, "You are not far from the kingdom of God."

And no one after that dared to ask him any more questions.

While the Pharisees were still gathered together, Jesus asked them, saying, "What do you think of the Messiah? Whose son is he? For the scribes say that the Messiah is the Son of David."

They answered him, "He *is* the Son of David."

Then Jesus said to them, "How then does David, *himself*, in the book of Psalms, while in the Spirit; call the Messiah Lord, saying, 'The LORD said unto my Lord, "Sit on my right hand, till I make your enemies your footstool?"' If David, therefore, called him Lord, how, then, is the Messiah his son?"

And no man was able to answer him a word; neither dared anyone, from that day forward, to ask him any more questions. And the common people heard him gladly.

Then Jesus spoke to his disciples, in the audience of all the people, saying to them in his doctrine, "The scribes and the Pharisees sit in Moses's seat. All, therefore, whatever they bid you to observe, that observe and do. But do not after their works, for they say, and do not. For they bind heavy burdens and grievous to be borne, and lay them on men's shoulders, but they themselves will not move them with one of their fingers. But all their works, they do to be seen of men. Beware of the scribes and Pharisees, who love to walk in long robes, and love greetings in the marketplaces, and the chief seats in the synagogues, and the uppermost rooms at feasts. They make broad their phylacteries, and enlarge the borders of their garments, and love to be called of men, Rabbi, Rabbi.

"But, *you*, be not called rabbi; neither be called masters, for one is your Master, even the Messiah, and *you* are all brethren. But he that is greatest among you shall be your servant. And call no man your father upon the earth, for one is your Father, which is in heaven. And whoever shall exalt himself shall be abased, and he that shall humble himself shall be exalted."

And while Jesus taught, he sat over against the treasury, and he looked up and beheld how the people cast money into the treasury, and many that were rich cast in much. And there came, also, a certain poor widow, and she threw in two *lepta*, the smallest of bronze coins.

When he saw it, he called to him his disciples, pointing out the poor widow, and said to them, "Truly, I say unto you, that this poor widow has cast more in than all they which have cast into the treasury, for all these have of their abundance cast in to the offerings of God, but she of her poverty has cast in all that she had, even all her living."

Then he turned upon the religious leaders, who continued to judge him for his ministry, while neglecting their own, and he cried to them, "But woe unto *you*, scribes and Pharisees, hypocrites! For you shut up the kingdom of heaven against men, for you neither go in yourselves, neither allow them that are entering to go in. Woe unto you, scribes and Pharisees, hypocrites! For you devour widows' houses, and for a pretense make long prayers; therefore, you shall receive the greater damnation. Woe unto you, scribes and Pharisees, hypocrites! For you compass sea and land to make one proselyte, and when he is made, you make him twofold more the child of hell than yourselves.

"Woe unto you, you blind guides, who say, 'Whoever shall take an oath regarding the temple, it is nothing; but whoever shall take an oath regarding the gold of the temple, he is bound by it!' You fools and blind, for which is greater, the gold, or the temple that sanctifies the gold? And, 'Whoever shall take an oath regarding the altar, it is nothing; but whoever takes an oath regarding the gift that is upon it, he is bound by it!' You fools, and blind, for which is greater, the gift, or the altar that sanctifies the gift? Whoever, therefore, shall take an oath regarding the altar, takes an oath regarding it and all things thereon. And whoever shall take an oath regarding the temple, takes an oath regarding it and him that dwells therein. And he that shall take an oath regarding heaven, takes an oath regarding the throne of God and him that sits thereon.

"Woe unto you, scribes and Pharisees, hypocrites! For you pay tithe of mint, and anise, and cumin; and have omitted the weightier matters of the Law—judgment, mercy, and faith: these you ought to have done, and not to have left the other undone. You blind guides, who strain at a gnat, and swallow a camel.

"Woe unto you, scribes and Pharisees, hypocrites! For you make clean the outside of the cup and platter, but within are full of extortion and excess. You blind Pharisees, cleanse first that which is within the cup and platter, that the outside of them may be clean also. Woe unto you, scribes and Pharisees, hypocrites! For you are like unto whitewashed tombs, which indeed appear beautiful on the outside, but are within full of dead men's bones, and of all uncleanness. Even so, you also outwardly appear righteous unto men, but within you are full of hypocrisy and iniquity.

"Woe unto you, scribes and Pharisees, hypocrites! Because you build the tombs of the prophets, and garnish the tombs of the righteous, and say, 'If we had been in the days of our fathers, we would not have been partakers with them in the blood of the prophets.' In so saying, you are witnesses unto yourselves, that you *are* the children of them which killed the prophets. Fill yourselves up, then, to the measure of your fathers. You serpents, you generation of vipers, how can you escape the damnation of hell?

"For this very reason, behold, I send unto you prophets, and wise men, and scribes, and some of them you shall kill and crucify, and some of them you shall scourge in your synagogues, and persecute them from city to city, that upon you may come all the righteous blood shed upon the earth, from the blood of righteous Abel to the blood of Zachariah son of Barachiah, whom you slew between the temple and the altar. Truly, I say unto you, all these things shall come upon *this* generation. Oh Jerusalem, Jerusalem, you that kill the prophets, and stone them who are sent to you, how often would I have gathered your children together, even as a hen gathers her chicks under her wings, and you would not! Behold, your house is left unto you desolate. For I say unto you, you shall not see me henceforth, till you shall say, 'Blessed is he that comes in the name of the Lord.'"

Mark 11:20–33   Matthew 21:20–27   Luke 20:1–8
Matthew 21:28–46   Mark 12:1–12   Luke 20:9–19
Psalms 118:22–23   Matthew 22:1–14   Luke 20:20–40
Mark 12:13–37   Matthew 22:15–46   Luke 20:41–44
Deuteronomy 25:5–6   Tobit 3:7–17   Exodus 3:1–6
Deuteronomy 6:4–5   Leviticus 19:18   Jeremiah 23:5
Psalms 110:1   Matthew 23:1–12   Luke 20:45–47
Mark 12:38–44   Luke 21:1–4   Matthew 23:13–39
Genesis 4:1–8   2 Chronicles 24:20–21   Zechariah 1:1
Psalms 118:26

Chapter 55

WEDNESDAY'S END-TIME WARNING

As he went out of the temple, Judas Iscariot, who made it a point, now, to stay close to Jesus, said to him, "Master, see how the temple buildings are adorned with such beautiful stones!"

Now the stones that had so impressed Judas were ornamental stones, donated as gifts, from the rich, to Herod's rebuilding project; they bore the names of those who donated them, to honor them and their contribution. Judas, therefore, out of envy for the honor bestowed upon those who donated them, marveled over them.

Jesus turned to his disciples, and said to them, "See these great buildings? Do you not discern all these things? As for these things, which you behold, truly I say unto you, the days will come, in which there shall not be left here one stone upon another that shall not be thrown down."

Judas took offense at his words, and became silent, brooding. Jesus's disciples became silent, as well, contemplating the magnitude and horror of such a catastrophic event. So they all walked in silence. Evening approached, as they departed, plodding their way up the Mount of Olives, where they would spend the night.

Later, while Jesus sat upon the Mount of Olives, in the dimly lit view of the temple, Peter, James, John, and Andrew came to him, privately, asking him, "Master, tell us. When shall these things be?

And what shall be the sign of your coming, and the end of the world, when all these things shall be fulfilled?"

And Jesus answered them, "Take heed that no man deceives you. For many shall come in my name, saying, 'I am the Messiah,' and 'The time draws near,' and shall deceive many. Go not, therefore, after them. And when you shall hear of wars and rumors of wars, be not greatly troubled, for these things must, of necessity, first come to pass, but the end is not yet. For nation shall rise against nation, and kingdom against kingdom; there shall be famines, and pestilences, and great earthquakes in various places; there shall be troubles, accompanied by fearful sights, and great signs shall there be from heaven. All these are the beginning of sorrows.

"But take heed unto *yourselves*, for, before all these things, they shall persecute *you*! They shall lay their hands upon you, and deliver you up to councils to be afflicted. In the synagogues, you shall be beaten; they shall put you into prisons, and bring you before rulers and kings for my sake. But when they shall lead you, and deliver you up, take no thought, beforehand, what you shall speak, for it shall turn into an opportunity of testimony for you. Settle it, therefore, in your hearts, not to meditate beforehand what you shall answer. Whatever shall be given you in that hour, that speak, for I will give you a mouth and wisdom, which all your adversaries shall not be able to refute nor resist. It is not you who speaks but the Holy Spirit! Now a brother shall betray his brother to death, and a father his son, and children shall rise up against their parents, and shall cause them to be put to death. So shall *you* be betrayed by both parents, brethren, kinsmen, and friends, and some of you they shall cause to be put to death. Indeed, you shall be hated of all men, in all nations, for my name's sake! For this reason, many shall become offended, and shall betray one another, and shall hate one another. Many false prophets shall rise, and shall deceive many. And because iniquity shall abound, the love of many shall become cold. But there shall not a hair of your head perish. In your patience, possess you your *souls*. For he that shall endure unto the end, the same shall be saved."

Jesus paused, and looked away from them. He stared nostalgically at the city below.

Then he turned to them again, and continued, "When you, therefore, shall see Jerusalem compassed with armies, then know that the desolation thereof is near. Then let them which are in Judea flee to the mountains, and let them which are in the midst of it depart out, and let not them that are in the country enter therein. For these are the days of vengeance, that all things which are written may be fulfilled. But woe unto them that are with child, and to them that give suck, in those days! For there shall be great distress in the land, and wrath upon this people. And they shall fall by the edge of the sword, and shall be led away captive into all nations, and Jerusalem shall be trodden down of the Gentiles, until the times of the Gentiles is fulfilled. For this gospel of the kingdom must first be preached among all nations of the world, for a witness unto all nations, and then the end shall come.

"Then, when you shall see the abomination of desolation, spoken of by Daniel the prophet, standing where it ought not to be, in the holy place: again, let them which be in Judea flee into the mountains. Let him which is on the housetop not come down into the house, neither enter therein, to take anything out of his house: neither let him which is in the field turn back to take his clothes. But woe unto them that are with child, and to them that give suck in *those* days! Pray also that your flight is not in the winter, neither on the Sabbath day, for in those days, shall be great tribulation, such as was not from the beginning of the creation of the world, which God created, to this time; no, nor ever shall be. And except those days should be shortened by the Lord, there should no flesh be saved, but for the elect's sake, whom he has chosen, he shall shorten those days.

"Then if any man shall say to you, 'Lo, here is the Messiah,' or, 'Lo, he is there,' believe it not, for false messiahs and false prophets shall rise, and shall show great signs and wonders, to seduce, if it were possible, even the very elect. But take heed: behold, I have told you all things beforehand. So if they shall say to you, 'Behold, he is in the desert,' go not forth: 'Behold, he is in the secret chambers,' believe it not. For in those days, immediately after the tribulation of those days, there shall be signs in the sun, in the moon, and in the stars, for the sun shall be darkened, the moon shall not give her light, and the stars of heaven shall fall. And upon the earth there shall be, also, distress of nations, with perplexity; the sea and the waves roaring; men's hearts failing them for fear, and for looking after those things which are coming on the earth, for the powers of heaven shall be shaken.

"After these things, the sign of the Son of man shall appear in heaven; then shall all the tribes of the earth mourn, for they shall see the Son of man coming in the clouds of heaven with power and great glory. And he shall send his angels with a great sound of a trumpet, and they shall gather together his elect from the four winds, from the uttermost part of the earth to the uttermost part of heaven, from one end of heaven to the other. When these things begin to come to pass, then look up, and lift up your heads, for your redemption draws near!"

Jesus smiled at them, imagining the event. The disciples fidgeted, smiling back at him, and at one another. They were almost giddy with anticipation of the day.

"But of that day and that hour knows no man," Jesus cautioned them, "no, not the angels which are in heaven, neither the Son, but the Father only."

Then he spoke to them a parable, saying, "Now, behold, learn a parable of the fig tree, when her branch is yet tender and puts forth leaves; and all the trees, when they now shoot forth; you know that summer is near, even at the doors. So you, in like manner, when you see all these things come to pass, know that the kingdom of God is near at hand."

Then, to reemphasize his enthusiasm, he lifted his hands toward them, as if to embrace them, saying, "Truly, I say unto you, *this* generation shall not pass away, till all is fulfilled. Heaven and earth shall pass away, but my words shall not pass away."

The disciples, feeling his excitement again, all nodded with nervous laughter; and not knowing what to do with themselves, they shifted their bodies to relieve their natural eagerness.

"The days *will* come," Jesus continued, "when you shall desire to see one of the days of the Son of man, and you shall not see it. And they shall say to you, 'See here,' or, 'See there'; go not after them, nor follow them." "For as the lightning, that lightens out of the one part of heaven in the east," he said, demonstrating with his hands, "and shines to the other part of heaven in the west, so shall also the coming of the Son of man be in his day.

"And take heed to yourselves, lest at any time your hearts be besieged with overindulging, and drunkenness and cares of this life, so that that day comes upon you unawares. For as a snare, shall it come on all them that dwell on the face of the whole earth. Watch, therefore, and pray always, that you may be counted worthy to escape all these things that shall come to pass, and to stand before the Son of man."

Jesus paused briefly, and then raised his index finger for emphasis.

"But first," he said thoughtfully, "he must suffer many things, and be rejected of *this* generation."

This he said, indicating the temple; and by implication, those who attended to it. "Take heed, watch and pray," he continued, "for you know not when the time is. For the Son of man is as a man taking a far journey, who left his house, and gave authority to his servants, and to every man his work, and commanded the porter to watch. Watch, therefore, for you know not when the master of the house comes, at even, or at midnight, or at the cockcrowing, or in the morning, lest coming suddenly he finds you sleeping. And what I say to you, I say to all: watch."

Jesus's anxiety was evident this evening, for he rarely spoke to them at such length. The four had come to comfort him with their support, for they knew that Jesus was troubled, but they could not get enough of his teaching, now, and they looked for him to continue. Jesus welcomed their presence; he felt there was so much still left to be said, and teaching them seemed to soothe his anxiety.

He continued, "As it was in the days of Noah, so shall it be also in the days of the Son of man. For as in the days that were before the flood, they were eating and drinking, marrying and giving in marriage, until the day that Noah entered into the ark, and knew not until the flood came, and took them all away; so shall also the coming of the Son of man be. Then shall two be in the field; the one shall be taken, and the other left. Two women shall be grinding at the mill; the one shall be taken, and the other left. Watch, therefore, for you know not what hour your Lord does come. But know this, that if the good man of the house had known in what watch the thief would come, he would have watched, and would not have allowed his house to be broken into. You, therefore, be also ready, for in such an hour as you think not, the Son of man will come.

"Likewise, also, as it was in the days of Lot; they did eat, they drank, they bought, they sold, they planted, they built; but the same day that Lot went out of Sodom, it rained fire and brimstone from heaven, and destroyed them all. Even thus shall it be in the day when the Son of man is revealed. In that day, he which shall be upon the housetop, having his stuff in the house, let him not come down to take it away, and he that is in the field, let him, likewise, not return back. Remember Lot's wife! Whoever shall seek to save his life shall lose it, and whoever shall lose his life shall preserve it. I tell you, in that night, there shall be two in one bed; the one shall be taken, and the other shall be left. Two women shall be grinding together; the one shall be taken, and the other left. Two men shall be in the field; the one shall be taken, and the other left."

And his disciples answered, and said to him, "Where, Lord?"

And he said to them, "Wherever the body *is*, and wherever the carcass is, *there* will the eagles be gathered together.

"Then shall the kingdom of heaven be likened unto ten virgins, who took their lamps, and went forth to meet the bridegroom. And five of them were wise, and five were foolish. They that were foolish took their lamps, and took no oil with them, but the wise took oil in their vessels with their lamps. While the bridegroom tarried, they all slumbered and slept. And at midnight there was a cry made, 'Behold, the bridegroom comes; go out to meet him.' Then all those virgins arose, and trimmed their lamps. And the foolish said unto the wise, 'Give us some of your oil, for our lamps are gone out.' But the wise answered, saying, 'Not so, lest there be not enough for us and you, but go rather to them that sell, and buy for yourselves.' And while they went to buy, the bridegroom came, and they that were ready went in with him to the marriage, and the door was shut. Afterward, the other virgins came also, saying, 'Lord, Lord, open unto us.' But he answered and said, 'Truly, I say unto you, I know you not.' Watch therefore, for you know neither the day nor the hour when the Son of man comes."

The four, still showing interest, drew closer around him as he taught them by parables.

Jesus explained, "The kingdom of heaven is as a man traveling into a far country, who called his own servants, and delivered unto them his goods. And to one, he gave five *talents* (one talent being worth roughly sixteen years' wages); to another, two; and to another, one; to every man, according to his various abilities. And immediately thereafter, the man took his journey. Then he that had received the five talents went and traded with them, and made five more talents. And, likewise, he that had received two, he also gained two more. But he that had received one, went and dug in the earth, and hid his lord's money. After a long time the lord of those servants came back, and reckoned with them. So he that had received five talents came and brought the other five talents, saying, 'Lord, you delivered to me five talents; behold, I have gained beside them five talents more.' His lord said to him, 'Well done, good and faithful servant; you have been faithful over a few things, I will make you ruler over many things; enter into the joy of your lord.' He, also, that had received two talents came and said, 'Lord, you delivered to me two talents; behold, I have gained two other talents besides them.' His lord said to him, 'Well done, good and faithful servant; you have been faithful over a few things, I will make you ruler over many things; enter into the joy of your lord.' Then he which had received the one talent came and said, 'Lord, I know that you are a hard man, reaping where you have not sown, and gathering where you have not winnowed, and I was afraid, and went and hid your talent in the earth; lo, there, you have what is yours.' His lord answered and said to him, 'You wicked and slothful servant, you knew that I reap where I have not sown, and gather where I have not winnowed; you ought, therefore, to have given my money to the exchangers; then at my coming I should have received my own with interest. Take, therefore, the talent from him, and give it to him who has ten talents. For to everyone who has, shall be given, and he shall have abundance, but from him that has not, shall be taken away even that which he has. Cast the unprofitable servant into outer darkness: there shall be weeping and gnashing of teeth.'"

The story was somewhat familiar, for Jesus had spoken a similar version to the multitudes. But hearing it again, within the context of the rest of his current teaching, made it seem more practical, especially given the ominous talk of Jesus's impending death, which had become like a dark cloud over all of them.

Jesus continued his teaching, wanting to invest in them still more of his wisdom. "When the Son of man shall come in his glory, and all the holy angels with him, then shall he sit upon the throne of his glory, and before him shall be gathered all nations, and he shall separate them one from another, as a shepherd divides his sheep from the goats, and he shall set the sheep on his right hand but the goats on the left. Then shall the King say unto them on his right hand, 'Come, you blessed of my Father, inherit the kingdom prepared for you from the foundation of the world, for I was hungry, and you gave me food; I was thirsty, and you gave me drink; I was a stranger, and you took me in; naked, and you clothed me; I was sick, and you visited me; I was in prison, and you came unto me.' Then shall the righteous answer him, saying, 'Lord, when did we see you hungry, and feed you? Or thirsty, and give you drink? When did we see you as a stranger, and take you in? Or naked, and clothe you? Or when did we see you sick, or in prison, and come to you?' And the King shall answer and say to them, 'Truly, I say unto you, inasmuch as you have done it to one of the least of these my brethren, you have done it to me.' Then shall he say, also, to them on the left hand, 'Depart from me, you cursed, into everlasting fire, prepared for the devil and his angels, for I was hungry, and you gave me no food; I was thirsty, and you gave me no drink; I was a stranger, and you took me not in; naked, and you clothed me not; sick, and in prison, and you visited me not.' Then shall they also answer him, saying, 'Lord, when did we see you hungry, or thirsty, or a stranger, or naked, or sick, or in prison, and did not minister to you?' Then shall he answer them, saying, 'Truly, I say unto you, inasmuch as you did it not to one of the least of these, you did it not to me.' And these shall go away into everlasting punishment, but the righteous into life eternal."

Luke 21:5–19	Mark 13:1–13	Matthew 24:1–8
Matthew 24:9–13	Luke 21:20–24	Matthew 24:14–26
Mark 13:14–25	Matthew 24:29	Luke 21:25–26
Matthew 24:30–31	Mark 13:26–27	Luke 21:27–28
Mark 13:32	Matthew 24:36	Luke 21:29–33
Matthew 24:32–35	Mark 13:28–31	Luke 17:22–24
Matthew 24:27	Luke 21:34–36	Luke 17:25
Mark 13:33–37	Luke 17:26–27	Matthew 24:37–44
Genesis 7:1–24	Luke 17:28–32	Genesis 9:1–29
Luke 17:33–37	Matthew 24:28	Matthew 25:1–46

Chapter 56

THURSDAY'S PASSOVER PREPARATIONS

As they sat on the Mount of Olives, after Jesus had finished all these sayings, he said to his disciples, "You know that after two days comes the feast of the Passover, and the Son of man will be betrayed to be crucified."

The four nodded solemnly, not knowing what to say to him. They sat with him in silent support for some time, until Andrew disturbed the silence by taking a great whiff of their dinner, wafting through the cool evening air. He followed it with an ambiguous sigh—one wrought in both inadequacy and satisfaction. He smiled a melancholy smile at Jesus, rose to his feet, and beckoned for the others to follow. Peter, James, and John followed his lead. Peter turned to Jesus, hoping he would join them, but Jesus just stared out toward the horizon, beyond the city. They left him, there, contemplating the last glimpses of daylight.

Now, at the same time Jesus had been speaking with his four closest disciples on the Mount of Olives, the chief priests were assembled together with the scribes, and the elders of the people, at the palace of the high priest, Caiaphas. These men continued their previous discussions about how they might take Jesus by subtlety, and kill him.

They concluded their meeting, agreeing to the demands of Caiaphas, who insisted, saying, "Not on the feast day, lest there be an uproar among the people."

This he said concerning the fifteenth of Nisan, which was the first day of the Feast of Unleavened Bread; it was a high Sabbath according the Law of Moses, for this year it fell on the weekly Sabbath, as well. His demand, however, would leave them little time to accomplish their goals, if they were to carry out their plan beforehand. The Passover sacrifice took place on the fourteenth, that very next evening, at sunset. They would have only Thursday, the thirteenth, preparation day for the Passover; and Friday, the fourteenth, which was both the Passover and preparation day for the high Sabbath of the Feast of Unleavened Bread. This afforded them a very tight window of opportunity, for they could not be certain that, after the feasts, Jesus would remain in Jerusalem. By then, also, it might be too late to win the people back from his influence. Caiaphas and the others were counting heavily upon the assistance of Judas Iscariot, whom they hoped would be able to identify a time and place, away from the crowds, where they could take him.

Now there were two schools of interpretation as to the timing of the Passover events. The difference surrounded the killing of the Passover lambs. One school believed that the lambs were to be killed between late afternoon and sunset on the fourteenth of Nisan, while the other school believed that they should be killed just after sunset on the fourteenth. Because the Jewish day began at sunset, this variation meant that some would begin their Passover feast at the beginning of the day, while others would begin their Passover feast at the end of the day. This also meant that those who began the day with the Passover feast could conclude all of the Passover events on the same day. In contrast, those who ended the day with the Passover feast would continue the events of Passover from the fourteenth to the fifteenth.

Jesus would keep the tradition, according to scripture, of killing the Passover lamb after sunset, at the beginning of the fourteenth; thereby consolidating all of the Passover events to that one day.

Pondering the coming Passover, he sat there on the Mount of Olives, as evening fell, the beginning of Thursday, the thirteenth; there he prayed alone, well into the night, for he knew that his time was short.

He awoke early in the morning, as usual, and went out again to pray. Seeing the old potter with his oxcart moving slowly along the road, it being the morning of the thirteenth, preparation day for the Passover, he spoke to the old man concerning his route for the day.

"Deliver for me, a water pot," he requested, "to the man who rents his rooms for religious feasts; his name is Samuel. You know him?"

"Yes," the man nodded.

"Make your delivery later this morning at the fifth hour (11:00 a.m.), can you?" Jesus asked him. "I will send my disciples to meet you on the outskirts of the city. Direct them to the man's house, and they will pay you there."

"Certainly, master. A water jar," the man said thoughtfully, "I was told of the day you turned water into wine, at Cana, in Galilee."

Jesus nodded, smiling.

"Those were my water jars!" he beamed, "Imagine that."

Jesus smiled broadly, and touched the old man on the arm.

"Thank you, Topheth, my friend," he said, then strode off down the road, disappearing from the man's view.

"He called me friend," Topheth said to himself, while moving farther along the road toward the city, "Friend. And he knew my name!"

When Jesus returned to the Mount of Olives, later that morning, he sent Peter and John, saying, "Go and prepare us the Passover, that we may eat."

And they said to him, "Where will we prepare?"

And he said to them, "Behold, when you enter into the city, there a man shall meet you, bearing a pitcher of water; follow him into the house that he enters. And you shall say to the good man of the house, 'The Master says unto you, "My time is at hand; I will keep the Passover at your house. Where is the guest chamber, where I shall eat the Passover with my disciples?"' And he shall show you a large upper room furnished; there make ready."

And they went, and found it as he had said to them. Topheth met them on the outskirts of the city, at the fifth hour, with his oxcart bearing the water jar. From there, he took them to Samuel's house, and entered in, greeting the man. Peter and John delivered Jesus's message, and when the man heard his words, he marveled. And with great joy, he showed them the upper chamber of his house, which was well furnished, suited for the richest of Jerusalem's upper class. Samuel remembered the teaching of Jesus that evening at Simon's house, not so long ago, around the Feast of Dedication, when Jesus had spoken with him afterward concerning his corroborating words.

"The rich are not the only ones who warrant great honor," Samuel had told him. "You'll always have the uppermost room at my house."

He hadn't really expected Jesus to take him up on his offer, but he was nonetheless pleased to serve him.

Peter and John marveled as much as Samuel had, for they hadn't known Jesus to arrange his other affairs in such detail, or at all, for that matter. After paying the potter, and thanking their host, they began to prepare the Passover.

Topheth, having finished his schedule later that day, went to his field at the southern end of the Valley of Hinnom. The potter had purchased this field when he was young, because its proximity to Jerusalem made it a very convenient location for his fledgling business. The rich red clay from this field he found superior to others for making his pottery. He made the familiar climb up the terrace to the field, where he released his ox and lay his weary old body down upon the earth. Resting there, he reflected on the day's events, smiling over thoughts of being of some service to Jesus once more.

Matthew 26:1–5	Mark 14:1–2	Luke 22:1–13
Mark 14:12–16	Matthew 26:17–19	Exodus 12:3–14
Numbers 9:2–3	Leviticus 23:5–6	John 18:28

Chapter 57

FRIDAY'S LAST SUPPER

Now before the feast of the Passover, when Jesus knew that his hour had come that he should depart out of this world to the Father, he came with the twelve, in the evening, to the upper room. And when the hour had come, he sat down with the twelve.

And he said to them, "With desire I have desired to eat this Passover with you before I suffer, for I say unto you, I will not any more eat thereof, until it is fulfilled in the kingdom of God."

And he took the cup, and gave thanks, and said, "Take this, and divide it among yourselves, for I say unto you, I will not drink of the fruit of the vine, until that day that I drink it new in the kingdom of God."

And they all drank of it.

And he took bread, and gave thanks, and broke it, and gave it to them, saying, "Take, eat; this is my body, which is broken for you; this do in remembrance of me."

Likewise, also, he took the cup, after supper; and gave thanks, and gave it to them, saying, "Drink you all of it, for this is my blood of the new testament, which is shed for many for the remission of sins; this do, as often as you drink it, in remembrance of me. But truly, I will not drink now of the fruit of the vine until that day when the kingdom of God shall come, and I drink it new with you in my Father's kingdom."

With supper being ended, and the devil having now put into the heart of Judas Iscariot, Simon's son, to betray him; Jesus knew that the Father had given all things into his hands, and that he had come from God, and was returning to God. He, therefore, rose from supper, and laid aside his garments, and took a towel, and girded himself. Then he poured water into a basin, and began to wash the disciples' feet, and to wipe them with the towel with which he was girded.

When he came to Peter, Peter said to him, "Lord, do *you* wash *my* feet?"

Jesus answered, and said to him, "What I do, you know not now, but you shall know hereafter."

Peter said to him, "You shall *never* wash my feet."

Jesus shrugged and sighed, then answered him, "If I wash you not, you have no part with me."

Peter frowned thoughtfully, then replied to him enthusiastically, "Lord, not my feet only, but also my hands and my head."

Jesus smiled at him, and explained, "He that is washed, has no other need than to wash his feet, but is wholly clean, and you are clean, but not all."

For he knew who would betray him; that's why he said, "You are not all clean."

So after he had washed their feet, and had taken his garments, and sat down again, he said to them, "Do you know what I have done to you? You call me Master and Lord, and you say well, for so I am. If I then, your Lord and Master, have washed your feet, you also ought to wash one another's feet. For I have given you an example, that you should do as I have done to you. Truly, truly, I say unto you, the servant is not greater than his lord; neither is he that is sent, greater than he that sent him. If you know these things, happy are you if you do them. I speak not of you all; I know whom I have chosen, but it is so that the scripture may be fulfilled, 'He that eats bread with me has lifted up his heel against me.' Now I tell you before it comes, that when it comes to pass, you may believe that I

AM. Truly, truly, I say unto you, he that receives whomever I send, receives me, and he that receives me, receives him that sent me."

When Jesus had said this, he was troubled in spirit, and testified, and said, "Truly, truly, I say unto you, that one of you shall betray me."

Then the disciples looked at one another, doubting of whom he spoke. And they began to inquire among themselves, which of them it was that should do this thing.

They became extremely sorrowful, and said to him one by one, "It's not I, is it Lord?"

And he answered, and said to them, "Behold, the hand of him that betrays me is with me on this table. It is one of the twelve that dips with me in the dish. The Son of man, indeed, goes as it is written of him, but woe to that man by whom the Son of man is betrayed! It had been good for that man if he had not been born."

Then Judas Iscariot answered and said, "It's not I, is it, Rabbi?"

But Jesus said to him, "*You* tell *me!*"

Now John was reclining upon one elbow, so that his head was directly in front of Jesus, who was sitting up, and leaning forward upon one outstretched arm. Peter, who was in front of John, told him to ask Jesus who it was that would betray him.

John, then leaning his head back upon Jesus's chest, said to him, "Lord, who is it?"

Jesus answered him, "It is he to whom I shall give a sop, a peace offering, when I have dipped it."

And when he had broken off a piece of bread, he dipped the sop in wine, and gave it to Judas Iscariot, the son of Simon. And after Judas took the sop, Satan entered into him.

Then Jesus said to him, "What you do, do quickly."

Now no man at the table knew for what intent he spoke this to him. For some of them thought, because Judas had the bag, that Jesus had said to him, "Buy those things that we have need of against the feast," or that he should give something to the poor.

He, then having received the sop, went immediately out, and it was night.

Therefore, when he was gone out, Jesus said, "Now is the Son of man glorified, and God is glorified in him. If God is glorified in him, God shall also glorify him in himself, and shall immediately glorify him. Little children, only a little while I am with you. You shall seek me, and as I said to the Jewish leaders, so, now, I say to you, 'Where I go, you cannot come.' A new commandment I give to you, that you love one another—even as I have loved you, that you, likewise, love one another. By this shall all men know that you are my disciples, if you have love for one another."

Peter, taking offense at his words, said to him, "Lord, where do you go?"

Jesus answered him, "Where I go, you cannot follow me, now, but you shall follow me afterward."

But Peter protested, boasting to him before the others, "Lord, *I* am ready to go with you, both into prison, and unto death."

So there arose strife among them, which of them should be accounted the greatest.

And he said to them, "The kings of the Gentiles exercise lordship over them, and they that exercise authority upon them are called benefactors. But you shall not be so, but he that is greatest among you, let him be as the younger, and he that is chief, as he that serves. For which is greater, he that sits to eat, or he that serves? Is it not he that sits to eat? But I am among you as he that serves. You are they which have continued with me in my temptations. And I appoint unto you a kingdom, as my Father has appointed unto me, that you may eat and drink at my table in my kingdom, and sit on thrones judging the twelve tribes of Israel." Then Jesus said to Peter, "Simon, Simon, behold, Satan has desired to have you, that he may sift you as wheat, but I have prayed for you, that your faith fails not, and when you are restored, strengthen your brethren."

Peter said to him, "Lord, why can't I follow you, *now*? I will lay down my life for your sake."

Jesus answered him, "Will you lay down your life for my sake? Truly, truly, I say unto you, the cock shall not crow this day, till you have denied three times that you know me."

Peter lowered his gaze in apparent humiliation. The others lost heart, as well.

"Let not your heart be troubled," Jesus reassured them; "you believe in God, believe also in me. In my Father's house are many mansions; if it were not so, I would have told you. I go to prepare a place for you. And if I go and prepare a place for you, I will come again, and receive you unto myself, that where I am, there you may be also. And where I go, you know, and the way you know."

Thomas said to him, "Lord, we know not where you go, and how can we know the way?"

Jesus said to him, "I am the way, the truth, and the life; no man comes unto the Father, but by me. If you had known me, you should have known my Father also, and from henceforth you know him, and have seen him."

Philip said to him, "Lord, show us the Father, and it will satisfy us."

Jesus said to him, "Have I been so long a time with you, and yet you have not known me, Philip? He that has seen me has seen the Father, and how say you then, 'Show us the Father?' Don't you believe that I am in the Father, and the Father in me? The words that I speak to you, I speak not of myself, but the Father that dwells in me, he does the works. Believe me that I am in the Father, and the Father in me, or else believe me for the very works' sake. Truly, truly, I say unto you, he that believes in me, the works that I do shall he do also, and greater works than these shall he do, because I go to my Father. And whatever you shall ask in my name, that will I do, that the Father may be glorified in the Son. If you shall ask anything in my name, I will do it. If you love me, keep my commandments, and I will pray the Father, and he shall give you another Comforter, that he may abide with you forever, even the Spirit of truth, whom the world cannot receive, because it sees him not, neither knows him.

But you know him, for he dwells with you, and shall be in you. I will not leave you comfortless; I will come to you. Yet a little while, and the world sees me no more, but you see me; because I live, you shall live also. At that day you shall know that I am in my Father, and you in me, and I in you. He that has my commandments, and keeps them, he it is that loves me, and he that loves me shall be loved of my Father, and I will love him, and will manifest myself to him."

Judas said to him, not Iscariot, "Lord, how is it that you will manifest yourself to us, and not to the world?"

Jesus answered, and said to him, "If a man loves me, he will keep my words, and my Father will love him, and we will come to him, and make our abode with him. He that loves me not, keeps not my sayings, and the word which you hear is not mine, but the Father's which sent me. These things have I spoken to you, being yet present with you. But the Comforter, which is the Holy Spirit, whom the Father will send in my name, he shall teach you all things, and bring all things to your remembrance, whatever I have said unto you. Peace I leave with you; my peace I give to you; not as the world gives, give I unto you. Let not your heart be troubled, neither let it be afraid. You have heard how I said unto you, 'I go away, and come again unto you.' If you loved me, you would rejoice, because I said, I go to the Father, for my Father is greater than I. And now I have told you before it comes to pass, that when it comes to pass, you might believe. Hereafter I will not talk much with you, for the prince of this world comes, and has nothing on me. But that the world may know that I love the Father: as the Father gave me a commandment, even so I do likewise."

And he said to them, "When I sent you without purse, and scrip, and shoes, did you lack anything?"

And they said, "Nothing."

Then he said to them, "But now, he that has a purse, let him take it, and likewise his scrip, and he that has no sword, let him sell his garment, and buy one. For I say unto you that this that is written must yet be accomplished in me, 'And he was reckoned among the transgressors,' for the things concerning me have an end."

And they said, "Lord, behold, here are two swords."

And he said to them, "It is enough; I am ready. Arise, let us go from here."

And when they had sung a hymn, he went out, according to his custom, to the Mount of Olives, and his disciples followed him.

John 13:1	Mark 14:17	Matthew 26:20
Luke 22:14–18	Mark 14:25	Matthew 26:26
Mark 14:22	Luke 22:19	1Corinthians 11:23–24
Luke 22:20	1 Corinthians 11:25	Matthew 26:27–29
Mark 14:23–24	John 13:2–22	Matthew 26:18–21
Luke 22:21–23	Matthew 26:21–25	John 13:23–36
Luke 22:33	Luke 22:24–32	John 13:37–38
Luke 22:34	John 14:1–31	Luke 22:35–38
John 14:31	Matthew 26:30	Mark 14:26
Luke 22:39	Psalms 41:9	Isaiah 53:12

Chapter 58

THE MOUNT OF OLIVES

The procession was quiet, as they made their way toward the Mount of Olives. When they came upon the tiered grape vines, Jesus stopped, and turning to his disciples, he taught them, "I AM the true vine, and my Father is the vinedresser. Every branch in me that bears not fruit he takes away, and every branch that bears fruit, he cleans by pruning, that it may bring forth more fruit. Now you are pruned clean through the word, which I have spoken to you. Remain in me, and I in you. As the branch cannot bear fruit of itself, unless it remains in the vine, no more can you, unless you abide in me. I AM the vine; you are the branches: he that remains in me, and I in him, the same brings forth much fruit, for apart from me, you can do nothing. If a man remains not in me, he is cast forth as a branch, and is withered; and men gather them, and cast them into the fire, and they are burned. If you remain in me, and my words remain in you, you shall ask what you will, and it shall be done unto you. Herein is my Father glorified, that you bear much fruit; so shall you be my disciples.

"As the Father has loved me, so have I loved you; remain in my love. If you keep my commandments, you shall remain in my love, even as I have kept my Father's commandments, and remain in his love. These things have I spoken unto you, that my joy might remain in you, and that your joy might be full. This is my commandment, that you love one another, as I have loved you. Greater love has no man than this, that a man lay down his life for his friends. You are my friends, if you do whatever I command you. Henceforth, I call you not servants, for the servant knows not what his lord does; but I have called you friends, for all things that I have heard of my Father, I have made known unto you. You have not chosen me, but I have chosen you, and ordained you, that you should go and bring forth fruit, and that your fruit should remain; that whatever you ask the Father, in my name, he may give you. These things I command you, so that you love one another.

"If the world hates you, you know that it hated me before it hated you. If you were of the world, the world would love its own. But I have chosen you out of the world, because you are not of the world; therefore, the world hates you. Remember the word that I said unto you, 'The servant is not greater than his lord.' If they have persecuted me, they will also persecute you; if they have kept my saying, they will keep yours also. But all these things will they do unto you for my name's sake, because they know not him that sent me. If I had not come and spoken to them, they had not had sin, but now they have no cloak for their sin. He that hates me hates my Father also. If I had not done among them the works, which no other man did, they had not had sin, but now have they both seen and hated both me and my Father. But this came to pass, that the word might be fulfilled that is written in their Law, 'They hated me without a cause.' But when the Comforter is come, whom I will send unto you from the Father, even the Spirit of truth, which proceeds from the Father, he shall testify of me, and you also shall bear witness, because you have been with me from the beginning. These things have I spoken unto you, that you should not be offended. They shall put you out of the synagogues; yes, the time comes, that whoever kills you will think that he does God service. And these things will they do to you, because they have not known the Father, nor me. But these things have I told you, that when the time shall come, you may remember that I told you of them. And these things I said not to you at the beginning, because I was with you.

"But now I go my way to him that sent me, and none of you asks me, 'Why do you go?' But because I have said these things to you, sorrow has filled your hearts. Nevertheless, I tell you the truth; it is expedient for you that I go away, for if I go not away, the Comforter will not come unto you. But if I depart, I will send him to you. And when he has come, he will reprove the world of sin, and of righteousness, and of judgment: of sin, because they believe not in me; of righteousness, because I go to my Father, and you see me no more; of judgment, because the prince of this world is judged. I still have many things to say to you, but you cannot bear them now. Howbeit, when he, the Spirit of truth, is come, he will guide you into all truth; for he shall not speak of himself, but whatever he shall hear, that shall he speak, and he will show you things to come. He shall glorify me, for he shall receive of mine, and shall show it to you. All things that the Father has are mine; therefore, I said that he shall take of mine, and shall show it to you. A little while, and you shall not see me; and again, a little while, and you shall see me, because I go to the Father."

Then some of his disciples said among themselves, "What is this that he said to us, 'A little while, and you shall not see me; and again, a little while, and you shall see me,' and, 'because I go to the Father?'" They said, therefore, "What is this that he said, 'A little while?' We cannot tell what he said."

Now Jesus knew that they were desirous to ask him, and he said to them, "Do you inquire among yourselves of what I said, 'A little while, and you shall not see me; and again, a little while, and you shall see me?' Truly, truly, I say unto you, that you shall weep and lament, but the world shall rejoice; and you shall be sorrowful, but your sorrow shall be turned into joy. A woman has sorrow when she is in labor, because her hour has come, but as soon as she has been delivered of the child, she remembers no more the tribulation, for joy that a man is born into the world. And you, now, therefore, have sorrow, but I will see you again, and your heart shall rejoice, and your joy no man shall take from you. And in that day you shall ask me nothing. Truly, truly, I say unto you, whatever you shall ask the Father in my name, he will give you. Hitherto, you have asked nothing in my name: ask, and you shall receive, that your joy may be full. These things have I spoken to you in proverbs, but the time comes, when I shall no more speak to you in proverbs, but I shall show you plainly of the Father. At that day, you shall ask in my name; and I say not to you that I will pray to the Father for you, for the Father himself loves you, because you have loved me, and have believed that I came out from God. I came forth from the Father, and am come into the world; again, I leave the world, and go to the Father."

His disciples said to him, "Lo, now you speak plainly, and speak no proverb. Now we are sure that you know all things, and need not that any man should ask you; by this we believe that you came forth from God."

Jesus answered them, "Do you now believe? Behold, the hour comes; yes, has now come, that you shall be scattered, every man to his own, and shall leave me alone; and yet I am not alone, because the Father is with me. These things I have spoken unto you, that in me you might have peace. In the world you shall have tribulation, but be of good cheer; I have overcome the world."

Then Jesus said to them, "All you shall be offended, because of me this night, for it is written, 'I will smite the shepherd, and the sheep of the flock shall be scattered abroad.' But after I am risen again, I will go before you into Galilee."

Peter answered, and said to him, "Though all men shall be offended, because of you, yet *I* will never be offended."

Jesus said to him, "Truly, I say unto you, that this day, even in this night, before the cock crows twice, you shall deny me three times."

But Peter spoke the more vehemently to him, saying, "Though I should die with you, yet will I not deny you in any way."

Likewise, also, said all the disciples.

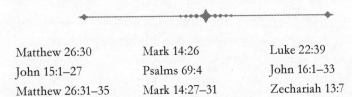

Matthew 26:30   Mark 14:26   Luke 22:39
John 15:1–27   Psalms 69:4   John 16:1–33
Matthew 26:31–35   Mark 14:27–31   Zechariah 13:7

Chapter 59

THE GARDEN BETRAYAL

Jesus, having spoken his words, went forth with his disciples over the brook Kidron, where there was a garden, called Gethsemane, into which he entered with his disciples.

And when Jesus had come to a certain place with his disciples, he said to them, "You sit here, while I go over there to pray. Pray that you enter not into temptation."

Then he took with him Peter and James and John, and became greatly distressed and very heavy in spirit, and he said to them, "My soul is exceedingly sorrowful, even unto death; you wait here, and watch with me."

He withdrew himself from them also, continuing forward a little farther, about a stone's throw away. Then he kneeled down, and fell upon his face, and prayed in the Spirit, crying out, "Abba, Father." Not knowing what to pray, the Spirit prayed for him in his anguish, in an unknown tongue, and Jesus's spirit, bearing witness with the Holy Spirit, prayed the interpretation, "All things are possible unto you, Father. If you are willing, let this cup pass from me; nevertheless, not my will, but yours be done."

And there appeared unto him an angel from heaven, strengthening him. And being in agony, he prayed more earnestly, and his sweat was as great drops of blood falling down to the ground.

And when he rose up from prayer, and had come again to his disciples, he found them sleeping for sorrow, and he said to Peter, "Simon, you *sleep*? *What*, could you not watch with me one hour? Watch and pray, that you enter not into temptation; the spirit indeed is willing, but the flesh is weak."

So he went away, again, the second time, and prayed, saying, "Oh, my Father, if this cup may not pass away from me, except I drink it, your will be done."

And he came and found them asleep again, for their eyes were heavy; neither knew they what to say to him. So he left them there and went away again, and prayed the third time, saying the same words.

When he returned to his disciples, he said to them, "Sleep on now, and take your rest; it is enough, for I am ready; behold, the hour is at hand, and the Son of man is betrayed into the hands of sinners."

Now Judas Iscariot knew the garden place in Gethsemane, for Jesus often resorted there with his disciples. Judas then, having received a band of men and officers from the chief priests and Pharisees, came there with lanterns and torches and weapons.

And Jesus, when he knew that the hour had come, woke his disciples, saying, "Rise up, let us be going; behold, he that betrays me is at hand."

And as he spoke, Judas came, with a great multitude from the chief priests and scribes, and the elders of the people, and they were brandishing their swords and staves.

Jesus, therefore, knowing all things that should come upon him went forth and said to them, "Whom do you seek?"

They answered him, "Jesus of Nazareth."

Jesus said to them, "I AM."

As soon, then, as he had said to them, "I AM," they went backward, and fell to the ground.

Then he asked them again, "Whom do you seek?"

And they said, "Jesus of Nazareth."

Jesus answered, "I have told you that I AM. If, therefore, you seek me, let these go their way."

This he did to protect his disciples, that the saying might be fulfilled, of which he spoke, "Of them which you gave me, I have lost none."

Now, trying to regain their composure, the leaders of the multitude stood, yet off at a distance, for fear. Judas, who also stood with them, gave them a sign, saying, "Whomever I shall kiss, he is the one; take him, hold him fast, and lead him away safely."

And as soon as he had directed them, he went straight to Jesus, and said, "Hail, master," and drew near to Jesus to kiss him.

Jesus said to him, "Friend, why have *you* come?"

But Judas lowered his eyes in silence, and kissed him.

And Jesus replied, "Judas, do you betray the Son of man with a *kiss*?" Then he whispered to himself, in the hearing of Judas, "They do honor me with their lips, but their hearts are far from me."

Judas's eyes flashed in anger, as he turned his back on Jesus to face the religious leaders.

When Jesus's disciples, who were now gathered about him, realized what would follow, they said to him, "Lord, shall we smite with the sword?"

Then the temple guards came, and they laid their hands on Jesus to take him. At this, Peter, having a sword, drew it; and struck Malchus, a servant of the high priest, and cut off his right ear.

But Jesus cried to Peter, pleading with him, "Put up your sword into its sheath, for all they that take up the sword shall perish by the sword. Don't you know that I can pray, now, to my Father, and he will immediately give me more than twelve legions of angels? But how, then, shall the scriptures be fulfilled? The cup, which my Father has given me, shall I not drink it? Allow even this; for thus, it must be."

He turned from Peter, reluctantly. And demonstrating compassion in the midst of his own pain, Jesus touched the ear of Malchus, and healed him. All present marveled at the gesture.

Then Jesus rebuked the chief priests, and captains of the temple, and the elders, which had come to him, saying, "Have you come out, as against a thief, with swords and staves to take me? When I was with you daily in the temple, you stretched forth no hands against me, but *this* is your hour, and the power of darkness." Then he added, "And the scriptures *must* be fulfilled."

After hearing his words and having witnessed his compassionate gesture, the band, being humbled, proceeded with less bravado. Led by the captain and the officers of the Jewish religious leaders, they reluctantly took Jesus; and, as was their duty, they bound him.

Peter and the other disciples discerned, now, that they were forbidden to fight for Jesus. Confused and frustrated, they reluctantly forsook him, and fled. Dazed and half naked, they scattered, as sheep having no shepherd.

———————————◆———————————

John 18:1	Mark 14:32–36	Romans 8:13–16
Matthew 26:36–39	Luke 22:40–46	Mark 14:37–41
Matthew 26:40–45	John 18:2–3	Mark 14:42–43
Matthew 26:46–47	John 18:4–9	Matthew 26:48–50
Mark 14:44–45	Luke 22:47–49	Isaiah 29:13–14
Mark 14:46–47	Matthew 26:51–54	John 18:10–11
Luke 22:50–53	Mark 14:48–49	Matthew 26:55
John 18:12	Matthew 26:56	Mark 14:50–52

Chapter 60

DELIVERED TO THE HIGH PRIEST

The soldiers led Jesus away to the palace of the high priest. But this band of men sent to apprehend Jesus was still shaken by what they had witnessed and heard in the garden, and they sought confirmation to the legitimacy of their mission. So instead of taking him directly to the high priest and the council, they brought him first to Annas, the former high priest, for he was father-in-law to Caiaphas, who was the high priest that same year.

From a safe distance, Peter and John followed Jesus. Now John was acquainted with the high priest, and went in with Jesus into the palace; but Peter stood at the door without. Then John went out and spoke to the woman that kept the door, and brought in Peter.

When the woman saw Peter, she asked him, "Are you not also one of this man's disciples?"

He said, "I am not."

Now the servants and officers who stood there had made a fire of coals in the hall, for it was cold, and they warmed themselves. And Peter stood with them, and warmed himself.

Within, Annas asked Jesus about his disciples, and his doctrine.

Jesus answered him, "I spoke openly to the world; I often taught in the synagogue, and in the temple, where the Jews always resort, and I have said nothing in secret. Why do you ask me? Ask them who heard me, what I have said to them; behold, they know what I said."

And when he had thus spoken, one of the officers, who stood by, struck Jesus with the palm of his hand, saying, "Do you answer the high priest, so?"

Jesus answered him, "If I have spoken evil, bear witness of the evil, but if well, why do you strike me?"

Then Annas, his pride being wounded by having his counsel unwelcomed by Jesus, sent him, still bound, to Caiaphas, his son-in-law, the current high priest. And John followed Jesus there, but Peter moved outside to the porch beneath the palace, for fear of being recognized again. There, he warmed himself by the fire, and sat with the servants, to see the end. And the cock crowed, as the night's darkness gave way to the morning light.

Inside the palace, the chief priests and scribes came together; and they led Jesus into their council, saying "Are you the Messiah? Tell us."

And he said to them, "If I *tell* you, you will not believe. And if I also *ask* you, you will not answer me, nor let me go. But hereafter shall the Son of man sit on the right hand of the power of God."

Then they all said to him, "Are you, then, the Son of God?"

And he answered them, "*You* tell *me*, for I AM!"

And they said, "Why do we still have need of testimony? For we ourselves have heard from *his* mouth."

Nevertheless, all the council sought those who would bear witness against Jesus to put him to death, and found none. For many bore false witness against him, but taken together, their witness did not agreed.

Two of the last witnesses came, saying, "We heard him say, 'I will destroy this temple that is made with hands, and within three days I will build another made without hands.'"

But not even on this account did their witness, taken together, agree.

So Caiaphas arose, and said to Jesus, "Do you answer nothing? What is it that these witness against you?"

But Jesus held his peace.

Then the high priest answered his silence, and said to him, "I adjure you, by the living God, that you tell us whether you are the Messiah, the Son of God."

Jesus said to him, "*You* tell *me*!"

Then the high priest, in his anger, drew near to him and demanded of him, shouting, "Are you the Messiah, the Son of the Blessed?"

His voice echoed throughout the hall.

Jesus waited for the echo to subside, and then said to him, in an equaling loud voice, yet without malice, "I AM! And you shall see the Son of man sitting on the right hand of power, and coming in the clouds of heaven."

The hall reverberated, and then fell silent for quite some time.

At last, the silence was broken by the echoing sound of tearing cloth as the high priest rent his clothes. This was followed by his anguished cry: "He has spoken blasphemy. What further need have we of witnesses? Behold, now you have heard his blasphemy. What is your judgment?"

And they all agreed, saying, "He is guilty of death."

Some began to spit upon him, and to cover his face, and to buffet him, and to say to him, "Prophesy unto us, you messiah. Who is it that smote you?"

Then they led him away, down the stairs, past the porch where Peter awaited word of his fate.

About that time, a maid recognized Peter, and pointed him out to those around the fire.

And a man, accusing him, demanded, "Aren't you also one of his disciples?"

He denied it, and said, "Man, I am not."

Then one of the servants of the high priest, being kinsman to the man whose ear Peter had cut off, said, "Didn't I see you in the garden with him? Of a truth, this fellow also was with him, for he is a Galilean."

And Peter said, "Man, I don't know what you're talking about."

As Jesus reached the bottom of the stairs, led by the palace guard onto the porch, he passed from behind Peter, who began to curse and to swear, saying, "I don't know the man."

Immediately the cock crowed the second time. And Jesus turned back, and looked at Peter. Peter was startled to see him; Jesus was looking at him with an expressionless stare. Then Peter remembered Jesus's words, how he said to him, "Before the cock crows twice, you shall deny me three times." And Peter, humiliated, went quickly out from the midst of them, and wept bitterly.

John 18:13–18	Luke 22:55–57	John 18:19–24
Matthew 26:57	Mark 14:53	Mark 14:54
Matthew 26:58	Mark 14:66–68	Matthew 26:69–71
Luke 22:66–71	Matthew 26:59–61	Mark 14:55–59
Matthew 26:62–64	Mark 14:60–64	Matthew 26:65–66
Mark 14:65	Matthew 26:67–68	Luke 22:63–65
Matthew 26:71–72	John 18:25	Luke 22:58
Mark 14:69–70	John 18:26–27	Luke 22:59–60
Matthew 26:73–75	Mark 14:70–72	Luke 22:61–62

Chapter 61

DELIVERED TO PILATE

The entire council, consisting of chief priests, elders, and scribes, who had come together to decide the fate of Jesus, concluded their business on the morning of the fourteenth with a decision against him to put him to death. So they led him away, bound, from Caiaphas to the Hall of Judgment; and delivered him to Pontius Pilate, the governor. When Judas Iscariot saw that Jesus was condemned by the council, and was being turned over to the Romans, he repented.

Judas brought again the thirty pieces of silver to the chief priests and elders, saying, "I have sinned in that I have betrayed innocent blood."

And they said to him, "What is that to *us? You* deal with it."

So he cast down the pieces of silver in the temple, and departed, and went and hanged himself, in the view of the high priest's palace.

Now, when the Jewish leaders came to the Roman Hall of Judgment, they would not enter in themselves, lest they should be defiled, for they had not yet eaten the Passover.

Pilate, therefore, went out to them, and said, "What accusation do you bring against this man?"

They answered, and said to him, "If he were not an evildoer, we would not have delivered him up to you."

But Pilate said to them, "*You* take him, and judge him according to *your* Law."

Then the Jewish leaders said to him, "It is not lawful for us to put any man to death."

Now the political environment had dramatically changed for Pilate in the recent months. Lucius Aelius Sejanus, whom Tiberius had given power to rule in his stead while he retired to Capri, had been executed for conspiring to overthrow Tiberius as emperor. To rid the empire of his influence, Tiberius began a reign of terror against those appointed by Sejanus, which included Pontius Pilate. Pilate's rule was now under constant scrutiny from Rome; and the anti-Hebrew sentiments held by Sejanus, and Pilate, were under particular criticism. The Jewish leadership now had the ear of the emperor, and executing Jews had become frowned upon. Pilate, therefore, refused to yield to their demands, insisting that a valid accusation was required to carry out a sentence of death. He took some pleasure in doing so, too, for in the wake of Sejanus's execution these emboldened Jewish leaders had complained to Tiberius about the way Roman rule was being conducted in Palestine. They had complained in particular how death sentences were being carried out indiscriminately upon the Jewish population.

Incited by the smugness of Pilate's reply, and the irony in it, the religious leaders began to vehemently accuse Jesus before him, saying, "We found this fellow perverting the nation, and forbidding Jews to give tribute to Caesar, saying that he himself is the Messiah, our King."

Then Pilate entered into the Judgment Hall again, and calling Jesus he said to him, "You are the king of the Jews."

He had phrased his words as a statement, but followed them by leaning his head forward and raising his eyebrows, waiting for Jesus to respond. His gesture, in essence, had changed his words from a statement into a question.

Jesus, seizing the opportunity to minister to Pilate, chose to answer him as if he had meant them as a statement. "Do you say this thing of yourself, or did others tell it to you of me?"

Pilate, somewhat embarrassed and offended by Jesus's wit,

snapped at him, "Am I a Jew?" Then composing himself, he returned to his interrogation, saying, "Your own nation and the chief priests have delivered you to me. What have you done?"

Jesus answered, "My kingdom is not of this world; if my kingdom were of this world, then would my servants fight, that I should not be delivered to the Jewish leaders; but, now, is my kingdom not from here."

Pilate, therefore, said to him, "Are you a king, then?"

Jesus answered, "*You* tell *me*, for I am a king."

These words, for Pilate's benefit also, Jesus delivered as Pilate had, phrasing them as a statement. He then leaned his head forward, raised his eyebrows, and waited for Pilate to respond to his questioning gaze. Jesus's obvious astuteness was not lost on Pilate. He paused at the comic relief Jesus brought to the gravity of the situation, and then he smirked, looking at Jesus admiringly.

Jesus continued ministering. "To this end was I born, and for this cause came I into the world, that I should bear witness unto the truth. Every one that is of the truth hears my voice."

Pilate crossed his arms, as if protecting his heart from scrutiny. His eyes narrowed, and his lips pursed; he felt strangely afraid, yet was inexplicably drawn to Jesus. He stepped closer to him.

Pondering Jesus's words, Pilate lifted a hand to his chin, and asked the question, "What *is* truth?"

This he said looking intently into Jesus's eyes, yet his question was not entirely addressed toward him; he questioned himself, as well.

Jesus's eyes softened ever-so-slightly to the hint of a smile. His almost imperceptible gesture dramatically affected Pilate, who immediately had to look away. Jesus did not answer his question, instead leaving the Roman governor to contemplate his own words.

And when he had considered them momentarily, Pilate brought Jesus out again to the Jewish leaders, and testified to them, "I find in him no fault at all."

But they were all the more fierce, saying, "He stirs up the

people, teaching throughout all Judea, beginning from Galilee to this place."

Jesus, however, having been accused by the chief priests and elders, answered nothing.

Then Pilate said to him, "Do you answer nothing? Don't you hear how many things they witness against you?"

But he answered him not a word, insomuch that the governor marveled greatly.

Nevertheless, when Pilate heard them speak of Galilee, he asked them if Jesus was a Galilean. And as soon as he knew that he belonged to Herod's jurisdiction, he sent him to Herod, who was also in Jerusalem at that time.

When Herod saw Jesus, he was exceedingly glad, for he had desired to see him for a long time. He hoped to witness some miracle done by him, because he had heard so many things about him. So Herod questioned him with many words, but Jesus answered him nothing, knowing that like the other Jewish leaders he sought a sign. Nevertheless, the chief priests and scribes stood by and vehemently accused him. Herod, then, with his men of war, treated Jesus with distain. Mocking him, they arrayed him in a gorgeous robe, and sent him back to Pilate.

Now the chief priests took the silver pieces that were discarded by Judas, and said, "It is not lawful to put them into the treasury, because it is the price of blood."

So they took counsel; and being informed of the discovery of the body of Topheth, the potter, they bought with the blood money the potter's field, in which they intended to bury strangers. And when the high priest discovered the horror of Judas's suicide, they buried his body there to cover up the ugliness of their conspiracy against Jesus. Therefore, that field has been called "the field of blood" unto this day. By this was fulfilled that which was spoken by Jeremiah, the prophet, saying, "And they took the thirty pieces of silver, the price of him on whom a price had been set by those of the sons of Israel, and gave them for the potter's field, just as the Lord had set it in order before me."

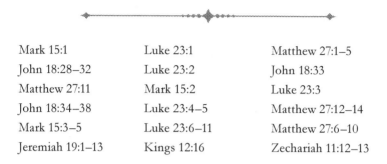

Mark 15:1	Luke 23:1	Matthew 27:1–5
John 18:28–32	Luke 23:2	John 18:33
Matthew 27:11	Mark 15:2	Luke 23:3
John 18:34–38	Luke 23:4–5	Matthew 27:12–14
Mark 15:3–5	Luke 23:6–11	Matthew 27:6–10
Jeremiah 19:1–13	Kings 12:16	Zechariah 11:12–13

Chapter 62

THE ROMAN TRIAL

Pilate, when he had called together the chief priests and the rulers and the people, said to them, "You have brought this man to me, as one that perverts the people, and, behold, I, having examined him before you, have found no fault in this man touching those things whereof you accuse him. No, nor yet has Herod, for I sent you to him; and he also judged that nothing worthy of death was done by him. I will, therefore, chastise him and release him to fulfill the custom that I should release to you one prisoner at the Passover."

But they cried out all at once, saying, "Not *this* man! Away with this man, and release unto us Barabbas."

Now Barabbas was a robber imprisoned for insurrection and for murder.

Pilate, more willing to release Jesus, spoke again to them, saying, "He says he is the king of truth. What is truth, that its power should frighten you so?"

But they cried, saying, "Crucify him, crucify him."

And he said to them the third time, "Why, what evil has he done? I have found no cause of death in him."

The Jewish leaders answered him, "We have a law, and by our law he ought to die, because he made himself the Son of God."

When Pilate, therefore, heard these words, he was even more

afraid, and went again into the Judgment Hall, and said to Jesus, "Where are you from?"

But Jesus gave him no answer.

Then Pilate said to him, "Will you not speak to *me*? Know you not that I have power to crucify you, and have power to release you?"

Jesus answered, "You could have no power at all against me, except it were given to you from above; therefore, he that delivered me unto you has the greater sin."

From that point forward, Pilate sought to release him. Pilate knew that, out of envy, the Jewish leaders sought to kill Jesus. He thought that if he could show them that Jesus was just a man, instead of the Son of God, perhaps their thirst for his death might be placated. He hoped that seeing Jesus scourged, and bleeding like any normal man, would satisfy their lust for revenge.

Pilate, reaffirming his intentions to the priests, insisted, "I will chastise him, and let him go."

For this reason, Pilate took Jesus, and had him scourged.

The soldiers led him away into the hall called Praetorium, and they stripped him, and platted a crown of thorns and put it on his head. They put on him Herod's purple robe, and put a reed in his right hand; and they bowed on their knees before him, and mocked him, saying, "Hail, king of the Jews!"

They smote him with their hands, and hit him with the blunt end of their spears. And they spit upon him, and took the reed, and smote him on the head. And they tore out the corners of his beard by his *peyot*; these were long curled sideburns, the tzitzit of his head. And when they had scourged him the customary "forty lashes less one," they reported back to Pilate.

Having received their report, Pilate went out again, and said to the Jewish leaders, "Behold, I bring him forth to you, that you may know that I find no fault in him."

Then came Jesus forth, wearing the crown of thorns, and the purple robe. When Pilate saw him, he was horrified.

Trying with great difficulty to compose himself, Pilate finally said to them, "Behold, the *man!*"

When the chief priests and officers saw him, they were altogether horrified, as well, at his broken visage.

Pilate, believing he had thoroughly demonstrated Jesus's human frailty, asked them in a manner revealing his disgust over the unpleasantness, "Will you, *now,* have me release unto you the king of the Jews?"

But the leaders, offended that the Romans mocked their Jewish heritage, became enraged, and cried aloud, saying, "Crucify him; crucify him. If you let this man go, you are not Caesar's friend: whoever makes himself a king speaks against Caesar."

Their reaction alarmed Pilate, for he knew that Tiberius had ambassadors in Jerusalem, monitoring the governor's every move. When Pilate, therefore, heard their words, he brought Jesus forward; and he sat down in the official judgment seat, in a place that is called the Pavement; but in the Hebrew: Gabbatha.

And it was the Preparation Day of the Passover for these Jewish leaders, before nine in the morning; and Pilate, looking for a way out, appealing instead to the growing Jewish multitude, said to them, "Behold your king!"

But the Jewish leaders cried out, "Away with him, away with him, crucify him."

Pilate, ignoring the leaders, said to the crowd, "Shall I crucify your king?"

The chief priests answered, "We have no king but Caesar."

The crowd, which had grown restless trying to understand these strange proceedings, now became quiet, as they fully grasped the situation. Pilate was obviously ignoring the demands of their religious leaders, and waiting upon them to decide.

Therefore, when the crowd had come together, settling down to hear him, Pilate said to them, "Whom will you have me release unto you, Barabbas or Jesus, who is called the Christ?"

Now, when Pilate sat down on the judgment seat, his wife sent word to him, saying, "Have nothing to do with that just man, for I have suffered many things this day in a dream because of him."

But, while the proceedings were being interrupted by the delivery of her message, the chief priests and elders persuaded the multitude that they should ask for Barabbas to be released, and that Pilate might destroy Jesus.

After receiving her message, and contemplating to some degree its significance, the governor returned to protocol, and addressed the crowd, again, saying, "Which of the two will you have me release unto you?"

The overwhelming majority shouted, "Barabbas."

Pilate said to them, "What shall I do, then, with Jesus, who is called the Christ, the king of the Jews?"

Looking upon this broken and humiliated man from Galilee, whom the Romans were mocking as the representative of all Israel's strength; the crowd began to shout in unified indignation, "Let him be crucified."

And the governor said, "Why, what evil has he done?"

But they cried out all the more, chanting repeatedly, "Let him be crucified."

When Pilate saw that he could prevail no further, but that rather a tumult was made, he called for a basin of water.

Now Annas, the former high priest, was there among them. And when he saw the spectacle, he was given a revelation, and he marveled at how much the trial paralleled the rituals of the Day of Atonement. There was Jesus, chosen as the sacrifice, and Barabbas as the scapegoat was being set free.

The water basin was brought to Pilate, and before the religious leaders, the multitude, and the ambassadors of Rome, he washed his hands, saying, "I am innocent of the blood of this just one; *you* see to it."

Annas pondered the proceedings, trying to grasp the revelation. Just then, however, all the people screamed in a frenzied response to Pilate, saying, "His blood be upon us, and upon our children!"

At this, Annas gasped, seeing in his vision the sprinkling of the blood upon the mercy seat of the Ark of the Covenant. Others nearby looked at him briefly to understand his reaction. But the old man shook his head in bewilderment.

Unwittingly, the cry of the people had become an oath of consent to the New Covenant in the blood of the Messiah, even as their ancestors had consented to the first covenant on Mount Sinai, when Moses sprinkled the blood of the sacrifice upon all the people.

Annas, observing by the wayside, watched as Pilate released Barabbas and turned Jesus over to be sacrificed. The Roman soldiers took hold upon Jesus to take him outside the city, there to be offered up by crucifixion. As Annas watched them take Jesus away, the revelation passed quickly from him, and the old man gave it no more thought.

Luke 23:13–17
John 18:39–40
Mark 15:7–8
Matthew 27:18
Mark 15:16–19
Micah 5:1
Mark 15:9
Matthew 27:17
Matthew 27:22–23
Luke 23:24–25
Mark 15:15
Hebrews 9:13-22

Matthew 27:15
Luke 23:18–19
Luke 23:20–22
Mark 15:10
Matthew 27:27–30
Leviticus 19:27
John 19:6
Matthew 27:19–21
Luke 23:23
John 19:16
Leviticus 16:7–10

Mark 15:6
Matthew 27:16
John 19:7–12
John 19:1–3
Isaiah 50:6
John 19:4–5
John 19:12–15
Mark 15:11–14
Matthew 27:24–25
Matthew 27:26
Exodus 24:6-8

Chapter 63

THE CRUCIFIXION

After the Roman soldiers had mocked him to scorn, they removed the purple robe from him, replacing it with his own clothes, and led him away to be crucified. And he went forth bearing his cross to a place called the place of the skull, which is called in the Hebrew: Golgotha; and in Latin: Calvary. They proceeded very slowly, because Jesus was so badly beaten; too slowly for the impatience of the soldiers, who continued to harass him. So as they came out along the way, they found a man of Cyrene, Simon by name, who was passing by, coming out of the country; and they laid hold upon him. On him they laid the cross, and compelled him to follow after Jesus. A great company of people followed Jesus, as well, among them many women, which also bewailed and lamented over him.

But Jesus, turning to them, said, "Daughters of Jerusalem, weep not for me, but weep for yourselves, and for your children. For, behold, the days are coming, in which they shall say, 'Blessed are the barren, and the wombs that never bore, and the breasts which never gave suck.' Then shall they begin to say to the mountains, 'Fall on us,' and to the hills, 'Cover us.' For if they do these things while the tree is green, what shall be done when it is dry?'"

And there were also two other thieves, led with him to be put to death.

When they reached Golgotha, the soldiers gave Jesus vinegar

to drink, mingled with gall, a bitter mixture of myrrh. But when he had tasted it, he would not drink it, for the vinegar was made from the fruit of the vine, which he had vowed to abstain from until the kingdom of God had come.

Now Pilate wrote a title to be put on his cross. And the writing was: "THIS IS JESUS OF NAZARETH THE KING OF THE JEWS." Many of the Jews, therefore, read this title, for the place where Jesus was crucified was near to the city, and it was written in Hebrew, and Greek, and Latin.

When the chief priests of the Jews saw it, they came protesting to Pilate, saying, "Write not, 'The King of the Jews,' but that he *said*, 'I am King of the Jews.'"

But Pilate answered them, "What I have written, I have written."

And it was about the third hour, around nine in the morning, when they crucified him.

When they had stripped him of his clothes; nailed him to the cross; and raised it up, setting it firmly in place; Jesus said, in the hearing of his torturers, "Father, forgive them, for they know not what they do."

The centurion who was overseeing his execution marveled at his words; so did many of the onlookers.

Alongside Jesus, they crucified the two thieves, the one on his right hand, and the other on his left. And the scripture was fulfilled, which said, "And he was numbered with the transgressors."

When they had crucified Jesus, the soldiers set up over his head his accusation, and sitting down, they watched him there. Then they took his garments, and made four parts, to every soldier a part. And they confiscated also his coat. Now the coat was without seam, woven from the top throughout.

They said, therefore, among themselves, "Let us not tear it, but cast lots for it, to determine whose it shall be."

This was done, despite their ignorance of it, that the scripture might be fulfilled, which said, "They parted my garments among them, and for my vesture they did cast lots." These things, therefore, the soldiers did, unknowingly.

And many people stood by beholding him. And they that passed by were appalled by his appearance, so they railed on him, wagging their heads, and saying, "Ah, you who destroys the temple, and builds it in three days, save yourself. If you are the Son of God, come down from the cross."

Likewise, also, the chief priests, mocking him, with the scribes and elders, said among themselves, "He saved others; himself he cannot save. Let him save himself, if he is the Messiah, the chosen of God. Let the Messiah, the King of Israel, descend now from the cross that we may see and believe. He trusted in God; let him deliver him now, if he will have him, for he said, 'I am the Son of God.'"

The soldiers continued also to mock him, coming to him, and offering him vinegar, and saying, "If you are the king of the Jews, save yourself."

Even the thief to the left of Jesus that was crucified with him, being appalled by him also, likewise railed against him, saying, "If you are the Messiah, save yourself and us."

But the other, answering, rebuked him, saying, "Do you not fear God, seeing you suffer the same condemnation? And we, indeed, justly, for we receive the due reward of our deeds, but this man has done nothing amiss." Then he said to Jesus, "Lord, remember me when you come into your kingdom."

And Jesus said to him, "Truly, I say unto you, today you shall be with me in paradise."

When he had said these words, a raven descended upon the head of the thief to his left, pecked out his right eye, and flew off, leaving the man wailing in agony.

Time dragged on, as the three condemned men suffered the physical rigors of crucifixion: acute pain in their hands and feet, where pierced by the nails; severe aching pain in their shoulders, elbows and wrists due to dislocation; chest pain and labored breathing, caused by the strain that their own bodyweight was exerting upon their heart and lungs as they continually shifted up and down the cross to breathe; headache, nausea, extreme sweating, chills, and dizziness from shock; severe thirst, cramping, and dehydration caused by the ordeal and the intensifying heat of the sun as it rose higher in the morning sky. People came and went, passing before them, as they endured also the humiliation of their public nakedness and suffering before the gaping crowd.

Now there stood by the cross of Jesus, women: his mother and his mother's sister; Mary, the wife of Cleophas; and Mary Magdalene.

When Jesus, therefore, saw his mother; and his disciple, John, standing nearby, he said to his mother, "Woman, behold your son!" Then he said to John, "Behold your mother!"

Mary began to weep, for she understood the meaning of his words; Jesus was letting her and John know that she was, now, not just his earthly mother, but one of his disciples, as well. And from that hour, John took her to his own home.

Now, when the sixth hour approached, high noon; the heavens grew dark, and there was darkness over the whole earth until the ninth hour, around three in the afternoon.

And about the ninth hour, Jesus cried with a loud voice, saying, "Eli, Eli, lama sabachthani?" which is to be interpreted, "My God, my God, why have you forsaken me?"

He said this, quoting the psalm, for he recognized that the sins of the world were now upon him, because his Father also had abandoned him, leaving him incomprehensibly and utterly alone.

Some of them that stood nearby, when they heard his laboring speech, said mistakenly, "Behold, this man, he calls for Elijah."

And at Jesus's words, one of them ran, immediately, took a sponge, filled it with vinegar, put it on a reed, and gave it to him to drink.

The rest said, "Let him be; let us see whether Elijah will come take him down to save him."

After this, Jesus, despising the sin, and yearning to be clothed in righteousness, knowing that all things were now accomplished, that the scriptures might be fulfilled, said, "I thirst."

So they refilled the sponge from a vessel full of vinegar, and they put it upon hyssop, and put it to his mouth. When Jesus knew that he had fulfilled his vow, he received the vinegar, therefore, and said, "It is finished."

Having faith, then, that his Father would accept his selfless sacrifice, Jesus cried with a loud voice, saying, "Father, into your hands I commend my spirit."

When he had said this, he bowed his head, and gave up the ghost.

At the temple, the priests were preparing the killing of the Passover lamb. This was interrupted; for behold, the veil of the temple was rent in two from the top to the bottom the moment Jesus died, and the earth did quake, and the rocks rent.

Now when the centurion, and they that were with him watching Jesus, saw the earthquake and those things that were done when he so cried out, they feared greatly, saying, "Truly this was the Son of God. Indeed, this was a righteous man."

Matthew 27:31	Mark 15:20	John 19:17
Luke 23:33	Luke 23:26	Mark 15:21
Matthew 27:32	Luke 23:27–32	Matthew 27:33–34
Mark 15:22–23	John 19:19–22	Mark 15:25
Luke 23:33–34	Matthew 27:38	John 19:17–18
Mark 15:27–28	Isaiah 53:12	Matthew 27:36–37
Mark 15:26	Luke 23:38	Mark 15:24
John 19:23–24	Matthew 27:35	Psalms 22:18
Matthew 27:39–44	Luke 23:35–37	Mark 15:29–32
Luke 23:39–43	Proverbs 30:17	John 19:25–27
Luke 23:44	Matthew 27:45–46	Mark 15:33–34
Psalms 22:1	Matthew 27:47–49	Mark 15:35–36
John 19:28–30	Luke 23:45–46	Matthew 27:50–51
Mark 15:37–38	Matthew 27:54	Mark 15:39
Luke 23:47		

Chapter 64

BURIAL BEFORE THE SABBATH

The Jewish religious leaders, because it was the Preparation Day, desired that the bodies of those crucified should not remain upon the cross on the Sabbath day, for this Sabbath, being also the day they celebrated their Passover, was, therefore, considered a High Holy Day. To hasten their deaths, therefore, they besought Pilate that the legs of the condemned might be broken, and that their bodies might be taken away. The soldiers then came, and broke the legs of the first man, and of the other one also, who was crucified with him. But when they came to Jesus, and saw that he was dead already, they neglected to break his legs. One of the soldiers, instead, pierced his side with a spear to make sure he was dead, and immediately there came out blood and water, indicating that his heart had ruptured.

And all the people that came together to that sight, beholding the things which were done, smote their breasts, and returned to their homes. But all his acquaintances, and the women that followed him from Galilee, stood afar off, beholding these things.

There were among them: Mary Magdalene; and Jesus's mother, Mary, who was also the mother of James, Joses, and Salome; the mother of Zebedee's children; and many other women who came up with him to Jerusalem. With them was John, who was also a witness and bore record to the truth of these things. For these things were done that the scripture should be fulfilled, "A bone of him shall not be broken." And again another scripture said, "They shall look on him whom they have pierced."

Now, when the evening had nearly come, while it was still the Preparation Day; that is, the day before the Sabbath, there came a rich man of Arimathaea named Joseph. He was a good and just man, who also waited for the kingdom of God; he was himself a disciple of Jesus, but secretly, for fear of the other Jewish leaders. Being an honorable counselor, he had not consented to the counsel and deed of the others who had condemned Jesus. This man went boldly before Pilate, and besought him, begging him, that he might take away Jesus's body. And Pilate marveled that Jesus was already dead, so he called the centurion to him, and asked him whether he had been dead for any length of time. And when the centurion confirmed Jesus's death, Pilate commanded that his body be delivered to Joseph.

Joseph bought fine linen; then he came, and took down the body of Jesus, and wrapped it in the clean linen cloth. There came with him also Nicodemus, who had come to Jesus by night at the beginning of Jesus's ministry, and he brought with him to the cross a mixture of myrrh and aloe, about a hundred-pound weight. Now in the place where Jesus was crucified there was a garden, and in the garden a new tomb, Joseph's own new tomb, which he had hewn out of the rock, wherein never before a body was laid. So they took the body of Jesus, and bound it in the linen cloth with the spices, as the manner of the Jews was to bury their dead. And they laid Jesus's body there, because the Jewish Preparation Day was nearing its end, and the tomb was near at hand. When they had finished, they rolled a great stone before the door of the tomb, and departed. Now Mary Magdalene and Mary the mother of Jesus were sitting over near the tomb, and they beheld how and where his body was laid. They also departed, and returned to their lodgings, where they prepared their own spices and ointments, and rested on the Sabbath day according to the commandment.

Now the next day that followed the Day of the Preparation,

just after the sun had set, a blood moon rose over the eastern sky, emerging from a lunar eclipse, under the feet of the constellation Virgo. Being startled by the heavenly sign, before they began their Passover meal on the Sabbath, the chief priests and Pharisees hastened therefore again to Pilate, saying, "Sir, we remember that this deceiver said, while he was yet alive, 'After three days I will rise again.' Command, therefore, that the tomb be made sure until the third day, lest his disciples come by night, and steal him away, and say to the people, 'He is risen from the dead,' so that the last error shall be worse than the first."

But Pilate said to them, "You have a watch of Roman guards; go your way, make it as sure as you can."

So they went, and made the tomb sure, sealing the stone, and setting a watch.

John 19:31–34   Luke 23:48–49   Matthew 27:55–56
Mark 15:40–41   John 19:35–37   Psalms 34:17–20
Zechariah 12:10   Psalms 22:14   Luke 23:50–52
Mark 15:42–43   Matthew 27:57–58   Mark 15:44–45
John 19:38–42   Matthew 27:59–60   Mark 15:46
Luke 23:53–54   Mark 15:47   Matthew 27:61
Luke 23:55–56   Matthew 27:62–66

Chapter 65

SUNDAY MORNING RESURRECTION

When the Sabbath was past, Mary Magdalene; and Mary, the mother of Jesus, James, and Salome; thought to return to the tomb, that they might come and anoint the body of Jesus.

So very early in the morning on the first day of the week, they went to the tomb at the rising of the sun, when it was yet dark, bringing with them the sweet spices that they had bought and prepared, and there were certain others with them.

And they discussed among themselves, "Who shall roll us away the stone from the door of the tomb?" For it was very great.

And, behold, there was a great earthquake, for the angel of the Lord descended from heaven, and came and rolled back the stone from the door, and sat upon it. His countenance was like lightning, and his raiment white as snow, and for fear of him, the keepers of the watch did shake, and became as dead men.

When the women came to the tomb, therefore, and looked, they saw that the stone was rolled away, and that the men of the watch were still lying about, as if sleeping. In fear, they returned in haste to tell the disciples. Then Mary Magdalene ran ahead to tell Peter and John what they had seen.

Now while the rest of the women were following, behold, some of the watch passed them, coming also into the city, to show the chief priests all the things that were done.

When Mary Magdalene reached Peter and John, she said to them, "They have taken away the Lord out of the tomb, and we know not where they have laid him."

Peter and John, therefore, went forth immediately, returning to the tomb. So they ran together, with Mary Magdalene in pursuit, passing the other women along the way, and John outran Peter, and came first to the tomb. And he found the tomb abandoned. Then stooping down and looking in, he saw the linen cloths, yet he went not in. Then came Peter following him, and went into the tomb, and saw the linen cloths lying there, and the napkin that had been about his head, not lying with the linen cloths, but wrapped together in a place by itself. Then John went in also, and he saw. And the disciples went away again to their own place of lodging.

But Mary, arriving at the tomb after them, beheld them leaving, and stood without the tomb weeping; and as she wept, she stooped down and looked into the tomb, and saw two angels in white sitting, the one at the head, and the other at the feet, where the body of Jesus had lain.

And they said to her, "Woman, why do you weep?"

She said to them, "Because they have taken away my Lord, and I know not where they have laid him."

And when she had said this, she turned herself back briefly, and saw Jesus standing there, and knew not that it was Jesus, for his head was shorn, and he was clean-shaven.

Jesus said to her, "Woman, why do you weep? Whom do you seek?"

She, supposing him to be the gardener, said to him between sobs, "Sir, if you have carried him off, tell me where you have laid him, and I will take him away."

Then turning back to the linens, she continued to sob.

Jesus said to her, "Mary."

When she heard how he said her name, she knew it was Jesus, and she turned herself again toward him, saying, "Rabboni;" which is to say, "Master."

Jesus said to her, "Touch me not, for I am not yet ascended to my Father, but go to my brethren, and say to them, 'I ascend unto my Father, and your Father, and to my God, and your God.'"

So she went and told his disciples, them that had been with him, as they mourned and wept, that she had seen the Lord, and that he had spoken these things to her. And they, when they heard that he was alive, and had been seen of her, believed her not.

Because they did not believe her, Mary Magdalene became indignant, complaining to the other women. And they consoled her, and went with her again to the tomb, hoping that perhaps Jesus might appear to them also.

Then they entered into the tomb, and found not the body of the Lord Jesus. And it came to pass, as they were very perplexed about the situation, behold, two men stood by them in shining garments, and they saw a young man sitting on the right side, clothed in a long white garment, and they were frightened.

Now, as they bowed down their faces to the earth in fear, the angel answered, and said to them, "Be not afraid, for I know that you seek Jesus of Nazareth, who was crucified. Why do you seek the living among the dead? He is not here, for he is risen, as he said. Come; behold the place where they laid him."

The women, finding courage, looked up to see.

So the angel continued speaking to them. "Remember how he spoke to you when he was yet in Galilee, saying, 'The Son of man must be delivered into the hands of sinful men, and be crucified, and on the third day rise again.' Go your way quickly, and tell his disciples, and Peter, that he is risen from the dead, and, behold, he goes before you into Galilee; there you shall see him, as he said unto you. Lo, I have told you."

And they departed quickly, and fled from the tomb with fear and great joy, for they trembled and were amazed, and they ran to bring his disciples word.

As they went to tell his disciples, behold, Jesus met them, saying, "All hail."

And when they recognized him, they came and held him by the feet, and worshiped him.

Then Jesus said to them, "Be not afraid; go tell my brethren, so that they go into Galilee, and there shall they see me."

So they remembered his words, and returned from the tomb; neither said they anything to anyone along the way, for they were afraid. When they got to the disciples, they told all these things to the eleven and to all the rest. It was Mary Magdalene; and Joanna; and Mary, the mother of Jesus and James; and other women that were with them, that told these things to the apostles. But their words seemed to them as idle tales, so they believed them not. Then Peter arose and ran to the tomb, and stooping down, he beheld, again, the linen cloths laid by themselves. And he remained there for some time, pondering in profound reflection, before he departed, wondering within himself at that which had come to pass.

Meanwhile, when the priests were assembled with the elders, and had taken counsel, they gave a large amount of money to the soldiers of the watch, saying, "You say, 'His disciples came by night, and stole him away while we slept.' And if this comes to the governor's ears, we will persuade him, and protect you."

This they said, because the penalty for Roman soldiers neglecting the duty of their watch was death. So like good soldiers, they took the money, and did as they were told.

Matthew 28:1	Luke 24:1	Mark 16:1–3
Matthew 28:2–4	John 20:1	Luke 24:2
Mark 16:4	John 20:2	Matthew 28:11
John 20:3–18	Mark 16:9–11	Luke 24:3–4
Mark 16:5–6	Luke 24:5–7	Matthew 28:5–7
Mark 16:7	Matthew 28:8	Matthew 28:9–10
Luke 24:8	Mark 16:8	Luke 24:9–12
Matthew 28:12–15		

Chapter 66

JESUS APPEARS TO HIS DISCIPLES

Throughout that day, around Jerusalem and beyond, the people of Judea began to stir; for the graves were opened, and many bodies of the saints that slept, arose and came out of their graves, and went into the holy city, and appeared to many.

And, behold, two of Jesus's disciples went that same day to a village called Emmaus, which was less than a half day's journey from Jerusalem. And as they walked, and went into the country, they talked together of all these things that had happened. And it came to pass that while they communed together and reasoned, Jesus himself drew near and went with them, but their eyes were not opened that they might recognize him.

Then he said to them, "What manner of communications are these that you have one to another, as you walk, and are sad?"

And one of them, whose name was Cleopas, answering, said to him, "Are you the only stranger in Jerusalem who has not known the things that have come to pass there in these days?"

And Jesus said to them, "What things?"

And they said to him, "Concerning Jesus of Nazareth, who was a prophet mighty in deed and word before God and all the people, and how the chief priests and our rulers delivered him to be condemned to death, and have crucified him. But we trusted that it had been he who should have redeemed Israel, and beside all this, today is the third day since these things were done. Yes, and certain women also of our company made us astonished, who were early at the tomb, and when they found not his body, they came, saying that they had also seen a vision of angels, who said that he was alive. And certain of them who were with us went to the tomb, and found it even as the women had said, but him they saw not."

Then he said to them, "Oh fools, and slow of heart to believe all that the prophets have spoken; ought not the Messiah to have suffered these things, and to enter into his glory?"

Then beginning at Moses and all the Prophets, he expounded to them, in all the scriptures, the things concerning himself. And they drew near to the village, where they went, and he made as though he would have gone on farther.

But they constrained him, saying, "Abide with us, for it is toward evening, and the day is far spent."

So he went in to tarry with them. And it came to pass, as he sat to eat with them, he took bread, and blessed it, and broke it, and gave it to them. Then their eyes were opened, and they knew him, but he vanished out of their sight.

Then they said one to another, "Did not our hearts burn within us, while he talked with us by the way, and while he opened to us the scriptures?"

So they rose up the same hour, and returned to Jerusalem, finding the eleven still gathered together there, with others in attendance. They came in the early evening, just before the sun had set, while it was still the first day of the week; and the doors were shut, where the disciples were assembled, for fear of the Jewish religious leaders. This remnant had not believed the witness of the women; neither had they gone to Galilee, obeying Jesus's words to them.

It was here, in Jerusalem, that Cleopas and the other disciple sat down with the remnant to eat, and were told by them, "The Lord is risen, indeed, and has appeared unto Peter."

Then the two, likewise, told them what things were done in

the way, and how Jesus was known of them in the breaking of the bread. But like the women who had testified that they saw Jesus at the tomb, neither did the remnant believe them.

Nevertheless, when they had spoken this, Jesus, himself, came and stood in the midst of them, and said to them, "Peace be unto you."

But they then became terrified, and supposed that they had seen a spirit.

And he said to them, "Why are you troubled? And why do thoughts arise in your hearts? Behold my hands and my feet, that it is I myself; handle me, and see, for a spirit has not flesh and bones as you see me have."

And when he had spoken this, he showed them his hands and his feet and his side.

And while they yet believed not for joy, and wondered, he said to them, "Have you here any food?"

And they gave him a piece of a broiled fish, and part of a honeycomb. And he took it, and ate it before them.

And he said to them, "These are the words which I spoke to you, while I was yet with you, that all things must be fulfilled, which were written in the Law of Moses, and in the Prophets, and in the Psalms, concerning me." Then he opened their understanding, that they might understand the scriptures, and said to them, "Thus it is written, and thus it was necessary for the Messiah to suffer, and to rise from the dead on the third day, and that repentance and remission of sins should be preached in his name among all nations beginning at Jerusalem. You are witnesses of these things."

When he had said these things, he upbraided them for their unbelief and hardness of heart, because they believed not the witness of those who had seen him after he had risen. Then were the disciples glad, when they saw it was the Lord.

Now when Jesus had left them, they gathered their belongings together, deciding to obey the commandment he had given them at

the first. But Thomas, one of the twelve, called Didymus, was not
with them when Jesus had come to them.

The other disciples, therefore, explained to him as they prepared.
"We have *seen* the Lord!"

But he said to them, "Except I shall see in his hands the print
of the nails, and put my finger into the print of the nails, and thrust
my hand into his side, I will not believe."

Nevertheless, they convinced him to join them, and they
departed for Galilee. And they assembled at Peter's house, shutting
themselves inside, still fearing retribution from the religious leaders
and the nonbelievers.

Another eight days his disciples remained within the house, and
Thomas was with them; then Jesus came, the doors being shut, and
stood in their midst, and said, "Peace be unto you."

Then he said to Thomas, "Reach here your finger, and behold
my hands; and reach here your hand, and thrust it into my side, and
be not faithless, but believing."

When Thomas had complied, he answered, and said to him,
"My Lord and my God."

Jesus said to him, "Thomas, because you have seen me, you have
believed: blessed are they that have not seen, and have yet believed."

And he stayed with them a short while, before departing from
them again, in like manner as he had appeared.

After these things, Jesus showed himself again, to the disciples,
at the Sea of Galilee. There were together, then: Peter, and Thomas
called Didymus, and Nathanael of Cana in Galilee, and the sons of
Zebedee, and two other of his disciples.

Peter said to them, "I am going fishing."

And they said to him, "We will go with you."

So they went out, and entered into a ship immediately, so as
not to be seen, and that night they caught nothing. But when the
morning had come, Jesus stood on the shore, but the disciples did
not know that it was Jesus.

Then Jesus said to them, "Children, have you caught any fish to eat?"

They answered him, "No."

And he said to them, "Cast the net on the right side of the ship, and you shall find some."

They cast, therefore, and then were not able to draw up the net for the multitude of fishes.

Therefore John, remembering the "miraculous catch," said to Peter, "It is the Lord!"

Now, when Peter heard that it was the Lord, he put on his fisherman's coat to cover his nakedness, and dove into the sea. And the other disciples came in a little ship dragging the net with fishes, for they were not far from land. Then, as soon as they had reached the shoreline, they saw a fire of coals there, with fish and bread laid thereon.

Jesus said to them, "Bring some of the fish, which you have just caught."

Peter got up, helping them draw the net to land, for it was full of great fishes, 153, and even though there were so many, still the net was not broken.

Then Jesus shouted to them, smiling broadly, "Come and dine."

And none of the disciples dared to ask him "Who are you?" because they knew that it was the Lord.

Jesus rose and took bread and gave it to them, and fish likewise. This was now the third time that Jesus showed himself to his disciples after he had risen from the dead. And Peter and the others were contented to be there with him, among such familiar and comfortable surroundings, but no one more than Peter.

So when they had dined, Jesus, gesturing to the fish, the nets, the boats, and the sea, said to Peter, "Simon, son of Jonah, do you truly love me more than *these*?"

Peter said to him, "Yes, Lord; you know that I love and believe in you."

Jesus answered him, "Feed my lambs." Then he said to him, a second time, "Simon, son of Jonah, do you *truly* love me?"

Peter sat up, wondering why Jesus questioned him again; then he said to him, "Yes, Lord, you *know* that I love and believe in you."

Then Jesus said to him, "Take care of my sheep." A third time, Jesus said to him, "Simon, son of Jonah, *do* you love and believe in me?"

Peter was grieved, because he asked him a third time, "*Do* you love and believe in me?"

So he said to him, "Lord, you know *all* things; you *know* that I do love and believe in you."

Then Jesus said to him, "Feed my sheep. Truly, truly, I say unto you, when you were young, you girded yourself, and walked wherever you would; but when you shall be old, you shall stretch forth your hands, and another shall gird you, and carry you where you would not."

The other disciples sitting with them marveled, for he spoke, signifying by what death Peter should glorify God.

And when he had spoken this, Jesus said to Peter, "Follow me."

Peter pondered Jesus's words, for they cut him to the heart, meaning more to him than by what manner he should die. He understood this conversation to mean that he should not waste his good time and strength concentrating on worldly activities, such as fishing; instead, he should devote what time and strength he had left toward furthering the kingdom of God.

Later, as Peter walked with Jesus along the beach, he turned, and saw John following them, and said, "Lord, and what shall *he* do?"

Jesus said to him, "If it is my will that he shall tarry till I come, what is that to you? *You* follow me."

Then this saying went abroad among the brethren that John should not die: yet Jesus did not say to him, "He shall not die," but, "If it is my will that he shall tarry till I come, what is that to you?"

Before Jesus left them there at the sea, Peter knew in his heart that he must forsake his life of fishing, and return again to Jerusalem to promote the kingdom of God. So when Jesus had left them, Peter set out, with the others in tow, and returned to Jerusalem. There, they took up residence in the upper room, where they had eaten the last supper with Jesus; the man of the house welcomed them, for he too believed.

On the fortieth day after his resurrection, Pentecost being yet ten days away, the eleven were assembled together with others also, in the upper room.

Then Jesus appeared to them, and said unto them, again, "Peace be unto you."

And they were very glad to see him, for they hoped for more instruction as to how to approach their ministry.

Knowing their concern, therefore, he said to them, "All power is given unto me in heaven and in earth. Behold, I send the promise of my Father upon you."

Then he commanded them, saying, "But wait for the promise of the Father, which you have heard of me, until you are endued with power from on high. For John truly baptized with water, but you shall be baptized with the Holy Spirit not many days from now. Therefore, tarry in the city of Jerusalem."

When they, therefore, had gathered closer to him, they asked of him, saying, "Lord, will you, at this time, restore again the kingdom to Israel?"

And he said to them, "It is not for you to know the times or the seasons, which the Father has put in his own power. But you shall receive power, after that the Holy Spirit has come upon you; and you shall be witnesses unto me both in Jerusalem, and in all Judea, and in Samaria, and unto the uttermost parts of the earth."

And when he had said this, he breathed on them, and said to them, "Receive the Holy Spirit: whose ever sins you forgive, are forgiven them; and whose ever you hold unforgiven, they are held unforgiven.

"As my Father has sent me, even so I send you. Go you, therefore, into all the world, and preach the gospel to every creature, teaching all nations, and baptizing them in the name of the Father, and of the Son, and of the Holy Spirit. He that believes and is baptized shall be saved, but he that believes not shall be damned. And these signs shall follow those who believe; in my name shall they cast out devils; they shall speak with new tongues; they shall take up serpents; and if they drink any deadly thing, it shall not hurt them; they shall lay hands on the sick, and they shall recover. Teach them to observe all things whatsoever I have commanded you, and, lo, I am with you always, even unto the end of the world."

Then he led them out toward Bethany, and as they walked, they were joined by many others who believed in him. When they came to the Mount of Olives, he stopped and lifted up his hands, and blessed them. And it came to pass, while he blessed them, he was parted from them, and carried up into heaven to be seated on the right hand of God. And they beheld him as he was taken up, and a cloud received him out of their sight.

As Elijah had been taken up before Elisha, leaving him with the promise of a double blessing of his spirit, Jesus ascended before a multitude of over five hundred of his disciples, leaving them with the promise of God's gift, the baptism of the Holy Spirit.

And while Jesus's disciples looked steadfastly toward heaven as he went up, behold, two men stood by them in white apparel; who also said, "You men of Galilee, why stand you gazing up into heaven? This same Jesus, who is taken up from you into heaven, shall so come in like manner as you have seen him go into heaven."

***

Matthew 27:52–53	Luke 24:13–35	Mark 16:12–13
Luke 24:36–48	Mark 16:14	John 20:19–20
John 20:24–29	John 21:1–23	Acts 1:2–4
John 20:21	Matthew 28:18	Luke 24:49

Acts 1:4–8

Matthew 28:19

Luke 24:50–51

2 Kings 2:4–15

John 20:21–23

Mark 16:16–18

Mark 16:19

Acts 1:10–11

Mark 16:15

Matthew 28:20

Acts 1:9

1 Corinthians 15:3–9

Chapter 67

PENTECOST

When the day of Pentecost had fully come, they were all with one accord in one place. Then, suddenly, there came a sound from heaven, as of a rushing mighty wind, and it filled the whole house where they were sitting. And there appeared unto them cloven tongues like as of fire, and it sat upon each of them. And they were all filled with the Holy Spirit and began to speak with other tongues as the Spirit gave them utterance.

Now there were those dwelling at Jerusalem, Jews, devout men, out of every nation under heaven. So when this was noised abroad, the multitudes came together and were confounded, because that every man heard them speak in his own language.

When they heard them, they were all amazed and marveled, saying one to another, "Behold, are not all these who speak Galileans? And how do we hear every man in our own tongue in which we were born? Parthians, and Medes, and Elamites, and those who dwell in Mesopotamia, and in Judea, and Cappadocia, in Pontus, and Asia, Phrygia, and Pamphylia, in Egypt, and in the parts of Libya about Cyrene, and strangers of Rome, Jews and proselytes, Cretes and Arabians, we do hear them speak in our tongues the wonderful works of God."

They were all amazed, and were in doubt, saying one to another, "What does this mean?"

Others, mocking, said, "These men are full of new wine."

But Peter, standing up on behalf of the eleven, lifted up his voice, and said to them, "You men of Judea, and all you that dwell at Jerusalem, be this known unto you, and hearken to my words, for these are not drunken, as you suppose, seeing it is but the third hour of the day. But this is that which was spoken by the prophet Joel; 'And it shall come to pass in the last days, says God, "I will pour out my Spirit upon all flesh: and your sons and your daughters shall prophesy, and your young men shall see visions, and your old men shall dream dreams. And on my servants and on my handmaidens I will pour out in those days my Spirit, and they shall prophesy. And I will show wonders in heaven above, and signs in the earth beneath: blood, and fire, and vapor of smoke; the sun shall be turned into darkness, and the moon into blood, before that great and notable day of the Lord comes. And it shall come to pass, that whoever shall call on the name of the Lord shall be saved."'

"You men of Israel, hear these words; Jesus of Nazareth, a man approved of God among you by miracles and wonders and signs, which God did by him in the midst of you, as you yourselves also know: him, being delivered by the ordained purpose and foreknowledge of God, you have taken, and by wicked hands, have crucified and slain: whom God has raised up, having loosed the pains of death, because it was not possible that he should be held of it. For David spoke concerning him, 'I foresaw the Lord always before my face, for he is on my right hand, that I should not be moved; therefore, did my heart rejoice, and my tongue was glad; moreover also my flesh shall rest in hope, because you will not leave my soul in hell, neither will you allow your Holy One to see corruption. You have made known to me the ways of life; you shall make me full of joy with your countenance.' Men and brethren, let me freely speak to you of the patriarch David that he is both dead and buried, and his tomb is with us to this day. Therefore, being a prophet, and knowing that God had sworn with an oath to him, that of the fruit of his loins, according to the flesh, he would raise up the Messiah to sit on his throne; he, seeing this beforehand, spoke of the resurrection of the Messiah, that his soul was not left in hell, neither his flesh did see corruption. This Jesus has God raised up, of which we all are witnesses. Therefore, being by the right hand of God exalted, and having received from the Father the promise of the Holy Spirit, he has shed forth this, which you now see and hear. For David is not ascended into the heavens, but he said himself, 'The LORD said to my Lord, "Sit on my right hand, until I make your foes your footstool."' Therefore, let all the house of Israel know assuredly, that God has made this same Jesus, whom you have crucified, both Lord and Messiah."

Now when they heard this, they were cut to the heart, and said to Peter and to the rest of the apostles, "Men and brethren, what shall we do?"

Then Peter said to them, "Repent, and be baptized every one of you in the name of Jesus the Messiah, for the remission of sins, and you shall receive the gift of the Holy Spirit. For the promise is unto you, and to your children, and to all that are afar off, even as many as the Lord our God shall call."

And with many other words did he testify and exhort them, saying, "Save yourselves from this habitually disobedient generation."

Then they that gladly received his word were baptized, and the same day there were added unto them about three thousand souls. And they continued steadfastly in the apostles' doctrine and fellowship, in the breaking of bread, and in prayers. And fear came upon every soul, for many signs and wonders were done by the apostles. And all that believed were together, and had all things in common; they sold their goods and possessions, and parted them to all men, as every man had need. And they, continuing daily with one accord in the temple; and breaking bread from house to house, did eat their food with gladness and oneness of heart, praising God, and having favor with all the people. And they went forth, and preached everywhere, with the Lord working through them, and confirming the word with signs following. And the Lord added to the church daily such as should be saved. Amen.

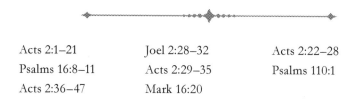

Acts 2:1–21	Joel 2:28–32	Acts 2:22–28
Psalms 16:8–11	Acts 2:29–35	Psalms 110:1
Acts 2:36–47	Mark 16:20	

Bibliography

Print

The Bible in the King James Version. na

Friberg, Timothy, Barbara Friberg, and Neva F. Miller. *Analytical Lexicon of the Greek New Testament.* Victoria: Trafford, 2005. Print.

Green, Jay P. *The Interlinear Bible including the Hebrew-Aramaic Old Testament and the Greek-English New Testament: With Strong's Concordance Numbers above Each Word.* Peabody, MA: Hendrickson, 1985. Print.

Holy Bible in the Revised Standard Version. na

Ruopp, Jonathan E. Sr. *A Table Prepared: Keys of the Kingdom.* USA: Xulon, 2005. Print.

The Scofield Study Bible, New International Version. New York: Oxford UP, 2004. Print.

Strong, James. *The New Strong's Exhaustive Concordance of the Bible.* Nashville: Thomas Nelson, 1990. Print.

Tenney, Merrill C., and J. D. Douglas. *New International Bible Dictionary: Based on the NIV.* Grand Rapids, MI: Zondervan, 1987. Print.

VanderPool, Charles D. 1941. *The Apostolic Bible Polyglot: He Palaia Kai He Kaine Diatheke.* Newport, OR: Apostolic, 1996. Print.

Walvoord, John F., and Roy B. Zuck. *The Bible Knowledge Commentary: New Testament.* Colorado Springs: Cook, 1984. Print.

Walvoord, John F., and Roy B. Zuck. *The Bible Knowledge Commentary: Old Testament.* Colorado Springs: Cook, 1984. Print.

Web

"The 7 Biblical Feasts." *Luzius Schneider.* Luzius Schneider, Feb. 2000. Web. 31 July 2016. http://www.luziusschneider.com/Papers/JewishFeasts.htm

"7 Clues Tell Us *precisely* When Jesus Died (the Year, Month, Day, and Hour Revealed)." *National Catholic Register.* EWTN News, 2016. Web. 31 July 2016. http://www.ncregister.com/blog/jimmy-akin/when-precisely-did-jesus-die-the-year-month-day-and-hour-revealed

"Abomination of the Desolation Fulfilled?" *Revelation Now.* Revelation Now, n.d. Web. 31 July 2016. http://revelationnow.net/2012/08/11/abomination-of-the-desolation-fulfilled/

"After the Crucifixion—The Three Days and the Three Nights."
Blue Letter Bible. Blue Letter Bible, 2016. Web. 31 July 2016.
https://www.blueletterbible.org/faq/crux.cfm

"All about Tallit and Tzitzit—The forget-me-not knots." *Chabad.
org*. Chabad-Lubavitch Media Center, 1993–2016. Web. 31
July 2016.
http://www.chabad.org/library/article_cdo/aid/110306/
jewish/Tallit-and-Tzitzit.htm

"The Apostolic Bible Polyglot." *Septuagint-Interlinear-Greek-Bible.com*.
N.p., n.d. Web. 31 July 2016.
http://septuagint-interlinear-greek-bible.com/

"As (Roman Coin)." *Wikipedia*. Wikimedia Foundation, n.d. Web.
31 July 2016.
https://en.wikipedia.org/wiki/As_(Roman_coin)

Badillo, Tony. "Israel's Amazing Jordan River Crossing." *Temple
Secrets*. Tony Badillo, 2008. Web. 31 July 2016.
http://www.templesecrets.info/jordan.html

"The Beginning of the 490 years: 457 BC." *dedication.www3.50megs*.
N.p., n.d. Web. 31 July 2016.
http://dedication.www3.50megs.com/457.html

BibleStudyTools.com. Bible Study Tools, 2014. Web. 31 July 2016.
http://www.biblestudytools.com/

"Biblical (Hebrew) Time Chart." *The Israel of God RC.com*. The Israel
of God Research Committee, n.d. Web. 31 July 2016.
http://www.theisraelofgodrc.com/Hebrew_Time_Chart.pdf

"Birth of Christ Recalculated." *Versebyverse.org*. Maranatha Church, 1998. Web. 31 July 2016.
http://www.versebyverse.org/doctrine/birthofchrist.pdf

"Blood Moons and Solar Eclipses." *Jesus on My Mind*. Magic Website Maker.com, 2007–14. Web. 31 July 2016.
http://www.jesusonmymind.com/services

Brooks, Carol. "The Feasts of Israel." *In Plain Site*. N.p., n.d. Web. 31 July 2016.
http://www.inplainsite.org/html/seven_feasts_of_israel.html

"Calendar Converter." *diagnosis2012.co.uk*. Dire Gnosis, 2012. Web. 31 July 2016.
http://www.diagnosis2012.co.uk/conv.htm

Cartwright, Mark. "Roman Coinage." *Ancient History Encyclopedia*. Ancient History Encyclopedia Limited, 2009–16. Web. 31 July 2016.
http://www.ancient.eu/Roman_Coinage/

Chaffey, Timothy. "Was Jesus Wrong about Zechariah's Father?" *Answers in Genesis*. Answers in Genesis, 28 Feb. 2012. Web. 31 July 2016.
https://answersingenesis.org/jesus-christ/jesus-is-god/was-jesus-wrong-about-zechariahs-father/

"Day of Atonement." *Jewish Virtual Library*. American-Israeli Cooperative Enterprise, 2013. Web. 31 July 2016.
http://www.jewishvirtuallibrary.org/jsource/judaica/ejud_0002_0005_0_04999.html

Editors of Encyclopædia Britannica. "Lucius Aelius Sejanus." *Encyclopedia Britannica Online*. Encyclopedia Britannica, 2016. Web. 31 July 2016. https://www.britannica.com/biography/Lucius-Aelius-Sejanus

Evans, M. Steven. "Date Calculator." *MSEvans.com*. M. Steven Evans, 2003. Web. 31 July 2016. http://www.msevans.com/calendar/daysbetweendatesapplet.php

"Guide to Ancient Roman Coinage." *Littleton Coin Company*. Littleton Coin Company, 1998–2016. Web. 31 July 2016. http://www.littletoncoin.com/webapp/wcs/stores/servlet/Display%7C10001%7C10001%7C-1%7C%7CLearnNav%7CGuide-to-Ancient-Roman-Coinage.html

"Greek OT (Septuagint/LXX) UTF8." *Bible Database*. BibleDatabase, n.d. Web. 31 July 2016. http://bibledatabase.net/html/septuagint/

Hamm, Greg. "When Was Jesus Born, When Was He Crucified?" *Here I Stand*. N.p., 4 Mar. 2014. Web. 31 July 2016. http://greghamm55.blogspot.com/2014/03/when-was-jesus-born-when-was-he.html

"The Harvest Cycle and the Holidays of Pesach, Shavuoth and Succoth." *AHBJewishCenter.org*. N.p., n.d. Web. 31 July 2016. http://www.ahbjewishcenter.org/harvest.htm

"Harvest Times in Israel?" *Joy by Surprise*. N.p., n.d. Web. 31 July 2016. http://www.joybysurprise.com/Harvest_Times_In_Israel_.html

"Harvest Times in the Last Days." *Heaven Awaits.* Wordpress.com, 11 July 2009. Web. 31 July 2016. https://heavenawaits.wordpress.com/ harvest-times-in-the-end-times/

Heroman, Bill. "Antipas' 'Birthday' after Purim." *NT/History Blog.* N.p., 23 Dec. 2008. Web. 31 July 2016. http://www.billheroman.com/2008/12/antipas-birthday-after-purim.html

"Hebrew Interlinear Bible (OT)." *Scripture4all.org.* Scripture4All, 2015. Web. 31 July 2016. http://www.scripture4all.org/OnlineInterlinear/ Hebrew_Index.htm

"Hebrew OT—Transliteration—Holy Name KJV." *QBible.* N.p., n.d. Web. 31 July 2016. http://www.qbible.com/hebrew-old-testament/

Hirsch, Emil G. "High Priest." *Jewish Encyclopedia.* Jewish Encyclopedia, 2002–11. Web. 31 July 2016. http://www.jewishencyclopedia.com/ articles/7689-high-priest

"How Do We Explain the Passover Discrepancy." *Catholic Answers Magazine.* Catholic Answers, 1996–2016. Web. 31 July 2016. http://www.catholic.com/magazine/articles/ how-do-we-explain-the-passover-discrepancy

"Interlinear Bible: Greek, Hebrew, Transliterated, English, Strong's." *Bible Hub.* Bible Hub, 2004–16. Web. 31 July 2016. http://biblehub.com/interlinear/

"Jesus's Public Ministry and Preaching." *Risto Santala.* N.p., n.d. Web. 31 July 2016. http://www.ristosantala.com/rsla/Nt/NT12.html

"Jewish Holiday Calendars & Hebrew Date Converter." *Hebcal.* N.p., n.d. Web. 31 July 2016. http://www.hebcal.com/

"Keeping Passover at the Proper Time." *YRM.org.* Yahweh's Restoration Ministry, 1999-2016. Web. 31 July 2016. http://yrm.org/keeping-passover-at-the-proper-time/

"The KJV Bible with Strong's References." *Apostolic-Churches.net.* N.p., n.d. Web. 31 July 2016. http://www.apostolic-churches.net/bible/strongs.html

"Language Translators—English to Hebrew Translation מוגרת תילגנאל." *Stars21.com.* Stars21, 1999–2016. Web. 31 July 2016. http://www.stars21.com/translator/english_to_hebrew. html

Lee, Scott E. "Rosetta Calendar." *Rosetta Calendar.* N.p., 1993–2015. Web. 31 July 2016. http://www.rosettacalendar.com/

"The Life & Times of Jesus of Nazareth: Did You Know?" *Christian History Institute.* Disqus, 1998. Web. 31 July 2016. https://www.christianhistoryinstitute.org/magazine/ article/life-and-times-of-jesus-did-you-know/

Lyons, Eric, M. Min. "Zechariah Who?" *Apologetics Press.* Apologetics Press, 2007. Web. 31 July 2016. http://www.apologeticspress.org/apcontent. aspx?category=6&article=2078

"Map of New Testament Israel." *Bible-History*. N.p., n.d. Web. 31 July 2016.
http://www.bible-history.com/geography/ancient-israel/israel-first-century.html

Marcus, Yosef. "What Is the Significance of the Four Cups of Wine?" *Chabad.org*. Chabad-Lubavitch Media Center, 1993-2016. Web. 31 July 2016.
http://www.chabad.org/holidays/passover/pesach_cdo/aid/658520/jewish/What-is-the-significance-of-the-four-cups.htm

Mock, Robert, M.D. "The Abomination of Desolation, the Two Witnesses and the Final Days" *BibleSearchers*. N.p. Sep. 2007. Web. 31 Jul. 2016.
http://www.biblesearchers.com/hebrews/jewish/messiahtheprincetemple7.shtml

Montgomery, Ted. "How Do You Calculate the Timing of Shavuot or Pentecost?" *TedMontgomery.com*. N.p., n.d. Web. 31 July 2016.
http://www.tedmontgomery.com/bblovrvw/emails/Pentecost.html

Moss, Vladimir. "The Feast of Tabernacles." *Orthodox Christian Books*. Marvellous Media, n.d. Web. 31 July 2016.
http://www.orthodoxchristianbooks.com/articles/473/-feast-tabernacles/

"The Mystery of the Passover Cup." *Jews for Jesus*. Jews for Jesus, 2016. Web. 31 July 2016.
http://jewsforjesus.org/publications/newsletter/march-2002/mystery

Odaughterofzion888. "The Star of Bethlehem (Full Movie)." *YouTube*. YouTube, 19 Dec. 2013. Web. 06 Aug. 2016. https://www.youtube.com/watch?v=gzWi0tWKoxo

"Online Greek Interlinear Bible." *Scripture4All.org*. Scripture4All Publishing, 2015. Web. 31 July 2016. http://www.scripture4all.org/OnlineInterlinear/ Greek_Index.htm

"On What Day Are We Supposed to Eat the Passover Meal?" *TheRefinersFire.org*. The Refiner's Fire, n.d. Web. 31 July 2016. http://www.therefinersfire.org/celebrating_passover.htm

Palmer, Ken. "Harmony of the Gospels." *Life of Christ*. Life of Christ, 1998–2016. Web. 31 July 2016. http://www.lifeofchrist.com/life/harmony/

Parsons, John J. "When Does Passover Begin?" *Hebrew4Christians*. Hebrew4Christians, n.d. Web. 31 July 2016. http://www.hebrew4christians.com/Holidays/ Spring_Holidays/Pesach/Zman_Seder/zman_seder.html

Parsons, John J. "Yom Kippur—The Day of Atonement." *Hebrew4Christians*. Hebrew4Christians, n.d. Web. 31 July 2016. http://www.hebrew4christians.com/Holidays/ Fall_Holidays/Yom_Kippur/yom_kippur.html

"The Passover Calendar—2016: An Overview of the Days of Passover in 2016." *Chabad.org*. Chabad-Lubavitch Media Center, 1993-2016. Web. 31 July 2016. http://www.chabad.org/holidays/passover/pesach_cdo/ aid/1723/jewish/Passover-Calendar.htm

"Passover—the Meal." *Different Spirit*. Living Word Bible School, 2008–16. Web. 31 July 2016.
http://www.differentspirit.org/articles/passover_meal.php

Powell, Mark Allan. "Coins Mentioned in the New Testament." *assets.bakerpublishinggroup.com*. Baker Academic, a division of Baker Publishing, 2009. Web. 31 July 2016.
http://assets.bakerpublishinggroup.com/processed/
esource-assets/files/332/original/hyperlink-01-09.
pdf?1375201519

"Quadrans." *Wikipedia*. Wikimedia Foundation, n.d. Web. 31 July 2016.
https://en.wikipedia.org/wiki/Quadrans

Rich, Tracey R. "Judaism 101: Jewish Calendar." *Jewfaq.org*. Tracey R. Rich, 1995–2011. Web. 31 July 2016.
http://www.jewfaq.org/calendar.htm

Rich, Tracey R. "Judaism 101: Shavu'ot." *Jewfaq*. Tracey R. Rich, 1995–2011. Web. 31 July 2016.
http://www.jewfaq.org/holidayc.htm

Rudd, Steve. "The Date of Exodus: 1446 BC." *Bible.Ca*. N.p., n.d. Web. 31 July 2016.
http://www.bible.ca/archeology/bible-archeology-exodus-date-1440bc.htm

"Semite Pentecontad Calendar." *Essene*. Nazarenes of Mount Carmel, 1999–2016. Web. 31 July 2016.
http://www.essene.com/Church/
SemitePentecontadCalendar.htm

Slonim, Rivkah. "The Mikvah." *Chabad.org/The Jewish Woman.org*. Chabad-Lubavitch Media Center, 1993–2016. Web. 31 July 2016.
http://www.chabad.org/theJewishWoman/article_cdo/aid/1541/jewish/The-Mikvah.htm

Somerville, Robert. "The Hours of Prayer." *Awareness Ministry*. N.p., n.d. Web. 31 July 2016.
http://awarenessministry.org/the-hours-of-prayer-%e2%80%93-biblical-times-of-memorial.html

"The Star of Bethlehem | Exploring the Evidence about the Star that Marked History." *The Star of Bethlehem*. FA Larson, 2016. Web. 06 Aug. 2016.
http://www.bethlehemstar.com/

"Synagogue Worship—Alfred Edersheim." *Piney*. N.p., n.d. Web. 31 July 2016.
http://www.piney.com/Synagogue1.html

"Tabor (Mount Tabor)." *Bible Atlas.org*. Bible Hub, 2004–15. Web. 31 July 2016.
http://bibleatlas.org/full/tabor.htm

"Tiberius." *Wikipedia*. Wikimedia Foundation, n.d. Web. 31 July
https://en.wikipedia.org/wiki/Tiberius

"Tophet." *Wikipedia*. Wikimedia Foundation, n.d. Web. 31 July 2016.
https://en.wikipedia.org/wiki/Tophet

"The Two Sabbaths of Passover." *The Way of the Messiah*. N.p., n.d. Web. 31 July 2016.
http://thewayofthemessiah.org/tsp.html

"Was the Law Given at Mount Sinai on the *Traditional* Shavuot?"
   Hope of Israel Ministries (Ecclesia of YEHOVAH). N.p., n.d.
   Web. 31 July 2016.
   http://www.hope-of-israel.org/sinailaw.html

"The Widows Mite." *RomanCoins.net*. RomanCoins.net, 2003. Web.
   31 July 2016.
   http://www.romancoins.net/newsletter/v2n2.htm

"The Whole Scriptures Interlining with the Hebrew, Greek, English
   Translated and Translitered Colored Words to Compare."
   Bayit haMashiyach. N.p., 2015. Web. 31 July 2016.
   http://www.bayithamashiyach.com/Scriptures.html

"Yom Kippur." *Shalomnyc.org*. N.p., n.d. Web. 31 July 2016.
   http://www.shalomnyc.org/feasts/yom_kippur.htm

"Yom Kippur." *Wikipedia*. Wikimedia Foundation, 2016. Web. 31 July
   https://en.wikipedia.org/wiki/Yom_Kippur

Printed in the United States
By Bookmasters